Duty & Desire

J.D. RAGHAV

AMARYLLIS
An imprint of Manjul Publishing House

AMARYLLIS

An imprint of Manjul Publishing House Pvt. Ltd.
• C-16, Sector 3, Noida, Uttar Pradesh 201 301, India
Website: www.manjulindia.com
Registered Office:
• 2nd Floor, Usha Preet Complex, 42 Malviya Nagar,
Bhopal 462 003 – India
Distribution Centres
Ahmedabad, Bengaluru, Chennai, Hyderabad,
Kochi, Kolkata, Mumbai, Noida, Pune

Duty & Desire by J.D. Raghav

This paperback edition first published in India in 2026

ISBN 978-93-7317-189-0

Cover design by Raghav House

Printed and bound in India by Repro India Limited

DEDICATION

To my sisters-in-law, my niece and nephew for their support. Also for proofreading and being the voice of reason.

To Pimmy, for calling out my collapsible walls—ones that somehow found their way into my heroine.

To my husband, for his steady support through all the late nights and the relentless sound of keystrokes while he patiently watched TV. For once telling me I had a book in me, even when I doubted it.

And finally, to my brother, who once said that where we come from and the things we have seen give us a unique perspective. That even when I believed I had no story in me, our experiences were more than enough. You saw the stories in me before I did and I know you continue to watch over me from above.

CONTENTS

PROLOGUE

The wedding dais was prepared. Karan begrudgingly walked to the *mandap* and took his seat. He recalled the conversation with his father on his deathbed two weeks ago.

"Promise me you will marry her."

Karan's eyes had protested, but his voice was caught in his throat. He had found his resolve weakening under a mix of trepidation and grief at the impending loss of his father.

He felt the small bony fingers of his grandmother on his wrists. He turned to look down at her tear-stricken face, pleading with him to accept a dying man's wishes. To let her only son be at peace.

The pundit called for the bride to be brought to the mandap. Karan felt numb, unsure how to feel with the memories from the past few weeks playing in his mind on loop.

He recalled where he had been when the phone call came from Jaisalmer.

He had been at the rooftop restaurant of Hotel Indigo in Lower East Side New York. His hand was in his pocket, fumbling excitedly with the ring box, waiting for the right moment, when the lights would dim and the violinists would start playing. Anya had been giddy with champagne. They were celebrating three years of being together.

If only she hadn't insisted that he answer right away. Maybe things could have gone differently.

He had answered the incessant ringing, fully intending to tell the caller he would call back. But it was the grave tone of Bakshi Uncle on the line that warned Karan that something wasn't right. He had felt his heart sink when Bakshi Uncle asked him to catch the next flight home. With the phone to his ear, listening to Bakshi Uncle speak with urgency on his father's ailment, Karan had walked to the back of the restaurant kitchen and had gestured to the manager to call off the proposal plan. Little did he know then that the opportunity would never come again.

By the time he arrived in Jaisalmer, his father had been declared to be in the terminal stage of his illness. Karan was furious at first and frantically tried to find out why he had been kept in the dark about his father's condition for so long. But in time, he came to the sad realisation that the diagnosis was as much a shock to his father as it was to the doctors. There was nothing anyone could do.

The sound of chiming anklets brought him back to the present. They had just brought the bride to the *mandap* and were helping her get seated on his right. Karan couldn't bring himself to look up. The grief of having lost both his father and the love of his life in a matter of days had rendered him devoid of all emotion. He had been offered up to the wheel of fate and fortune like a lamb to the slaughter.

Karan still didn't look up when his right hand was pulled between him and the bride nor even when the bride's trembling right hand was placed atop his, palm up.

The pundit continued the *mantra* recitation as someone poured a drop of water on their hands as part of the *kanyadaan* ritual. Karan was in such a daze that he had no awareness of who anyone was around him. The slight recoil of the bride's hand from the mild shock of cold water caused her *hathphool* to scrape on the stitches on his palm. The sting of which reminded him of how he got it.

He had been on the phone with Anya explaining to her what had passed in his father's hospital room. It had taken every ounce of his strength to deliver the news of his impending nuptials to the only woman he had ever loved so passionately.

He could feel her silent tears through the phone. She hadn't screamed or cried. Instead, she was understanding of his predicament and consoled him despite her grief. Even though she hid it well, he knew she was distraught by the way her voice had hitched when she said goodbye.

Later, as he sat in the dark silence of his room, cradling a neat glass of bourbon, he felt his tight composure finally slip. He felt himself let out an anguished cry at both his and Anya's pain. In his helplessness, he had gripped the glass in his hand with such force that it shattered into fragments that cut and gashed at his hand.

The pundit announced it was time for the pheras around the holy fire. Karan stood up but his mind was elsewhere. As Karan walked with his bride in tow, he thought of the conversation he had had with Bakshi Uncle after his father's funeral.

It turned out that Karan's father had not only expressed his wishes verbally but he had also penned them down in his last will. The will stipulated that unless and until Karan is married to a girl of his father's choosing, Karan's access to his own estate and the estate of his father would be restricted. Karan had spent years building the tech branch of his father's business. He had worked his way up from high school to college to finally earning an MBA from Harvard all in the pursuit of the growth of his pride and joy, inSense.

In essence, his father's wishes had not only jeopardised Karan's relationship with Anya but had also put on hold his entire life.

"You have to marry her," Bakshi Uncle had said.

They had been seated in his father's office. Bakshi Uncle was not only their family attorney but also a close family friend. Karan was desperate for any help or loophole he could use to get out of this mess. He had explained his situation. His ambitions for the business and his relationship with Anya. And Bakshi Uncle was sympathetic. But the terms of the will were clear. Bakshi Uncle had drawn them up himself at the behest of his father.

"What if I refuse?" Karan had asked.

"Then, the estate and all your family possessions will be owned by the state. You can contest it all you want. But it will be a long and hard battle. I don't recommend it. With your reputation and standing in society, it

could quickly become a scandal. Look, if you like, why don't you meet her first? It might help you see your father's point of view. She and her—"

"What difference would it make?" Karan had asked furiously. "I will still have to marry her, wouldn't I?"

After the *pheras,* they were asked to be seated again, this time his bride sat on his left. Karan gazed distractedly into the fire. He didn't hear what the pundit said, but someone placed a *mangalsutra* in his hands. Karan moved robotically toward the bride, whose face was partially covered with the bridal *dupatta.* He felt his way behind her nape and worked quickly to tie the *mangalsutra,* not desiring to look in her direction and keeping his gaze firmly fixed on the fire.

"Is annulment an option? I can explain it to her. She would be well compensated," he had asked Bakshi Uncle.

"Unfortunately, not. Your father's will is watertight on that account. If the marriage dissolves within the first three years, then the same clause applies."

The pundit placed a sindoor dibba in Karan's hands.

"Three years? So, after that, I can consider divorce?"

Bakshi Uncle hesitated.

"Yes, you can break free at this point provided the marriage remains valid for three years. But I'll just say this one last thing. If it were anyone else, I might have agreed. And while I completely sympathise with you, I also know she isn't a bad person. Maybe if you give her a chance, you could have a happy life. I'm sure your father would have wished the best for you. Besides, she's the daughter of an old friend your father had sworn to protect. But at the end of the day, this is your life and you must do what you think is right for you."

As they helped lift the bride's veil for the *sindoor daan,* Karan momentarily closed his eyes. All he saw was Anya's beautiful face, her bright deep, blue eyes and gorgeous smile. And he knew then, that he could never love another woman as deeply as he loved her.

Karan opened his eyes, took a pinch of *sindoor*, quickly applied a line of it between the bride's parted hair, not once letting his gaze drift to her face and returned to staring into the fire. He had made up his mind. This marriage was going to be in name only, a means to an end and nothing more. His heart belonged to Anya and always would.

Karan sat in the dark, on the edge of his bed, anxiously waiting for his bride to come in. The wedding was completed and he was officially a married man. He cringed at the thought.

He had already decided he was going to leave tonight. His bags were packed. He'd say what he wanted to say to the girl and leave. Each second he waited felt like a torturous eternity.

At long last, he heard the clinking sound of her anklets as she walked in the room hesitantly. Her face was still covered by her *ghunghat*.

She held a glass of milk in her hands, no doubt schooled by nosy aunts eager to pass on their legacy of old wives' tales. She looked around the room, looking for a light switch.

"Stop," he said.

She turned to look at him. He got up from the bed and walked toward her, stopping just three feet away. She instinctively stepped back in trepidation.

"You don't need to be afraid of me," Karan began. "Because nothing is going to be happening tonight."

Karan paused, trying to gauge if he could sense a reaction but she stood motionless holding the glass.

"Would you like to take a seat?" he asked while walking to the desk to grab a chair.

He heard a low tinkle of bangles and caught her shaking her head from the corner of his eye.

"Alright," he quipped.

He sauntered back to stand in front of her, deciding he should get to the point quickly before things became any more awkward.

Karan took a deep breath and began, "Here's the thing about me. My father and I have never seen eye-to-eye on anything in life. He was always a rigid, unemotional man. He carried his army discipline into all aspects of our family life. What he lacked in his expression of love, however, he made up for in his philanthropy. Brigadier General Rathore was a man of honour in Jaisalmer, respected by all.

"And don't get me wrong, I did too. But his lack of emotion planted a seed of resentment in my heart, which only grew with time, becoming deep-rooted after my mother's passing.

"Still, in a way he was a good father. He made sure I was never left wanting for anything in life. I had a comfortable upbringing; some would say lavish even. I was born into wealth. This manor had been in our family for seven generations. I think it's fair to say, I'm used to the good life.

"But my greatest passion in life has been business. For as long as I could remember, I had wanted to join our telecommunications business that my great grandfather had started and which my grandfather and father expanded over the years. I studied hard, continued my higher education in London and finished with an MBA in Harvard.

"After graduation, I joined a tech startup in New York and worked my way from the ground up to become partner and used that as a climbing stone in establishing inSense, the tech branch of my family business.

"And that's when I met Anya. She started as an intern in my company and with time, we began a relationship and eventually fell in love. I have had a handful of girlfriends prior to meeting her, but, my relationship with her felt different. Suffice it to say that she brought into my life the love and understanding that I always sought from my family growing up."

Karan paused here to check if his words were sinking in. She hadn't spoken a word and the veil and darkness hid away all the reaction she may have had. It was all well and good as he did not want to see her at all. He noticed her fingers had tightened around the glass. He gently pulled the glass out of her hands and set them on the desk near the window.

"Naturally, with the progression of our relationship," Karan continued, "we moved in together. And now we've been together for three years."

He watched her timidly wrap her hands around herself and dip her head lower. As painful as this was going to be, he had to say his part.

Karan continued, "Before I left New York, I was going to propose to her, but that didn't happen. I came here and well, you know the rest of the story.

"Whatever the reason may be, it was my father's express dying wish that I marry you. He also forced my hand by putting on the line my pride, my business inSense, by making this marriage a condition of his will and testament. I was left with no choice. So, in order to *a.* honour his last wish and *b.* for the sake of everything that I built, I agreed to this marriage.

"All I know is though, that I am in no way obligated to keep it."

Karan paused to catch a breath.

"My father's will stipulates that this marriage must last for three years to fulfill its conditions. After the end of that period, I will have secured my estate permanently, we will be divorced and you and I would be free to go our separate ways.

"Until then, I will return to New York and you are free to stay here in the *haveli*. You won't be lacking for anything and I will make sure that you are provided for, and at the end of our marriage, I'll also make sure that you are well compensated.

"In short, I *have* to go. I have fulfilled my promise to my father by marrying you, but I love someone else and I can't pretend I belong in Jaisalmer when my life is in New York."

Karan looked at her intently to see if she understood what he was saying but she hadn't moved or spoken a word. Without another word, Karan wheeled his packed suitcase out of the room.

The now lonely bride stood motionless, her fingers trembling slightly as they clutched the soft fabric of her bridal dupatta. For five long minutes, she remained rooted in place, her chest rising and falling with shallow breaths as the reality of her solitude settled around her like a thick, oppressive fog. Slowly, she walked to the edge of the bed, her footsteps echoing in the empty silence, and sank down onto the floor. She leaned her weary head against the bed's edge, the ache in her heart finally giving way as she closed her eyes, letting her tears spill over in silent streams.

1

HOLLOW HEIGHTS

Two and a half years later

Karan stood at the floor-to-ceiling glass window watching the busy streets of downtown Manhattan on a clear Thursday afternoon. In the last year, Karan's brainchild, inSense, had not only gone public but had also made the Forbes Global 2000 ranking last quarter. A celebration cocktail event was planned for tonight.

In the background, his interview was airing on the Business Channel.

Interviewer: Tell us more about inSense. How did this name come to be?

Karan: Well, it has a both personal and practical meaning. Growing up in India, my days would typically start with waking up to the scent of incense sticks that my grandmother or mother would light for the morning prayers. And it would also be the time I would be most productive, completing my homework, researching. Essentially those were the formative years of developing interest in my education. Later, when I was expanding our family's communications business to include wireless sensors, I coined inSense as a tribute to my past shaping my future.

Interviewer: That is absolutely remarkable. Now what would you say is the future of inSense?

Karan: At the moment, we are working on a collaboration with Delta Airlines to develop an advanced aviation comms system which I think will—

Karan looked behind to see Anya had just turned off the TV.

"How long have you been standing there?" Karan asked with a weak smile as he walked over to her.

"Long enough to see you flash your schoolboy charm at the interviewer on TV," Anya teased.

Karan put his arms around her waist.

"Good afternoon," he whispered.

"Back at ya," Anya replied back before they both kissed. As Karan leaned in to deepen their embrace, Anya turned her head to look at the view.

"It's a beautiful day today, isn't it?" Anya said.

Karan looked into Anya's bright blue eyes that took on a hue of green as they reflected the sunlight. Her eyes were what had drawn him to her in the first place. But today they looked distant. If he were being honest with himself, they had been looking distant every day these last few days.

"It is indeed," he said, flirtatiously, wondering if she would react.

Anya turned to look at him for a brief second before giving him a quick smile without saying anything.

"I've been waiting for you all day today," Karan said.

Anya smiled again without saying a word.

"Are you okay?" Karan asked.

"I'm okay," she responded smilingly but there was an uncertainty in her eyes when she spoke. "I'm really proud of you, you know. You've worked really hard to get here."

"Thanks Anya," said Karan. "I couldn't have done any of this without you. You have been with me every step of the way. It's as much a win for you as it is for me. But... are you sure you're okay?"

Anya forced a smile, "Yeah, just... a lot on my mind. You know how it is. Listen I—"

A clearing of throat made them jump. Nathan was standing at the door to Karan's office, grinning at them both.

"*Hello,* lovebirds."

"What do you want?" Karan asked nonchalantly as Anya moved ever so slightly away from him. Karan noticed her distance and felt something was definitely on her mind but decided to ask her later when they were alone again.

"It's not what I want, it's what I brought," said Nathan pulling out a bottle of champagne from behind him.

Karan shook his head in disbelief, "Aren't we celebrating already tonight?"

"*That is* for making the ranking," Nathan replied, "whereas *this* is for your new project. It's also a pre-party offering."

The two friends laughingly embraced one another before the three of them popped the bottle of champagne.

"Congratulations to you, mate," Nathan said softly as they tipped their glasses.

"And to you too," said Karan.

Nathan had been friends with Karan since their sophomore year at Harvard and after starting inSense, they had also been business partners. Together with Anya, the three of them frequently meet up socially after work with an occasional fourth person depending on who Nathan was dating that month, or even that week. Nathan had always been the designated Casanova even throughout university.

"So, when are we going to the venue?" Nathan asked.

"We need to be there at seven," said Karan looking at his watch, "so we have... another three and a half hours."

"Perfect timing," said Anya. "I just came in to say I'm going to call it an early day today. I need to go pick up my dress from the atelier and then get to my hair and makeup appointment. I'll see you back at the apartment."

"Okay, no problem," answered Karan, "but wait! Didn't you want to say something to me?"

"Um, maybe later, it can wait. Okay, bye guys."

"I'm heading out too to pick up our remote office colleague from the airport. Did you want me to give you a ride to the atelier?" Nathan offered.

"That'd be wonderful, thanks."

"No problem. Bye buddy. I'll see you tonight."

After they left, Karan sank back into his leather chair behind the desk and sighed. He had achieved so much in such a short span of time but instead of elation, all he felt was an unexplainable emptiness. He wondered if that was what Anya was feeling too. They had always been in sync emotionally, but in the last few months, things hadn't felt the same. His achievements, inSense's growth, his relationship with Anya—none of it seemed able to fill the void. Maybe he was just burnt out.

Despite his state of mind, two months ago, he had finally proposed to Anya. She was thrilled at the time, or at least pretended to be, but since then, she had been growing increasingly distant.

He opened the first drawer of his desk cabinet and took out an A4 manila envelope. It had arrived that morning from India via registered mail. Peeling it open, he pulled out a stack of divorce application forms. Eager to break free from his obligations, he had reached out to Bakshi Uncle, hoping that perhaps a fresh start with Anya would finally bring some clarity to both their lives and help everything fall into place once again.

They still had six months but the idea was to get started on the paperwork as these things took a lot of time in India's family courts.

He had already gone over the pre-filled PDF version that Bakshi Uncle had emailed him last week. But he still read over the printed version to make sure all his details were accurate.

Applicant: *Karan Singh Rathore*
Respondent: *Janvi Talvar*

He had wondered at the absurdity of how he had only just found out his wife's name when he read this form last week. It still took him aback reading it this second time on print. He remembered hastily signing the wedding certificate at his wedding to get it over and done with but was completely pre-occupied with thoughts of Anya at the time that his mind had never registered her name. All this while she was just *Papa ke dost ki beti*. How had he never even bothered to learn her name?

Even on his monthly phone calls with his grandmother, she'd somehow, thankfully so, had never brought her up and he'd never asked. It was just as well, because he didn't want to be reminded of the girl who became the reason for this constant guilt that ate at him. On occasional moments when he'd find himself harbouring a mild curiosity about her and her life in Jaisalmer, he'd nip those thoughts right in the bud.

He didn't want to know.

He'd never tried to hurt a soul in his life and somehow, his father in his death had put him in a position to make a decision so rash that it put so many people's lives on hold. It was a spur of the moment, panicked decision he had made when he realised that he did not want to lose Anya. He wasn't particularly proud of it. And he did not want to be reminded of that.

His only hope was that, after all this was over, he could somehow pay the girl back sufficiently to ensure it would be worth her while. Hell, he would set up a monthly fund for her. And one day, hopefully be brave enough to ask for her forgiveness.

Karan picked up the pen to sign but stopped, the tip hovering over the blank line. A strange heaviness filled his chest, and he couldn't understand why. He decided to put the forms away in his briefcase and come back to them once his heart and head were clearer.

Later that night.

The cocktail party was hosted in a lavish ballroom. Chandeliers hung like stars from the ceiling, casting a golden glow across the room, where waiters in sharp black suits weaved through the crowd with trays of champagne flutes. The hum of conversation, punctuated by bursts of laughter, filled the air—an orchestra of success.

Karan walked in dressed in a tuxedo, his posture exuding

calm confidence. Anya stood next to him, looking glamorous in a shimmering blue gown, her arm casually draped through his.

The room was filled with investors, industry leaders, and media figures, the titans of the business world, all sipping expensive drinks and exchanging ideas that could shape industries. Karan and Nathan gave speeches that moved their employees and impressed their investors.

As the evening wore on, Karan was pulled into conversation after conversation. He looked at Anya who was laughing at something a high-profile investor said, flashing her signature smile that could charm anyone in the room. She fit into his world of wealth and power so perfectly, always knowing the right thing to say, the right person to approach.

Despite his apparent success, however, his thoughts kept drifting to the emptiness that was now gnawing at his chest.

That night, when he went to bed, Anya asleep next to him, he lay awake for a long time with his thoughts. He was uncertain about everything; his career, his friendships and his relationship with Anya. He looked at Anya for a few seconds and then glanced at his briefcase on the desk in their room briefly before giving in to sleep.

2

FADING MIRAGE

Karan was sitting in a business class seat of an Emirates flight with an untouched glass of wine reflecting on how, once again, his life had changed in a matter of days. He recalled the events of Friday.

It was the day after the celebration event. Karan had flown to Atlanta in an early morning flight to meet with Delta Airlines' engineering team and have a first-hand feel of the prototype of their communications system incorporating inSense technology. He had decided to return to New York earlier than scheduled due to a bad weather forecast and he did not want to be left stranded in Atlanta the whole weekend as he had a project update meeting scheduled with his investors on Monday.

On his way back, he decided he wanted to work through his uneasiness and be a better person for Anya. He wanted to surprise Anya with a date night as he felt he had been so unduly busy with both work and his own conflicting thoughts that he suspected her recent disinterestedness was an outcome of his neglect.

When he arrived at their apartment that evening and went to his room to change, the scene that greeted him turned his entire world around its axis.

The first thing he noticed were the scattered clothes, Anya's familiar red dress and a suit jacket he didn't recognize lying carelessly on the floor. His gaze travelled to his bed, finding tangled there in his sheets, Nathan and Anya, their bodies intertwined in a height of passion.

Time felt as if it had stood still as Karan remained frozen at the door. He felt choked like life was slowly being drained out of him much like for a fish out of water. Anya, sat up in a panic when she spotted him desperately trying to cover herself.

"Anya...?" Karan's voice had cracked, barely above a whisper, at realizing that what he was witnessing was a betrayal of both love and friendship.

"Karan, I—" she started, her voice trembling unable to find the words, her fingers tightening around the sheets, the engagement ring in her hand twinkling in the dim light. But it was Nathan who interrupted as he was scrambling to grab his clothes from the floor.

"This isn't what it looks like..." Nathan's words faltered.

"Nathan," Karan his voice slowly steadying but devoid of all emotion, "from where I'm standing, it is exactly what it looks like."

Nathan looked down in shame, unable to meet Karan's eyes.

Karan turned around to leave, but Anya called out to him her voice choking with a mix of guilt and pain, desperate to explain. "Karan, I tried really hard to tell you...I didn't know how. I'm sorry."

Karan turned to looked at her with a menace in his eyes that scared her. "This was as clear as you could ever have ever been."

Karan left his bedroom, pulling the door close firmly behind him drowning Anya's guilt-filled sobs. He grabbed his keys and walked out of his apartment.

Upon landing at Mumbai Airport, Karan felt momentary relief as he was able to distract himself among the sea of travellers. Even as he boarded his Air India connecting flight to Jodhpur, he found himself feeling thankful for the brief reprieve that the cacophony of excited travellers brought helping his mind remain in the present moment. He landed just before lunch and without taking a break, grabbed the black, rental Range Rover that his assistant had organized for him and set off to Jaisalmer.

Driving along, National Highway 125, Karan passed through sparse desert fields, the dusty, parched landscape a reflection of his state of mind. Karan regretted the now uncomfortable silence of his car which forced him to keep revisiting the events of the weekend.

After leaving his apartment that evening, Karan had driven purposelessly for an hour or two. He couldn't really put a finger on how long because in his emotional state, he had lost all concept of time. He remembered checking into a hotel for the rest of the night. He was distraught and unable to think clearly and had nearly drunk himself to sleep that night. The next morning, he had woken up to multiple messages and phone calls from Anya and Nathan.

He went back to the apartment where Anya greeted him hesitantly but with some relief that he was okay. She had tried to talk to him but Karan was too hurt and angry to listen. He grabbed his clothes from their bedroom and went to the guest bathroom to shower. As the hot water poured over him, his muscles began to relax only then registering how wound up he was. He decided he would go back to the office despite it being a Saturday because he needed to take his mind off of everything. He packed a suitcase and left a note for Anya to say he was shifting into a hotel for the next few days before driving into the office.

However, work could neither give his aching heart any relief nor his racing mind some respite. His tired brain kept replaying the image of Anya's bare flesh rubbing against Nathan while they moved in unison, an image that had been painfully seared into his brain. With an anguished cry and an angry sweep of his hand, Karan pushed all the contents of his desk on the floor. Deafening silence followed the loud crash and he sat back in his chair defeated and finally overcome with a flood of grief.

That night Karan had a short-disturbed sleep. The next morning, Karan went for a two-hour run trying to burn off his grief and frustration. At the end of the run, when he sat at the pier catching his breath, he realized he couldn't trust himself to go to work on Monday and face either Nathan or Anya without losing his composure. Karan thought long and hard. At long last, he decided he needed a long break from everything, both his work and his now fragmented relationship. He called his assistant to put in an indefinite leave, cancel his meetings, send out a work status email on his behalf to Nathan to follow up on and book the earliest flight route to Jodhpur.

As Karan continued driving through the undulating landscape of the Thar desert, the sun casted shimmering mirages on the sand that danced like illusions before his eyes much like his relationship with Anya. The memories of joy he had experienced with her now feeling like cruel tricks of a harsh desert on a parched and weary traveller. All his dreams feeling like sand that have slipped through his fingers leaving behind an aching void.

After almost five hours of continuous driving, Karan felt nostalgia when the sandy dunes gave way to the familiar landscape of the *Sonar Quilla* as it basked in the warm, vermillion tinged rays of the setting sun that is synonymous to the Thar dessert. He drove through the narrow winding streets towards the Rathore *haveli* just on the outskirts of Jaisalmer, twilight turned to dusk. As the opulent Rathore *haveli* greeted him, Karan sighed in respite. Perhaps, spending time in his childhood home was exactly what he needed to take his mind off the harrowing heartbreak he just went through.

Entering the front foyer with a suitcase in tow, Karan was greeted with eerie quietness. The lights were off, and he wondered where everyone was. Just then, he heard the soft tinkle of anklets before a sharp whoosh filled the air—immediately he caught sight of an incoming strike of a cricket bat that was aimed perfectly at his head.

"Jesus!" Karan yelped, instinctively ducking. The bat whistled past him narrowly missing his skull.

A dim light flickered on, illuminating the foyer. Karan straightened, blinking in surprise, finding himself face to face with a girl in a pale pink salwar kameez, her hands over her mouth, her wide eyes locked on his, just as startled as he was.

Before he could even register what just happened, the girl ran to him with a cry and swung her arms around him pushing him back slightly with the sudden momentum. A confused Karan looked over her shoulder to find his grandmother who had been standing behind her, her expression morphing from shock to recognition.

Amidst his confusion, he felt the racing heartbeat of the girl on his chest, her trembling arms on his shoulders. He stood motionless for a moment unsure of what to do and just when he hesitantly tried to steady her with his free hand, she let him go, her cheeks turning crimson with embarrassment. She hurriedly stepped back and without another word, dashed up the stairs, the sound of her chiming anklets drifting away with her.

Karan stood there, still processing the whirlwind of events. "Daadi," he said again, his voice tinged with confusion. "What the hell's going on? Where is everyone?"

His grandmother, however, seemed too caught up in the excitement of his return to address his question directly. "Areh, you've come!" she exclaimed, her face lighting up. "How are you? When did you arrive?"

"Just now, Daadi," Karan replied, bowing slightly to touch her feet. But his thoughts were still on the girl. He straightened, and his grandmother, filled with joy, immediately pulled him into a tight embrace.

She pulled back and placed her slightly shaky hands on his face as if she couldn't quite believe Karan was actually there, her eyes tearing up. Karan felt aggrieved at her display of emotions and guilty at how he had left things in Jaisalmer. Seeing his grandmother so emotional made his own troubles fade into the background.

When she finally pulled away, wiping her tears, Karan managed to steady himself. "Daadi," he repeated, trying to refocus. "What's going on? Where is all the staff?"

"They wanted to go to the *Janmasthami* celebrations in town so Janvi gave them the night off," his grandmother responded, conveniently ignoring the first question.

So that was Janvi, Karan thought.

He still had no explanation for why she swung a cricket bat at him but he reckoned if he were entering into a house at night without any prior warning then it was probably to be expected. With the events of the last few days still fresh in his mind, it had not even occurred to him to let his grandmother know he was coming.

At least he could be thankful the girl wasn't deliberately trying to murder him for how he handled things the last time he was here by the shock on her face. On the other hand, he thought amusingly, she had an excellent aim.

"*Badri!*" His grandmother called out. "Badri, look Karan has come home."

A stout man with a dhoti, vest and turban ran out sleepily from the end of the hallway.

"*Chote Hukum!*" He exclaimed, bowing deeply, "*Khama ghani, chote hukum.*"

"*Ghani khama, Badri kaka,*" Karan replied with a smile.

"Badri, take Karan's luggage to his room upstairs," his grandmother ordered.

"No," Karan quickly interjected, "that's fine. It's just one bag, *daadi*. I'll be fine. *Kaka,* you can go to sleep."

"No," his grandmother opposed firmly, "Badri, at least go set up his room quickly."

Karan began to protest again but smilingly gave up. She was as stubborn as ever.

His grandmother asked him if he had eaten, but he responded by saying he was too tired and just wanted to go to bed. She understood as she knew how long a journey he had to have taken to get here. It was just good to be back home.

Upstairs in his bedroom, Badri had already cleared the dust from the top sheets and wiped down the side tables. Karan showered, changed, and sank into the comfort of his old bed, the familiar surroundings oddly soothing.

It hadn't registered to Karan that the last thought he had before he drifted to sleep was not about Anya and his heartbreak but of the girl who had just crashed into him downstairs.

Her scent still lingered in his senses, and the echo of her heartbeat was still vivid in his mind. The warmth of her sudden embrace, the softness of her body pressed against his. All of it swirled in his thoughts, more present than any of the heartbreak he had left behind.

As he lay there in the stillness of the room, his mind sharpened, the realization crystallizing.

He had just met his wife. Janvi.

The thought lingered with him as he drifted off to sleep.

3

A STRANGE OASIS

Karan awoke the next morning to the sound of hustle and bustle echoing through the walls. For a brief moment, he'd forgotten where he was and sighed in contentment as the memory returned. There was no better feeling than being at home. A cup of tea was already placed on the side table next to his bed, not too long ago judging by the hot steam. The unmissable scent of incense also lingered in the air.

As he sat up, stretching his neck, the lively sounds of movement in the courtyard continued to filter in. Curious, he picked up his tea, walked to the window, and took in the scene below. Staff and labourers were busy in the *mandap* area, hanging garlands and drapes from ladders, while others cleaned the pool. *What on earth was happening?*

After a quick shower, he threw on a pair of jeans and a charcoal, long sleeved T-shirt before heading downstairs for breakfast. Just outside the kitchen, he nearly bumped into his grandmother who was carefully balancing a large *thali* filled with *pooja* items.

"Good morning, *Daadi*," Karan greeted, stooping to touch her feet.

"Good morning to you too, *bete*. God bless you," a fond smile in her eyes. "Have you had breakfast yet?"

"No, no not yet, I was just abo—" he began, only to be interrupted.

"Badri! Karan *ke liye naashta lagao*!" she called out.

"*Daadi*, no, I'll get breakfast myself," he said, chuckling as poor Badri *kaka* scrambled to respond. A warm feeling settled over him;

she was as indulgent as ever. "But here–give me this *thali*. I'll help you. Where are we taking it?"

"To the *pooja* room," she replied, handing it over with a contented nod.

Together, as they walked to the *pooja* room, his grandmother re-iterated her sentiments from the night before.

"I'm can't tell you how happy I am that you are home," she began, her voice warm. "I thought of you every day and prayed you were doing well. When I heard about your company's success, I was bursting with pride. Every now and then, I'd see one of your interviews on TV. How is that sensor project going?"

Karan was stumped, "*Daadi,* how do you know about all that?" He couldn't recall his grandmother ever keeping track of anyone's work, whether it was his father's business, his own studies or his career. And he certainly never spoke at length about it on their brief phone calls. So naturally, her sudden awareness and curiosity about his achievements took him aback.

"Janvi showed me," she said as a matter-of-fact, "she showed me all your interviews whether it was in print or on TV. She even taught me how to use that pad... what is it...?"

"The iPad?" he asked, smiling.

"Yes, that," she nodded, a hint of pride in her tone.

Interesting, he thought, with a smile. Janvi. What else have you been up to?

He didn't want to admit it to himself but ever since meeting her for the first time last night, or rather her running into his arms, he was anxious to see her again.

And, as if in answer to an unspoken prayer, there she was in the *pooja* room.

She was sitting on a prayer cushion, wearing a simple white *salwar kameez,* her back turned to them. Her damp, wavy hair was pulled over her right shoulder. The oxidized earring in her left ear dangled, occasionally brushing against her bare shoulder. She was entirely focused, rolling cotton wicks and placing them neatly in the brass *diyas,* unaware of the way she held his gaze.

"Janvi, I think you better check on what Badri and Laxmi are doing in the kitchen. Those two are useless. Karan and I can finish up here. And tell Laxmi to come to my room afterward," his grandmother instructed.

"Yes, *Daadi,* I'm almost done here," Janvi replied, her *paayal* tinkling softly as she stood up and turned to face them.

She first glanced at his grandmother before looking directly at him. It was only for a fleeting moment before she averted her eyes to the *thali* in his hand. If she was surprised to see him, she didn't show it. The embarrassment she felt last night was no longer there. He had a sneaky suspicion that from henceforth, he was about to be ignored.

Aside from her cheeks being lightly flushed and a thin layer of barely visible gloss on her lips, she had almost no makeup on. A small red *bindi* nestled between her brows completed her look. She was stunning.

She walked past him, barely sparing him another glance but he caught the faint scent of her freshly shampooed hair. The edge of her *dupatta* brushed against his fingers. He hadn't realized he was holding his breath until his grandmother's voice cut through the moment.

"You can put the *thali* on the floor, Karan," she said.

After he finished helping his grandmother, she instructed him to go have breakfast.

As Karan approached the kitchen, he spotted Janvi gesturing to Laxmi *tai,* who rushed out nodding in response. The air buzzed with a sense of busyness; everyone was either cleaning, decorating or cooking. A feast no doubt judging by the delicious aromas wafting from the kitchen.

Laxmi *tai* nearly crashed into him in her hurry. When she saw him, her eyes widened with joy, and tears began to well up.

"Karan *beta,*" she mumbled, her voice trembling with emotion.

"How are you Laxmi *tai?*" Karan stooped to touch her feet but she wouldn't allow it, pulling him into a tight embrace instead.

"Badri told me you arrived last night," she started, her excitement bubbling over. "That's why I've been so eager to see you all morning! I've been messing everything up in the kitchen, putting salt in the *chai* and sugar in the *dal*."

Karan's brief laugh faltered as instantly as he realized what was about to come with Laxmi *tai*'s expression changing from warmth to disapproval. He braced himself for her impending reprimand.

Karan always felt he grew up in the presence of three mothers. The first was his own mother whose love was of gentle firmness that complemented her grace. The second was his grandmother whose love was an ocean of endless mercy. She viewed the world with rose-coloured glasses and wouldn't speak ill, either of or to anyone, even in her dreams.

Then there was Laxmi *tai*. She was first hired by the Rathore family to help his mother as a wet nurse and had remained with them ever since becoming like part of the family. She was also the one they relied on to discipline him. Memories of all the times she had twisted his ears for doing something wrong came rushing back. She was the mother who raised him with tough love.

Laxmi Tai was known for her straightforwardness, never mincing words. It was this very quality that made her the go-to person for all kinds of gossip. This time, however, Karan had a very specific person in mind he wanted to inquire about, so she was exactly who he needed. But first, he steeled himself for the drilling he was about to receive.

"Now, look here, Karan," she began, her tone firm. "I'm very disappointed in you. How could you abandon everyone like that? No messages, hardly a phone call for over two years. Is this how we raised you? Do you think just by sending money your responsibilities are over?"

Karan hung his head in shame, knowing she was right. His actions had been dishonourable, not just to those who loved him, but also to the memory of his parents who had raised him better than that. The way he left was cowardly. The dreams he went away to pursue had come at the expense of other people's pain. Now that those dream lay in ruins, he realized that what he had been chasing were mere illusions.

He had a lot of amends to make. To his Daadi, to Laxmi *tai*. And to Janvi.

Laxmi *tai* continued to berate him and he listened to every word in silence giving her his complete attention. He knew no one else would tell him what he needed to hear. When she finished, Karan looked into her eyes and apologized to her.

"*Tai*, I know what I've done is hard to forgive. You are right, you have raised me better than that. I can't change what I have done but I want to make amends. So could you please forgive me?" Karan said, his voice laced with sincerity.

"And besides," he continued with a cheeky smile, "haven't you always said, *'subah ka bhula sham ko ghar aaye'...?"*

"*Toh usse bhula nahi kehte,*" she finished, a smile breaking through her earlier disapproval.

"Naughty boy," she chided him lovingly. "You've always had a way with words. Come, give me a hug."

Karan wrapped Laxmi *tai* in his arms, towering over her. At almost six feet tall, he was used to towering over everyone. Far behind them in the kitchen, he saw Janvi, who had been trying to open a stainless-steel container, pause in her act when her eyes fell on them hugging. A strange emotion passed over her face but she shook it off as quickly as it had come resuming her task at hand.

What was that?

Anger, pain... longing?

He let go of Laxmi *tai*.

"See I've already forgotten what I was doing after seeing you." she complained, "Janvi told me to go see your *daadi*."

"Speaking of," Karan ventured trying his luck, "*how* is she?"

Laxmi *tai* smiled understanding exactly what he was asking.

"She's nice. But *very* strict." she whispered conspiratorially.

"Strict?" Karan raised an eyebrow, intrigued. "In what way?"

"Yes, just like a school *masterni.* No, I don't mean she is a mean person, she's just a very no-nonsense girl. If something needs to be done, there are no delays. She has it done right away. Everything that you'd want in the house, she'll know exactly where it is. Completely organized. And she looks after everyone especially your *daadi.* All day long, she runs around the *haveli* with that diary of hers.

"What needs to happen in the haveli, how it needs to happen, when it needs to happen, who needs to do what, what to cook, what to buy. She even keeps an updated list of grocery prices. Like this *Nand Utsav* that is happening today. She's planned the whole menu, bought and bargained for the vegetables, sent out the invites, organized the cleaners and decorators. In short, Janvi runs a tight ship."

Karan tried to take a breath on her behalf. But Laxmi *tai* continued, "Now that we are talking about her, I must add, I'm also extremely disappointed with you for what you did to that poor girl. Did you know because of you she had to—"

"Laxmi!" they were interrupted by their *daadi* calling out from her room who was no doubt wondering which ditch in the *haveli* Laxmi *tai* had decided to fall into this time.

"Coming," Laxmi *tai* shouted back. "We'll talk later," she promised Karan before she started rushing away.

"Oh," she came back looking concerned, "but you're here, *nah?* As in you're not going away again any time soon?"

Karan assured her that he was here for a while before marching her off and continuing his way to the kitchen. When Janvi saw him come in, she simply tipped her head towards the table indicating that he sits down. She didn't say anything else.

No nonsense indeed, he thought amusedly.

Karan took his seat at the small wooden table in the kitchen. With his elbow propped on the table and his head resting on his hand, he watched her in fascination as she pulled out a stainless-steel *thali* and quickly and efficiently filled it up.

She placed the *thali* on the kitchen table in front of him, poured him a glass of water and went back to stirring what looked like a large pot of *kheer* on a wood stove in the portico just outside the kitchen.

He looked down at this plate to find *baajre ki khichdi*. He tasted a spoonful of it. It tasted delicious. The warm, savory spices gave him a feeling of comfort. He wasn't hungry, but considering he hadn't eaten in over eighteen hours, he should be grateful for whatever he was getting.

Janvi walked back to the kitchen, picked up a mortar and a pestle and placed it in front of him on the table. She then took the elaichis that had already been deseeded, poured them into the mortar and began pounding them mercilessly.

Thump. Thump. Thump.

It reminded him of the cricket bat she swung at him the night before. The way she pounded the *elaichi*, he suspected she was imagining his brains in there.

Karan decided to see if he could attempt to break the ice. He cleared his throat.

"The *khichdi* is delicious," he said.

Thump. Thump. Thump.

"Did you make it?" he asked slowly.

Thump. Thump. Thump.

She looked at him without stopping and gave a brief nod before turning her focus back to the mortar. It was a subtle motion which he would have missed if he wasn't looking at her.

Okay, now we're getting somewhere, Karan thought hopefully.

"Did you also leave the chai in my room?"

Thump. Thump. Thump.

This time she didn't look up; she simply shook her head twice indicating she had not.

Karan opened his mouth to ask something else when she stopped, picked up the mortar and walked back outside to the pot of kheer in the portico. Karan's eyes continued to follow her, mesmerized by everything she was doing. First, she flipped the contents of the mortar into the kheer, put it down on the floor and then went back to stirring the pot. A soft gust of wind blew a stray lock of her hair in her eye which she flicked back with a blow of her mouth.

She then used the spatula to scoop a small amount of rice and checked the texture between the fingers of her other hand. Somehow, it brought back the memory of those hands holding a glass of milk on their wedding night, the night he told her he loved someone else and that he was leaving. Karan winced at the memory.

"Badri *kaka*!" she called out.

Badri *kaka* and another kitchen staff went running out to help with moving the pot while Janvi immediately started working on making dough for *puris*.

Karan could sense the awkwardness between them, knowing it was mostly his fault. Janvi looked incredibly busy today, her focus sharp as she worked diligently on her tasks. Unsure of how to approach the situation, he decided it was best to give her some space for the moment.

After finishing his breakfast, he glanced at her again, feeling an urge to help. But he hesitated, uncertain if she wanted assistance or simply needed to be left alone. With a silent promise to himself to find a way to bridge the gap between them later, Karan stood up and quietly left the kitchen.

4

BETWEEN THE LINES

Karan wandered through the halls of the *haveli*. Each corner of this house was steeped in memories. The walls adorned with family portraits. He passed his father's study, the door of which was left slightly ajar.

As he walked curiously into the dimly lit office, the familiar scent of old wood and leather wrapped around him like a forgotten embrace. Memories of his childhood flickered through his mind, of the laughter shared with his father and the lessons learned in this very space. His gaze drifted across the room, finally landing on his father's portrait above the desk, behind the leather chair. He remembered that the last time he was in this room was with Bakshi Uncle, so clear on his vision for life, his love for Anya and desperately trying to get out of marrying Janvi.

And now, he wasn't so sure.

He ran a hand on the carved frame of his father's chair, reliving his memories. He could almost smell the faint scent of his cologne mixed with single-malt. As he walked around, he noticed stacks of papers and ledgers on the desk. Clearly, the space was being used. Curiously, he looked through the contents.

As he leafed through the papers, confusion knitted his brows together. These bills were recent. The expenses listed for the current month were staggering, far surpassing the automated value he had been sending each month.

"What on earth?" he muttered under his breath. This didn't make sense. Where was this being spent, and did they need more money?

Suddenly, the sound of the door creaking open pulled him from his thoughts, followed by the soft tinkle of Janvi's *paayal*. She stepped inside, her presence filling the room with the sweet smell of her shampoo. Karan felt an unexpected warmth spread through him as he watched her, captivated by the way her hair cascaded over her shoulders and how the light caught her features.

She held a tray of fruits and a glass of water. "You didn't eat much at breakfast, so I brought you this."

His gaze lingered on her as she walked in, placing the tray on the table, her movements graceful and effortless.

"Also," she added, her voice soft but steady, "*Daadi Sa* wanted you to join the *puja* and lunch for Nand Utsav."

Karan nodded, the weight of his earlier thoughts momentarily lifting.

"Alright, I'll be there," he replied, his tone more agreeable than he felt.

While it felt odd being instructed in his own house by this strange, bewitching woman, Karan also couldn't help feeling drawn. There was an allure to her manner that made it hard to look away. It wasn't just the way she looked, she was beautiful no doubt, but there was a soft strength to her. An elegance of sorts. And despite the chaos of his thoughts, there was something even comforting about her presence, something that stirred a longing. A longing for what thought, he couldn't quite grasp.

As she turned to leave, a moment of hesitation crossed her features. She glanced back, her brow furrowed slightly, "Can I ask you something?"

"Sure," Karan replied, his tone amiable but his brows now furrowed in curiosity.

"Why exactly are you here?"

Karan's surprise flickered across his face. "It's...my house," he responded carefully, his voice steady despite the sudden tension.

Janvi's cheeks flushed, and she quickly added, "That's not what I meant. I mean, you said you were going to return in three years..." Her voice trailed off, leaving the unspoken question hanging in the air.

A wave of guilt washed over him as he realized the implication of her words. She still thought they would divorce. He wasn't ready to disclose that all his best laid plans were in shambles and he hadn't really had time to reflect on any of it yet.

"I just came to check on the state of affairs of the estate," he said, the words spilling out before he could think and hoping it sounded casual enough.

The response caught Janvi off guard, and her expression shifted, a flicker of hurt mixed with confusion.

"You came to check on the estate?" she repeated.

Noticing a slightly stronger reaction than her earlier coldness, Karan decided to quickly lean into his improvised pretext with a bit more flair, "I think I'm well within my rights to check on my estate, don't you think?"

He paused, letting a slight smirk tug at the corner of his mouth. "Or were you planning on tossing me out like you swung that bat at me last night?"

Janvi's face reddened as she shot him an indignant look, replaying his words. "That's because I thought you were that..." She trailed off, then finished, almost reluctantly, "I thought you were an intruder!"

He arched an eyebrow, catching her odd choice of words but not giving it much thought in the moment. Instead, he seized the chance to push her further.

"Fair enough," he said, unable to resist. "Do you also go running into the arms of every intruder who shows up at the door?"

The quiet room suddenly seemed charged with tension as his teasing landed. Janvi looked flustered, her pride prickling at his playful accusation as she struggled for a response. Karan couldn't help but notice the way her cheeks coloured as she met his gaze, her silence proving even more satisfying than any retort.

"What are you insinuating?" she asks annoyed.

Karan's gaze lingered on the ledgers before him, a smirk

flickering on his lips. "The expenses seem... a little higher than usual," he remarked, casting a sidelong look at her. "You don't happen to have a... boyfriend you're providing for, do you?"

Janvi's eyes widened, both shocked and affronted by his insinuation. "Excuse me?" she demanded, her voice barely concealing her indignation.

Karan walked around to the front of the desk, leaned on it with his hands in his pockets feigning a casual demeanour. "I mean, I wouldn't hold it against you," he continued smoothly. "Two and a half years is a long time for anyone to be left on their own. Just thought it'd explain a few things if you'd found... companionship."

Her face flushed, caught between embarrassment and anger. "If you think so little of me—" she began, but he cut her off with a slight, dismissive wave.

"Not at all," he replied, enjoying her reaction. "I'd say it would be practical, actually. Sensible, even." He looked at her, his expression unreadable, but there was a subtle, almost hopeful edge to his voice.

Janvi took a breath, gathering her composure. "For your information, Mr. Rathore, I don't *need* anyone else's support to handle the affairs here," she replied, her voice laced with defiance. "And if you think I'm here looking for anyone's companionship, least of all yours, you're entirely mistaken."

Karan's amusement didn't waver, though something softened in his gaze. Her admission of not needing anyone else perhaps relieved him in a way he wouldn't readily admit.

Janvi's eyes flashed with barely restrained anger. "And may I add, if you're so fond of snooping around in the first place, why don't you snoop at the ledgers more properly?"

With that last retort, Janvi whirled around and stormed out of the room, the soft clinking of her anklets following her, the sharp rustle of her *dupatta* and the defiant tilt of her chin rooting him in place, an unanticipated surge of attraction pulling at him. He hadn't expected her to be so... feisty. That flash of indignation in her eyes, the way her voice had trembled—not with fear but with restrained anger—had him feeling oddly off-kilter.

A slow grin spread across Karan's face. This was a side of her he hadn't expected, one with fire and bite, a world apart from her so far, distant composure. It was refreshing—and far more intriguing than the cold, polite silence she was so far greeting him with. Staring at the door she'd exited through, a faint smirk still playing at his lips. Perhaps, he thought, this visit would be far more interesting than he'd anticipated.

For a moment, he found himself wanting her to return, to throw another sharp look his way. His gaze lingered on the space where she had been, the trace of her sandalwood scent still in the air, disarming him more than he'd like to admit.

Shaking himself out of it, he turned back to the ledgers, curious to see what had driven her to such intensity. But as his eyes settled on the numbers, he forgot everything else, his respect for her deepening with every page he turned.

As Karan scanned each line from the first page, a creeping realization took hold. The figures, each carefully documented, told a story he wasn't expecting. Not only had they managed the monthly expenses, but she was somehow generating revenue each month with profits steadily increasing, expenses well-managed—and all of it without a single rupee from him. The money he sent remained in the primary account never once withdrawn. She was running the estate like clockwork. All without his help.

"What the...?" he muttered, flipping to another page as if expecting to find some hidden flaw. But there was none.

His respect for Janvi flared, sharp and sudden. The girl he'd dismissed as a mere responsibility and without a glance had been handling everything—and with more efficiency than he'd imagined. This estate, his estate, wasn't just surviving in his absence. It was thriving.

Karan paused, glancing up at the large portrait of his father hanging above the desk. The stern but warm eyes looked back at him, familiar yet haunting, as if seeing right through his guarded thoughts.

A strange sense of awe mixed with regret tugged at him. Had he underestimated all of this? Underestimated *her*?

His father had chosen her—a young woman who, against all odds and without anyone's help, had kept the estate alive, even growing it beyond his expectations.

"Did I get it all wrong, Dad?" he murmured softly, an unexpected warmth filling his chest. His father had left him more than an inheritance—he'd left him a partner, a gem that he'd overlooked until now.

Karan's gaze drifted back down from his father's portrait, his brows knitting as he replayed Janvi's words in his mind.

"*That... intruder,*" she'd said. It wasn't just a simple slip up—it was almost as if she'd caught herself mid-thought, trying to hide something. Why would she use that specific phrasing? She was far too composed for a random stumble.

A resonant sound of a *shankh* pierced the stillness, signalling the start of the *puja*. The echo reverberated through the room, pulling him back from his thoughts. He took a deep breath, his train of thought momentarily interrupted. He decided to come back to this later. As Karan left the office, he casted one last glance at the ledgers shaking his head in disbelief.

* * *

The sun hung high in the Rajasthan sky, casting a warm, golden hue over Rathore *Haveli*. The courtyard buzzed with life as villagers, neighbours, and extended family gathered to celebrate *Nand Utsav*. The scent of marigold garlands mingled with the smoke of incense, filling the air. In the centre of the *mandap*, Punditji had arranged a small throne for Bal Gopal, alongside the vessels for the *panchamrit abhishek* and *aarti*. Drums and folk songs echoed softly, heightening the festive atmosphere.

Karan observed from the portico, his heart tugging at the sight of this ancient courtyard now brimming with warmth. Suddenly, his grandmother spotted him and waved him over.

"Punditji, Karan is also home after such a long time for the celebrations," his grandmother said with pride as she introduced him.

"Oh, so this is Karan?" Punditji's eyes sparkled as he blessed Karan, who respectfully bent to touch his feet.

"Your grandson has come home at a very auspicious time, Renuka Devi ji," Punditji remarked, addressing Karan's grandmother. "Just like Gopal Krishna."

"Yes," *Daadi* chuckled, "he is our very own Krishna."

They all laughed, Karan could only smile with embarrassment.

"Speaking of Krishna, where is his Radha? Where is our Janvi *bitiyan*?" Punditji inquired, glancing around.

"She is bringing Bal Gopal from the *puja ghar*," Renuka Devi replied. "Ah, there she is."

Karan turned and saw Janvi descending the steps of the corridor leading to the courtyard, her smile bright and welcoming, her hair flowing gently in the breeze. She carried the murti of Bal Gopal with a look of reverence, each step measured and graceful. The soft sunlight cast a warm glow around her, making her seem almost ethereal.

After their tense encounter in the office, Karan was expecting her to go back to ignoring him but as he was fast coming to realize, she didn't let her personal grudges get in the way of her responsibilities. Her smile didn't falter even when she greeted Punditji. Her presence commanded respect, a stark contrast to the guarded demeanour she had shown him earlier.

After what he read in the ledgers, he had been feeling more disconnected to his ancestral home and with the demeanour of the rest of the family, feeling completely like an outsider looking in. He noticed *Dadi, Laxmi Tai,* Badri Kaka, all staff members and guests looking upon Janvi with admiration, their faces glowing with pride.

Even Punditji, with his white beard and wise eyes, regarded her as a virtuous girl deserving of the highest praise. Everyone looked on at Janvi with admiration as she placed Bal Gopal on the throne in the *mandap* and took her seat on the *puja asan*.

He didn't blame any of them because Karan could also not take his eyes off of her. This time though, Karan's heart swelled with an unexpected mixture of admiration and longing as he watched her.

"Go Karan," his *Daadi* nudged Karan forward, urging him to join her. "The last two years she did this *puja* alone, this time she'll do it with her husband, just as it should be."

Karan was convinced he saw Janvi stiffen at the very idea obviously hesitant to be sitting next to him but she didn't protest. She shifted slightly to give him room on the cushion. When Karan settled down, his hand brushed against hers—a barely-there touch that sent a subtle jolt through her. She stiffened, her fingers instinctively curling away, but the warmth lingered, leaving her unable to focus on the *puja* unfolding before them.

Karan, however, seemed to relish her discomfort, a hint of a smile playing on his lips as he deliberately stayed close. The subtle tension between them danced in the air, unnoticed by the others yet impossible for them to ignore. Janvi felt a flush creep up her cheeks, her heart fluttering unbidden, while Karan basked in the silent thrill of being near her.

As the *puja* progressed, the vibrant colours of the festivities enveloped the mandap area, but his focus remained on Janvi. She performed the Gopal Krishna *abhishek* with grace after which she sang the *aarti* with poise, her voice ringing clear and melodious.

After the *aarti* and *puja* had concluded, Karan stood in the periphery of the courtyard leaning against a column watching with fascination as Janvi interacted with the guests, villagers and their children. Her laughter rang like music, bright and genuine, a sound he didn't know he needed but now couldn't get enough of. She served each and every one food with her own hands with a smile, engaging each person with a warmth that revealed her true nature. It stirred a longing in him.

Janvi, he proudly realized, had rooted herself in the hearts of the villagers and family alike, embodying the essence of an ideal Rathore daughter-in-law and fulfilling her duties with grace. Despite his rejection on their wedding day, she had never let it tarnish the family's reputation or allow his estate to fall into neglect.

Karan's regret was running deep the more he learnt about her. He wondered if it would be a long road to redemption?

As the festivities continued, Karan caught sight of Daadi speaking with a police officer, her expression serious and focused. Karan observed the interaction from a distance, a nagging sense of unease creeping into his thoughts. Just as he made his way toward them, he noticed Daadi deftly shifting the conversation to mundane topics, her poise unwavering. The policeman nodded, receiving Daadi's blessings before he began to depart.

"Mr. Rathore," the officer greeted him with a respectful nod walking past him, but Karan's mind was focused on the subtle tension he sensed between Daadi and the police officer.

"Is everything alright?" Karan asked, feigning nonchalance as he approached his grandmother. But the way Daadi met his gaze told him something was amiss.

"Of course, my dear. Just a little chat," Daadi replied smoothly, her tone betraying nothing. Yet, Karan could feel the undercurrents of concern, the way his grandmother's gaze flickered towards Janvi, who stood at a distance, a shadow of worry crossing her features.

As the officer walked away, Karan wondered if they were all keeping something from him. Janvi's slip up in the office, her trembling in his arms the night before, Daadi's conversation with the police officer and looking at Janvi with concern. *What was going on?*

"Karan, beta," his grandmother said.

"Yes, Daadi?" Karan asked.

"Have you had *prasad* and lunch?"

"Not yet, I thought I'd wait for you and Janvi to finish helping the guests so we could all have lunch together," Karan said, tucking away his previous thought.

"Yes, that is an excellent idea. However, we might be a while as not everyone has eaten yet. Why don't you help out a little while you wait?" his grandmother asked.

"Sure, what do you need?" he asked.

"We're running low on *pattal* plates," Daadi said, gesturing toward the front entrance of the haveli. "I think they've already delivered some. Could you check and help bring them in?"

Karan nodded, setting off toward the entrance. As he reached the large wooden doors and stepped outside, he spotted a bundle of neatly stacked *pattal* plates waiting to be brought inside. Bending to pick up the bundle, he noticed a boy approaching on a bicycle, his face flushed from the exertion.

5

FROM THE HANDI

"Hey, watch out!" the boy called as he hopped off, skidding to a halt right in front of Karan.

"Has the *puja* started?" he asked, eyes wide with anticipation.

Karan smiled. "The *puja* just finished."

"Oh shoot!" the boy muttered, a pout forming on his face. "*Didi* is going to kill me."

"If you are here for lunch, though, they're still serving inside," Karan offered. "I can show you to the courtyard if you like."

The boy crossed his arms, indignation flashing in his eyes. "Uh, excuse me, mister, this is *my* house. I know where to go."

Karan raised an eyebrow, intrigued. "*Your* house?"

"Yup." The boy studied him with a mixture of suspicion and curiosity. "Who are *you*, anyway?"

"Karan," he replied, a smile tugging at his lips. "And you are?"

"I'm Aman," the boy declared proudly. "What are you doing here, Mr. Karan? Are you here for the *Nand Utsav* lunch?"

"I suppose I am," Karan replied, amused. "So, Aman, is this really your house? Isn't it a bit big for you?"

Aman laughed, shaking his head. "It's not just me, silly! I live here with my sister. Do you know her?"

Karan's expression softened with curiosity, wondering if he was perhaps related to one of the servants. "I don't think so. What's her name?"

"Janvi!" Aman's chest puffed with pride.

Karan's brow furrowed in surprise, taken aback. *Janvi has a brother?*

"Your sister... is Janvi?" he asked, masking his astonishment.

"Uh-huh," Aman replied with an enthusiastic nod.

Karan watched as Aman's expression shifted, his earlier cheer fading as he kicked a small stone on the ground.

"I really wanted to be here for the *puja*," Aman muttered, his shoulders slumping. "I promised *Didi* I'd be back in time, but... I went into town to get her favourite sweets for today." He pulled a small, neatly wrapped box from his bag, looking at it with regret. "She does so much for everyone, you know? I just wanted to do something nice for her, for once."

Karan's gaze softened, watching the boy wrestle with his disappointment. "I'm sure she'll appreciate it. Sometimes just the thought counts more than anything else."

Aman's lips quirked into a small smile, though it didn't quite reach his eyes. "Yeah... I hope so."

"I'm helping take these plates back. Should we walk to the courtyard together?" Karan offered.

"Sure," Aman agreed.

They walked in silence for a moment before Aman's face darkened. "She never asks for anything. She's always just... there, looking after everything and everyone. But she deserves better," he muttered, kicking the stone again. "Even her husband—my *jijaji*—left her right after their wedding. He didn't even stay for one night. Can you believe that?"

Karan's heart gave an unexpected pang. He forced himself to remain calm, curious to hear more from Aman's point of view.

"*Didi* never talks about him, but I know it hurt her. He just... left her, and now he's somewhere far away, probably not even thinking about her. She pretends she's fine, like she doesn't care, but I know she does," Aman added, his young face set with a mix of anger and sadness. "I can't stand him, you know? Whoever he is, he's just... selfish."

Karan swallowed, feeling the weight of Aman's words settle heavily on him. He didn't know how to respond, the guilt twisting in his chest.

After a moment, Karan spoke, his voice quiet. "Maybe... he didn't realize what he was leaving behind? Sometimes people make mistakes, and by the time they understand, it's already too late."

Aman shot him a dubious glance. "Well, I still think he's a jerk," he huffed. "He doesn't deserve her."

Karan nodded slowly, hearing the truth in Aman's words. "You're probably right."

They fell silent again, and Aman glanced at Karan with a mix of innocence and determination. "But I'll make it up to her, somehow. I promised I'd always take care of her, no matter what."

Karan felt a surge of unexpected respect for this boy and a renewed sense of responsibility weighing on him. *Maybe it's time I tried to make things right, too.*

As their conversation continued, Karan's curiosity about Janvi's efforts grew. "So, what else does your sister do?" he asked casually, hoping to lighten Aman's mood and hopefully to gain more insights into her life.

Aman perked up a little, happy to talk about his sister. "What doesn't she do?" he began, eyes widening with admiration. "She does *everything* around here. She handles all the estate stuff, helps with the villagers, and keeps track of all the money. And she even makes the best *laddoos* for festivals!"

Karan raised his eyebrows, genuinely impressed. "She sounds... pretty remarkable."

"Yeah, she's the best. Like today, for the Nand Utsav, she's been planning for weeks. She invited everyone from the village for lunch, just like last year. And you know what? Daadi *Sa* always tells her stories about our family history, and she helps Didi decide how to set everything up," Aman said, a proud grin on his face. "And then there's Laxmi Tai, who's been like a second mother to us. She helps Didi cook and always makes sure everything is perfect for the guests."

Karan smiled, picturing Janvi working alongside those familiar faces. "It sounds like she has a good team around her."

"Definitely! Badri Kaka is also a huge help. He's like the gardener, handyman and more and he knows everything about the estate. If Didi needs help, he's always there for her. But Didi does all the hard work too, you know? If she had it her way, she would climb up on the roof to fix leaks if she has to," Aman said, his admiration evident.

Karan felt a warmth spreading in his chest. *So, Janvi wasn't just managing his family's estate; she was practically holding it together single-handedly, with the support of people who cared about her.*

"Does she ever ask for help?" Karan asked, genuinely intrigued.

Aman shook his head, his expression serious. "Nope. She never wants anyone to worry about her. Even if something's wrong, she just pretends it's fine. I've seen her stay up all night to finish paperwork sometimes. But she never complains." He frowned, frustration evident in his youthful face. "Sometimes, I wish she'd let me help her, but she insists on doing everything herself."

Karan's gaze drifted toward the courtyard, where the soft hum of festivities continued. He felt a strange ache in his chest, an unfamiliar sense of regret and respect mingling as he considered how much of her life he'd missed.

"What about friends?" he asked gently. "Or... someone she can talk to?"

Aman shrugged, a shadow of sadness crossing his face. "Not really. It's just us now. She doesn't have many friends here, and she doesn't talk about... well, she doesn't really talk about *jijaji*, either." He looked down, frowning. "It's like she's all alone sometimes, even with *Daadi Sa* and everyone around."

The weight of those words settled over Karan. He'd once thought he could simply walk away, detached and unaffected, but learning more about Janvi and her how she was building her life all on her own—stirred something deep within him.

As they reached the courtyard, Karan found himself wondering how he'd even begin to make up for lost time—and, more importantly, if he'd even deserve the chance.

"Aman!"

Karan and Aman turned towards the mandap to find Janvi calling him out.

"Aman, where were you? You missed the *puja*." Janvi asked with a hint of concern.

"Sorry, didi, I went to get your favourite *mawa kachoris* for the *bhog*," Aman said, sounding a little disappointed.

"Acha, it's okay," Janvi softened, giving him a small smile. "At least come have some *prasad*."

"Yes, didi," Aman replied with a nod.

Janvi briefly glanced at Karan, the tension still thick between them, before turning to leave.

Karan opened his mouth to say something, but Daadi approached him first.

"Karan, there you are! Thank-you for helping with the plates. Now, hand those to Badri and come sit with us for lunch."

In the mandap area, Punditji, Daadi, *Aman*, and Karan sat cross-legged in a line on woven mats, awaiting to be served *prasad* and *lunch*. Daadi looked affectionately at Aman, her gaze slipping toward Karan.

"So, Aman," she said, her tone playful, "you finally get to meet your *jijaji*, hmm?"

Aman turned, his eyes widening in surprise as he looked at Karan. "You're my *jijaji*?" he asked, clearly taken aback.

"Guilty as charged," Karan replied, sheepishly scratching the back of his neck. "I know I've let you down, Aman, but... do you think you could forgive me? I promise to be a better *jijaji* from now.

Aman considered it for a moment, then broke into a bright grin. "Alright, I forgive you! But you have to promise me you'll save me from Didi's scolding when I don't finish my homework!"

Karan chuckled, sharing a quick, conspiratorial look with him. "Deal." Karan wondered if it could be as simple with Janvi.

The scent of spices filled the space as Janvi moved down the line, serving the *sabzi* with practiced grace. She offered a respectful portion to Punditji, then served Daadi and Aman, who accepted with a warm smile.

As Janvi leaned down to serve Karan with a large ladle, he instinctively reached out, placing a gentle hand on her wrist. "That's enough," he murmured, genuinely trying to stop her from piling more food onto his plate. But the moment his fingers brushed her skin, Janvi froze, her eyes darting to where his hand held hers.

Karan caught the flicker of surprise in her expression, a hint of nervousness she couldn't quite hide. Amused, he realized it was the first time he had ever touched her. Something stirred inside him—an unexpected mix of mischief and desire. The spark was undeniable.

Janvi attempted to pull away, but rather than let go, he tightened his hold ever so slightly unbridling her. Karan's thumb lightly traced along her wrist, lingering just a moment longer than necessary, his touch deliberate. Her skin was warm, impossibly smooth under his thumb. Janvi's breath caught in her throat.

With a subtle smirk, he leaned in closer and whispered, "Maybe save some space for something sweet?"

Janvi's cheeks flushed a deep shade of pink, her gaze flicking away as she quickly pulled her hand free. Flustered and clearly embarrassed, she turned and busied herself with getting more food, keeping her focus anywhere but on him.

Karan watched her with an amused glint in his eyes, savouring her reaction and the blush that lingered on her cheeks. But beyond the amusement, he felt a spark of something more—a desire that was new, yet undeniably real.

After lunch, Aman and Karan helped serve the guests in the courtyard while Janvi took a moment to eat, her expression a mix of contentment and exhaustion.

As the guests and villagers began to depart, Aman, bursting with energy, grabbed Karan's hand and pulled him around to the other side of the *haveli*. As Karan followed the excited boy, a sense of disorientation crept over him. He didn't recognize this part of the *haveli* at all. There had been something else here before, but what was it?

His mind raced as he struggled to recall the cluttered storage room that had once been filled with dust-covered antiques and forgotten relics.

Just then, Aman turned and led him toward a new entrance, and Karan's heart skipped a beat as they approached. The space had been completely reimagined. Ticket windows flanked the entrance, where visitors eagerly lined up, their laughter and chatter creating a vibrant atmosphere that contrasted sharply with the silence of the old storeroom.

Karan's eyes widened in disbelief; this was no longer a place of neglect but a lively museum, showcasing carefully restored artifacts that gleamed under the soft lighting. Each piece seemed to tell a story, a whisper of the past woven into its very fabric. Beside the museum, a bustling restaurant filled the air with the rich aromas of traditional dishes, inviting patrons to sit and savour the culture of their heritage.

"What's this?" Karan blurted out; the shock evident in his voice. "Is this... open to the public?"

Aman nodded with a grin. "*Didi* turned this into a museum! She had everything cleaned and restored. It's to share our history with everyone and to make money."

Karan's mind reeled, recalling the ledgers in his father's office. *This was how she was generating revenue.* The enormity of it struck him—she was maintaining the honour of the *haveli* while creating jobs for villagers and preserving their culture for a broader audience.

As he stood there, grappling with the realization that Janvi had not only transformed the space but had done so with remarkable vision and determination, he felt a profound sense of admiration. She had consulted with Jaisalmer's cultural centres and historians, sealing off the unused lounge room next to the museum to optimize the area.

She had not only rejuvenated the space but had also created a lifeline for the community, employing villagers and preserving their culture for a broader audience. The realization that she had accomplished this all on her own left him speechless, and he couldn't help but marvel at the woman he had once sworn to not even look at.

As Karan stood in the transformed space, taking in the vibrant atmosphere and the meticulous care Janvi had put into reviving the haveli's history, a memory flickered in his mind—the sharpness in Janvi's voice echoing from their ledger's earlier conversation in the office. *"And may I add, if you're so fond of snooping around in the first place, why don't you snoop at the ledgers more properly?"*

Her words resonated with him now, carrying a weight he hadn't fully grasped before. He had been so preoccupied with his own assumptions, that he had failed to see the bigger picture she was working to create. The jumbled story, the numbers on the ledgers were showing, now suddenly clear. But it wasn't merely about finances; it was about the legacy of the *haveli* and the community that surrounded it.

Karan's heart sank with a mix of shame and admiration. Janvi had known what she was doing all along, and she had done it without his input or support. Instead of being a burden, she had taken on the responsibility with grace, transforming the past and securing a future for herself, his Daadi, and the villagers.

The thought of divorce now seemed not only unthinkable but profoundly unfair. How could he ever justify removing her from Daadi's life or uprooting her from the community that relied on her? The idea of severing ties felt heavy, a choice that would ripple through everyone connected to them. Karan realized he could never separate her from this; she was far too intertwined with the heart of this place.

His perception of her shifted dramatically. Karan couldn't help but feel a pang of regret for never giving her the chance. Like Bakshi Uncle had told him to.

Aman, bursting with energy, darted off to join his friends, laughter trailing behind him as he ran. Karan watched the boy disappear around the corner of the *haveli*, the sound of his excitement fading into the distance leaving Karan alone with his thoughts.

Karan leaned against a pillar, trying to absorb the full weight of his ignorance. Just then he heard the now familiar tinkle of Janvi's *paayal* behind him.

He turned around to find Janvi, hesitating, almost seeking out his thoughts on the transformation of the storeroom.

"Janvi," he whispered.

"So, what do you think?" she asked, careful almost nervously.

Karan met Janvi's gaze, searching for the right words. "It's incredible," he finally said, his voice barely a whisper. "I can't believe how much you've done."

A small smile broke through her initial hesitation, but uncertainty flickered in her eyes. "It's your family's history. I wanted to honour that. I had *Daadi Sa's* blessings." Her tone was almost tentative. Karan sensed her underlying anxiety that he might not be pleased. But contrary to her fears, he felt genuinely impressed by her ingenuity.

"You've done more than honour it. You've breathed new life into it," he replied, feeling admiration swell within him. "This place feels vibrant now, like it has a purpose. Not to mention creating jobs and bringing people together!"

Regret washed over Karan. "I'm sorry," he whispered. "I was rude to you in the office."

Janvi shrugged it off with a small smile that didn't quite reach her eyes. "I'm going back to the courtyard to clean up."

Karan nodded as she left quietly, leaving him to simmer in his regret, reflecting on how wrong he had been about her.

* * *

That night, after the household had quieted and the staff had left, they all sat together in the lounge room, the warm, flickering glow of candlelight filling the space. Daadi sat in her armchair, busy with her crocheting, while Aman lay sprawled on his stomach on the floor, nose buried in a comic book. Karan sat beside them on the floor, his head resting against Daadi's knees, feeling a sense of ease settle over him.

Across from them, Janvi sat on the sofa, legs folded beneath her, mending Aman's uniform with a needle and thread.

Karan's voice softened as he spoke to Daadi. "The museum looks incredible, Daadi," he murmured, almost as if thinking aloud. "It's like the *haveli's* history has found a new life."

Daadi paused her crocheting, glancing over at him with a quiet smile. "All it needed was someone who understood its worth," she replied, her eyes flicking knowingly to Janvi.

Aman piped up without lifting his eyes from his comic, "And now tourists come to see it! *Didi* really made it special."

Karan agreed, "Yes, Janvi has done remarkably well."

Janvi looked up, meeting Karan's gaze for a fleeting moment before lowering her eyes back to the fabric in her hands. The gentle, shared silence stretched on, each of them lost in their own thoughts, yet bound by an unspoken understanding as the candlelight flickered softly around them.

Karan found his gaze drifting toward her constantly, stealing glances when he thought she wouldn't notice. The candlelight cast a soft, warm glow over her face, highlighting the delicate sparkle of her earrings and the smooth fall of her hair as it slipped over her shoulder each time she bent forward to check a stitch. She was serene and focused, her features softened yet striking in the dim light.

When she finished a line of stitches, he watched, captivated, as she lifted the thread to her lips, biting it to snap it off. There was a calm, practiced grace to her movements, and though she didn't smile or glance his way, seemingly intent on her work, he couldn't help but feel mesmerized.

Janvi let out a small sigh, carefully folding Aman's mended uniform on her lap. She looked up, her gaze passing over Daadi, Aman, and Karan without lingering, her face calm but visibly tired from the day's work.

"If you don't mind, Daadi Sa, I think I'll retire for the night," she said softly, gathering her sewing kit and rising gracefully from the sofa. She nodded politely to each of them, her expression still guarded as her eyes briefly met Karan's. He noticed the fatigue in her movements, and something in her look lingered with him, a trace of softness she was careful not to reveal.

"Goodnight, *beta*," *Daadi* replied warmly, watching her leave with a fond smile.

Karan couldn't take his eyes off Janvi as she made her way to the hallway, her form disappearing into the shadows. There was an ache of admiration and guilt within him, and as the candlelight dimmed, he realized he felt the absence of her presence immediately, a silence settling over the room.

"Can you believe she's only twenty?" *Daadi* said, her voice light, almost conversational as she continued crocheting, the flicking sound of her needle creating a rhythm in the air.

Karan blinked, his attention still on where Janvi had just been, the remnants of her presence in the air around him. *Daadi's* words barely penetrated at first, his mind too tangled in thoughts of Janvi. But then, something about the age twenty lingered in his thoughts.

Only twenty?

The words bounced around in his tired, jetlagged mind, their full meaning just out of reach. His eyes drifted absently toward the space where Janvi had been sitting. Karan blinked, trying to focus through the fog. His mind, still sluggish from the long flight, the drive from Jodhpur yesterday and the long day today. He tried to latch onto the numbers.

Twenty. That means...

He worked through it slowly, his brain struggling to adjust to the rapid shift in understanding.

Karan, don't be an idiot. You married her two years ago... His thoughts ran over the timeline, trying to piece things together, counting the years on his finger tips absently.

He sat up straighter, the fatigue suddenly replaced by an intense, nauseating wave. *Eighteen.* The number reverberated in his head, louder with every second. *Eighteen...*

She had been *eighteen* when they married.

He began to feel sick to his stomach. His throat tightened. He had married a girl, barely out of school.

She was just a child, he thought, his heart lurching in his chest.

The weight of the sudden realisation began to crush him, suffocating him with guilt. These two and half years, all this time, and he hadn't even considered it—hadn't taken the time to realize that she was still so young.

He stood up, slowly, trying to seem casual and gave his *Daadi* a tired smile. "I think I'll retire to my room," he said, his voice low and controlled, betraying none of the turmoil that had just erupted inside him. "It's been a long day."

Daadi looked up from her crocheting, studying him briefly with a soft, maternal gaze. "Of course, *beta*. You must be exhausted after all the travelling yesterday and the whole day of *Utsav* today. Rest well."

Her tone was gentle, unaware of the storm brewing within him. Karan simply nodded in response, offering a small, tight smile before turning toward the door.

The walk to his room felt like it took an eternity, his mind whirling, still processing the calculation that had only just hit him. He could feel the tightness in his chest, the sensation of his breath being too shallow, like he couldn't quite draw enough air into his lungs.

When he reached his room, he closed the door quietly behind him, as if the action would somehow block out the reality of what he had just realized. The room was dimly lit, still, and cold. He stood for a moment, letting his eyes wander over the familiar surroundings, but they felt foreign now, as though he had stepped into a different world entirely.

He sank down onto the edge of the bed, his elbows resting on his knees, his head in his hands. His body felt exhausted, but his mind refused to slow down. The guilt, the shock, the uncertainty—they all clawed at him, making it difficult to focus.

Karan sat in the stillness of his room, the weight of the revelation pressing down on him.

She was 18. And he had been 29 at the time!

The thought reverberated in his mind. He tried to recall their wedding day—so distant, so clouded by his own turmoil. She had been covered by the *ghunghat,* so he hadn't really seen her then. During the *mangalsutra* and sindoor ceremony, he could have looked at her, but he chose not to. He had turned away, consumed by his own grief and anger.

She was a child! God, only 18?

Karan ran his hand through his hair in frustration. His chest tightened as the thought tore through him. At that age, he had been packing his bags, excited to leave for London and start his life, full of dreams and opportunities. And she—she was thrust into a marriage with a man almost twelve years her senior, to someone she didn't know, someone who hadn't even bothered to look at her on their wedding night.

He clenched his fists, the weight of it sinking in. There he was, angry at his own life for being derailed, for the career he had to leave behind, for the love of his life who was about to slip away. And what had she been doing? Losing everything. Her youth, her freedom, her chance at a life of her own.

He had no right to feel sorry for himself, no reason to brood over the things he lost. She was the one who had lost it all. She had it worse—so much worse.

And what had he done to make up for it? Nothing.

The thought of it made his stomach twist. She'd been sacrificed for him. And there he was, wallowing in his own self-pity. Telling her on their wedding night that he loved someone else in this very room, when she never even had a chance to live. She was thrust into a life she never chose, a life of obligation and duty. And he—selfish, bitter, too caught up in his own pain—had added to it by cruelly declaring that his heart belonged elsewhere.

What the hell were you thinking, Karan? You're almost twelve years older than her, and you acted like an entitled teenager? You were ready to divorce her, and then what did you expect her to do afterward? Here you were, disillusioned by the love you thought was real, while she had been making the best of everything life had handed her—honouring the family legacy, taking on a responsibility that no one should ever have to bear at her age.

She's was a child! A child!

All this time, you had been so caught up in your own pain, your own escape, you didn't even realize it was your job to guide her. Not Daadi's, not Laxmi Tai's. Your job! It hit him like a truck. The weight of it slammed into his chest, suffocating him with the force of his realization.

What an entitled idiot I have been!

Karan sat still, his breath caught in his throat. All this time, he had thought he was the one bound—by duty, by obligation, by the promises his father had made. He thought he was the one sacrificing, trapped in a marriage he never wanted. But now, staring at the truth in front of him, it hit him with devastating clarity: *She* was the one who had it worse.

At eighteen, she had been thrust into this life—married to a stranger, left to navigate a world that had suddenly changed around her. No choice, no voice. He had been the one to leave, the one to escape into his own life, but she... she had stayed. And in doing so, she had to grow up faster than anyone should.

Karan exhaled sharply, the weight of his thoughts pressing down on him. He had always been consumed by his own pain, his own disappointment, and had failed to see the truth about Janvi. He hadn't been the one bound by their marriage—she had been. She was the one who had borne the weight of it all, alone.

His hand gripped the edge of the bed as the realization hit him like a truck. How had he been so blind, so selfish? He had left her to fend for herself when he should have been protecting her.

The stillness of the room felt suffocating. He couldn't change the past, but he knew now that he had to do better.

Karan stood, walked to the window, and looked out into the quiet night. Somewhere out there, Janvi was sleeping, just as she always had—alone.

He couldn't undo what had been done, but he could try to make it right. For once, he wouldn't run away.

He would stay.

6

THE ENIGMA THAT IS JANVI

Over the next week, Karan had learnt Janvi's daily schedule inside and out. She would wake up at six in the morning to prepare breakfast and lunch for Aman before getting him ready for school.

After the daily morning *puja*, she would make chai and breakfast for the rest of the household.

Mid-morning, she would either help out in the museum and restaurant, engaging with tourists or go to the markets in town to buy groceries for the *haveli*. She would leave lunch and dinner cooking to Badri *Kaka* and Laxmi *Tai* but occasionally prepared meals on Sundays and festival days.

After lunch, Janvi would do her's and Aman's laundry. Karan noted with concern that despite having so many servants in the *haveli*, Janvi insisted on doing her's and Aman's chores on her own. While she played the role of lady of the house remarkably in front of outsiders, internally she hadn't fully embraced that role. Karan suspected with some guilt that that was likely his fault for not having given her any clarity on their relationship.

In the afternoons, she would manage the estate accounts, in the evenings, she would walk to the village and tutor children. Her age and the fact that she did so much, still took him by surprise.

She still avoided Karan as much as she could during the day deliberately keeping herself busy and ensuring she didn't cross paths with him. It didn't take Karan long to figure that out and it bothered him but he couldn't blame her one bit.

He would look forward to dinners with Daadi and Aman though because then she wouldn't have any excuse to avoid him.

One morning, Bakshi Uncle arrived at Rathore *Haveli* to pay a visit.

"How are you, Bakshi Uncle?" Karan greeted him as he walked into the formal lounge room near the foyer.

"Oh, Karan, my dear boy!" exclaimed Bakshi Uncle, surprise lighting up his features as he embraced Karan. "When did you arrive? This is such a wonderful surprise!"

"It's been about a week," Karan replied.

"Really?" Bakshi Uncle pondered.

"I drove by your office to see you but was told you were out of town," Karan added.

"Yes, I—"

"Bakshi *chacha*!" Janvi's vibrant voice interrupted as she entered the foyer, her energy brightening the room. She stooped to touch Bakshi Uncle's feet.

"God bless you, my darling girl," he said warmly, pulling her into a hug.

Karan watched their interaction with intrigue. Janvi was particularly chirpy to see him and while Bakshi Uncle had always been warm to Karan, he had never seen him so... fatherly towards anyone.

"*Chacha*, where were you? You missed *Janmasthami*!" Janvi complained playfully.

"Ah yes, *bachche*, as I was just about to tell Karan here, I had gone to Bikaner for a few days to meet with a client," Bakshi Uncle explained. "And since you love *Rasgullas*, I brought along Bikaner's famous ones for you and Aman. When I got here, I was pleasantly surprised to see Karan!"

"Thank-you, *chacha*! I'll go put the Rasgullas away in the kitchen. Are you staying for lunch?" Janvi asked, completely ignoring Bakshi Uncle's surprise at Karan's arrival.

"No, not today. I have some urgent work at the office. I thought

I'd give you the Rasgullas while they're still fresh. I'll come by to visit this weekend," he replied.

"Okay, *chacha,* I have to go to the markets soon..." Janvi explained, but Karan interrupted.

"I'll see him out," Karan offered.

Janvi nodded at him her expression neutral.

"Bye, *chacha,*" she said, her voice brightening despite her apparent detachment.

"Bye, *beta,*" Bakshi Uncle responded as she left the room.

"Bakshi Uncle, I was wondering if I could come by the office tomorrow to see you?" Karan ventured as they walked together towards the entrance.

"Of course," Bakshi Uncle replied. "I'll let my PA know you'll be calling."

If Bakshi Uncle was wondering at Karan's motive for being in Jaisalmer after their previous Zoom call regarding divorce proceedings, he didn't voice it.

* * *

The next day, Karan found himself in Bakshi Uncle's office, seated in a newly renovated building in Jaisalmer town.

Narayan Bakshi was a man of remarkable integrity, his stature as imposing as his character. As far as Karan knew, Bakshi Uncle was never married, dedicating his life to law and justice. His honourable work and standing in society had earned him the respect that he enjoyed. Bakshi Uncle was also known to be frank so Karan knew to get to the point quickly.

"Bakshi Uncle, I know you didn't say anything yesterday, but I'm sure you were wondering why I'm here after previously denying your request to start the divorce proceedings in person," Karan began, meeting Bakshi Uncle's steady gaze.

"Without going into too much detail, I'd like to put that thought to rest. I've decided I'm not going to divorce Janvi."

Bakshi Uncle raised his eyebrow subtly surprised.

"At least... not without understanding where I stand with her," Karan clarified. "And that's partly why I am here. There are things I've learned about her from Daadi, Laxmi Tai, and even Aman. I've watched her closely these past few days, and I think I have a fair idea of who she is—her character, her personality, her strengths. But there's something about her that continues to elude me."

Karan exhaled, leaning forward slightly, "I realize the best way to do this is to talk to her directly, but we haven't exactly been able to get past the awkwardness that's between us and that's *entirely* my fault. I just don't know where to begin considering how I left things after our wedding. I know you once told me to give her chance and you obviously know her well. So, I'm hoping, maybe you could help me out. And I do have a lot questions."

"I see," Bakshi Uncle said, nodding thoughtfully. "Go on."

Karan hesitated for a beat before asking, "When we married, was she still in school?"

Bakshi Uncle gave a slow, thoughtful nod. "She... had just started her final term. So yes."

Karan leaned back in his chair, exhaling slowly. His jaw tightened.

"Did she at least finish?" his voice was slightly tight.

"With flying colours," Bakshi Uncle replied with a small smile. "96th percentile. She's always been a bright girl."

Karan nodded, processing the information. It was impressive—but it still didn't sit right with him.

"Why didn't you say anything?" Karan asked, his tone laced with frustration.

Bakshi Uncle tilted his head slightly. "To... you?"

"No..." Karan paused, running a hand through his hair. "I mean, to Dad. Or Daadi."

A sigh left Bakshi Uncle's lips. "Believe me, I tried my best to make your father see reason, but he had made up his mind. And we've gone through this before, Karan. Before your wedding."

Karan sighed, regret heavy in his voice. "Yes, yes we have. I just wasn't ready to listen properly back then. But it pains me that she was so young. She could have done so much more than just being married to me at eighteen."

Bakshi Uncle studied him carefully before responding. "You do realize that, in this country, statistically, 23% of women are married by that age, or earlier. I'm not justifying it, just stating a fact—it's not unheard of."

Karan nodded but frowned slightly, his concern deepening. "She was eighteen, at least, wasn't she?"

Bakshi Uncle smiled knowingly. "Just. Or, I can assure you, I of all people would have had something to say about that."

"Just?" Karan repeated, his voice edged with disbelief.

"She turned eighteen the month prior."

Karan scoffed, shaking his head. "I don't think that makes me feel any better. It may be legal, but was it moral?"

Bakshi Uncle exhaled, his voice patient. "Legality and morality have never been mutually exclusive. But your father truly considered securing her future his moral obligation. Anyway, it's done now. Any other questions?"

Karan's expression turned pensive. He hesitated before asking, "How did you and my father know her?"

Bakshi Uncle's gaze softened, his lips curling into a small, knowing smile.

"Ah," he murmured. "Now, that's a bit of a story."

Karan leaned forward. "I have all the time in the world, Bakshi Uncle. I don't have anywhere else to be right now."

Bakshi Uncle leaned back in his chair, fingers steepled, his expression thoughtful. "You've made some keen observations, Karan. Janvi is indeed a remarkable young woman, shaped by the circumstances of her life and your father's tutelage. He saw in her a lot of potential."

Karan nodded, absorbing Bakshi Uncle's words. "But why is she so determined to shoulder so much responsibility on her own? How can someone be so selfless? What motivates someone like her? She's clearly bright, but I also see so much of my father's influence in how she runs the house. And how did my dad know her?"

Bakshi Uncle regarded him with a knowing look as he began.

"Let me start from the beginning," he said finally. "As you may know, your father and I have been friends since childhood. We did a lot of things together—even joined the army at the same time."

Karan blinked in surprise. "Wait, you were in the army too?"

"Yes, indeed. I had put in ten years of service alongside Viren by the time we met Janvi's father. Ashok Talvar," Bakshi Uncle replied with a smile.

Karan's eyebrows shot up. *Janvi's father was in the army too?* Even before Bakshi Uncle could, the gears in Karan's mind had begun to turn. *Her father wasn't just a random friend or acquaintance of his father like he'd always assumed.*

"It was in 1997. We were in the Rajputana Rifles stationed at Srinagar. Viren was on field for peacekeeping and border patrol duties, and I was helping with logistical coordination and military legal matters," Bakshi Uncle continued. "Ashok was still a Lieutenant at the time."

Bakshi Uncle paused with a smile obviously reminiscing a funny incident.

"Viren and I were notorious for pulling pranks on new recruits. It was kind of like a rite of passage. So naturally, Ashok also had to go through it. It was a harmless prank. Hiding shoes of the new recruits. A bit of fun really but it was also a way to gauge how our recruits would react to the situation. You'd be amazed how much one can learn about someone this way. And you have to understand, that most army recruits don't come from well off families and shoes are an integral part of the uniform that is checked every day. So how someone handles the situation can be quite telling.

"Most men would panic or get frustrated. Those shoes aren't cheap either. It wasn't uncommon for recruits to steal, plead or scramble to borrow a pair just to avoid the wrath of the officers."

Bakshi Uncle's smile widened as he continued. "But Ashok

didn't do any of that. While others would be anxious or frantic, he kept his composure. Instead of searching desperately or trying to borrow a pair, he just dusted off his feet, straightened his posture, and showed up barefoot."

Karan's raised an eyebrow, an amused smile playing on his face at learning about his late father-in-law.

"Yes," Bakshi Uncle chuckled, nodding. "Stood there in line as if nothing was wrong, not a trace of worry on his face. It wasn't defiance—Ashok was always respectful—but he had this calmness about him. He was barely 20 years old but he had a sense of duty that overshadowed everything else. When the officer came over, Ashok looked him straight in the eye and said, 'Sir, I didn't want to be late to roll call. Reporting for duty was more important than anything else.'"

He already sounded a lot like Janvi, Karan thought with a surge of admiration.

"And they let it slide?" he asked.

Bakshi Uncle shook his head, a wave of nostalgia crossing his face. "No, they didn't let it slide entirely. The officer was impressed, but rules were rules. He told Ashok that while his dedication was admirable, discipline and proper attire were equally important. Ashok accepted the reprimand without a word, standing tall and respectful."

Karan's admiration deepened. "So, what did they do?"

"Well," Bakshi Uncle continued, chuckling, "they made him run drills—barefoot. All day. But Ashok didn't complain or ask for mercy. He took it all in stride, finished every drill, and earned a new level of respect from everyone around him. By the end of the day, those of us watching realized we'd tested not just his composure but his grit. From then on, no one ever questioned his resolve. He never let his circumstances come in the way of his responsibilities or his discipline."

Karan sat back, processing this with a newfound sense of respect. He could definitely draw the parallels between Janvi and her father—a dignified presence that didn't need words or displays but simply stood its ground, hardy and unwavering.

Bakshi Uncle leaned back, his gaze distant as if seeing into the past. "Ashok was the kind of man who made the best out of any situation. Never one to complain or let life's challenges shake him. He took everything in stride, no matter how tough it got. And I see so much of that in Janvi. She carries herself with the same grit. It's like they were both cut from the same cloth."

Karan nodded slowly, seeing his admiration reflected in the eyes of the older man. He couldn't deny it. She did seem to embody that same strength. Her stoic resilience, the way she ran the *haveli* with such care and precision, even though he hadn't been around to witness it. Not needing anyone's validation, and without a hint of complaint. It was something he had seen but couldn't quite comprehend.

Bakshi Uncle's voice broke through his thoughts. "We returned his shoes, apologized. But there was no anger, no need for retaliation. Ashok simply nodded, said it was done, and that was the end of it. There was no need for anything more."

Karan was quiet for a moment, his gaze fixed on the horizon. "It sounds like Ashok handled everything with grace," he said slowly, thinking about his own impulsive actions, about how quickly he had let his frustrations dictate his behaviour.

"Grace," Bakshi Uncle echoed with a smile, "that's exactly the word for it. Ashok understood something that many of us forget. That it's not the situation that defines a man, but how he handles it. And I see that in Janvi as well. She doesn't make a fuss, doesn't seek pity—she simply moves forward. I think that's what makes her so remarkable."

Karan, nodded absorbing the words. He couldn't deny it.

"We were best friends from then on, practically became like family," Bakshi Uncle continued, his eyes had a faraway look reflecting his nostalgia. "I left the army the following year transitioning fully into civilian legal practice but our bond had already strengthened by then. Viren remained in service as Ashok's direct senior. When Kargil War broke out in 1999, Ashok fought alongside Viren on the frontlines."

"Kargil?"

Karan's pursed his lips.

Kargil.

He had a hazy memory of that period. His mother, Gayatri, spending eventful mornings juggling meetings with managers and abiding anxious nights next to the phone hoping it wouldn't ring.

Bakshi Uncle nodded, his face growing more serious. "Yes. Rajputana Rifles was actively involved in reclaiming high-altitude positions held by Pakistani forces. Ashok was Captain by this time in charge of leading his company, so he was involved in close combat. Viren had progressed to Colonel, and he was in charge of the overall planning and coordination of the operations.

"There was a mission to reclaim Tololing Ridge, and your father entrusted the flank to Ashok's team. They crept up the treacherous slope under heavy fire, pinned down until Viren, hearing the commotion, broke from his own assault to back him up. Side by side, they fought through the night, silencing enemy fire and clearing the ridge for the battalion. By dawn, Tololing was back in Indian hands."

Karan listened, absorbing the weight of Bakshi Uncle's words, his respect for both men deepening. It was clear that the bond between them had been forged through shared hardship, mutual respect, and an unspoken understanding that transcended the battlefield.

Karan also realized how limited his view of his father had been at seven. Back then, all he saw was discipline and distance. But hearing of his father's bravery now, the man he once feared and resented felt completely different. Everything he thought he knew was shifting.

Bakshi Uncle paused, his expression softening. "Ashok married the next year. Viren and I had attended his wedding. After Ashok married, his life changed, as you'd expect. He had Janvi in 2004. A beautiful girl, strong like him. I wasn't around much, focused on my practice, but I remember Ashok always spoke of her with such pride. Even though I wasn't as involved after I left the army, I kept in touch. Viren and Ashok were still in the army, of course, serving side by side. Their bond only deepened over the years. They went through everything together—operations, peacekeeping, even the long stints away from home."

Karan was quiet, processing. He had been just over eleven when Janvi was born, and it struck him how much of his father's life had happened without him even knowing. And he somehow felt cheated. Not longer after, he had left for boarding school, and in that time, his father's life had continued to move on without him.

At school, Karan had buried his frustrations, lost in the routine of boarding life. But the distance only deepened. His father's rare visits felt like duty calls rather than father-son bonding, and Karan had learned to live with the absence, convincing himself it was normal. But deep down, he knew he had wanted more—more time, more attention, more of his father's warmth.

Karan snapped back to the present, blinking as Bakshi Uncle's voice pulled him from his thoughts. Bakshi Uncle's voice grew quieter, his gaze shifting slightly as he seemed to relive a painful memory.

"It was in 2012 when everything changed. Ashok and Viren were both deployed in Kashmir. It was war zone at the time. There was increasing unrest. The army had been tasked with maintaining order, which meant intense operations in hostile terrain. It was in the middle of one of these operations when disaster struck."

He paused, his hands folding over each other as if to steady himself.

"Ashok, along with their teams, were on a reconnaissance mission in a particularly dangerous part of the valley, near the Line of Control. They were making their way through a dense forest area. Viren wasn't supposed to be on field but he had insisted he wanted to join in to assess. Toward a dip in the road, the convoy hit a patch of IED which exploded."

Karan's breath hitched. The sense of danger, the tension of being in the field, hit him hard as Bakshi Uncle's words painted a vivid picture.

"Viren was knocked unconscious in the blast. He was trapped, pinned under debris, and if not for Ashok—" Bakshi Uncle's voice wavered, but he caught himself and pressed on. "Ashok didn't think twice. He dragged Viren to safety, under fire, despite the pain. He saved his life. But the cost... the cost was his leg."

Karan sat up straight, feeling the weight of the story settling over him. His mind went to the images of his father—strong, unbreakable Viren—and to Ashok, who had given so much in the name of duty.

Bakshi Uncle's eyes closed momentarily as he seemed to lose himself in the memory.

"It was... a brutal moment. Ashok was rushed to the field hospital, but the damage was irreparable. He lost his leg that day. It was a hard blow for everyone. A soldier without a leg."

Karan felt the gravity of the moment, the sacrifice that came with the job. He had never truly understood it before.

"Meanwhile, back home, Janvi's mother was in labour with their second child. It was a complicated delivery... and tragically, she passed away during childbirth. Aman, Janvi's younger brother, was born that day, but at the cost of her mother's life. Can you imagine? Ashok, fighting to stay alive in a military hospital, receiving the news of his wife's death while also trying to process the loss of his leg. And Janvi, only eight years old, losing her mother."

Bakshi Uncle exhaled deeply, his hands tightening into fists before he relaxed them again. "It was a hell of a year for them. Ashok was dealing with the loss of his leg, while also mourning his wife. Viren was recovering from his injuries, but more than that—he was dealing with the trauma of what happened, the fact that Ashok had saved him at such a great cost. There was no real time to recover, though. Both of them threw themselves back into their duties as best they could, but the emotional scars, they never go away."

Karan sat there, frozen, as Bakshi Uncle's words sank in. His mind was struggling to catch up with what he'd just heard. His father—Brigadier General Viren Singh Rathore—the man he'd always admired from a distance, had come so close to death, and Karan had never known.

He was nineteen years old in 2012, far away in London, fully immersed in his exciting university life. His father's near-death experience, had occurred while Karan was making friends, attending lectures, and moving through the routines of life.

Why was he never told?

His father had never mentioned it—never once in any of his calls home had Viren spoken of the attack. It had always been about duty, about his work, about getting back on his feet. Karan had assumed his father's military life was just that—his life. But now, with the full weight of what Bakshi Uncle had shared, Karan could see the cost of that life—the physical and emotional toll that had been buried beneath the stories of valour and honour.

He thought back to the times his father had come home, how he had always seemed distant, wrapped up in the quiet, unspoken pain of a man who had seen too much, given too much.

Had it always been this way?

Karan remembered how his father had kept him at arm's length. There was never much affection—no emotional displays, no words of reassurance.

Now, it made sense.

His father had been through hell and never said a word about it and the fact that Janvi's father had saved his life.

And for young Janvi to have lost her mother. Karan felt a sharp pang of sorrow for her.

Janvi would have been just eight years old.

The thought of her, standing beside her mother's pyre, watching her flame vanish into the sky, struck him. Along with her father's injury, they were a family shattered by tragedy. Karan couldn't imagine the depth of the pain that had coursed through their lives in that moment. And somehow, that young girl kept going. She'd been thrust into a new reality, one without the comfort of a mother's love and with a father who had become a different man after the blast.

How had Janvi endured this?

Karan's heart felt heavy as the realization hit him. Janvi, so oddly composed, so seemingly calm and unshakeable, had lived through things he couldn't even begin to fathom.

His mind spiralled, grappling with the realization that his whole world had been built on a foundation of ignorance. He had been so caught up in his own life, so focused on his own path, that he hadn't stopped to look beyond it.

He had so many questions—so many things he wished he had known. But for now, all he could do was sit there, stunned and silent, as the weight of Bakshi Uncle's story settled over him.

Bakshi Uncle continued; his voice steady yet heavy with emotion. "In 2013, Ashok, despite the loss of his leg, refused to let it define him. He transitioned to a training position, traveling across the country for his work. Janvi, though... she had to balance it all. She was a young girl but took on the role of mother to young Aman, an assistant to Ashok, and still carrying the weight of what she'd already endured, she kept moving forward, quietly."

Karan listened intently, but his mind was already drifting back to his own life. 2013 was the year his own mother passed away. It hadn't been sudden, and Karan had been there in Jaisalmer, facing the reality of losing his mother to a long-term illness. He had mourned, but it was different—it was expected, almost. His mother had been ill for so long that the grief didn't hit with the same intensity. And all he felt for his father was intense hatred. For all the times he had left them and his mother to navigate the *haveli* and their family business all on her own. That's when he finally stopped talking to his father.

He thought about Janvi. At that same time, she must have been going through something entirely different. Her own mother's passing, her father's injury. There was a gap of eleven years between them, a divide he hadn't fully grasped until now. As much as he thought he knew, Karan realized just how little he truly understood. He may have been much older than her, but she certainly was well and truly ahead of him in emotional maturity.

Bakshi Uncle's voice took on a sombre tone as he continued. "From 2013 to 2020, Ashok moved from post to post. Janvi, from the age of 9 to 16, travelled with him all over India. She had to grow up quickly, taking on responsibilities beyond her years, learning the ins and outs of each place they went."

Karan nodded, lost in thought. He'd been in London and then moved to US during those years, focused on his own growth. By 2016, he had begun his MBA in Harvard, while Janvi was still learning what life demanded of her in small towns and big cities alike.

Perspective really changes things. He thought he had struggled in life to get to where he was. But Janvi, all the while, had been out there in the world with Ashok, learning to be both a daughter and an independent young woman. He could barely imagine what that must have been like.

Bakshi Uncle paused, his voice a little shakier now. "2020 was the year that everything changed for Janvi. Ashok had a heart attack. Just like that—gone. Aman was too young to understand it fully, but Janvi... she was orphaned in the most brutal way."

Karan felt a pang of guilt at the contrast in their lives. He was 27 that year, wrapped up in his own success, his own growing relationship with Anya.

Bakshi Uncle sighed, his voice softening as he continued. "After that, the only people Janvi and Aman had left were Viren and me. Viren had once promised to take care of them if anything ever happened. And he did. He brought them to Jaisalmer, made sure they had everything they needed. He owed Ashok his life, and this was the least he could do."

To be orphaned at 16, with no one but the people who had been tied to her father's legacy... it explained so much about her, the way she carried herself with a maturity far beyond her years. Karan couldn't even begin to comprehend the depth of what she'd experienced.

Bakshi Uncle's words lingered in the air, as if the weight of the past was too heavy to simply brush aside.

"Your father taught her everything about the Rathore estate. She's a fast learner, you know," Bakshi uncle said with a proud smiled tinged with sadness. "After all, she's Ashok's daughter. Resilient, morally upright, disciplined..."

He paused, and Karan could almost hear the sorrow in his voice, as if these words carried the weight of a deep admiration for both Ashok and Janvi.

Karan's mind spun as he processed the gravity of the words. She had been learning everything—about the estate, the management, the complexities that came with the legacy his family had built. And here he was, thinking of her as just a child. She'd always been more than that. All this time since he'd married her, he had considered her an obligation and here she was taking on responsibilities he never could have comprehended.

He thought back to the last few years, the carefree moments he'd spent in New York. Not once thinking about the weight Janvi, his young wife, had carried alone all these years. She had to be strong for herself and for Aman, moving from post to post, facing loss, and then stepping into the role of a daughter-in-law in addition to being a surrogate mother.

In New York, he had been chasing his dreams. Janvi had been fighting to keep hers intact.

Karan sat in silence as Bakshi Uncle's words continued to echo in his mind. The weight of the past began to settle in, a slow realization creeping over him. His thoughts, once clouded with frustration and confusion about his father's choices, were now beginning to crystallize.

It wasn't about him. It never had been.

His father, Viren, had never seen the marriage to Janvi as a way to "chain" Karan. It wasn't about control, about keeping his son tethered to a promise made to his dying friend. No, it was always about Janvi.

The last piece of the puzzle clicked into place.

In the haze of Karan's resentment, he'd never stopped to consider the true gravity of his father's decision;. And now, he finally understood.

Viren had promised Ashok that he would look after Janvi. And that promise became his duty that he fulfilled even his death. He needed to ensure Janvi's future. She had no one left. No family, no foundation to fall back on.

And so, his father had arranged for Karan, at 29, to marry 18-year-old Janvi. She was young, yes, but the marriage wasn't about control or obligation for Karan—it was about securing her future. It wasn't a decision made out of malice or neglect. It had been an act of love—for Janvi and for Ashok. To ensure that the daughter of his dear friend would never be alone in the world. And Karan, for the first time, saw the gravity of that promise. His father had done it all because Janvi mattered.

Karan realized, with an almost overwhelming sense of guilt, how little he'd known about Janvi—the girl he'd married without ever bothering to know her name or face. Never once bothered to ask who she was beneath that veil. His heart sank for her in the aftermath of his misplaced cruelty. He closed his eyes, the weight of it all heavy on his chest.

Now, he had a new question hanging over him: What was he going to do with this knowledge?

"Bakshi Uncle, I—I need to go," Karan said hoarsely, before turning to leave, not waiting for a response.

Bakshi Uncle stopped him, "I understand Karan, but before you go, there is something else you need to hear." Karan's heart sank. This didn't bode well.

7

REVELATIONS

Bakshi Uncle hesitated for a moment, clearly weighing what he was about to say. "I should have told you this earlier, but... Janvi and your grandmother made me promise not to. But now that you're here, now that you've come back... I feel it's my duty to share this with you."

Karan's pulse quickened, his stomach knotting. Whatever it was, it couldn't be good.

"It's about Janvi," Bakshi Uncle began, his voice quiet but sharp with concern. "After you left her, Karan, she was only eighteen—a child, barely more than a girl. And you know how it is here, especially for women in her position. Even the Rathore daughter-in-law is not immune to labelling. A young girl abandoned by her husband. The kind of woman people think is fair game."

Karan felt his throat tighten, his pulse pounding in his ears. He couldn't believe what he was hearing.

Bakshi Uncle's eyes darkened with sadness as he continued, "Janvi had to face taunts, unwanted advances from men—men who thought that because her husband wasn't around, she was somehow up for grabs."

Karan felt a sharp pain pierce his chest.

"She was alone, Karan," Bakshi Uncle's voice cracked slightly, the words heavy with regret. "And despite all that, she never once raised her voice, never asked for help. She endured it all with quiet resilience. But it's worse than you think."

Karan's breath caught in his throat. "Worse?" he asked, his voice barely above a whisper, afraid of what was coming next.

Bakshi Uncle's eyes turned sombre, his next words a sharp blow to Karan's already shattered sense of guilt. "She has a stalker, Karan."

Karan's blood ran cold, his world suddenly spinning. "A what?"

Bakshi Uncle nodded gravely.

"It started with harmless letters, flowers. Nothing too threatening at first. But soon, it escalated. The letters became... disturbing. One day, there was blood in them. Then photographs—photographs of Janvi, taken without her knowledge, from a distance. She was being watched. Followed."

Karan felt his legs weaken beneath him, his head spinning. His mind flashed back to the night of Janmashtami—the night he had arrived at Rathore haveli, expecting to find everything the same.

Janvi had nearly swung a cricket bat at his head, only to run into his arms a moment later, seeking relief. It hadn't been surprise—it had been fear. She had been terrified, not of him, but of whoever had been stalking her.

And then, the slip-up the next morning, in his father's study, Janvi had almost said something. "I thought you were that... I thought you were an intruder."

She had caught herself, changed her words quickly. But now, Karan understood. It had all been connected.

"God," Karan breathed, his chest tightening with guilt. "I was the one who left her. I left her alone to deal with all of this."

Karan's hands shook, his heart heavy with the weight of his neglect. He had been so wrapped up in his own guilt, in his own confusion about their marriage, that he had completely ignored Janvi's suffering. She had been fighting battles alone—*battles that she had been fighting on account of him leaving.*

Bakshi Uncle placed a hand on Karan's shoulder, a silent understanding passing between them. "That's why I wanted to see you in person, Karan. That's why I've been urging you to come back to do the divorce proceedings in person. So I could get a chance to tell you. Because Janvi needs you. Now more than ever. And miracle of all miracles, you've come home just in time."

Karan's mind reeled as the weight of Bakshi Uncle's words sank in. He had been so wrapped up in his own plans, his own escape from a marriage he had never truly embraced. He had already proposed to Anya, dreaming of a future far from Jaisalmer, far from the responsibilities he had left behind. He had been so sure that, once the three years of his marriage to Janvi were up, he would divorce her, and they could both move on with their lives.

If he hadn't come back—if he had gone through with the divorce—what would Janvi's life have looked like? She would have been alone, a young woman with no protector, no one to turn to.

The consequences of that scenario hit him like a freight train. Would she have been driven to desperation? Would the man stalking her have escalated, crossing the line into something far worse? He shuddered to think of what could have happened. *Rape. Murder.*

The very thought made Karan's blood run cold. He had abandoned her. A child. His wife. The woman he was supposed to protect.

Karan's stomach churned with guilt, and his chest tightened as the full scope of his failure settled on him. He had been so blinded by his own selfishness, his own sense of entitlement, that he hadn't once stopped to consider what Janvi might have been going through. She was almost a child when they married—signing away her life to a man she had never met, placing all her trust in him because that's what his father's dying promise had demanded.

He had left her to fend for herself. Alone. At the mercy of the world.

And now, the consequences of that decision were clear to him. What if he hadn't come back? What if he hadn't learned the truth, hadn't found out about the stalker? What would have happened to Janvi?

His hands trembled as he thought about her, his mind flashing back to the moments he had spent with her since his return. She had been so distant, so closed off, but now Karan understood. It wasn't just because of their marriage; it wasn't just the past. It was because she had been fighting battles that he couldn't even imagine. Battles that, if he hadn't come back, could have taken her life.

"God, what have I done?" Karan whispered to himself; his voice hoarse with the crushing weight of his guilt. He couldn't change the past, but he could fight for her now. He could make it right. He would make it right, no matter the cost.

"I need to leave."

"Karan before you leave," Bakshi Uncle said, "I want to ask you something. The last time we met in person, I advocated your marriage from your side as you have been my best friend's son. But this time, I will choose Janvi's side whom I have seen first-hand grow from strength to strength. And now I feel, that though you are my client, personally my loyalty lies with her. So, what I want to ask you is, a question I should have asked two years ago. What are your intentions with my daughter?"

Karan looked into the eyes of the older man, with respect.

"Honourable, sir."

"Atta boy," Bakshi Uncle said. "Now go make things right."

* * *

Karan had left Bakshi Uncle's office. He drove in a daze, his hands gripping the steering wheel so tightly his knuckles turned white. The desert landscape stretched out before him, vast and empty, the horizon blurred by the heat that shimmered off the road.

The weight of everything, all of it—Janvi's childhood, both their fathers' heroism, the reason for his forced marriage, the promise he had failed to keep, the years of selfishness, and Janvi's helplessness—crushed him.

Suddenly, he couldn't breathe. The guilt was suffocating him. Without thinking, he pulled the car to the side of the road, the tires kicking up dust as he stopped in the middle of the barren desert.

He didn't care that he was alone in the vast emptiness. He didn't care that the only sound was the distant wind and the hum of the engine idling beneath him. All he could see, all he could feel, was Janvi—her face, her quiet strength, her eyes, and the deep hurt he had caused her. His hands trembled as he released the grip on the steering wheel. He slumped against the seat, his mind reeling with the image of Janvi, barely a child, left to face the world alone, abandoned by the very man who had vowed to protect her.

He had been so blind, so focused on himself, on his own escape, that he hadn't seen her. He hadn't seen the weight of her world. She had been alone, vulnerable—she had trusted his father's promise and him, and he had let her down.

And now, to think of the consequences. What could have happened to her?

Karan's stomach turned at the thought. His breath hitched in his throat as the full extent of his failure dawned on him. The letters, the blood, the photos. She had been stalked—watched. Terrified. And he had been so far away, so lost in his own selfish pursuits.

Could he have stopped it if he had been there? Could he have shielded her from that nightmare? The thought gnawed at him, tearing him apart inside.

His vision blurred in anger at himself. His chest ached, a raw, guttural pain that he hadn't known existed. He had risked everything—her safety, her peace of mind, her innocence.

He buried his face in his hands. Karan could feel his world cracking apart, the fragile shell of his self-justification shattering in the face of the truth.

The harsh reality settled like a weight on his soul, each word a piercing reminder of everything he had done wrong. He had a chance now, but how could he make up for the years of neglect? How could he undo the damage he had done? Could he ever make her feel safe again? Karan didn't have the answers. He didn't even know where to begin. But one thing was clear: he had to fight for her now. He had to protect her. He couldn't let her suffer any longer.

He took a deep breath, and straightened in his seat.

No more running.

He was going to fix this. And he wasn't leaving Jaisalmer again. Not until Janvi was safe.

No, he realized correcting himself. He wasn't leaving Jaisalmer again. Period.

8

AUSPICIOUS BEGINNINGS

Karan arrived at the *haveli*, still grappling with everything Bakshi Uncle had told him. His mind kept drifting, inevitably, back to Janvi.

He needed to find her.

He headed to the kitchen, hoping to catch a glimpse of her but finding Laxmi Tai there instead.

"Laxmi Tai," Karan asked, carefully masking the desperation in his voice, "Where is Janvi?"

"She's on the terrace, hanging the laundry," Laxmi Tai replied. "Would you like some lunch?"

"In a bit," Karan said quickly, not waiting for her response. He walked hastily up the stairs taking two steps at a time.

He didn't know what he was going to say to her but for the moment, all he wanted was to see her.

When he reached the terrace, he hesitated, slowing his pace when he spotted her. He remained hidden in the shadow of the arches, allowing himself a moment to simply watch her, the racing heart in his chest, steadying to a calm rhythm as he took in the sight of her.

She was standing in the sun next to the clothes line looking utterly divine in her yellow salwar kameez. Her dupatta, tied loosely around her waist, fluttered in the breeze. Her hair was pulled up in a messy bun, with stray strands dancing around her face with every movement.

He watched her for a while, her brows furrowed as she squinted against the bright glare of the noon sun. She was completely absorbed in her task—wringing out a wet towel, flicking the droplets into the air, then hanging and pinning it neatly on the line before moving on to the next piece of clothing in the steel bucket at her feet.

He felt as though he could stand there, watching her, for as long as the moment lasted.

Eventually, he took a deep breath and walked toward her slowly, each step deliberate, careful not to startle her.

She paused when she saw him, her hand halting mid-motion. The fabric on the clothesline caught the sunlight, and time seemed to stretch between them, suspended in the air.

She didn't appear alarmed, but regarded him with an intensity that seemed to strip away his composure, her gaze steady—almost unburdening him of his restraint.

What was she thinking?

"Hi," he began. He was nervous but managed to keep his composure.

"Hi," she responded softly, her gaze lingering on him for a beat longer before she returned to the task at hand of hanging the wet laundry.

Karan swallowed a lump in his throat, deciding to risk it all. Suddenly, he knew exactly what he needed to say to her. He wasn't sure what the outcome would be. If she shot him down—which was highly likely—he would retreat quietly for the moment before approaching her again. All he knew, though, was that he wasn't going to give up. He was going to have to start somewhere, so let it be *now*.

"Janvi," he began, his voice betraying a slight tremor, "I... I've been meaning to talk to you all week now. And I'm going to struggle, because essentially what I am about to ask of you might seem extremely unfair, considering how I left things after our wedding."

Karan paused to gauge if she was listening. There was a frown on her face, her attention focused on her hand, frozen mid-motion over the clothesline. An image of her standing in his dark room on the night of their wedding made its way into his consciousness. That night she had a veil over her, so he hadn't been able to see her reaction. This time, he could, and he knew he had her full attention.

He continued, choosing his words carefully. "I'm not going to ask you to forgive me. At least not yet. I think it's your right to be upset with me, and I'll bear your anger for as long as you need."

She was still looking away from him, but he could see clearly her expression had softened, her gaze lowering slightly as if she were absorbing his words. He caught a hint of confusion in her eyes.

Encouraged, Karan pressed on. "What I *am* asking, though, is the honour of your friendship."

Her gaze dipped even lower, her lips curling inward as though she were processing his request. He could almost see the wheels turning in her head—she had heard him loud and clear, and was considering him carefully. Karan paused, clutching hope to his chest like a drunk man clutches onto a bottle. He wasn't afraid of her anger or wrath or reprimand, but her distance was gnawing at him.

He could no longer stand in the sidelines, watching her interact with everyone around him while he yearned for a mere glance from her. He wanted to be a part of her life, in whatever capacity she was willing to allow. And if that meant enduring her anger, then he would welcome it with open arms.

"I know I'm probably not even worthy of your friendship," he continued, his voice softer now, "but would you please allow me to get to know you at least? Just a little bit." Karan shrugged, his sincerity clear. "That's all I'm asking."

He watched her with bated breath, waiting for her response. She continued to stare ahead, her expression unreadable. The seconds stretched, but no response came.

Finally, he sighed, a weak smile tugging at his lips. "I'll leave you to it for now. But just know this—I'm not going to give up on trying to be your friend."

Turning away, he took a step toward the stairs, but then he heard the soft clink of her bangles. He stopped in his tracks and turned back to her.

She was looking at him, her lips parted slightly as if she were about to speak. She licked her lips nervously, her voice hesitant. "I... I haven't had lunch yet. Do you... want to eat together?"

Karan felt air rush into his lungs, relief flooding him. It was as if he'd been buried in sand, trapped and breathless, and now—finally—had been lifted free. Her simple offer felt like a feast laid before a starving man.

Karan nodded, barely able to speak. Sensing his eagerness could betray him at any moment, with a steady voice, he managed, "I'll wait for you downstairs."

He turned, feeling the weight in his chest ease with every step. Her invitation, small as it was, felt monumental—a door cracked open that he hadn't expected. As he made his way down, he couldn't stop the slight smile tugging at his lips. For the first time in a long while, he felt as though he had a chance.

When Karan reached the kitchen, he found Laxmi Tai scrubbing dishes, her watchful gaze flicking to him as he entered. Noting his subtle grin and the lightness in his steps, she smirked knowingly.

"Wow, look at that. She hasn't thrown you off the terrace yet," she teased, raising her eyebrows.

Karan narrowed his eyes in mock warning. He knew Laxmi Tai had keenly observed the tension between him and Janvi, and, if anything, she seemed to take great pleasure in watching him get flustered over it. Her sly grin only confirmed it, and Karan couldn't help but shake his head, feeling both amused and slightly exposed under her gaze.

"You'd wish, wouldn't you?" he replied, leaning against the counter beside her. "No," he admitted, smiling sheepishly, "we're actually about to have lunch together."

Laxmi Tai's eyebrows shot up. "Progress, finally," she said, giving him a playful nudge with her elbow. "Well done."

Karan chuckled, feeling a renewed spark of optimism.

Just then, he heard the soft, distant chime of her anklets approaching the kitchen, and he straightened instantly, the easy smile slipping from his face as his posture shifted, tense yet expectant. Laxmi Tai's smile widened, clearly savouring his reaction, a glint of mischief in her eyes.

When Janvi entered the kitchen, she stopped in her tracks, momentarily taken aback to find both Karan and Laxmi Tai staring at her, a strange, almost guilty awkwardness hanging in the air.

Laxmi Tai, quick to break the silence, jumped to the rescue.

"Uh, Janvi, could you finish washing up these dishes? I need to help Badri set up the *aasan* in the living room for Ganesh Chaturthi."

Karan silently thanked Laxmi Tai, breathing a quiet sigh of relief. *God bless you, Laxmi Tai.*

As she walked out, Laxmi Tai threw a knowing wink his way from the doorway, her expression full of mischief.

Karan shook his head subtly, a faint blush of embarrassment colouring his cheeks as Janvi moved to the sink, seemingly unaware of the exchange that had just taken place. She began rolling up her sleeves, her movements unhurried and practiced, entirely absorbed in the simple task ahead.

Karan stood back for a moment, watching her, trying to calm the small flutter of nerves that had taken root. He knew he should say something, anything, to bridge the quiet between them.

"Here, let me help you," he offered.

As Karan's hands brushed lightly against hers under the stream of water, she quickly pulled her hands back, startled, as if she'd touched a live wire.

She blinked, flustered, her cheeks colouring faintly as she stammered, "I... I'll set up the plates."

Karan smiled to himself, a quiet satisfaction settling within him. *At least she wasn't immune to my touch.* It was a small victory, but it was enough to make his heart beat a little faster.

As they both continued their respective tasks, Karan asked casually, "So what time does Aman come home from school?"

"He should be home by 2," she said.

Finishing with the last dish, Karan straightened, wiping his hands with a towel. As he turned, he found Janvi moving pots from the stove to the table.

While waiting for her to finish, Karan took a moment to admire the grace with which she moved—effortless yet commanding. He couldn't help but be drawn to the rhythm of it all, the way she made something as simple as setting the table look like an art form.

When she finished, he pulled out a chair for her, the action almost automatic. She glanced at him briefly, her expression unreadable, but Karan's heart still skipped a beat at the brief exchange.

As they both sat, she began filling his steel *thali* with *dal, gatta sabzi,* and *bajra roti,* piling on more food with each spoonful.

"Whoa... that's enough," Karan said, holding up a hand to stop her. He was careful not to touch her again, aware that she might retreat from him once more.

Janvi paused with a subtle nod before slowly putting the ladle back in the pot.

"You don't eat much," she observed quietly, speaking more to herself, a flicker of curiosity in her voice.

Karan smiled at her simple, almost innocent remark. "Not usually. It's just lately..." He paused, his gaze drifting momentarily as he thought about his work and the lingering sting of his recent breakup with Anya—things he wasn't quite ready to talk about. "...I've been quite stressed, almost to the point of losing my appetite. It's taking me a little longer to get my usual fervour back."

"And in fact," he added as an afterthought, "that's actually why I'm home. It wasn't to spy on you all or check on the estate. I just... I needed a break from everything. And that day in the study, I was just teasing. I had absolutely no intention of hurting your feelings." Karan shrugged his shoulders apologetically. It was only the half-truth, but it was better than her assuming she did something wrong.

Janvi quickly shook her head, "Oh, it's okay, you don't need to apologise."

She added with a look of genuine sympathy in her eyes. "And I can understand... about the stress. I've seen your interviews on TV and read about your company in the news. I can imagine it's not so easy being in such a position." She hesitated, a soft smile tugging at her lips as she added, "Daadi Sa is really proud of you, you know."

Her words surprised him. He watched her, feeling oddly off-kilter. A mixture of elation and warmth flooded him at the acknowledgment of his progress, but a shadow of regret followed quickly. This beautiful, gentle soul—whom he had abandoned without a second thought—had been sharing his achievements with his grandmother. A man she shouldn't even care about.

The words Bakshi Uncle had spoken to him that morning echoed in his mind.

"We returned his shoes, apologized. But there was no anger, no need for retaliation. Ashok simply nodded, said it was done, and that was the end of it. There was no need for anything more."

Janvi was so much like her father. She made peace with what he'd done to her and moved on, without holding a grudge. The realization struck him hard. He suddenly wanted to pull her into his arms, hug her, weep at his stupidity, and beg for her forgiveness. But he forced himself to come back to the present moment, the reality of their situation weighing down on him.

He had no right to demand forgiveness. Not yet. All he could do was work on earning it—one step at a time.

He gave her an embarrassed smile, nodding in acknowledgment of her words, then decided to change the topic, eager to shift away from the weight of his unspoken words.

"So, what's happening this week? What was Laxmi Tai saying about Ganesh Chaturthi?" he asked, trying to sound casual, though the underlying tension still lingered.

Janvi looked up at him, her expression softening at the mention of the festival. "Ah, yes," she replied, her voice lightening. "We're bringing Ganpati Bappa home today, and the *visarjan* is on Wednesday." She smiled. "Of course, that means there's lots to get done. I think it's Aman's second favourite festival after Diwali. He gets so excited when we take Bappa to Gadisar Lake for the *visarjan*."

Her eyes lit up with an idea.

"You should come with us for the *visarjan* this year," she said. "It'll be fun, and Aman will be so happy."

Karan was momentarily stunned by the dimple that appeared on Janvi's cheek as she spoke. He hadn't noticed it before but she hadn't smiled so sincerely at him before either. Her smile, caught him off guard. It was genuine and there was none of that stiff politeness she was giving him all week since he arrived.

For a moment, everything else faded away. He couldn't help but feel a wave of attraction, something he struggled to keep in check. She was beautiful, and the intensity of the moment left him breathless.

Her words finally registered, and Karan blinked, realizing she'd just invited him to join them for the *visarjan*. The offer took him by surprise, but his heart raced with excitement. He didn't hesitate. He didn't care much for the tradition but whatever moment she was willing to share with him, he would take it.

"Absolutely, I'd love to. Thank-you." His smile was genuine, the warmth in his voice unmistakable.

Janvi's eyes softened, and for a brief moment, Karan thought he saw a flicker of something in her gaze—hope, perhaps. But before he could analyse it further, she quickly looked away, as if the moment had passed.

"Good," she said quietly, her voice carrying a note of finality. "I'll let *Daadi Sa* know. She'll be excited."

Karan watched her, his pulse still quick from the exchange.

As she moved to tidy up, the warmth of her smile lingered, filling him with hope. For the first time since his return, Karan felt like he might finally be able to make things right. One step at a time, he reminded himself—one step at a time.

⁂

After lunch, Karan strolled through the shaded courtyard, his mind weighed down by his thoughts. He caught sight of his grandmother sitting in the *chowk*, threading marigolds into garlands. She looked up as he approached, her face softening into a gentle smile.

"Come, Karan," she gestured, "have a seat."

He lowered himself onto the stone bench opposite her, feeling distant from the serene atmosphere around them. Daadi continued her work, the rhythm of her threading steady and soothing.

"I'm just making garlands for Ganesh *Bhagwaan*," she said, glancing at him. "I hear you will join us for the *visarjan*. I was very happy to hear that."

Karan offered a tight smile, though it didn't reach his eyes. He leaned back, his frustration simmering beneath his calm façade.

"So," he began slowly, keeping his voice quiet yet edged with tension, "when exactly were you planning to tell me that Janvi has a stalker?"

Daadi looked up, unsurprised. A faint smile curved her lips as she continued threading the marigolds, her hands never faltering.

"Ah, so Narayan told you?" she asked, her voice soft, as though it were nothing remarkable that Karan had finally learned what was going on.

"Yes," Karan replied, his hands clenched tightly in his lap. "Among other things."

She dismissed him with a wave, her focus back on the garland. "You're here now. That's all that matters."

Karan's patience thinned. He leaned forward, exasperated, and ran his hands down his face. "That's not the point, Daadi," he said, frustration thick in his voice. "The point is—why is it that every time, people try to keep things from me? I admit, regretfully, I haven't been around for over two years, but you didn't think that maybe—just maybe—you could have slipped it into one of our conversations on the phone or in the last eight days I've been back?"

His eyes darkened as he spoke, his chest tight with emotion. "Even as a child, I had to sneak information out of Laxmi Tai because someone always forgot to tell me something." He shook his head in disbelief. "And Dad... for a man who was in the army, I'm sorry to say, his communication skills were abysmal. It's a wonder he lasted as long as he did. Transparency, Daadi, it's everything. Like, why wasn't I told the truth about why I was marrying Janvi in the first place? Maybe I would've understood, or maybe I would've tried to handle things differently."

Karan's tone softened, his voice heavy with regret as the memories flooded back. "Even when he was on his deathbed, it was just, 'Here, do this. Marry my friend's daughter.' That was it. No introduction, no context. I didn't even know she was eighteen! And now her life is at risk because someone decided she was an easy target."

His voice hardened with frustration. "The sad part is, if I hadn't asked Bakshi Uncle anything, I probably wouldn't have found out. And just what were you planning to do if her stalker took things too far?"

He leaned back again, his gaze distant, pain etched on his face. "And don't think I don't understand what you're doing, Daadi," he continued, his voice quieter but resolute. "We never used to have these celebrations so publicly before. Yes, we did *puja* privately, but it wasn't this grand, this lavish. We didn't invite the whole town. You're using these festivals, these *pujas,* these gatherings—as a distraction for Janvi and Aman. A distraction from the emptiness you think they're feeling because of my abandonment." He sighed, his shoulders slumping. "I'm not complaining. I just... I see it. I know what you're doing."

Karan paused, his chest tight with emotion, as he looked at Daadi, her back slightly bent over the garlands, seemingly unaffected by his words. He exhaled sharply. "But Daadi, you didn't have to do this," he said, his voice low. "Any of it. You all could've just told me the truth. I would've found another way. There had to be something else. If it was about Janvi and Aman, I could've been there for them in some other way. But instead, you all had me marry her... and ruin her life. She was just eighteen, with a whole future ahead of her. Now she's stuck here, tied to this house—married to a stranger who ran off into the sunset."

A dry laugh escaped him. "But no, oh no. Why should Karan

know anything? And now... here we are." Karan threw his hands up in defeat.

He fell silent, his gaze fixed on his grandmother, the weight of everything still pressing down on him.

Daadi finally looked up at him, completely unfazed, a smile on her face.

"Did I just crack a joke?" Karan asked, with a hint of dry amusement.

She gave a small shrug, her expression unchanged.

"Are you done?" she asked, her voice soft, almost amused.

"Yes," Karan muttered, breathing indignantly, like a child who'd just thrown a tantrum.

"The question," she began, her voice carrying the weight of experience, "isn't what has happened. The real question is, what will you do now that you know everything?"

And there, Karan was stumped.

"I'm still... working that part out," he admitted guiltily.

"Well then, let me know when you do." she said getting up. "I'll be right here, ready to listen."

With that, she tapped him on his shoulder and walked off, leaving him in the quiet of the chowk, confused but, perhaps, a little lighter in spirit.

"Jijaji!" Aman's voice rang out, breaking Karan's reverie.

Karan looked up, finding the 12-year-old by the entrance, grinning ear to ear, eager for the celebration to start. He waved back, feeling the warmth of Aman's enthusiasm.

"Oh, hey Aman," Karan replied, a slight lift in his tone. "You're back from school already?"

"Yes!" Aman bounced on his feet, clearly full of energy. "*Challo*, let's bring Bappa home."

Karan smiled at the child's excitement and followed him into the living room, where everything had been set for the homecoming of Lord Ganesh. The room was filled with the fragrance of *mogras* and sandalwood. Sounds of chatter buzzed in the air. Laxmi Tai and

Badri Kaka were arranging flowers, ensuring the Ganesh idol was placed on its pedestal with care. The rest of the staff stood around momentarily pausing their activities for this short spiritual respite. The atmosphere was bustling with an air of devotion.

Aman, full of focus despite his age, carefully set the idol onto the pedestal, looking up at Karan to ensure he was watching. Karan gave him an encouraging nod, admiring his sincerity. It was a far cry from the carefree chaos of a few minutes ago.

Janvi, standing nearby, applied a small tikka to Ganesh's forehead, her fingers steady and precise. She then reached for the garland Daadi had threaded earlier in the chowk, a chain of marigolds woven together with patience and devotion. With gentle hands, she draped it over the idol, and the simple gesture seemed to carry a weight that Karan couldn't explain.

As she did so, Karan thought back to the conversation he had with Daadi earlier, her calmness in the face of his frustrations. Her wisdom, the quiet way she carried the family's traditions, now felt more meaningful than it ever had before. Perhaps, just perhaps, that wisdom could help him understand how he fit into this web of tradition. How Janvi fit into it.

Punditji, standing near the idol, began to explain the significance of Ganesh, the remover of obstacles, the one who brings auspicious beginnings. Karan listened intently, more out of respect than belief. Though he wasn't particularly religious, the meaning behind Punditji's words struck him. Ganesh as a symbol of new beginnings—a fresh start—reminded Karan of the very thing he desperately needed. His life, his relationship with Janvi, and the road ahead all seemed clouded with things he couldn't control. But in this moment, surrounded by family, he felt a fleeting sense of clarity.

The ritual began. The air was thick with devotion, the light from the *diya* flickering in the room, casting warm shadows. The sound of the *aarti* began, and Badri Kaka rang the *ghanti* in rhythm, its resonance echoing through the house. Karan's gaze landed on Aman, who stood next to him, his face shining with pride and excitement.

Karan placed a hand on Aman's shoulder. Together, they sang the aarti, their voices blending with the others. For a moment, Karan wasn't thinking about the obstacles in his life or the weight of his responsibilities. He was just a part of something larger than himself.

Daadi and Laxmi Tai stood nearby, their eyes soft as they watched Janvi, who carefully passed the aarti plate to Daadi to continue the ritual. When it came time for Karan's turn, Daadi gave him a gentle nudge.

"Come, Karan, Janvi," she said, her voice soft but firm. "Do the aarti together."

Janvi, a little shy but not as hesitant as before, moved to stand beside Karan. Their hands met the plate together, and Karan felt a rush of warmth. The flirtatious tension in him was long gone, replaced with something far gentler—respect, perhaps, or understanding. As they waved the aarti, Karan felt the weight of it, the significance of the moment. Not just for the family, but for him. For Janvi.

The room hummed with the energy of their collective prayers, the vibrations of the aarti lingering in the air long after it ended. Karan closed his eyes for a moment, letting the reverberations fill him. Peace. It was brief, but it was there.

The puja concluded, and Janvi, with her usual elegance, moved around the room, offering prasad to everyone. Karan accepted a piece, the *laddoos* sweet and comforting in his mouth.

As the last of the prasad was distributed, Karan stood there, looking at Ganesh, a silent prayer forming in his heart. There were still many things to work out, but in this moment, there was the faintest sense of new beginnings. A new beginning, with Janvi.

9

REFLECTIONS

The soft sunlight and sounds of peacocks drifted through the *jharoka* rousing Janvi from her sleep. She stretched, embracing the calmness of the early morning. Rising, she picked up her notebook from the bedside table and reviewed her to-do list for the day.

The museum and restaurant were closed on Sundays, and Aman didn't have school, so it was going to be a quieter day. But there was still *prasad* and *bhog* to prepare for Ganesh ji, and Bakshi Uncle was coming for lunch.

As she prepared for the day, made her bed and got ready, her thoughts inevitably turned to Karan, unsettling her slightly.

He'd been here for almost two weeks now, but she still wasn't used to his presence. When he arrived on the night of *Janmasthami,* she'd almost cried in relief, instinctively running into his arms, seeking safety. Though she wouldn't admit it to him—or even to herself—she felt happy that he was here, yet at the same time, he unnerved her in a way she couldn't quite understand.

She wondered if he'd be awake already.

If she were being perfectly honest with herself, she had forgiven him a long time ago. In truth, she never expected much from the marriage. She was simply fulfilling Viren Uncle's wishes, repaying him for everything he had done for her and Aman. Still, it hurt when he walked away so suddenly after the wedding—she was only human. But because her expectations had been so low, she had come to terms with it fairly quickly.

Now that he was here, she was trying hard not to form any

attachment to him. As always, she kept her expectations low. He had told her they'd be divorced at the end of three years, and so far, he hadn't given her any reason to think otherwise—even if he said he was just here to take a break from work. And then there was also his girlfriend, Anya.

She paused midway, comb in hand, contemplating that relationship.

She'd seen Anya in one of his pictures from his company's success party. The woman was standing next to him, looking beautiful, his arm around her waist. Janvi couldn't help but feel a pang of envy, a longing that made her feel small.

She shook herself, pushing the thought away.

That's why she always kept her focus on her tasks, careful not to get too comfortable with life in the haveli or to rely on him—or anyone else—for anything. She needed to stay busy, constantly reminding herself that all this was temporary. Eventually, she would have to move out and build a life for herself.

As she moved to the dresser to pick up her earrings her mind wandered to the stalker, the letters in blood, the photographs. He had called the landline on *Janmasthami* night, the first time she'd heard him. Until then, he was simply an unknown man in the shadows sending vulgar letters and photographs taken from unsuspecting places. But hearing his breathy, menacing voice speaking to her, telling her how he was going to drag her away from the *haveli* and make her his, made everything more real. When she heard the noise of the car and the door open, she had been so scared he was there, ready to make good on his threats. She had picked up Aman's cricket bat, ready to defend herself, only to find it was Karan.

Janvi closed her eyes tightly, trying to push the thoughts away. Even that, she thought painfully, was her burden to bear. She wouldn't endanger Karan's life.

She put on her *mangalsutra, bindi,* slipped on her leather watch, and did a final check in the mirror before heading out.

As she walked to the kitchen, she ran into a flustered Karan.

He was dressed in a loose t-shirt and shorts, his mid-length black hair tousled and damp with sweat. He must have just returned from a run. His tall frame filled the doorway, his narrow waist and broad shoulders unmistakable in his dishevelled state. A flush crept up her cheeks, so she quickly moved around him to avoid him catching her reaction.

"Good morning!" she said, trying to keep her voice bright, though nerves stirred inside her.

She placed a steel pot on the stove to make *chai* for everyone.

"Good morning," he replied, following close behind her.

As Janvi filled the pitcher with water, Karan bent around her to fill his water bottle. His tall frame, with broad shoulders, almost seemed to surround her. The heat of his body, mixed with the faint scent of cologne and sweat, made it hard to focus. Her heart raced, and she struggled to catch her breath at the closeness.

Eventually, he walked away to sit at the dining table, chugging water, and Janvi managed to calm her nerves enough to remember she was making *chai*.

She poured the water from the pitcher in the steel pot and set it to boil as she moved to pull out the tea leaves, chai masala and sugar from the cabinets.

"So," Karan asked, "what's the plan for today?"

"Um, we have Bakshi Uncle over for lunch, then bhog, prasad and aarti for Ganesh ji. Oh, I have to wash the outer courtyard and do rangoli."

As she reached for her notebook to jot it down, Karan sauntered over, leaning against the counter to sneak a look. Janvi instinctively clutched the notebook to her chest and looked up to find a hint of a smirk playing on his lips.

"What is it that you keep writing in there?" he asked, clearly amused.

"Everything I have to do during the day," she replied curtly.

Isn't it obvious? she thought.

Janvi sighed, shifting the notebook out of his view and moving to the other side of the kitchen, acutely aware of his gaze following her. She'd been perfectly fine ignoring him all this time. Why, oh why, did he have to come to her, asking to be friends? And why did she have to give in to his puppy-dog eyes like some goody two shoes?

As the tea boiled, Janvi quickly pulled the pot off the stove and poured it into a teapot.

"Will you have chai now?" she asked Karan.

He nodded.

"Where is everyone else?" he asked as she filled up two cups.

Janvi, while putting a heat cover over the teapot, replied, "Daadi is probably getting ready but I'll take it to her room in a while. Aman is most definitely sleeping, Laxmi Tai hasn't come yet from her village and Badri kaka is probably watering the garden."

As she finished, she looked up to find Karan watching her quietly, making her heart skip a beat.

What was wrong with her?

Janvi cleared her throat, trying to shake off the tension. Karan's eyes followed her as she picked up their cups. She couldn't decide if it was comforting or unnerving.

When she handed him his cup, her fingers brushing against his for a brief, electrifying second. She quickly pulled her hand back, pretending not to notice the warmth that spread up her arm.

Definitely unnerving.

"Thank-you," he said, his voice low but sincere.

She nodded, retreating to the other side of the table, not trusting herself to say anything more. They sat in silence for a moment, each of them lost in their own thoughts, the only sound being the soft clink of the porcelain cups against the table.

Karan took a sip of his tea, then set the cup down with a soft sigh. "You really do have a lot to manage around here, don't you?" he said, breaking the silence.

Janvi looked up, startled. "I guess I do," she replied, shrugging again. "It's not so bad. I'm used to it."

He leaned back in his chair, considering her for a moment. "I'm sorry if I've made things harder for you."

The sincerity in his voice caught her off guard. She blinked, not knowing how to respond. Instead, she focused on her own tea, hoping the warm liquid would settle her nerves.

"Um, sorry, I forgot to pull out the biscuits," she said, desperate to change the subject. "Would you like some now?"

Karan shook his head, his lips quirking into a tight smile. "No, thank-you. I'm fine," he said, finishing his tea. "I'm going to go shower now. I'll see you in a bit."

He took his cup to the sink, and without waiting for her to protest, began to wash it.

"Oh, you don't have to do that," Janvi said, embarrassed by the gesture.

Karan met her eyes with a steady, unwavering gaze. "I have to," he said simply, his words laced with something she couldn't quite place.

He finished washing the cup, and as he left the kitchen, Janvi found herself staring at the empty space he left behind. A strange emptiness settled in her chest, like she had somehow missed his presence more than she expected.

Focus, Janvi!

She finished her tea and started on her to-do list by first making *modak*, followed by preparing lunch.

* * *

By the time Janvi had finished cooking and all her other tasks for the day were done with the help of Laxmi Tai and Badri Kaka, Bakshi Uncle had arrived. The whole family gathered together for *puja* and *aarti* before they all sat down to lunch in the dining room.

Bakshi Uncle took his place at the head of the table, with Aman and Daadi on either side of him. Karan sat beside Aman, and Janvi sat opposite him next to Daadi. A feast was spread out on the glossy, teak table—golden fried *kachoris, gatte ki sabzi,* and the earthy *ker sangri,* served alongside soft *bajra rotis* and fragrant *panchmel dal. Raita, papad,* and *aachar,* in brass *katoris,* were placed around the curries.

As they settled in, Daadi looked over at Janvi with a soft smile. "Beta, you've outdone yourself today. Everything looks so delicious!"

"Really, Janvi," said Bakshi Uncle, "my mouth is already watering."

Karan nodded, his expression genuine. "I have to agree, everything looks delicious."

Janvi smiled, grateful for the praise, and thanked them all.

Aman, eager as always, leaned forward. "Didi, where's the *moong dal halwa*?"

"Aman," Daadi admonished with a playful tone, "we'll have dessert after lunch."

Everyone chuckled at Aman's eagerness.

"So, Aman," Bakshi Uncle began, shifting gears, "how's school going?"

"School's okay, Bakshi Chacha," Aman replied casually. "Why wouldn't it be? My teacher is way less strict than Janvi didi."

Janvi shot him a mock glare across the table. "Excuse me?" she said, raising an eyebrow. "At least I'm the reason you get good marks."

Aman shrugged with a grin. "I get good marks because everyone else in my class is stupid."

Everyone burst into laughter.

"Karan was just as naughty as you," Daadi added with a knowing smile.

Karan chuckled nervously. "Daadi, what are you saying?"

Aman leaned forward with excitement. "Daadi sa, tell us a story about him!"

Daadi looked mischievously at Karan, who was shaking his head at her with a look of horror.

"Okay," she decided with amusement.

Karan groaned and threw his head back in defeat.

"When Karan was young, he was incredibly competitive. One day, there was a fair just outside of town with a camel race. Now, Karan had also developed a little crush on a girl in his class—he must've been about 10 years old."

"Daadi, no! Please stop!" Karan pleaded, as everyone else giggled, already enjoying the story.

Aman and Janvi leaned forward, intrigued.

Ignoring Karan's discomfort, Daadi continued, her voice full of amusement, "So, of course, he wanted to impress her. He borrowed a camel from some villager and started practicing without telling any of us. On the day of the race, he insisted we take him to the fair, where he and his camel were waiting. Gayatri, Narayan, and I went along. Some of his classmates were there too, including the girl. Viren was away on duty at the time."

"Oh, yes, I remember this story," Bakshi Uncle chimed with a chuckle, suddenly realizing what was coming next.

Karan shot him a side glance, "Oh, come on. Not you too."

Daadi continued, her voice full of mischief, "Naturally, we were all shocked to see Karan on his camel at the starting line. Then, the signal to start the race went off, and all the camels began moving... except Karan's!"

"What!?" Aman exclaimed, bursting into laughter. Janvi couldn't help but giggle, and Karan buried his face in his hands, mortified.

"Yes," Daadi said, unable to contain her laughter, "it just wouldn't move. Karan kept prodding it with his legs, trying to get it to budge, but the camel just stayed right there, as stubborn as anything."

The table erupted in laughter, and Karan, grinning despite his embarrassment, said, "Alright, alright, everyone, the joke's over now."

"Areh, the real story hasn't even been told yet!" Bakshi Uncle chimed in, his eyes twinkling with mischief.

"Bakshi Uncle, please don't, that's enough," Karan pleaded, his face completely red with embarrassment.

Ignoring Karan's protests, Bakshi Uncle grinned mischievously and continued, "Now Karan is desperately prodding the camel, trying everything he could think of to get it to move. Just as he was about to give it a final push, the camel suddenly stood up—and poor Karan—well, he went flying off and faceplanted straight into the sand! At first, we all rushed to check if he was okay, but once we saw he wasn't hurt, we couldn't stop laughing. We laughed so much that we had to hold our stomachs! I swear, we were all in tears."

Daadi joined in, unable to contain herself, "After that, Karan never spoke to that girl in his class again. In fact, he never went near her! We couldn't stop laughing for days. Every time he tried to act all serious about anything, all we'd see was that image of him flying off the camel and faceplanting right into the sand! And let me tell you, he never lived that one down."

The table erupted into laughter again, and Karan sat back in his chair, groaning in mock defeat. "I will never hear the end of this, will I?" he muttered, trying to cover his embarrassment with a smile.

"Not anytime soon," Bakshi Uncle chuckled.

As everyone continued laughing, Karan shook his head with mock defeat, amused. But as his gaze fell on Janvi, her laughter bright and carefree, he felt as if all his embarrassment were worth it. Her cheeks flushed, her hair bouncing with each giggle, and her smile seemed to light up the room. In that moment, something stirred inside him—an urge to close the distance between them.

Then, their eyes met.

Her laughter quieted, and for a brief moment, time seemed to stretch. Karan's heart quickened with excitement, while Janvi's thudded with a flicker of nervousness. The sounds of the room faded, and all that remained was the connection between them—unspoken, yet so palpable.

Eventually, the sound of Aman's spoon clattering to the floor broke the spell. Karan blinked, watching as Janvi quickly looked away, though a soft smile still lingered on her lips. The meal continued, but Karan's thoughts remained locked in place.

What the hell was happening to him?

On their wedding night, he hadn't even bothered to look at Janvi. He'd been too focused on his plans—on Anya, on the life he thought he was meant to have in New York.

Now, here he was, heart racing, chest tight, drawn to her smile, the way her hair moved, the way she laughed. It hit him all at once, a pull so strong he couldn't ignore it.

What had he been doing all this time?

Two and a half years wasted, chasing something that never even came close to what he truly needed. He had turned his back on the life he was meant to have, on the woman who was right in front of him. And now, for the first time, he couldn't deny the force of attraction pulling him toward her.

What an idiot he had been.

10

AN AFTERNOON OUT

After lunch, Bakshi Uncle left, Daadi was taking a nap and Aman was engrossed in building a model plane for school.

Janvi sat curled up on a sofa in the living room, her book balanced in her hands. Her legs were tucked beneath her, and her *dupatta* fell loosely over one shoulder, swaying slightly in the faint breeze from the open balcony doors. The lattice windows let in streams of soft sunlight, creating intricate patterns on the tiled floor. The room was tranquil, with its rustic charm softened by potted plants and the muted sounds of the courtyard below.

She was engrossed in her reading when movement by the door drew her attention. Karan leaned casually against the frame, his sleeves rolled up and his expression carrying the faintest trace of amusement.

"I didn't know you knew how to relax," he teased, a small smile playing on his lips.

Janvi's fingers tightened on the book. Her heart gave a small jolt, but she kept her composure, even if his easy confidence always unsettled her. "It's Sunday," she replied, her tone light, accompanied by a casual shrug.

"Is that so?" he asked, his eyes narrowing playfully. "I wouldn't know, considering you spent last Sunday avoiding me."

Her breath hitched for a fraction of a second before she masked it with another shrug. How could she admit that she hadn't trusted herself to act normally around him? That she had no idea how to navigate his presence?

"I was busy," she said evenly, keeping her eyes firmly on the page, though her mind couldn't focus on a single word.

"If you say so," Karan responded, his smile still plastered on his face.

Karan pushed off the doorframe and walked toward her, his steps steady but unhurried. He took the chair opposite hers and sat down, his presence deliberate yet calm, as if giving her space while still commanding her attention.

Janvi tried to control her breathing.

He was watching her intently. Why?

After a moment of silence, he spoke, his voice thoughtful. "It's still early. I was thinking we could take a ride to the *Quilla*." He paused, watching her reaction. "You, me and Aman. A little fresh air and sightseeing could be nice."

Janvi blinked, caught off guard by the suggestion. *A car ride with him? Sightseeing, in close proximity?* She hesitated.

"Um, I'm not sure," she began carefully, glancing down at her book, "I need to prepare for the evening aarti."

Karan nodded as though considering her words, his gaze steady but kind. "I'll bring you back in plenty of time for that," he said simply, a hint of a smile in his voice. "Scout's honour."

Janvi felt her resolve wavering. He had a way of doing that—nudging her without pressuring, coaxing her into lowering her guard. It was infuriating, in a way. But also... disarming.

Her gaze flicked toward the table where Aman's half-finished plane lay, glue and scraps of paper scattered around. At least Aman would be there. He'd act as a buffer, a safe distraction from the weight of Karan's attention.

"Fine," she said at last, her voice quieter than she intended. "But only for a little while."

Karan's smile deepened—not triumphant, but satisfied, as though he'd been confident of her agreement all along.

"Perfect," he said, rising smoothly to his feet. "I'll tell Aman. He'll be thrilled."

"Tell me what?" Aman asked, walking back into the room, glue still smeared across his hands.

Karan turned to him, his tone light. "We're going to *Sonar Quilla* for an outing. What do you say?"

Aman groaned, shaking his head. "No way! I went there last week with school, Di. I'm not going again. I've seen it so many times already!"

Karan sighed in mock disappointment, glancing briefly at Janvi. "You mean you're leaving your sister to go with me alone? What kind of brother are you?"

Aman grinned, completely unbothered. "You two will be fine. I have a plane to finish."

He turned and strolled off, leaving the sound of scissors snipping in the distance.

Janvi froze. Just the two of us?

Her hands instinctively tightened on the edges of her dupatta, her pulse quickening. She wasn't sure what unnerved her more: the thought of being alone with him or the ease with which he made her second-guess herself.

"You're still coming, aren't you?" he asked, his voice calm but his gaze steady.

Her conviction faltered. Why was he so good at doing that—unravelling her resolve without so much as raising his voice? At least Aman would have been a good cushion between them, she'd told herself. But now...

Reluctantly, she nodded. "Let me get my sandals."

"Good. I'll bring the car around," Karan said smoothly, his tone casual.

As she walked toward her room, her thoughts swirled in turmoil. The haveli suddenly felt too quiet, the sounds of the courtyard distant and muted. *Aman, you traitor,* she thought, her steps heavy with a growing sense of unease.

* * *

The car hummed softly as it made its way down the winding road toward the Quilla, the late afternoon sun casting a warm glow over the landscape. Karan stole a glance at Janvi beside him. She was sitting stiffly, her hands tightly clutching a worn leather-bound notebook. He'd noticed it earlier—how she carried it everywhere. It was different from the wallets girls usually carried, and he found it strangely endearing. Laxmi Tai had mentioned more than once how Janvi was always scribbling in it, making lists, organizing her thoughts. Karan found himself wondering what was in it.

Janvi sat quietly, her gaze fixed ahead, seemingly absorbed in the passing scenery. Karan couldn't help but notice how guarded she was, how tightly she kept herself together. He could tell she was on edge, but he was patient. He had orchestrated this whole situation, after all. Aman's refusal to come along had been part of the plan, leaving just the two of them alone. The car ride was his opportunity—an intimate moment that he was determined to make the most of.

"Everything alright?" he asked, keeping his voice casual but carrying a trace of amusement.

Janvi's eyes flicked toward him for a brief second before darting away again. "Yes," she said, her voice tight.

"You sure?" Karan pressed, sensing her discomfort.

She shrugged slightly, still clutching her notebook. "I'm fine."

Karan couldn't resist teasing. "You're awfully quiet for someone who's 'fine.'" He leaned back, watching her, enjoying the way she seemed to shrink in on herself at his words.

Janvi didn't answer, but the tension between them hung in the air. Karan felt a slight satisfaction—this was exactly what he wanted. Alone time with her, just the two of them, with no distractions.

"I'll tell you, though," Karan continued, his voice taking on a playful note, "I don't think I've ever seen you so tense. You've been like this since we left the *haveli*."

Janvi's jaw tightened, but she remained silent. Karan watched her, letting the silence linger. He didn't need to push her further. He knew she was slowly letting her guard down, even if just a little.

"Well," he said finally, his smile softening, "I'm sure you'll warm up to the idea soon enough."

Janvi didn't respond, her attention still fixed firmly on the road ahead. Karan's gaze lingered on her for a moment longer, his amusement tempered by something else—something deeper. He had all the time in the world.

The car came to a stop near the entrance of the Jaisalmer Fort, and Karan turned off the engine, his eyes briefly catching Janvi's expression as she looked out the window. She hadn't said much on the drive over, but Karan was used to that now. He knew how to give people space when they needed it. Still, the silence felt oddly comfortable, like an unspoken understanding between them.

Janvi's hand still rested on the worn leather notebook, and Karan's curiosity about it hadn't waned since they were in the kitchen together. The edges were frayed, like it had been well-loved. She'd been scribbling in it occasionally during the drive, but he hadn't pushed her to explain. There was time for that later.

"So, have you been to the fort before?" Karan asked, stepping out of the car, stretching his legs.

Janvi nodded, lifting her eyes from the notebook for the first time in a while. "Yes, a couple of times. Not much to do in Jaisalmer, after all."

Karan chuckled, feeling a small pang of nostalgia for the place. "I know. I grew up here. But there's something about it... always something new to discover."

They started walking, Karan leading the way with a natural ease, like he knew the fort as well as the back of his hand. His voice carried as he explained, pointing to the grand merchant *havelis* tucked within the walls of the fort. "My ancestors used to live here, in the heart of the fort, in those houses." He paused, a hint of fondness in his tone. "At least, that's what my grandfather used to tell me."

Janvi's gaze followed his pointing finger, her attention piqued. "I didn't know your family used to live here. Viren uncle and Daadi told me about your family's history, but this part, I didn't know."

Karan shrugged, his expression softening as he looked out over the fort. "A lot of families still live in the fort, but my ancestors decided to move out to the outskirts of Jaisalmer. They wanted more space... and to be closer to village life, you know? They wanted to make an impact on the locals, the villagers, the nomads. It was never just about wealth, it was about community."

Janvi listened attentively, nodding as she absorbed the information. Her notebook was in her hands again, and Karan couldn't help but watch with a raised brow as she scribbled something down.

"You write in that thing a lot," he observed, his voice laced with amusement.

Janvi's eyes flickered up to meet his for a moment before returning to her notebook. "I have a lot to remember."

Karan was intrigued but chose not to press her for now. They walked on, heading toward the Raj Mahal. He guided her through the rooms, showing her the intricate carvings, the age-old murals, and the grand courtyards.

"This courtyard," Karan pointed out as they walked through a large, open space, "was the inspiration for the one at the Rathore Haveli. My family wanted the same checkerboard design, but on a slightly larger scale." He grinned slightly, the memories of childhood visits to the fort coming to him in waves. "I spent a lot of time here with my grandfather."

Janvi nodded thoughtfully and jotted something down in her notebook again, but Karan didn't say anything. There was something about the way she wrote that he couldn't quite place—like she was cataloguing everything, even the smallest details.

Eventually, they reached a spot at the edge of the fort where the view stretched out over all of Jaisalmer. The golden city shimmered under the fading sunlight, and the wind carried the scent of desert sand. They stood there in comfortable silence, taking in the expansive view, the stillness of the moment.

Karan, unable to contain his curiosity, spoke first. "You know, my father used to bring me here. Said it was one of his favourite spots to reflect." He paused, glancing at Janvi. "It's peaceful here, don't you think?"

Janvi nodded, but she was already scribbling in her notebook, her focus unwavering.

Karan chuckled, almost to himself. "You know, I'm starting to think you write more than I talk."

Janvi flushed slightly, closing her notebook with a soft snap. "Sorry. I just—" She hesitated for a moment before speaking again. "I keep notes on everything. It helps me remember things. Important things."

Her voice had softened as she spoke, and Karan felt a small sense of tenderness towards her—her dedication, her quiet attentiveness. But his curiosity got the better of him.

"Alright," he asked, trying to sound casual, "what's so important that you keep writing down?"

Janvi shifted uncomfortably, but there was a flicker of trust in her eyes. "It's been with me since I was a child," she started, her voice quieter now, "this notebook. I write down things I don't want to forget—places I've been, things I've learned. My father was an Army trainer, so we travelled a lot. I would write about the places we went, the people we met, the things I wanted to remember. Local customs, recipes, just... whatever caught my interest."

Karan was quiet, surprised at her openness. "That's... beautiful. You've always had a love for learning, huh?"

Janvi smiled, though it was tinged with a hint of sadness. "Yes. And now, I'm trying to write everything down about the Rathore Haveli. I'm working on a project to revive it. My hope is to turn it into something that people can visit and learn about. And I'm also putting it all together for a guidebook—something tourists can use when they come to Jaisalmer."

Karan was speechless for a moment, taking in the depth of her ambition, her passion.

Janvi's eyes brightened, and she flipped the notebook open, her fingers eagerly skimming the pages. "Look," she said, showing him notes about his family's history with the haveli, even referencing things she'd learned when visiting with his father. Dates, references.

Karan's chest tightened with an unexpected warmth as he saw her notes. There was something so... familiar about it. Almost as if he could feel the presence of his father again, even though he was gone.

Janvi turned the pages more excitedly now, her voice full of energy as she shared more of her project with him. "See? I made notes when I learned about your father's time here, what he did for the haveli..."

Karan couldn't help but smile, but then his gaze fell on the leather cover of the notebook, and a strange sense of recognition washed over him. He traced his finger along it, wondering why it seemed so familiar.

Janvi's voice interrupted his thoughts. "Your mother gave it to me, you know."

Karan froze, his breath catching in his throat. "My mother?"

"Yes," Janvi said softly, her voice carrying a trace of sadness. "She came to see us after my mother's funeral. She was very kind to me... She gave me this notebook as a gift, and I've kept it with me ever since."

Karan's heart gave an unexpected lurch. His mother had met Janvi? He hadn't known, but the thought settled like a warmth inside him. It felt like a sign, a blessing, something guiding him toward her.

But Janvi's voice broke through his thoughts. "It's almost full, though. I'll have to get a new one soon," she said, a slight frown on her face. "I'll miss this design, though. I haven't been able to find another one like it."

Karan's mind raced as his fingers traced the leather cover, the familiar design, an engraving of a pair of compasses. He blinked, a sudden, strange thought entering his mind. Could it be?

Karan tucked that thought away to dwell on it later and continued flipping pages. Her daily ticked off, to do lists, Rajasthani recipes, ideas for the estate. Occasional diary entries. Eventually he reached a particularly longer one.

"February 22, 2022..." he read aloud.

Janvi quickly snatched the notebook from his hands, her eyes wide with panic. "It's getting late," she said, her voice tight. "We should go back to the haveli. I need to do aarti."

Karan, his heart racing, tried to mask his confusion, but the realization hit him like a sudden blow. February 22... That was the day of their wedding.

He watched her as she hurriedly walked away, his mind spinning with the implications.

11

BACK TO WORK

Yesterday was the most relaxing day Karan had ever experienced in a long time. He also enjoyed interacting with Janvi. Although he could still sense some hesitation on her part, she was more open and welcoming which was a clear progression from her earlier avoidance of him.

But now it was Monday, and he couldn't escape it. Even though he'd taken two weeks of proper leave from his role as CEO, a rarity in itself, but he couldn't ignore the responsibilities waiting for him on the other side of the world. Projects, emails, meetings—his absence wouldn't make them disappear.

Still, he had no intention of diving into work too early—he had to remember the time difference between New York and Jaisalmer. But he couldn't afford to let the day slip by either. He began setting up his workspace in his room, deliberately steering clear of the study.

The study was Janvi's domain now. He hadn't been here in over two years, and it didn't feel right to encroach on that space. Besides, he'd spent most of his life in that study, and now it felt like one more place in the haveli that didn't belong to him anymore.

As the clock ticked toward late morning, Karan stretched and tried to decide how to spend the rest of the day. Daadi, of course, had already made that decision for him. She'd insisted—firmly—that he take Janvi to the bazaar for her usual grocery run. The way she'd said it left no room for argument, and Karan didn't mind. He'd take any opportunity to spend time with Janvi, especially after the moments they'd shared yesterday.

"I'll go with you," he said as Janvi stood by the door, her shopping list in hand, ready to leave.

She paused and turned to him, brows slightly furrowed. "You don't have to," she said softly, her tone polite but hesitant.

"I want to," Karan replied, already stepping past her toward the car. "It's not a problem."

Janvi didn't argue further, though he caught the brief flicker of something—uncertainty, maybe—in her expression. He could tell she wasn't entirely comfortable. Her tension was subtle but palpable, like the way her fingers tightened around the list or the distance she kept as they walked toward the car.

Yesterday had been a start, a shift in their strained dynamic. Spending the day at the fort with her had felt... right. She'd been more open, more herself. But then he'd seen the date in her notebook—22nd February 2022—and everything had changed. The walls had gone back up, and the warmth she'd shown had vanished into the cold politeness she wore like armour.

It didn't help that she now knew he'd enlisted Aman to nudge her into spending time alone with him. While she hadn't openly confronted him, her quiet disapproval was clear.

Still, Karan wasn't discouraged. If anything, her restraint felt like a quiet challenge, one he was more than willing to take on. He wasn't looking to win her over with grand gestures or force her to trust him. He just wanted to get past the layers of hesitation—to see her smile, to hear her speak without that careful edge to her voice.

The drive to the bazaar was quiet, the only sound the steady purr of the engine. Karan stole a glance at Janvi, who sat with her hands folded neatly in her lap, her eyes fixed on the passing scenery. She seemed lost in thought, miles away from the moment they were sharing.

She had no idea how much he wanted to bridge the gap between them—to make things easier, to make her feel comfortable, to make her feel seen. But every attempt so far had felt like walking a tightrope, unsure if the next step would lead to progress or send him tumbling.

Karan slowed as they approached the outskirts of the town, the streets growing livelier with vendors setting up their stalls. He parked on a side street, and Janvi grabbed her *jholas*, turning to him. "I'll be quick," she said, her voice neutral.

Karan leaned against the car, watching her for a moment before responding. "Take your time," he said, his tone steady. He pulled out his phone to catch up on emails, though his eyes often wandered back to her as she moved through the market.

"*Kaisi ho,* Janvi *beta,*" called a turbaned man from the first stall.

"*Theek hoon,* Madhav *Kaka,*" Janvi replied, her tone respectful but brisk. "*Aap kaise ho?*"

"*Hum bhi badhiya,*" Madhav Kaka said warmly. "So, what can I get you?"

"Two kilos of *urad* and two kilos of *masoor dal,*" she said, adjusting the *jholas* on her arm.

Madhav passed her the bag with a nod. "*Daadi sa, kaisi hai?*"

"She's okay, Madhav Kaka," Janvi replied, handing him the exact amount of rupees. Before leaving, she crossed off the items from her notebook with a pen tucked neatly in its spine. Karan noticed the notebook, the same one she seemed to carry everywhere—a steady companion to her meticulous routine.

"*Acha,* I'll go now—I still need to buy vegetables and get back to the haveli. There's a lot to do today," she said as she waved goodbye to Madhav.

Karan's gaze lingered on her, a flicker of fascination playing across his face. For someone so young, she carried herself with the poise of someone far more experienced, navigating the market with brisk efficiency. It amused him, how effortlessly she managed it all, and yet there was something captivating about seeing her in her element.

As Janvi disappeared deeper into the market, Karan's gaze occasionally flicked up to watch her, noting the way she weaved through the crowd, her head bobbing above the sea of shoppers. He saw her bargaining with the vendors, her determination clear as she moved from one stall to the next, checking things off her list.

As Janvi finished her shopping and started making her way back to the car, the air around her shifted. A group of men loitering near the market's entrance began to jeer at her. At first, it was the usual crude remarks—unpleasant, but nothing she hadn't heard before. But then, as she walked closer to the group, their taunts grew louder and more direct. One of the men stepped forward, making a mock grab for her jhola, sneering with a cruel comment about her being "the abandoned bride."

Karan's blood ran cold. His fingers clenched into fists, and he straightened from the car, every muscle in his body tensing with a surge of protective instinct.

Janvi froze mid-step, her face tightening. Her eyes flicked between the men and him, but there was no fear in her stance—just a weary, quiet resolve, the kind that came from facing this kind of thing more times than she should have had to.

Madhav Kaka was already on his way toward her, shouting at the men to back off, but Karan didn't wait for him. His feet moved before he even realized it, his steps swift and unyielding. In a flash, he was in front of the men, his hand grabbing the ringleader by the collar.

"You have something to say?" Karan's voice was low, but it cut through the air with a sharpness that left no room for misinterpretation.

The man stumbled, caught off guard. He tried to sneer, pushing against Karan's grip. "Who the hell are you to—"

Before he could finish, Madhav Kaka's voice rang out, urgent and panicked. "*Bhai*, no! Rathore sir, Rathore sir!"

The older shopkeeper rushed forward, his eyes wide with fear. "This is Rathore sir, the heir of Rathore haveli. You don't know him?"

The thug's face paled as the words registered, and in an instant, his cocky demeanour evaporated. He glanced at his companions, then back at Karan, realizing his mistake. "Rathore *sahab*?" The fear in his voice was unmistakable.

Karan's eyes darkened, and his voice dropped to a dangerous level, laced with authority.

"SHE. IS. MY. WIFE!"

The words came out slow and deliberate, each one punctuated with a firm grip on the man's collar. There was a raw possessiveness in his tone, as if claiming what was his in front of the whole market. "You will show her respect, or I will make sure you regret it."

The thug's arrogance vanished, replaced by sheer panic. His lips moved, but no words came out until Karan shoved him back with a sharp, final push. He stumbled, dragging his companions with him as they scurried away. "Apologies, sir! Apologies!" the man stammered, nearly tripping over himself in his haste to flee.

Karan stood rooted, his chest heaving, eyes fixed on their retreating forms. Even as the men disappeared into the crowd, the simmering anger in his gaze remained, refusing to dissipate.

Karan's gaze shifted to Janvi, standing a few steps away, her *jholas* clutched tightly. Her expression was unreadable, but something about the way she stood, the way her eyes flickered between him and the retreating men, made Karan's chest tighten. He realized the weight of the words he had just spoken—the emphasis on *my wife*. He hadn't just claimed her in front of those men; it was more than that. It was a declaration. And something about it triggered a reaction in Janvi. He could see it in her eyes, though she didn't say a word.

But Karan couldn't focus on any of that now. He couldn't dwell on how she seemed to withdraw or the subtle shift in her expression. His mind was clouded with guilt, still seething at himself for leaving her to face this alone. If he hadn't walked away, none of this would have happened.

Without a word, Karan stepped toward Janvi. He didn't need to say anything; he simply took the *jholas* from her hands, walking behind her as she slowly made her way back to the car.

The drive back to Rathore Haveli was quiet, the weight of Karan's internal battle and Janvi's uncertainty filling the air between them. He was too lost in his own guilt to speak, and Janvi, unsure of how to break the silence or how to process what had just happened, remained silent as well.

When they arrived back at the haveli, Karan was still filled with frustration, his emotions coiled tightly. His mind replaying the scene in the markets over and over. If he hadn't left her... If he had only been there for her, none of this would have happened. His chest tightened, the weight of his guilt suffocating him. This was all his fault.

Once inside the haveli, Karan silently helped Janvi with the bags, taking them from her and carrying them into the kitchen. He didn't say anything, his movements efficient, but distant. The silence between them stretched, thick and heavy, each lost in their own thoughts.

When the task was finished, Karan gave a quick nod to Janvi, but his expression remained tight. Without another word, he turned on his heel and swiftly ascended the stairs. The frustration inside him was raw, his emotions too tangled to face anyone, even her.

He didn't want to think about what had just happened. Didn't want to confront the way Janvi had looked at him when he'd said *"my wife."* The guilt, the anger, the pain—it was all too much.

He retreated to his room, shutting the door behind him with a soft click. The moment he was alone, he collapsed onto the bed, staring at the ceiling. The guilt ate at him, gnawing at his insides. The silence of the room felt suffocating, but it was the only place where he could try to make sense of everything.

His wife?

She was his. *His wife.*

The realization hit him like a wave, pulling him upright as every thought, every feeling, aligned in a single moment. He understood now. His chest tightened as the truth settled deep within him—he wanted her. He wanted this life, her in his family, in this home, by his side. Permanently.

* * *

Janvi finished putting away the groceries, but her thoughts were far from the task at hand. The incident at the *bazaar* kept replaying in her mind. Karan's sudden fury, the way he'd grabbed one of the men by the collar, the force in his voice when he declared, *"She's my wife."*

For a fleeting moment, she had felt a sense of safety, something she hadn't known in a long time. But it was quickly followed by a flood of confusion. His wife? The words seemed to echo in her mind. Karan had left her on their wedding night. He had made it clear—he was in love with another woman, Anya, and had promised her they'd be divorced in three years. He'd walked away, and she had accepted it.

At first, she had been hurt, deeply. But she had forgiven him. She had to, for her own peace of mind. And she had accepted that her marriage would be nothing more than a formality. She'd decided to be okay with it.

But today... today something had changed. His declaration, his possessiveness, had stirred something inside her—something she couldn't quite place. *His wife*. The words were like a trigger, igniting a mix of emotions she hadn't expected to feel. It made her question everything—what had happened between them, what could happen now? Was she really his?

She quickly shook her head, trying to push the thought away. No, he was just trying to protect her, to scare the men away. That was all it was. There was no deeper meaning.

She sighed and pushed the thoughts away. There was work to be done. She couldn't afford to dwell on this right now. She had tasks waiting for her in the haveli. Still, as she worked, the thought lingered, a small nagging feeling she couldn't quite ignore.

She had forgiven him for the past, but with him back, everything felt different. The uncertainty of it all unsettled her, and she knew she couldn't keep pushing it aside forever. Sooner or later, she would have to face it.

12

A WALK TO THE VILLAGE

Karan sat at the desk in his room, laptop open, but his focus wavered. He had been working through the afternoon, but something was still off. It was rare for him to feel unsettled like this, especially when it came to work. Yet, today, everything seemed harder to concentrate on. The guilt from earlier that morning gnawed at him, and no matter how much he tried to immerse himself in his emails, his mind kept drifting back to Janvi.

He hadn't realized how much he'd skipped lunch until he felt the slight pang of hunger in his stomach. He checked the time—it was already 2:00 PM.

There was a knock at the door, followed by a familiar voice. "*Chothe hukum*, are you hungry? I've prepared something for you."

Karan smiled at the sound of Badri Kaka's soft voice. The old man had been taking care of him since he was a child, and even now, Badri Kaka was as devoted as ever. "I'm not hungry, Kaka, but thank-you," Karan called out, his voice warm with affection.

Badri Kaka didn't take no for an answer. "You're a busy man, I know. But you must eat. It won't do any good for you to work on an empty stomach."

Karan sighed, then relented. "Alright, I'll be down in a minute." He sympathized with the old man. Badri Kaka was just trying to make sure Karan didn't forget to take care of himself.

As Karan made his way downstairs, the faint smell of food filled the air, reminding him of home. After a quick but satisfying bite in the kitchen, Karan stood up to return to his room.

As he walked down the hallway, he paused when he heard voices coming from the study. It was Janvi and Aman.

Janvi's voice was clear, though tinged with frustration. "Aman, you can't keep distracting me with this. I need you to focus on your studies, not on the estate accounts. You're not ready for this yet."

Aman's voice was quieter, filled with hurt. "But I want to help. I don't want to sit here and do nothing while you handle everything."

Janvi's tone softened, but it was still firm. "You will help in your own time, but right now, your priority is school. Understand?"

Karan couldn't help but smile slightly. There was something endearing about the way Janvi was trying to be both a sister and a mother to Aman. It was so typical of her, the way she always took charge and tried to protect everyone, even when they didn't ask for it.

He cleared his throat before entering the study, hoping to interrupt the moment with a little humour. "Aman, I think you've got a good point there. Maybe Janvi could use some help with—"

"You stay out of this!" Janvi shot him a look that was a mixture of frustration and amusement.

Karan couldn't suppress the laugh that bubbled up. He raised his hands in mock surrender. "Alright, alright. I was just trying to help."

Amused by her reaction, he retreated from the study, shaking his head with a smile.

Back to Work.

* * *

It was nearly 4:00 PM, and Janvi was in the middle of sorting through some estate papers when she glanced out the window. Her thoughts wandered, and her mind replayed the events of the morning—Karan's protective outburst at the market, the men's taunts, and Karan's fury. She still wasn't sure how to feel about it all. There was safety in his presence, but there was also something unsettling about the way he handled the situation.

Janvi knew Karan had been gone for over two years, and although they'd had the wedding, they were still very much strangers. She was so used to handling things alone that having him back in her life, even in this distant way, created an unease she couldn't shake.

She stood up, deciding it was time to head out for her tutoring session. She always walked to the village to teach the children—it was a routine that gave her comfort, away from the weight of family expectations. The walk was about 20 minutes each way, and the fresh air helped her think. And it was also cooler at this time of day.

As she stepped outside, she was surprised to hear a voice call after her. "Janvi, wait."

She turned to see Karan standing by the door, his hands in his pockets. He looked... different than he had this morning, slightly more at ease.

"I was wondering if I could join you," Karan said, his voice casual but with an underlying sincerity. "I've been stuck in my room all day, and I could use some air. Is that alright?"

Janvi hesitated. She wasn't sure how to handle being around him after their earlier interaction. She had hoped to go alone, to have a moment of quiet, but something in his request made her pause.

She opened her mouth to decline, but before she could, he added, "I need a break from the work, too."

Janvi gave a short nod. "Fine."

They walked together in silence, each wrapped in their thoughts. The distance between them felt palpable, even though they were side by side. Karan made an effort to break the silence after a while, asking, "How long have you been tutoring the village children?"

Janvi glanced at him, surprised by the question. She hadn't expected him to be interested in such a small detail.

"I've been teaching them for a few years now," she answered, keeping her voice steady. "It's something I feel strongly about. I want to help them... give them opportunities they wouldn't otherwise have."

Karan nodded, his expression thoughtful. "That's admirable," he said quietly, his voice carrying a depth of respect that surprised her.

They continued walking, the silence between them no longer

as heavy. Yet, Janvi couldn't shake the feeling that Karan was still a stranger in her life, someone she wanted to trust but was unsure how to.

Karan, for his part, felt the weight of her words and the softening in her tone. It wasn't much, but it was a start.

* * *

As Janvi walked ahead toward the village, the familiar faces of the villagers greeted her with warmth. But when they saw Karan, the atmosphere shifted. It wasn't the excitement of the children this time. Instead, it was the elders—men and women who had witnessed Karan grow up—that recognized him. Their eyes lit up in recognition, and they murmured among themselves, nodding respectfully.

"You're back, young sir," one of the older men said, his voice full of reverence.

Karan nodded, his gaze sweeping over the familiar faces of those who had been a part of his life, whether he realized it or not. The elders offered him polite, even somewhat deferential, greetings. One or two of them raised their hands in a slight gesture of respect. Karan felt a warmth settle in his chest. It wasn't just the official respect that came with his family's name; it was a more genuine recognition of who he was to them, of his role in this community.

Janvi stood slightly apart, watching this interaction with a mixture of pride and quiet satisfaction. Karan could see the way her eyes softened, seeing how they welcomed him not as just the 'young sir' of the Rathore family but as a part of their lives.

The village had a certain rhythm to it—simple, unaffected by the world outside. And Karan, for a brief moment, felt like he had stepped into a world where he belonged, not because of his title but because of his connection to these people.

After a few moments, the village elders resumed their tasks, and Janvi moved toward the centre of the gathering, pulling out a small tablet from her bag. Karan, still standing nearby, couldn't help but watch as she interacted with the children.

She didn't follow the traditional ways of teaching. Instead, Janvi brought something new to them: YouTube, podcasts, free online courses—all tools she used to help these children discover their passions. Whether it was science, fashion, or pottery, each child seemed to find something that sparked their interest. Karan found himself absorbed by it—by the way Janvi blended technology with learning in a way he had never seen before.

He had always been taught through a rigid curriculum, expected to excel in certain subjects to meet a set standard. But here, in this small village, Janvi was teaching the children to find their own path, to pursue what excited them. It was a refreshing contrast. He couldn't help but be impressed by her approach.

As the lesson continued, something dawned on him. Janvi had created a space where the children could pursue their individual passions, but what about Aman? Why hadn't she extended that same openness to him? The thought lingered in his mind as he silently watched her teach.

He made a mental note of it. Maybe she needed to give Aman the same freedom to find his own way.

* * *

After the lessons with the village children, Janvi and Karan began their walk back to the haveli. The sun was lower in the sky now, casting a warm glow over the path, but her mind was elsewhere, still turning over Karan's words.

He had been so quietly observant, offering his approval of her tutoring methods. "I'm really impressed, Janvi," he had said. "The way you've found ways for each child to pursue their passions... it's refreshing."

His praise, though sincere, hadn't made her feel any less unsure about what he had added next: "But don't you think you should consider holding the same space for Aman? Giving him a role in this?"

She glanced sideways at him, a slight frown knitting her brow. His words caught her off guard. She had always thought she was protecting Aman from the weight of the family's legacy, keeping him away from the responsibilities that had burdened Karan and their father. But Karan's perspective made her pause. Was she unintentionally sheltering Aman too much? Was there a risk in not allowing him to grow into his role in the estate?

Karan's voice cut through her thoughts, soft but certain. "My parents used to keep things from me about what was happening in the estate. They thought they were protecting me, but I regret it now. I wish they had been more transparent. Maybe if they had let me help out, I would've found my passion earlier."

Janvi took in his words, her mind spinning. She had always thought it was better to shield Aman from everything, but what if he was right? What if she was making the same mistake with her brother that his parents had made with him?

She didn't respond immediately, her mind still grappling with the idea as she walked ahead, lost in thought. Her eyes were down, her steps measured as she tried to make sense of Karan's advice. She didn't even notice that she had walked too close to the edge of the path.

Then, she felt a sudden pull on her wrist. It was strong, firm, and unexpected, causing her to stumble forward. Everything seemed to slow down in that moment. The warm breeze, the sound of footsteps on the gravel, the soft murmur of distant voices—all of it faded as her body jerked slightly, and her heart skipped a beat. Karan's hand was on her wrist, holding her with an intensity that was both protective and calming.

She looked up, startled by the sudden motion and the proximity between them. Her breath caught in her throat, her pulse quickening as she locked eyes with him. Her heartbeat was louder than anything else, each beat reverberating in her chest.

For a brief second, it felt like the world had paused, and there was nothing but the two of them—standing close, her hand still in his grip. She could feel the warmth of his touch, the tension between them thick in the air. It was as though time had stretched, each second hanging longer than the last, and Janvi was suddenly acutely aware of how close they were, how she could feel the steady pressure of his fingers around her wrist.

Then, as if nothing had happened, Karan's gaze flickered toward something ahead. He didn't say anything, but his expression softened as he pointed his head, his brow slightly furrowed.

Janvi blinked, still in a daze from the unexpected pull, and slowly turned her head to follow his gaze.

She saw it then—a pile of camel dung just ahead, barely noticeable against the path.

Karan had pulled her away just in time, preventing her from stepping right into it.

A flush of embarrassment surged through Janvi, and she mentally admonished herself for being so lost in her thoughts. How careless she had been. Her hand, still warm from where Karan had held her, now felt strangely empty. She quickly shook her head to clear the thoughts that had begun to crowd her mind. *Focus, Janvi*, she told herself.

Without a word, she looked away from him, feeling a mix of embarrassment and a strange fluttering in her chest. They continued their walk back to the haveli, each step slow and heavy with the weight of unspoken words.

The conversation, the touch, the tension—all of it lingered, hanging between them. And as they walked in silence, Janvi couldn't shake the feeling that things were changing between them, in ways she wasn't yet ready to understand.

13

SHARING SPACES

After the walk, Karan continued on with his work. Daadi, Aman and Janvi were downstairs, and from the faint sounds of bells and chanting, they were doing the third day *puja* and *aarti* for Ganesh ji. Karan was feeling a little more settled after the walk with Janvi.

A knock on the door broke his concentration. He looked up in surprise to find Janvi standing there, a steel bowl in her hand, her expression hesitant. As always, the sight of her sent a familiar lurch through his heart.

"Hey, Janvi," he greeted, standing to meet her. "Please, come in."

She lingered just beyond the threshold, shaking her head lightly. "Um, no, I don't want to keep you. I just came to give you prasad."

"Sure," Karan said, stepping closer and extending his right hand to accept a generous serving of *halwa*.

Janvi gave him a brief smile before turning to leave. "Will you come down for dinner soon?" she asked, her voice soft but firm.

Karan nodded, offering a reassuring smile. "I'll be done in 10 minutes, just finishing up an email."

As she walked away, Karan watched her for a moment, noticing how quickly she'd retreated—almost as if she was in a hurry to leave. It struck him as odd, but the thought quickly slipped away as he turned his attention back to his work.

Dinner was a casual affair with Daadi, Aman, and Janvi. Laxmi Tai and Badri Kaka joined in as well, and the atmosphere was light, filled with easy conversation and laughter. Karan, however, felt a slight tickle in his throat as he reached for a piece of *roti*. He tried to suppress the sneezing that followed, but the third one made him pause.

Janvi, who had been talking to Aman, glanced at him with a furrowed brow. "Are you okay?" she asked, her voice laced with concern.

Karan wiped his nose with a napkin, managing a smile. "I think I'm coming down with something," he said casually, not wanting to worry her. "But it doesn't feel bad. I'll probably be able to sleep it off."

Janvi's eyes lingered on him for a moment longer, her concern still evident. "You should rest if you're feeling unwell," she said, her voice softer now.

Karan felt a warmth spread through him at the attention. Typical Janvi, always taking care of everything and everyone, even the ones she wasn't sure about. Despite her usual distance, there was something comforting about her care.

"I will, don't worry," he reassured her, giving a light chuckle to ease the moment.

As the conversation moved on, Karan couldn't help but notice how much he enjoyed the rare moments when she seemed to genuinely care, even if she kept her distance otherwise. It made him feel... seen.

After dinner, Karan was back at his desk, absorbed in his work, when he heard a soft knock at the door. He looked up to find Badri Kaka standing there, holding a warm glass of turmeric milk.

"Janvi Bitiya noticed you seemed to be coming down with something, so she asked me to bring this," Badri Kaka said, his smile warm and kind. "Drink it while it's warm."

Karan smiled at the thought. Sweet, beautiful Janvi.

He gratefully accepted the glass, offering a brief thank-you as he took it from the old man's hands and placed it on his desk.

"Will you be done soon, Beta?" Badri Kaka asked as he turned to leave.

Karan, still distracted by his work, nodded. "In about ten minutes."

Badri Kaka paused, his voice casual. "Ah, alright. Can I come back then to take the glass? I'm accompanying Laxmi to her village later as they have Ganesh Utsav celebrations, so I will return to the *haveli* late."

Karan, not thinking much of it, responded absently, "That's okay, you can go on ahead, Janvi can take it back when she comes up."

Badri Kaka gave a small, innocent shrug. "But she doesn't come in this room."

Karan's fingers froze over the keyboard as the words sank in. He looked up, his confusion evident. "What do you mean?"

Badri Kaka gave another shrug, his expression still light and unbothered. "She doesn't come in this room," he repeated, as if it were an everyday fact.

Karan's mind raced as he processed the casual comment. He sat back in his chair, staring at the glass of turmeric milk on his desk, a question stirred inside him. He blinked, trying to shake off the thought, but it lingered.

After a long moment, Karan cleared his throat and quickly replied, "Um, that's okay. I'll take it to the kitchen myself."

Badri Kaka gave a nod, his face still innocent. "*Theek hai*. I'll be going now. Goodnight, *Bete*."

With that, he left, leaving Karan sitting there, the question echoing in his mind. *Janvi doesn't come in this room?*

Karan remained still for a moment, uncertainty gnawing at him. His focus on his work had completely faltered now, the strange comment lingering like a puzzle that he couldn't yet solve.

The next morning when Karan woke up, Badri Kaka's words were still in his mind. At first, he dismissed it as the ramblings of an old man, but the more he thought about it, the more it started to make sense.

The way Janvi lingered at the threshold when she came to give him *prasad* the night before. And on the first day when he'd asked if she left the *chai* in his room, she had shaken her head.

But Karan knew by now that she made chai every morning

and took it to Daadi's room. She knew every nook and cranny of the *haveli*, had a sense of where everything was, managed the house and took care of it all and everyone in it.

And yet, he had hardly seen her even stumble outside his room before last night.

The question was: *why?*

Karan needed to find his grandmother. Even as he walked, a suspicion gnawed at him, but he no longer wanted to operate on assumptions when it came to Janvi because that's what has brought him in this predicament in the first place.

He found his grandmother in the living room, reciting the *Hanuman Chalisa*. She looked up with a gentle smile and invited him to come in.

"I'll come by later after you're done with *puja*," he said, trying to sound casual.

"That's okay," she replied, setting aside her glasses, "Come sit."

Karan took a seat opposite her.

"I can no longer sit on the cushions in the puja room anymore," Daadi continued. "So Janvi suggested I sit in here and do my reading. She says God is everywhere, not just in the *puja* room."

The warmth in Daadi's tone infecting Karan as well.

"You really are fond of her, aren't you Daadi?" Karan asked, his voice softening. "You always speak of her with so much affection and praise."

"Yes," Daadi agreed, her eyes shining. "She's like an oasis in the desert."

Karan smiled at that description of Janvi. He couldn't deny any of it. Her presence felt like a stream of water in a barren land, nourishing and soothing, just like her name.

"So young man, why are you here?" Daadi asked with a mischievous glean in her eyes. "You obviously aren't here to listen to my chanting."

"No," Karan said with a sigh. Normally he'd be amused at her perceptiveness but today, he was too bothered to care.

"Badri Kaka said something that caught my... concern," Karan began hesitantly. "Does Janvi really not come in to my room?"

"Ah," Daadi said, setting her book and her glasses aside. "No, she does not."

Karan's chest tightened at the weight of Daadi's words.

"Why?" he asked again, though deep down, he already knew the answer.

"Since the night you left on your wedding, she hasn't stepped foot into that room again."

Karan's heart felt heavy. He repeated what she said questioningly, though more to himself than anyone else.

"Since the night of the wedding?" His voice was thick, but his eyes were distant. He'd suspected as much but hadn't wanted to believe it. Didn't want to add another feather to his already full guilt-cap.

Daadi sighed, looking at him with a mix of understanding and sympathy.

"Look here, Karan," Daadi continued gently, "I don't know the details of the conversation you had with Janvi on the night you left. And to be very honest with you, I really don't need to know. I can see now that you were suffering too. We weren't exactly fair to you. But in the last five years I have known her, I have had the opportunity to see Janvi closely. She is not in the habit of opening her heart out to people but in everyday life she is nothing but consistent so it doesn't take a genius to put two and two together. She clearly does not do anything without reason."

Karan let her words sink in. Daadi's observations about Janvi were accurate—she was quiet, reserved even at times, but not complicated. There was no grand revelation here. The answer was simple, staring him right in the face.

She doesn't do anything without reason. So, if she hadn't stepped into his room since the night of their wedding... then the obvious answer was that he hadn't given her a reason to.

And how could she? He thought back to that night—the

speech about lacking his father's attention, the mention of his love for someone else in New York, and the cold, final declaration that they would divorce in three years. He had left her with nothing but the weight of those words. No surprise, then, that she couldn't bring herself to cross the threshold of a room where he had told her, in no uncertain terms, that she was merely a duty fulfilled.

How could she ever believe she had a place in his life—much less in his room?

"You're absolutely right, Daadi." Karan said as he stood up to leave, "Anyway, I'll let you get back to your reading."

Daadi nodded with a smile before adjusting her glasses and setting them firmly on her nose.

As Karan walked to his room, one thought rung sharp and clear in his mind. Janvi was too proud. She wouldn't go where she believed she wasn't wanted.

Then there was only one solution, Karan thought. If the mountain will not come to Muhammad, then Muhammad must go to the mountain.

Without wasting any more time, Karan called out to Badri Kaka.

"Badri Kaka, I need your help. Can you please move the desk in my room to the study? I'll be working from there now."

Badri Kaka nodded without question, "Ji, hukum. Right away."

* * *

Janvi stepped into the study after lunch, ready to continue her work on the estate accounts, but she stopped when she saw the unexpected sight before her. Badri Kaka and Karan were moving Karan's smaller desk from his room into the corner of the study, near the window. The larger, oakwood desk—Karan's father's desk—remained in the centre of the room.

Karan grinned at her, looking pleased with the change. "Janvi!" he greeted with a cheerful tone. "I hope I didn't surprise you. I decided to move my desk in here—my room was starting to feel a bit... suffocating, you know? Work there, sleep there, then go back to work—it didn't feel right. So, I thought I'd change things up a bit."

He glanced toward the large desk in the middle of the room. "If you don't mind, I thought I could work over here, in the corner, just for a change of scenery."

Janvi stood by the door, watching the scene with a slight surprise. She had grown accustomed to the study as her space over the past two and a half years, especially the desk she had been using—Karan's father's desk, which had always been the centrepiece of the room.

Karan, sensing her hesitation, added quickly, "I haven't touched Dad's desk. You've made it your space. I wouldn't take that from you, Janvi."

Her gaze softened at his words. It was clear that Karan was not going to claim the desk—he was simply trying to adjust to a new environment for his work. Janvi, understanding his thoughtful gesture, responded, "If you'd prefer the larger desk, you can take it. It's yours after all. I don't mind using the smaller one."

Karan smiled, but there was a quiet hesitation in his expression. "No, I couldn't do that," he said, shaking his head. "It's been your space all this time. I'm happy here in the corner." His voice was firm, but there was a tenderness to it, a respect for the arrangement Janvi had made for herself over the years.

Janvi nodded, appreciating his understanding. "Thank-you. But I'll get used to the smaller one. You can have the bigger one." She reassured him, her voice warm and kind.

"And I said, that's your space and you will continue to keep it. Besides," Karan gave her a small, almost sheepish smile, "I like the view from here."

Janvi laughed, "Alright".

"Thanks for being understanding. It's just... good to have a change, you know?"

Janvi nodded before walking to her own desk and settling into her usual routine. She couldn't help but feel the shift in the air. Karan's desk was now in her line of sight, and she couldn't ignore the way his presence in the study had altered the dynamic of the room.

She tried to focus on her work, but the subtle spark in the air made it difficult. Karan's presence in the room, so close, was impossible to ignore. But she couldn't afford to entertain those feelings. Their marriage would end in a few months, and she had to accept that. The spark between them was just a fleeting moment—nothing more. She pushed the thought aside, burying her hopes with it.

14

AN OFFERING

After ending his update meeting call, Karan sat back in his chair, stretching his neck. He glanced over at Janvi, who was fully focused at the oak desk, writing in the ledger. After each line, she punched the numbers on the pocket calculator with a pen between her fingers. He watched her for a while in fascination.

Intrigued, he asked, "Why don't you use a computer?"

"It's not that complicated," Janvi said, a hint of a smile tugging at her lips as she continued writing. "Besides, I only do the basic entries. Himanshu handles all the complicated stuff."

Karan's brows furrowed in confusion. "Who's Himanshu?"

"Our accountant," Janvi replied matter-of-factly.

Karan tilted his head slightly, his concern rising, "I thought our accountant was Kuldeep Sodha?"

"Oh, yes, we still use the same firm," Janvi clarified. "But Kuldeep Kaka retired three years ago, and his son took over soon after."

Recognition clicked in Karan's mind. "Oh, Himanshu Sodha!" he said, a hint of recollection in his voice. "Yes, I remember him. We were friends in Primary School."

"Yes, he told me," Janvi said.

Of course he did, thought Karan, his mind lingering on the fact that they were clearly on a first-name basis too. Something about that didn't sit well with him. Himanshu had been his childhood friend, but Karan remembered him as a flirt—a bloody flirt, to be precise.

Karan watched as Janvi laughed softly to herself.

"What's so funny?" Karan asked.

"Nothing, it's just...," Janvi said shaking her head with a chuckle, "something I remembered Himanshu had said. He is funny. He's always making me laugh.

Karan's stomach tightened, a tinge of jealousy creeping up his spine before he could suppress it.

Run a knife through me, Janvi, why don't you?

"Yes, I know, he is... quite the charmer," Karan added dryly, though Janvi didn't notice.

Karan couldn't shake the thought. Himanshu had always been charming—too charming, if he was being honest. The idea of Janvi laughing at his jokes made him uncomfortable.

He watched Janvi continue working until her smile slowly faded. A ping on his laptop announced that the project update from his R&D team had arrived in his inbox, but his mind still lingered on the unexpected possessiveness he was feeling, bothering him more than he cared to admit. With a sigh, he returned his focus on work.

After Karan finished his shareholder meetings and went over the audit and research approvals, he walked to the kitchen to have a break and fill up his water bottle. Janvi was already in the kitchen after finishing up her estate paperwork and returning from her daily walk to the village.

Janvi was standing at the dining table rolling *boondi laddoos* for the fourth day of Ganesh Utsav. Laxmi Tai was making dinner and Aman was sitting across from Janvi doing homework on the kitchen table.

"Hey, Aman," Karan said as he walked behind Aman over to the sink.

"Hi Jij!" Aman greeted him brightly, but then winced. "Ow!"

Karan turned just in time to see Janvi swat Aman's hand, which had crept dangerously close to the plate of *laddoos*.

"Aman," Janvi scolded sharply. "How many times do I have to tell you? First we give *prasad* to God, then we eat!"

Laxmi Tai, who was stirring the pot, looked on and smiled.

"Karan was also just like this," Laxmi Tai added with a laugh while stirring her pot. "No matter how many times you tell him not to do something, he'll keep doing it.

Karan froze, his hand still on the faucet. He looked over at Janvi, who was watching him with a barely suppressed smile, clearly amused.

"Laxmi Tai," Karan said slowly, his voice dripping with mock seriousness as he finished filling up his bottle. "How about we do this? I'll bring a loudspeaker for you, and you can go up on the terrace and announce all my misdeeds to the entire neighbourhood."

"That's probably a good idea for my benefit," Aman piped in. "They say learning from other's mistakes is wisdom."

Karan turned and shot an amused glance at Aman before turning to Laxmi Tai and Janvi who were laughing at his expense.

Karan walked over to the table and sat across from Aman, beside Janvi.

"In that case, watch and learn," Karan said mischievously as he quickly grabbed a *laddoo* from Janvi's *thali*.

Janvi let out a shocked sound, looking at him speechless.

"What?" he asked, raising an eyebrow. "I'm following Shabri's rule. Taste first and then offer to God." He winked, clearly enjoying the chaos he was causing.

Laxmi Tai and Aman now laughing at Janvi's frustration.

"By the way, these are delicious. Ganesh ji will absolutely love them." Karan said.

Karan reached out for another one saying "Here, you try one Aman."

But Janvi, desperate to stop him, caught his wrist. Her fingers were sticky with sugar, leaving a faint tackiness on his skin. She gasped softly, realizing what she'd done, her eyes darting up to meet his with a mix of embarrassment and defiance.

Karan was momentarily stunned by her sudden action, her fingers warm and sticky around his wrist. For a second, neither of them moved, caught in the unexpected moment. But then, Karan's playful smirk returned. With a gentle tug on his wrist, he pulled her toward him.

In an instant, Janvi lost her balance and stumbled, falling forward into Karan's chest. She gasped, eyes wide with surprise, as she landed against him, her face inches from his. Karan's hand wrapped around her to steady her.

Aman's laughter filled the room, and even Laxmi Tai couldn't suppress her smile. Janvi, flustered and wide-eyed, immediately tried to push herself away, her cheeks flushed red, but Karan wouldn't let go. She glanced at him nervously. His dark eyes held a gaze for a moment. His lips curved into a slow, mischievous smirk. Without another word, he let her go.

Janvi quickly straightened and returned to her task, her cheeks glowing red as she rolled the remaining *laddoos* with shaky hands. She avoided his gaze, but her heart refused to settle, fluttering wildly at the unexpected moment.

Karan watched her for a few seconds longer, his smile lingering as though he could still feel the warmth of her against him. Finally, he picked up his water bottle and straightened.

"I'll see you all at dinner after the *puja* and *aarti*," he announced, his tone light but steady.

Aman and Laxmi Tai nodded, settling back into their tasks as the laughter faded.

"See you jij," Aman called back.

Janvi kept her focus on the *laddoos*, though her hands moved slower now.

Just as Karan was about to leave, he paused mid-step. His sharp eyes caught Janvi jerking her head to swat away a loose strand of hair that had fallen into her face, her hands too sticky with sugar to brush it away. She huffed in mild frustration, determined to finish her task despite the distraction.

Karan glanced at Aman, who was engrossed in his homework, and Laxmi Tai, still busy at the stove. Satisfied they weren't paying attention, he took a quiet step closer.

Without a word, he reached out and tucked the stray strand gently behind her ear. His fingers barely grazed her skin, but the light touch sent a small shiver through Janvi. She froze, her breath catching, and her eyes widened in surprise, though she didn't dare look up.

Karan stepped back quietly, his expression calm and unreadable now, but his lips quirked just slightly before he turned and walked away.

Janvi stood there for a moment, stunned and flustered, her heart racing faster than ever.

* * *

Dinner was a buzz of conversation and Karan was feeling completely left out of it. The women were making lists and plans for *visarjan*. With Aman piping in on all his demands every now and then.

"*Acha,*" Daadi instructed Janvi in her usual gentle manner, "have we arranged for the *shikara*?"

"Yes, Daadi Sa," Janvi replied looking into her notebook.

"We've also told the *phoolwala* to come here first thing in the morning," Laxmi Tai added. "Oh, and Janvi, did you tell *punditji* what time to come?"

"Yes, Laxmi Tai," replied Janvi, "He said he'll be here at 2:30pm sharp and Aman will also be home by then. Aman make sure you're showered and ready. I've left your kurta in the room."

"And, yes," Daadi added, "make sure you pack all the extra *laddoos* for the children."

"Don't worry," Laxmi Tai assured her, "Janvi and I will pack it after dinner."

"Don't pack everything," Aman cried out, "I want to take some for my school friends tomorrow."

"I've already packed the *laddoos* for your friends, Aman bete," Laxmi Tai assured him.

"And for goodness' sake, Laxmi," Daadi cautioned, "please don't wear anything fancy like last year. Remember last year you dropped your bangle in the lake? And Janvi you too. There'll be a crowd."

Karan ate in silence watching the scene in front of him. Even though he felt completely excluded, paradoxically, he felt like he completely belonged. He felt a swell of affection in his heart for them.

His eyes fell on Janvi, her eyes furrowed, turning pages, writing notes, ticking off items. Every now and then, she'd stop to peruse the contents and while doing so hold the top of the pen with her teeth. The way she flicked her hair when she'd look up to speak. The way she'd smile when Aman said something innocently obvious and laugh at Laxmi Tai rolling her eyes at Daadi.

Karan's gaze flickered to Janvi's notebook, the worn leather cover sparking a memory from Sunday afternoon. The one his own mother had given her. She had spoken fondly of it, lamenting that it was nearly full and she hadn't found another like it. The thought stayed with him now, nudging at something buried in his memory.

Could it be?

He made a mental note to check his room later.

* * *

Later that night in his room, Karan sifted through old boxes in the top shelf of his wardrobe until he found the exact one he was searching for. He opened the dusty box.

Bingo!

With the box securely in his hands, Karan stepped into the dimly lit corridor towards Janvi's room. Daadi and Aman were already in bed, but Janvi was still finishing up with the packing of the last *laddoos* when Karan had come up. She should already be in her room now.

Karan reached the last room, the faint light spilling from beneath the door confirming his assumptions. He hesitated for a moment, taking a few seconds to calm his nerves before knocking softly.

The door creaked open, revealing Janvi, still dressed in her pale pink *salwar kameez*, her messy hair tied up. She looked at him with a mix of curiosity and weariness, her expression turning to confusion as she saw the box in his hands.

Karan adjusted the box in his hands. "I brought you something. I think... you might like what's inside," he said carefully. "May I come in?"

Janvi nodded, moving aside to let him in. He could sense she was nervous but her curiosity was getting the better of her.

He noted, she kept the door deliberately wide open, probably wary of him. Karan felt a mix of amusement and sadness. As he looked around, he realized, this was the first time he'd seen her room.

It was exactly like her. Simple, efficient and minimalistic. He walked in slowly, setting the box on her dresser, her leather watch placed neatly in its box on top of it.

"What is it?" she asked softly.

"Open it," Karan said as he stepped back to lean against the door, his arms folded watching her carefully.

Janvi opened the box slowly. As she removed the old newspaper on top, Karan watched in satisfaction as Janvi's expression morphed from confusion, to surprise to pure happiness.

She gasped, her hands covering her mouth. As she turned to look at him, she dropped her hands, "How?"

Karan shrugged a single shoulder.

She didn't wait for him to answer as she pulled out the contents of the box. One, two, three... leather notebooks. The exact same kind she owned with the compasses engraved on the back. There was at least a dozen more in the box. She flipped them. They were all blank.

Karan smiled as his hands slipped into his pockets. "You can write and document as much as you want," Karan said.

Janvi was rendered speechless with pure happiness, squealing like a child in a candy shop. Janvi's gaze darted back to the open box, then to the notebook she held, her excitement barely contained. "Right? This is perfect!" she exclaimed, her voice rising with joy. Her hands clutched the notebook tightly to her chest as her grin widened, radiating pure, unrestrained happiness.

And before she even realized what she was doing, she stepped forward and threw her arms around him.

Karan stiffened, surprised by the sudden contact, but before he could process it fully, she pulled back just as quickly. Her cheeks flared red as she stumbled over her words. "Oh! I—I'm so sorry! I didn't mean to—"

"Janvi," Karan interrupted, his voice calm and laced with an unmistakable warmth. "It's okay."

He was still reeling, though he kept his expression composed. Her sudden burst of excitement, the feel of her arms around him, the way her happiness had spilled over—it was... endearing. More than that, he had enjoyed it, far more than he had expected.

"How did you even find these?" she asked.

Karan swallowed before he answered. "My mother had bought a boxful of them for my 12th birthday so I could give it to my classmates. It was my first year at boarding school in Dehradun. I only gave it to a few friends and somehow the rest remained. She kept the box in my room. And I had completely forgotten about them until that day at the *Quilla* when you showed me yours."

With a distant gaze and a shrug, he continued. "She loved writing. I think she'd be very happy knowing I gave them to someone who'd understand their worth. I was never a note-taker. And I'm happy they have finally found a purpose after gathering dust in my bedroom for all these years."

Janvi looked down at the notebook in her hands, her fingers tracing the compass engraving on the back. Her eyes glistened, and for a moment, Karan thought she might cry. But she quickly recovered and looked up to give him the brightest smile she had ever given him.

She continued looking at him, her gratitude shining. "Thank-you! Really. This means so much to me."

Her sincerity was disarming. Karan felt a tug in his chest, an urge to pull her back in his arms. But he fisted his hands in his pocket to calm the feeling and smiled instead.

"Well," he said after a pause, clearing his throat, "I'll leave you to it. You have a long day tomorrow."

Karan turned toward the door to leave but before he could take another step, Janvi's voice stopped him.

"Um, wait?"

He turned, and she hesitated, looking like she wanted to say something more. Instead, she smiled again, her cheeks still faintly pink. "Goodnight."

"Goodnight, Janvi," he replied, his voice quieter this time, before stepping out and closing the door behind him.

As he walked back to his room, Karan felt an unfamiliar warmth settle in his chest. Her joy, her gratitude, and even that impulsive hug lingered in his thoughts.

15

VISARJAN

Lunch was chaotic. Karan couldn't decide whether he should have helped or just stayed out of everyone's way. *And who were all these people, anyway?* The haveli was buzzing with activity—friends, extended family, and villagers all preparing to take Ganesh ji to the lake for visarjan.

He shook his head, still incredulous at everyone's earlier plan: walking to Gadisar Lake from Rathore Haveli—a 40-minute trek in this heat!

"No fucking way! It's 37 degrees out today! We are NOT walking there!" Karan declared, adamant.

Karan was already dressed in his linen kurta, waiting for everyone else to get ready. He was reviewing the System Integration Plan for the airline communication project that his lead engineer had emailed when his phone rang.

It was Nathan.

Karan's stomach tightened. He hadn't spoken to Nathan since that day.

Hesitantly, he picked up the phone.

"Hello," Karan answered.

"Hey..." Nathan's voice came through, followed by a long sigh. "I—" Nathan hesitated, "I wasn't sure you would pick up."

Karan laughed awkwardly. "I wasn't sure I would either."

Nathan laughed nervously and then paused.

Karan looked at the time on his clock. It was almost 3:30 in the morning for Nathan.

"Can't sleep?"

"No." Nathan sighed again. "I... uh... wanted to talk. Been trying to work out what to say. I realize I—"

Nathan broke off, and Karan noticed his phone's network was low. He stood and walked out of the study, heading up to the terrace.

As he made his way to the terrace, Karan realized that deep down, he was no longer upset with either of them. Because if it weren't for them, he would have still been living under a rock when it came to Janvi.

* * *

As Janvi pleated her sari, she thought about Karan and his gesture yesterday. She had been so busy since morning that she never got a chance to speak to him today. He had been in the study all morning, busy with work.

Lunch had also been rushed so it was just a brief nod here and there. She almost laughed at his frustration earlier. He looked at them as though they'd all lost their marbles when they suggested walking to Gadisar Lake. It wasn't like they hadn't done it before, but it still felt good to hear him have his say.

He made her feel safe. The way he came to her aid at the markets the other day, the way he listened to her, his awareness of her, and care for Aman. And then there were the notebooks.

Her smile turned wistful. *Anya was very lucky to have him.* She thought back to that day on the terrace when he had asked to be her friend. She realized that if not as a partner, she could still happily spend the rest of her life with him as a friend.

Janvi did a final check in the mirror before leaving her room. Downstairs, everyone was gathered, ready to take Ganesh ji for the visarjan.

"Where's Karan?" someone asked.

"I think I saw him head to the terrace," Laxmi Tai said.

"Janvi, go check and let him know we're ready to leave," Daadi instructed.

"Yes, Daadi sa," Janvi replied with a nod.

* * *

"... so do you recall Garret's suggestion on the night of the cocktail party?" said Nathan.

"Vaguely. Remind me again?" Karan replied trying to think back on that night.

Nathan paused before continuing. "They specialize in medical device sensors. Remember how we both thought he was just throwing darts in the dark? Well, they reached out to me directly yesterday. They're very serious about an acquisition. They've got potential, but what do you think?"

As they spoke, Karan felt as if a weight had been lifted off his shoulders at resolving the tension between Nathan and himself. Nathan's feelings for Anya had been genuine. In hindsight, Karan should have seen the signs. Girlfriends came and went but his affection for Anya was constant. Maybe what began as friendship took the form of love. Karan was glad they could all see past that and get back on track with their shared passion, their work.

His thoughts returned to the call. Leaning back on the terrace ledge, he let out a slow sigh. "I think that's flattering, but... medical devices are a whole different ballgame," Karan replied cautiously. "We're talking about dealing with FDA, medical regulations. Not to mention getting investors on board with it."

Nathan's voice broke through. "I get your point. Even I'm not certain if we are ready for that level of scrutiny. On one hand, we've got the tech but we'd need a dedicated regulatory team..."

As Nathan spoke, the familiar soft jingle of anklets drew Karan's attention to the terrace entrance and Nathan's voice disappeared into oblivion. Karan's breath caught in his throat, his brain stopped functioning and his heartbeat began to race.

Janvi walked toward him, a vision in gold. She was draped in a marigold yellow *saree* with a gold and pink embroidered border. Her hair was swept into a neat low bun, a loose wavy fringe framing one side of her face, softening her features. Her simple, gold necklace and matching earrings glinted in the sun as she moved. Her right hand rested gently over the pleats of her saree, her fingers subtly adjusting the fabric as she walked. Bangles adorned her slender wrists, the gold and pink designs mirroring the delicate embroidery on her saree, chiming faintly as she moved. Her pink lips were curved in a soft, shy smile.

As Karan regained his composure, he became aware of his phone still pressed against his ear, Nathan still talking.

"Nathan, can I talk to you later?" Karan spoke quietly, his eyes never leaving Janvi. Without waiting for a response, he cut the call and slipped the phone in his pocket.

Janvi came to a stop in front of him, and Karan's body tensed, a sudden heat rising in him. Unable to tear his eyes off her, his gaze helplessly trailed downward, taking in every curve and contour highlighted by the yellow fabric, hugging her frame in a way that felt both innocent and dangerously provocative. It wasn't intentional; that's what made it worse. She wasn't trying to be sensual—she just was.

He shifted awkwardly, trying to maintain his composure, but the magnetic pull was impossible to ignore. The faint smell of jasmine only made it harder to think straight. It took every ounce of his strength to resist the urge to close the distance between them, to reach out and touch her. He was struggling to breathe, and his heart beat in a way that felt both urgent and dangerous.

"Hi," she spoke first. "I'm sorry, I didn't mean to interrupt."

"You didn't," Karan replied too quickly. His voice sounded strained, even to his own ears. He cleared his throat, forcing himself to take a steadying breath before speaking again. "You... you look stunning."

He watched her smile deepen and a faint blush creep up her cheeks. "Thank-you," she said. "You look good too."

Her brows furrowed as her hand hesitantly moved towards his left chest. She paused midway, unsure, "May I?". Karan followed her fingers to a lone red thread on his kurta. She picked it and flicked it out but not before her fingers brushed against his chest. The feeling was electric. She was close, so close. He tightened both his fists digging his nails into the palm of his hands to control his urges.

"*Challe?*" she asked.

Karan merely nodded, too afraid of his own emotions to speak.

As she turned to lead the way, his eyes lingered, against his better judgment, on the delicate curve of her bare waist. The dip of her back, the gentle sway of her hips. Karan clenched his jaw, forcing himself to look away, but the image lingered, vivid and relentless, etched into his mind. He moved to walk beside her instead, hoping to steady his erratic thoughts.

The air between them was thick with unspoken words and barely contained emotions. Every step felt like a test of his self-control.

Suddenly, Janvi's heel caught the edge of her saree. She stumbled, letting out a soft gasp as her hand instinctively shot out, grabbing his arm for balance.

"You okay?" Karan asked, his voice taut with concern, though his heart hammered against his chest at the contact.

"Yes," she laughed nervously. "I'm not used to wearing a saree."

I can help you take it off.

He stiffened, horrified at himself. Where had *that* come from?

Janvi seemed unaware of his inner turmoil as they resumed walking. The moment should have passed, but the weight of his inappropriate thought clung to him like a shadow.

"Um," Karan blurted out, his voice too sharp as they neared the stairs. "You go on ahead. I'll be down in five minutes. I just need to grab something from my room."

"Alright," said Janvi curiously. She turned and continued down the steps, leaving behind the faint scent of jasmine.

The moment she was out of sight, Karan inhaled sharply and strode to his room, each step an effort to put physical distance between himself and the overwhelming pull she had on him. Once inside, he shut the door with a firm click and leaned against it, closing his eyes and exhaling shakily. His heart was still pounding, the memory of her touch—however fleeting—seared into his senses.

Crossing to the bathroom, he turned on the faucet and splashed cold water onto his face, the shock of it grounding him. He gripped the edge of the sink tightly, drops of water trailing down his face as he lifted his eyes to meet his reflection in the mirror. His jaw was clenched, his chest rising and falling with uneven breaths.

"Get it, the fuck, together!" he muttered, his voice low and sharp.

He raked a hand through his hair, his mind racing. He had been drawn to other women before, but this... this was different. The way she looked, moved, and smiled—it was as if every part of her was designed to test his self-control.

Karan straightened, wiping his face with a towel. He couldn't afford to let his emotions spiral. Not now. Not when he was still trying to earn her trust, to rebuild whatever fragile connection they had begun to forge. He had to focus on her comfort, not his desires.

Taking a deep breath, he squared his shoulders and stepped out of the bathroom.

* * *

Janvi carefully adjusted the Ganesh idol in her lap as Karan came down the haveli steps, his steps brisk and purposeful. He opened the passenger door and offered her a steadying hand. "Watch your step," he said quietly, his voice unusually low.

Janvi slid into her seat, murmuring her thanks, though he was already rounding the car to the driver's side. Daadi, Laxmi Tai, and Aman settled in the backseat, chattering softly about the festivities as the car hummed to life.

As Karan gripped the steering wheel, Janvi noticed how tightly his hands held it, the tendons in his forearms flexing. His expression was unreadable, but there was a tension about him that made her wonder. Was he still thinking about work, or was it something else entirely?

"Everything okay?" she asked tentatively.

He nodded curtly. "Fine."

The festive chants of "Ganpati Bappa Morya!" grew louder as they neared Gadisar Lake, where a crowd of villagers and family friends had gathered. Colourful trucks and cars lined the lakeside, adorned with garlands and idols as other groups of people gathered for the visarjan of their Ganesh ji.

When they arrived, Karan stepped out and came around to help her. His hand brushed her arm as she adjusted the Ganesh idol in her arms, sending a fleeting warmth through her. He turned away quickly, his jaw tight as he focused on organizing their small group.

They made their way to a waiting *shikara*, the boat's bright paint gleaming under the lantern-lit sky. Aman, practically bouncing with excitement, climbed aboard after them. Together, they rowed to the middle of the lake, where Janvi, with Karan's steadying hand, immersed the Ganesh idol into the serene waters.

The chants of "Ganpati Bappa Morya, Mangal Murti Morya!" echoed across the lake, the sound filling Janvi with a strange sense of peace. But when she glanced at Karan, his face lit by the soft glow of lanterns, the tension hadn't left him. If anything, it seemed to deepen.

She couldn't help but wonder: what was weighing so heavily on his mind?

* * *

From the edge of the crowd, the stalker lingered, his eyes glued to her. Janvi. She looked radiant, her *saree* catching the golden hues of the festival lights. Her laughter, soft yet musical, reached him even amidst the chants of "*Ganpati Bappa Morya!*". It was meant for him.

But then he saw *him*.

Karan Rathore. The man walked beside her, his presence imposing, his hand resting lightly at Janvi's back as he guided her through the crowd. The sight made the stalker's stomach churn with rage.

Who was he? Her husband? The thought burned like acid. Janvi didn't belong to him. She couldn't. She belonged to *him*. And if she couldn't be his, then no one would have her. Not even this towering stranger who dared to stand by her side.

The crowd thickened as they returned from the lake, the Rathore family blending into the festive chaos. The stalker pulled the tattered scarf over his face, his movements masked by the bustle of people. His grip tightened around the blade hidden beneath his shawl. His pulse raced, the moment of reckoning close.

Janvi walked just ahead of him now, her head tilted toward Karan as she spoke to him. She didn't see it coming.

The stalker moved swiftly, his blade arcing toward her. But before it reached her, Karan turned instinctively, the motion almost unconscious, and the blade sank into his arm instead.

Karan hissed, more from shock than pain, his eyes snapping to the attacker. For a moment, their eyes met—the stalker's wild with jealousy and rage, Karan's sharp with realization. But before he could react, the man was already retreating, melting into the throng like smoke.

"Karan!" Janvi's scream cut through the noise, her voice trembling as she grabbed his injured arm. Blood seeped through the fabric of his kurta, staining it crimson.

Karan's gaze darted around, scanning the crowd for the man, but he was gone, vanished as if he'd never been there.

"Karan, you're hurt!" Janvi's voice cracked as she pressed her hand against the wound, her face pale with fear.

"I'm fine," Karan muttered, his voice low, though the strain was evident. His focus remained on the crowd, his jaw tightening. "He's gone."

The chants of "Ganpati Bappa Morya!" carried on, oblivious to the moment of danger that had passed. Around them, the villagers and family members began to notice the commotion, their voices rising in concern.

But for Janvi, the world seemed to narrow to Karan—the blood on his arm, the tension in his jaw, the protective way he had stood between her and harm. Her heart pounded, not just from fear but from the realization of how close she had been to danger—and how Karan had shielded her without hesitation.

The stalker had disappeared, but his threat lingered like a shadow. And as the family gathered around them, Karan's protective instincts only hardened further. Whoever this man was, he had made one thing clear.

Janvi's safety would not come without a fight.

* * *

Karan's arm throbbed as he waved off Daadi's worried questions, assuring her it was just a scratch. Laxmi Tai and Aman hovered nearby, their faces pale with alarm, while Janvi pressed her dupatta firmly against the wound, her hands trembling.

"It could've been worse," Karan said quietly, his voice steady but his gaze distant, still scanning the crowd as though willing the attacker to reappear.

Janvi shook her head, her eyes brimming with unshed tears. "Why didn't you move? You could've—"

Karan cut her off, his voice soft yet firm. "Because I wasn't going to let anything happen to you."

Her breath caught at his words, but before she could respond, Daadi placed a calming hand on her shoulder. "Let's go home," she said, her voice shaking slightly. "We'll clean the wound there and call the doctor."

The ride back was silent, the festive chants fading into the distance. The family huddled close, but Karan's thoughts remained on the faceless man who had dared to harm Janvi. Whoever he was, Karan would find him. And he would end this.

Beside him, Janvi stole a glance at his profile, her heart twisting with guilt and gratitude. She clutched her trembling hands in her lap, her mind reeling. Today had been a joyous day, but the shadow of danger now loomed large.

As the Rathore family entered the haveli, the Ganesh Chaturthi celebrations felt far behind them. Karan allowed himself to be led toward the study where the doctor would soon arrive. But even as the wound was tended to, his mind was elsewhere.

He would protect Janvi at all costs.

No one would hurt her again.

16

WHY DON'T YOU UNDERSTAND

"So, what have you found out so far?" Karan asked.

Karan was in the study with the Superintendent of Police. Earlier at the lake, the women were in hysterics. Aman had luckily not seen anything as he had run off to get candy floss on the other side of the lake as soon as they had returned to the steps from the lake. By the time they found him, the women had calmed down enough to not alarm Aman, even though he could sense the change in their demeanours.

The door to the study creaked open before SP Bhargav could respond. Janvi stepped in. She still looked frazzled. Her hair was undone, streaks of dried tears stained her cheeks and the edge of her *saree* was torn because she had used it to tie up Karan's wound.

"Daadi's resting," she explained. "Tai is making dinner."

Karan nodded and gestured to SP Bhargav to continue.

"As I was saying," SP Bhargav began, "we have been working on this case for a while now. Ever since, Renuka Deviji and Bakshi Saheb reached out to us. From the patterns we have observed till date, the stalker hasn't been consistent with his approach. Sometimes, he would send multiple messages in a span of a few days and then there would be weeks of silence. This has led us to assume that perhaps the man isn't local to Jaisalmer or he works as an out-of-town labourer or a truck driver. That would explain his weeks of absence between each stalking episode."

Karan's expression must have conveyed disbelief because SP Bhargav's next words were carefully delivered. "But until tonight, we had had no reason to believe he was capable of being violent."

"You had no reason to believe he was capable of being violent?" Karan repeated the question calmly, struggling to keep his frustration in check. He took a deep breath reminding himself that civility was the only way he was going to get any help from the police. "He has been sending notes, photographs, calling my house and you had no reason to believe he could be capable of being violent."

Janvi looked up at him in shock at the fact that Karan was aware of everything.

"Mr. Rathore. We understand your frustration. And in light of this recent escalation, our department will do everything in its power to get the culprit apprehended. Our patrol team is also outside. We have taken the statements of all the family members and we will look into any CCTV footage we can get our hands on between here and the area of incident."

Karan nodded, "Keep me posted with updates."

Karan closed the study door after SP Bhargav departed.

"How long have you..." Janvi trailed off.

"Known about your stalker? Since Saturday morning." Karan gave a clipped response.

Janvi looked down, her brows furrowing at the implications.

"Is that why you asked to be my friend? And accompany me to market, the village and *visarjan*? So you could keep watch over me?" Janvi asked hurt in her voice.

"What?" Karan looked at her in incredulously. "*No*, I-"

"I don't need your help!" Janvi spat out in anger. "I can take care of myself."

Janvi's gaze fell on the wound on his arm. "This is my problem. There is no need to endanger yourself for me."

"Endanger myself?" Karan held himself back with barely restrained anger, speaking slowly but clearly with gritted teeth. "Janvi, I have *immense* respect for you. However, right now, I am *this* close to losing my patience with you. I only saw the glint of the blade and instinctively stepped in front of you. But that man's knife was aimed at *you*, not me. Now I get that you are so used to doing things on your own, but there is a limit to even what you can do."

The room fell into a heavy silence.

Janvi hugged herself, her fingers gripping the torn edge of her *saree*. Her lips pressed into a thin line as she avoided his gaze. When she finally spoke, her voice shook with unsaid emotions.

"And how long?"

"How long, what?" Karan asked confused.

"How long will you stand by me? 5 months? And what about after we divorce? Will you still stand by me? Even after you marry Anya?" Janvi's eyes flowed with tears. "You're patronizing me now because I didn't tell you I have a stalker? That I didn't ask you for your *help?*" Janvi's voice trembled, but there was a quiet strength behind her words, the kind that made them cut deeper.

Karan stiffened, his mouth opening to respond, but she cut him off with a sharp breath.

"Kis haq se madad maangti aapse!?" Her voice cracked, the words spilling out before she could stop them. Her gaze locked on his, her eyes glistening with unshed tears. *"Kya rishta hai hamaara!?"*

Karan flinched at the force of her question, his throat tightening as he struggled to find the right words.

"I've been alone for so long," she continued, her voice trembling as she pressed on. "My father passed away, and then Viren uncle..." Her breath hitched, and she gripped the torn edge of her *saree* with both hands, her knuckles turning white. "And then you came—into a marriage that was just... an obligation for you. A duty. I barely knew you!"

Her lips twisted bitterly around the word obligation, and she shook her head, her hair falling loosely around her face.

"All you ever wanted was for this marriage to be done with. For it to be over, so you could go back to your life—back to Anya," she whispered, her voice a jagged edge. "So why now? Why all of this? Why pretend that you care?"

Karan's chest tightened, his hand twitching as if he wanted to reach for her, but he held himself back.

"Why should I rely on you? When I know, in just a few months... you'll leave. And what about me? I'll be alone again." Her voice cracked with a sudden pain that tore through her.

She blinked back tears, but her gaze remained hard. "The stalker will come back. Or someone else will. And then? Then who will protect me? Who will stand by me?"

Her words rose with a restrained fury, the anger fuelled by her deep sense of betrayal and fear. "I've always had to take care of myself. I've always been on my own. So why should I ask you for anything now? You'll be gone, and I'll be left to fend for myself again."

Her voice broke slightly as she finished, the bitterness of her words still hanging in the air. "I can't ask for your help," she said softly, her tears falling freely now. "Because I know that in the end, I'll have to survive on my own as I have always done."

She turned toward the door and ran out, leaving Karan standing alone in the thick silence of the study. Karan stood there, staring at the closed door, her words reverberating in his mind, each one like a fresh wound.

* * *

Karan sat in his father's chair in the study, dimly lit with the table lamp, his head resting against the leather back, eyes closed. A couple of hours had passed since Janvi left. The house was quiet now—staff gone, Aman and Daadi likely asleep.

Janvi's words echoed in his mind, cutting deeper with each repetition. *"I can't ask for your help. I'll have to survive on my own, like I always have."*

He ran a hand through his hair, frustration bubbling up. How could he have expected her to turn to him? She had been alone for so long, learning to fend for herself. And what had he done? Abandoned her from the very beginning, never giving her a reason to trust him.

She doesn't know me. How could she?

The realization hit hard. He had failed her—left her to navigate their marriage alone, while he continued his life, oblivious to the damage he'd done. *How could I expect her to need me now?*

Karan's eyes opened, staring blankly at the desk. The guilt gnawed at him.

Where do I even start?

The door creaked open softly, and the faint sound of Janvi's *paayal* broke the silence. Karan straightened, his heart lurching unexpectedly. He thought she would never want to see him again. Yet, there she stood. Still in her *saree,* holding a first aid box, looking as fragile as ever.

His eyes followed her as she walked toward him hesitantly, pulled a chair, and sat beside him. Karan's breath caught in his chest as he watched her, unable to look away. The sight of her—so fragile, so tender—dismantled every defence he had built. His heart pounded in his ears, each beat heavy with guilt, regret, and longing.

She didn't say a word, but the tears that slid down her cheeks spoke volumes. She carefully unwrapped the makeshift bandage she had tied around his wound earlier, her fingers trembling as she worked, her eyes never meeting his. The sight of her tears, unspoken and raw, pierced through him like a blade.

As she tended to his wound, he realized she still cared. Despite all her pain, her anger, and distrust of him, she cared. Kind, sweet Janvi. His eyes travelled down to the *mangalsutra* around her neck, a symbol of her loyalty to him as his wife, even though he hadn't given her any reason to deserve it. *My wife.*

When she finished, her hands lingered for a moment on his skin, almost as if she needed the touch to steady herself. Her eyes stayed downcast, as though she couldn't look at him for too long, afraid of what she might see in his gaze. Karan's heart ached, every part of him wanting to say the words he hadn't said before.

Janvi slowly stood up, her fingers brushing against the first aid box as she turned to leave.

Karan wasn't ready to let her go. He reached out, his hand wrapping gently around her wrist, stopping her mid-step.

"Wait, Janvi," he whispered, his voice raw, pleading.

Janvi froze at his touch. Her wrist felt warm where his fingers held her, firm but not forceful. Slowly, she turned to face him, her wide, tear-filled eyes searching his. Karan stood up, his hand still holding hers, as though afraid she might vanish if he let go.

"Don't go," he said, his voice hoarse, carrying the weight of everything he hadn't been able to say before. "Please, sit. Just... for a moment."

Janvi hesitated, then allowed him to guide her back to the chair.

Karan knelt in front of her, his hands holding on to hers on her lap. The lamplight cast shadows across his face, highlighting the vulnerability in his expression. He met her gaze, his eyes raw, unguarded.

"I haven't been entirely honest with you about why I'm here. And it's not because I was deliberately trying to keep you in the dark. I just wanted you to see me for who I was and feel what I feel for you. Without you thinking, I'm treating you like a second fiddle or some kind of rebound. Because you're not."

Karan paused, looking down at their hands tightening his hold on her just a little bit afraid to let her go.

"I'm not with Anya anymore. I don't want to go into the details of my breakup. But just know that when I arrived here, I was distraught. I was just trying to get away from my life in New York. I wasn't even thinking about this marriage, or the divorce. And then I met you for the first time."

Karan looked up, meeting her gaze with raw unbridled emotion.

"I have never regretted a decision so much in my life as I do now the one where I pushed you away from me. I wasted two and a half years of this marriage running away from it only to realise how much I want it now. Janvi, I am willing to spend the rest of my life making up to you but I do not want to let go of this marriage."

She looked down at him then, her eyes glistening with unshed tears.

"I don't want a divorce. Not now, not in five months, not ever." His voice broke on the last word, the rawness of his confession laid bare between them. "I'm not asking you to forgive me—not yet. I know I have to earn that. But I'm asking for a chance. A chance to fix what I've broken. A chance to be your husband. *Please, Janvi.*"

Her lips parted, as though to speak, but no words came. Instead, a single tear escaped, rolling down her cheek. Karan raised a hand, brushing it away gently with his thumb.

"I'll spend the rest of my life making up to you if that's what it takes," he whispered.

Janvi took a shuddering breath, her hands slipping from his grasp as she rose from the chair.

She looked hesitantly down at Karan, unsure of what to say. Finally, she settled on, "I need to think. I need time."

With that, without waiting for another word, she walked slowly towards the door.

Before she could reach it, Karan said with finality, "Take as much time as you need, Janvi. I'll wait. For as long as it takes."

Janvi paused momentarily at the door, her hand on the knob, as if contemplating his words. Eventually with a shuddering breath, she left the room, leaving Karan alone once again—but this time, with a flicker of hope. She hadn't said yes, but she hadn't said no either.

17

AN INVITATION

Janvi awoke the next day extremely tired. She sat up in bed with great difficulty. As she took in her appearance in the mirror, memories of the previous day's incident came flooding back. She was still wearing the same *saree*, having been too exhausted to change. The tattered edge reminding her of the incident at the lake.

Everything had happened so fast. One minute, she was happily walking through the crowd towards the rest of the family. The next minute, she had been pulled back by Karan to one side. She heard the whoosh of the blade though she hadn't known what it was at the time. Then came Karan's grunt and the crowd had erupted in screams. But it was Karan's bleeding arm that had really put things into perspective for her.

As she looked at her swollen eyes in the mirror, she thought about their argument in the study. Perhaps he was right. She should have tried to ask for help. Maybe things wouldn't have escalated to this. How would she have been able to live with the guilt if something had happened to Karan?

Janvi's eyes drifted to the reflection of the mangalsutra, placing her fingers on it. And did he really mean what he said? That he wanted to remain in this relationship.

She wasn't sure how she felt about that. It was easier to forget the past when she didn't have any reason to be attached to him. Now she wasn't so sure. She had already planned her life after the end of their marriage.

At night she had been filling out Aman's admission forms to

schools in Pune. She had already looked up apartment rentals in the area and a night school for book-keeping classes. Bakshi Chacha had agreed to help her get a secretarial job at his friend's law firm to get by. She knew she would be sad to leave Daadi Sa, Laxmi Tai and Badri Kaka but she had made up her mind to bring Aman back every school holidays.

All of that was now up in the air after Karan's disclosure the night before. Would it be so bad to continue her life in Jaisalmer with him? He was respectful, kind and thoughtful. She couldn't deny feeling safe in his presence. And he cared about Aman. Aman would have a family. And she wouldn't be so alone anymore. She also couldn't deny she was attracted to him.

Shaking her head to dismiss those thoughts, Janvi looked at the time. It was 6:30 am. She was already behind on her schedule for the day. Aman had to get ready for school. Brushing aside her dilemma for the moment, she turned over her notebook to quickly make a to-do list she had forgotten to make after the drama of yesterday afternoon. She asked Karan for time and it wouldn't do well to make a decision so soon without considering all her options. She owed it to herself and Aman. And to Karan.

A thought crossed her mind as she wrote. *Was it safe to send Aman to school so soon after the incident yesterday? Should she ask Karan?*

Janvi quickly got ready so she could go talk to Karan. He should be up by now, shouldn't he? She also needed to change Karan's bandage but the first aid kit was still in the study. As she entered the study, she noticed it was darker than usual as the curtains were drawn. Did Karan draw them last night? She spotted the kit on the study. As she walked towards it, she almost stumbled on an outstretched hand.

Karan?

He was sprawled on the sofa, fast asleep. Did he sleep here the whole night? Why? An open laptop and paperwork on the coffee table suggested he was working in the night.

And were those haveli schematics?

Her heart wrenched in sympathy at his state. He looked exhausted. His arm, still bandaged from the attack, hung awkwardly off the edge of the sofa. Even in sleep, his brow was faintly furrowed, as though the weight of the world hadn't left him.

Quietly, she picked up the first-aid kit from the study table and walked back to the sofa. For a moment, she stood still, clutching the kit as she debated what to do. Should she wake him? He looked so worn out, his face softened in sleep, and she knew he needed rest. But his bandage needed changing, and the sight of the dried blood seeping through tugged at her conscience.

As she stood there, caught between her thoughts, he stirred. His brow furrowed slightly, and then his eyes fluttered open, meeting hers. Her heart skipped, a soft warmth unfurling in her chest, followed by a flutter—like butterflies dancing inside her. For a moment, neither of them spoke.

Janvi's voice faltered as she shifted the kit in her hands, trying to break the tension. "I was just here to change your bandage," she said, her words a little too fast.

Karan blinked groggily, his gaze sharpening as he sat up on the sofa. "You didn't have to," he murmured, his voice rough from sleep. His good hand moved to his bandaged arm, wincing slightly at the tug of dried blood.

"You need it cleaned," Janvi said, clutching the first-aid kit tighter. "It's bleeding again."

He looked at the bandage with a grimace. "I'll handle it after a shower."

"You can't," she replied quickly, her voice firm but not unkind. "If it gets wet, it'll only make things worse. Let me re-bandage it now. You can cover it before your shower."

Karan raised an eyebrow at her matter-of-fact tone but didn't argue. "Efficient," he muttered, sitting up straighter.

"Practical," she countered, lowering herself to sit on the edge of the coffee table. Avoiding his gaze, she opened the kit and began unwrapping the old bandage.

The silence between them stretched, broken only by the soft rustle of gauze and her careful, deliberate movements. Karan's steady gaze didn't help her focus. Her fingers faltered as she cleaned the wound, but she refused to let it show.

"You don't have to fuss over me, Janvi," he said quietly, his voice gentler now.

"I'm not fussing," she replied, keeping her eyes on the wound. "This is just... necessary."

Her words came out sharper than she intended, and she bit the inside of her cheek. She finished tying off the fresh bandage and stood quickly, brushing her hands on her dupatta. "That should hold."

Before she could turn to leave, she hesitated. Her shoulders stiffened slightly, and then she faced him again, clutching the first-aid kit tightly.

"I also wanted to ask... Do you think it's safe for Aman to go to school today?" she asked, her voice quieter now, almost hesitant.

Karan frowned slightly, sitting up straighter. "I doubt anyone will try anything so soon, but we can't be careless. I'll have Aman dropped off and picked up by Badri Kaka, just to be safe."

Janvi nodded, visibly relieved. "Thank-you. I didn't want him to miss his lessons, but..." She trailed off, her fingers nervously gripping the kit. "I wasn't sure what to do. I'll leave you to your shower. I'll keep breakfast for you in the kitchen."

Karan stretched slightly, groaning as he got to his feet. He glanced at the papers and laptop on the coffee table. "Leave this. I'll handle it later."

"You're already late for breakfast," she said briskly. "Go shower."

Karan hesitated, studying her for a moment, but then nodded. She watched him leave the study before turning her attention to the coffee table.

Stacking the scattered papers and closing the laptop, Janvi let out a slow breath. As sunlight streamed in when she pulled back the heavy curtains, she stood for a moment, gazing at the empty sofa.

Her fingers brushed her *mangalsutra* absently, the memory of

Karan's words flickering in her mind. She'd promised herself she wouldn't dwell on it—not yet. For now, there were practical matters to handle.

Straightening her shoulders, Janvi turned and walked out of the study to quickly prepare breakfast and pack Aman's lunch.

* * *

Laughter travelled from the living room, diverting Karan's attention as he walked to the study after a much-needed shower. That sounded like Janvi. Who was she with?

Karan stopped at the threshold to find Janvi speaking animatedly to a man near the window. She looked beautiful. Her hair flowed in the breeze, her lips were curved in a smile. But envy gripped him at the thought that it wasn't directed at him. He continued watching her until she eventually noticed him.

"Ah, there he is," Karan heard her say in a soft voice, his frown deepening with curiosity.

The man turned to see him. *Himanshu Sodha.*

"Hey, buddy!" Himanshu walked over as Karan took further steps into the living area, meeting Himanshu's over-enthusiastic hug with equal enough gusto so as not to betray his otherwise conflicting emotions. What was he doing here? Janvi said he was their accountant; he must be here for the ledgers.

"It's so great to see you after all this while? How have you been?" Himanshu began with pleasantries.

Karan gave a clipped response, "Quite well. And yourself?"

"I am in excellent spirits, especially after seeing Janvi *bhabhi* here and having *chai* made by her lovely hands. She sure makes the best chai in all of Jaisalmer."

Karan understood he was being polite, albeit rather generously, however, something about his referring to Janvi's lovely hands didn't sit right with him. His use of *bhabhi* however, offered an excellent opportunity to step right into the role of her husband.

"That she does!" Karan responded with a wide smile as he

stepped behind Himanshu to stand next to Janvi and placed his hand on her waist. He felt her tense up and before her face could betray her shock, he pulled her even closer and whispered as loud as he could for Himanshu to hear. "Darling, could fix me a cup as well?"

Janvi blinked at him for a moment, like a deer caught in headlights before finally letting out a weak "Of course". He knew he had startled her and especially after the promise that he was going to give her time but the pang of jealousy he had felt at her exchanging pleasantries with Himanshu in that easy, unguarded way made him want to stake his claim on her. To let him know in not-so-subtle terms that she belonged to him.

She turned quickly to the pot of chai on the coffee table as Karan continued his conversation with Himanshu.

"So, what brings you here? The account books?" Karan asked.

"Actually, yes and no," Himanshu replied, settling back into a lounge chair. "I did come by to grab the ledgers, but truthfully, I also heard you were in town and thought it would be nice to catch up. Plus," he added with a grin, "Janvi *bhabhi's* chai was the perfect excuse."

Karan's jaw tightened again at the continuous casual mention of Janvi, though he kept his expression composed. "I see. How thoughtful."

Janvi returned with Karan's cup of chai, placing it on the side table without a word, her demeanour calm blissfully unaware of the tension simmering in him.

Himanshu took another sip of his own tea before sighing theatrically. "You know, I was just telling Janvi *bhabhi* how unfortunate it was that my wife and I had to cancel our honeymoon last month. Bad weather at Maldives ruined everything. Such a disappointment."

Karan's brows furrowed. "Your wife?"

Himanshu looked at him, puzzled. "Of course, my wife! Didn't Janvi mention it?"

Karan caught the slight shift in Janvi's posture as she stiffened, her eyes darting to her teacup like it held all the answers in the world.

It was clear she didn't know how to respond, and for once, Karan felt an overwhelming wave of empathy for her.

"Ah, yes," Karan said smoothly, stepping in before the awkwardness could thicken further. "She did mention the wedding, Himanshu. I must have forgotten—I was in the middle of a major project at the time. Things were quite hectic." He glanced at Janvi as he spoke, silently willing her to trust him.

Her eyes flicked to his, a mixture of relief and gratitude passing between them before she added as a matter-of-factly, "I couldn't make it to the wedding. It was in Jodhpur, and Aman's school schedule made it impossible to travel."

"Ah, yes," Himanshu said with a wistful smile. "You were missed, *bhabhi*. But it was a beautiful ceremony. Still, the cancelled honeymoon was a bummer. Now we're planning a quick getaway to a desert camp a few hours outside of Jodhpur to make up for it."

Karan felt a strange mix of emotions flood through him—relief that Himanshu was married, followed by shame for having assumed otherwise. He glanced at Janvi, who was now entirely focused on stirring her own tea, completely oblivious to all the subtle changes in his demeanour.

"Speaking of the camp," Himanshu continued, his tone turning conspiratorial, "and the reason for why I'm here, I wanted to invite you two to join us. It's a beautiful place—luxury tents, starry skies, and cultural evenings. Perfect for some quality time together. And I thought, since it's quite a drive away, and I didn't want to hire a driver, it would make sense for two couples to travel together and who better than you two! And I haven't been able to spend time with Karan in so long."

Karan raised a brow at the implication, but Himanshu wasn't done. Leaning slightly toward him, he added in a quieter tone, "After all, you've been away for so long. A little break might do you both good. Consider this your honeymoon as well since you had to leave before you could get yours."

Daadi, who had entered the room just in time to catch the tail end of the suggestion, clapped her hands together in approval. "What a wonderful idea! Janvi, Karan, you should absolutely go. It will be good for both of you to get out of the house for a while."

Janvi opened her mouth to protest, but Daadi cut her off with a knowing smile. "Don't worry about us, beta. Aman and I will manage just fine here. You two deserve a little time away."

Karan glanced at Janvi, noting the discomfort in her expression. She clearly wasn't thrilled.

"Then it's settled!" Himanshu said enthusiastically without waiting for Janvi's response, clapping Karan on the shoulder. "I'll make the arrangements and send you the details. Trust me, it'll be a trip to remember."

Karan nodded, offering a polite smile, though deep down, he felt something stir within him—an unfamiliar blend of anticipation and hope. This trip, he realized, could be exactly what they needed.

Janvi, on the other hand, remained quiet, her fingers tightening around her cup as she stared into its depths, as though searching for answers she wasn't ready to confront.

⁂

Over the next few days, Karan observed, with the least bit of compunction and perhaps a sliver of satisfaction, Janvi's vain attempts to thwart all plans of their impending excursion. She came up with every possible excuse under the sun to not go on the camping trip. Aman's school, Daadi's health, her students in the village or the weather... anything to get out of going away with him.

To be perfectly honest, part of him wanted to help put her out of her misery too because of *who* they were going with. He had barely tolerated Himanshu growing up and had zero interest in spending any time whatsoever in close proximity with him. The man had been insufferable growing up, the kind of friend who thrived on teasing and pushing boundaries. Karan could already imagine the smug grin Himanshu would wear during the trip, his self-satisfied remarks barely masking his curiosity about Karan and Janvi's unconventional marriage. But his desire to win over Janvi trumped his contempt for the man.

When Himanshu first suggested the idea, sensing her discomfort, Karan was ready to decline on Janvi's behalf. But after giving it some thought, he concluded that this trip could be an answer to his prayers at completely breaking down Janvi's somewhat collapsible wall when it came to him. And Lord knows, after that night in the study, he needed every bit of luck in this matter. She had barely started to open up to him before that night but the walls that he was trying so hard to break brick by brick had gone up quickly when he finally told her the whole truth of why he was there.

They hadn't spoken about it since that night, instead, slipping back into their previous routine—more her than him—of mundane greetings or occasional polite conversations when they were in presence of other people. Yet, he was absolutely certain she wasn't completely immune to him by the way her face flushed when they were alone together or by the way her breath would catch when they would accidentally touch passing along some of the narrower corridors of the haveli.

More than once, he had caught her watching him, considering him, sometimes when she waited on him at meals or from her desk when they both worked in the study, running her index finger around her *mangalsutra*. He knew what that meant, or so he would like to imagine. The *mangalsutra*, the symbol of married Hindu women from time immemorial. Was she considering her marriage? Their marriage? Considering him, as her husband? Despite her best efforts to appear unaffected, she was far from it.

It was for this reason that he hadn't thrown in the towel. Even when he had found the application forms in her room for Aman's school admission in Pune. He had gone to her room looking for her on Daadi's behest one evening calling her for dinner and seen them on her desk. He understood the implications. She had every right to choose to leave him at the end of their contract. After all, as she put it so succinctly, her relationship to him was in name only. And he had no one to blame for this but himself.

But by some strange grace, that he had begun to matter to her was becoming evident. The way she'd find an excuse to be near him on the pretext of changing his bandage even though it wasn't as bad. Or asking him for his suggestions for their daily menu or selecting a piece of furniture or artwork for the museum or restaurant. One could be forgiven for mistaking these gestures as an act of kindness she bestowed on everyone as a result of who she was as a person. Except, Karan had suddenly realized with a thrill one night, it wasn't just out of kindness.

Returning from an evening run after an especially exhausting work day, he decided to sit outside on the bench on the front portico of the haveli to watch the skies change hue from pink to dark blue from the setting sun. As Karan stretched out on the bench, letting the cool night breeze soothe his muscles, his gaze had wandered toward the glowing windows on the ground floor of the haveli just past the main entrance. The warm light spilled out into the courtyard, framing the silhouette of a figure behind the curtains.

Janvi?

From his vantage point under the portico, hidden in the shadows, he could see her clearly. She was standing by the window, her dupatta loosely draped over her shoulder, one hand clutching the edge of the curtain. Her head tilted slightly, as if she were straining to peer into the darkness outside.

He froze, watching her. She stood there for a while, shifting her weight from one foot to the other, her fingers fiddling absentmindedly with the fabric of the curtain. He could almost see the slight furrow of her brows, the faint worry etched into her expression.

Was she looking for him? The thought sent an unexpected thrill through him, followed by the more practical consideration that perhaps she was merely concerned for his safety after everything that had happened with the stalker. But then, he noticed something else—a hesitance, almost like she didn't want to be caught doing whatever she was doing.

She lingered for another moment before abruptly stepping

back, letting the curtain fall into place. When Karan finally stood and walked into the haveli, he found her in the corridor, near the staircase. She looked up at him, startled, clutching a small tray of flowers.

"Oh," she said, her voice unnaturally casual. "You're back."

He raised an eyebrow, his lips quirking into a faint smile. "Didn't know you were waiting for me."

Her grip on the tray tightened ever so slightly. "I wasn't," she replied quickly, a little too quickly. "I was just... sorting these for tomorrow's puja."

He bit back a laugh, glancing at the flowers she claimed to have been sorting. They were arranged in neat, untouched piles, as if they had been ready for hours.

"Of course," he said, his tone light, as if he believed her. "Don't let me disturb you."

He walked past her, catching the faintest scent of jasmine as she turned and hurried away. He didn't miss the slight stiffness in her posture, the way she avoided meeting his eyes.

The realization struck him then, unbidden but undeniable: she had been waiting for him. Not just tonight, but in subtle ways he had started to notice more and more.

Like the way she would linger at the dining table after meals, pretending to be preoccupied with Aman or Daadi but always glancing toward the doorway as if expecting him to walk in. Or how she'd sit with Daadi during their evening chats, a book in her hands but never actually turning the pages. Then there were the mornings in the kitchen. She'd insist she was too busy to join him for breakfast, only to hover by the counter, slicing fruit or arranging plates, her movements slowing every time he spoke. And when he finally looked up, she'd dart out of the room, muttering something about being late for her lessons in the village.

It was maddeningly endearing.

She wasn't ready to admit it—not to him, and maybe not even to herself. But her actions spoke louder than her carefully constructed indifference. She liked him, even if she was pretending otherwise. The realization made him want to be more ambitious, but he tempered the urge. Instead, he resolved to play along.

So it was that the resolve had cemented in his mind. There was no way he was backing out of their forced honeymoon. He already knew he wasn't going to compel her to do anything she didn't want to do but he still needed her to feel safe enough to express herself more freely in front of him.

18

UNDER THE KHEJRI

"You want me to drive this monstrosity?" Karan asked indignantly, his eyebrows climbing dangerously high.

"Yes," Himanshu replied, deadpan.

Karan stared at the hideous car parked in the driveway of the haveli. Supposedly, if the catalogues were to be believed, it was a Mahindra Bolero in a Power Plus Diamond White model. In reality, it looked like a 100-year-old carcass that had been dunked in diluted coffee and left to crisp under the merciless desert sun.

"And remind me again why we can't take my car?" Karan pressed, his voice sharp.

"Because we'll be taking turns driving, and I can't afford the insurance on your car if something happens to it," Himanshu retorted without missing a beat.

Karan considered taking his car and driving all the way himself. At least they'd be comfortable, and he'd done solo trips to Jodhpur countless times. But then, he wouldn't be able to focus on Janvi and that somehow felt worse than enduring this rattling tin-box.

With a resigned sigh, he muttered under his breath, "The things we do for love," before placing his hand on the door handle, half-expecting it to crumble under his touch.

Settling into the driver's seat, Karan adjusted his aviator shades as Janvi and Meghna walked out with the remaining bags and baskets of snacks. From behind the dark lenses of his glasses, Karan allowed his gaze to linger on Janvi, unabashed and unseen. She was looking radiant in a flowy, maroon salwar kameez, laughing at something

Meghna had said. She reached up to tuck an unruly strand of her straight hair dancing in the wind behind her ear and Karan felt all his prior inhibitions of this trip, if he had any, melting way.

Meghna climbed into the back seat, settling directly behind Karan. He continued to watch, his fingers tightening slightly on the steering wheel when Janvi hesitated near the passenger door. For a moment, his chest tightened in near-panic as she turned toward the back seat, about to sit beside Meghna. Did she seriously plan to sit there the entire ride? Behind him? Out of his line of sight?

Himanshu was still busy stacking the luggage in the trunk, oblivious to the silent turmoil unfolding in Karan's head.

Luckily, Himanshu finished stacking the luggage just in time.

"Bhabhi, it's my honeymoon," Himanshu said with a playful grin as he stepped forward. "If you don't mind, I'd like to sit with my wife. You sit here in the front seat."

Karan could barely hide his smirk as Himanshu gently guided a hesitant Janvi toward the passenger seat beside him. Her uncertainty only made the moment sweeter, and he didn't bother to fight the satisfaction that curled at the corners of his mouth.

"Hi darling," Karan teased, with mischievous tilt of head as Janvi fastened her seatbelt.

Janvi stared back wordlessly, unimpressed.

Karan took a deep breath, turning his focus to the front. *If looks could kill,* he thought.

"Okay, let's go," Karan said, kicking off the ignition and pulling out of the driveway, the car coming to life as they headed toward their destination.

They drove in relative silence as the Bolero wound its way through the narrow streets of Jaisalmer towards National Highway 11. The staggering clammer of the vehicle as it ground along the uneven terrain making up for any need for further sound. As they reached the smoother roads of the highway, it became a bit more bearable.

The journey would take at least four hours but they planned to stop between each hour for snacks and lunch which would make it a gradual six hours before they reached the campsite.

Karan adjusted the air conditioning, the cool air battling the desert heat. Meghna, however, reached for the window button, rolling it down and letting in a gust of warm wind laced with fine particles of sand.

"Oh, this is so romantic," Meghna said.

Karan's fingers tightened on the steering wheel. He wanted to protest—the AC was already working overtime in the Thar heat—but he caught himself. Not worth it. Instead, he glanced at the others. Himanshu seemed unbothered, fiddling with his phone, and Janvi, seated beside him, stared quietly out of her own window, her dupatta fluttering slightly in the breeze

"So, Karan," Meghna asked, "what is it that you do?"

Janvi looked at him curiously, interested in what he had to say. Karan looked into the rearview mirror to respond.

"I own a tech company. We make sensors for communication systems."

"Wow, that is impressive," Meghna said, turning in her seat.

"It is," Himanshu chimed in beside her, grinning. "He was always the brainiac in our class. We all knew he'd make it big one day."

Karan glanced in the rearview mirror, a faint smile tugging at his lips. "You haven't done too badly yourself, Himanshu. Taking over your father's accounting firm and expanding it? That's no small feat. I saw you won an ICAI award recently."

Himanshu's eyes widened in elation. "Hey! How'd you know that?"

Karan shrugged. "I keep tabs on my friends."

And on people who flirt with my wife, he thought. He had looked up Himanshu that very night that Janvi had first mentioned him.

"Thanks, buddy," Himanshu said, clearly pleased.

Janvi looked back at Himanshu, "Even I didn't know that! Congratulations Himanshu."

"Thanks Bhabhi," Himanshu said cheerfully.

Beside him, Janvi smiled faintly, her expression softening for a moment before she turned back to the window.

"Yes, I'm so proud of my bae," Meghna squealed. "And what about you Janvi, what do you do?"

Janvi smiled modestly. "Oh, I don't work. I just help Daadi Sa manage the haveli and handle a few things here and there."

Karan glanced at her, shaking his head, his grip tightening on the steering wheel. "Oh, come on. She's being overly modest," Karan said, turning toward Meghna in the rearview mirror. "Janvi runs the haveli like a well-oiled machine. She handles everything—maintenance schedules, staffing, financials. She turned an old storeroom of artifacts into a museum and an unused living area into a profitable restaurant. She manages the logistics and bookkeeping with an efficiency I haven't seen from anyone, not even the managers I've hired at my own company."

Himanshu, nodding, chimed in, "Karan's not exaggerating. As the accountant, I can tell you her financials are flawless. I'd trust her numbers over anyone's. She's got a mind for organization."

Karan's tone grew even more serious, his admiration evident. "I've worked with some of the best professionals in the business, but I've rarely seen someone handle so much with such high competence. And on top of running everything smoothly, she takes care of Daadi, her brother Aman, tutors village children, cooks, and cleans."

Meghna's eyes widened. "Wow, Janvi! That's incredible."

Janvi, a slight blush creeping up her neck, looked at Karan for a moment, touched by his words. "It's really nothing," she said, her voice soft.

Karan shook his head, refusing to agree, his tone still firm but warm. "It's not nothing, Janvi. There are few who can juggle it all as well as you do. Don't sell yourself short."

Meghna grinned. "Aw! You two are so sweet—hashtag *couplegoals*!"

Himanshu laughed. "She's not wrong. Karan, you're one lucky guy."

A surge of warmth spread through Janvi's heart as she watched Karan, the genuine sincerity in his voice wrapping around her like a comforting embrace. In that moment, she realized how deeply he respected her—not just for her work, but for who she was.

The journey continued in relative silence, with the occasional hum of the car breaking through the stillness. Karan's eyes remained on the road, though his thoughts drifted occasionally. The golden desert stretched endlessly on either side, dotted with sparse bushes and the occasional camel cart.

He adjusted the rearview mirror slightly and caught sight of Himanshu and Meghna in the backseat. At first, they seemed to be leaning closer to each other, sharing a whispered conversation. But a moment later, Himanshu's hand slid over Meghna's, and she tilted her head toward him.

Karan's brow arched, amusement flickering in his eyes. He knew where this was headed. His gaze darted to Janvi beside him. She was sitting upright, her hands resting neatly in her lap, entirely unaware of the scene unfolding behind her. Her attention was fixed on the passing landscape, her expression calm and serene.

Karan wondered how she'd react if she noticed. The thought entertained him for a moment.

He glanced at the rearview mirror again. Himanshu and Meghna were entirely engrossed in each other now, their whispered words replaced by the unmistakable sound of soft kisses. Karan shook his head slightly, the corner of his mouth twitching upward.

Let's see how long it takes for Janvi to notice.

For a while, she didn't. Her focus remained on the road ahead, her fingers absently fiddling with the edge of her dupatta.

Then came a soft sound—barely audible but enough to catch her attention. Janvi's brows furrowed, and she tilted her head slightly, as if trying to discern the noise.

Karan watched her out of the corner of his eye, fighting the urge to grin.

Another faint sound, and this time, Janvi stiffened. She turned her head just enough to catch a glimpse of what was happening in the backseat.

Janvi's face turned crimson, and she quickly looked away. She reached for the radio, fumbling with the buttons in a clear attempt to block out the sounds behind them. The faint rustle from the backseat continued, only slightly muffled by the music now playing in the car. Karan's grin widened as he kept his eyes on the road, watching her from the corner of his vision.

His gaze flickered back to the rearview mirror. Himanshu and Meghna were no longer hiding their actions, lost in each other as if they were the only two people in the world. Karan's amusement grew, though he felt a touch of satisfaction seeing that Janvi was clearly uncomfortable.

Without warning, he reached over and gently took her hand, his fingers brushing lightly against hers. The contact was enough to make her jump, her heart rate picking up instantly. She turned to him in surprise, her breath hitching for a brief moment. Karan didn't let go.

"Everything okay?" he asked casually, keeping his voice steady but with a hint of amusement.

Janvi's cheeks flushed, her gaze flickering to his hand before quickly pulling her own away. Her breath quickened, and she nodded, though her eyes betrayed her unease. "I—I'm fine," she stammered, her voice a little higher than usual.

Karan's lips curled into a mischievous smile, and he leaned back slightly in his seat, the weight of his words falling lightly. "Don't worry. We'll switch seats soon when Himanshu takes over the driving. In case you're missing out."

Janvi's eyes widened, and for a moment, she froze, unsure of how to respond. Her pulse quickened as her thoughts raced. The idea of switching seats with Himanshu and Meghna felt like a distant, almost absurd concept, but she couldn't help the surge of nervousness that it brought.

Karan chuckled softly, clearly enjoying the effect his teasing had on her. He kept his tone light, though there was a trace of warmth in his voice. "Relax, Janvi. I'm just kidding."

Janvi took a steadying breath, still feeling the heat in her cheeks, but she couldn't suppress the faint smile tugging at the corner of her lips. Her gaze darted to the road ahead, anything to avoid looking directly at him.

The car wound along between the golden desert stretching endlessly on either side eventually coming behind a herd of camel drivers. Karan took the opportunity to pull over.

"We needed a break anyway," Karan said, cutting the engine.

The camel owners, who had noticed the vehicle pulling up, approached them with wide, welcoming smiles. "Would you like to ride?" one of them asked. "A short trip through the dunes, it'll be a good experience."

Himanshu and Meghna, ever the adventurous couple, immediately agreed with enthusiasm. "This sounds amazing!" Meghna exclaimed, tugging Himanshu by the arm, and soon they were climbing onto camels, ready for the ride.

Karan watched them with a slight smirk, then turned to Janvi, who was already making her way over to a large stone under a nearby *khejri* tree. He followed her, feeling a quiet shift between them, and sat beside her, their shoulders brushing slightly as they settled down.

The silence stretched comfortably between them for a moment. Karan looked out over the desert, watching Himanshu and Meghna in the distance. He wasn't exactly the type for these kinds of excursions, but there was something calming about the desert air, about the stillness that surrounded them. He found himself lost in thought for a moment before glancing at Janvi who had a soft smile on her lips.

"What's so funny?" he asked.

"I just remembered that story Daadi and Bakshi chacha told us about your camel race," she answered.

Karan chuckled softly, rubbing the back of his neck.

"I've done more stupid things than that," he offered.

"Go on. I want to hear them," Janvi said, resting her chin on her hand, her elbow propped up on her knee, her eyes sparkling with curiosity.

"Okay, here goes," Karan began, "Do you know that odd turbaned man who sits outside the Quilla with the colourful baskets?"

"Yes?" answered Janvi, unsure of where this was headed.

"He's been there for years. Someone at school had said he sold magic rubber flowers that you could morph into a rubber snake with a sleight of hand. I thought it would be a neat trick to learn. I was, I think about seven or eight, at the time."

Karan paused almost laughing at the memory.

"Anyway, so one day after school, I went to the Quilla looking for him. Told him I wanted to learn the snake trick and if he could sell it to me. So, he walks behind one of the juice stalls, where he kept all his wares and other stock and pulls out a black cotton bag. Charged me 100 rupees. I paid him and came straight home.

"By the time I got home, my parents had to go to an event and they wanted me to come along. It was one of those rare occasions when dad was home. So, I left the bag in my bedroom, got ready and went out. When I returned home that night, I opened the bag to find it completely empty. I was furious and went to bed with my mind made up that the next day I would find the old man and give him a piece of my mind for scamming me out of my 100 rupees.

"The next morning, we all woke up to screams from the kitchen. The whole house rushed there to find ourselves witnessing a peculiar scene. Laxmi Tai was cooped up on the kitchen counter with a broom pointed at a snake that was well and truly alive, and oddly, with a plastic bouquet of flowers stuck to its tail."

Janvi brought a hand to her mouth to cover her gasp.

"And then what happened?" she asked.

"Well, then, my dad quickly threw a basket on it, called a snake catcher who promptly came and took it away. Luckily, we were told, it was an Indian rat snake which isn't venomous. They all wondered why it was dragging a bouquet of plastic flowers and assumed it must have gotten stuck by accident. Needless to say, I have kept my mouth shut since."

Janvi was laughing freely now, her dimples deep and prominent. Karan watched her gleefully, his heart warming at the beautiful sound.

She suddenly stopped, a thoughtful expression on her face.

"Were you afraid of Viren uncle growing up?" she asked.

"I was," Karan answered softly, his tone sincere, his gaze distant.

"But that fear has since grown into respect for him," Karan continued. "He was a distant father but a good man. He's given me a lot of good things in life. Comfort, education, recognition in the community. But the most important thing he has ever given me is... you."

The last word was spoken softly, barely louder than a whisper, but she heard it loud and clear. Silence stretched between them. Karan watched her calmly, his vulnerability laid bare before her, and she looked at him nervously struggling to find the right words.

Before she could speak, Himanshu's voice drifted over breaking whatever spell that had been cast between them.

"Guys, we're back. Let's hit the road."

Karan helped her up before slowly making his way to the car.

"Wait," Janvi urged, her voice unsure. He turned back to face her waiting patiently as she debated whether to speak her next words or not, tangling her fingers in her dupatta.

"That night, in the study. Did you mean what you said? About wanting to stay in this marriage?"

Karan looked deeply into her eyes, his intentions unwavering, his voice clear and certain, "Every word."

For a long moment, their gazes locked, as if each searching for something unspoken in the other's eyes. Then, without another word, Karan turned and made his way back to the car.

As she followed slowly in his steps, her eyes fixed firmly on his retreating back, she realised a fact that was as true as the pulse that was raging in her heart. That she was fighting a losing battle against Karan Rathore.

* * *

The four of them continued on their journey, their positions swapped. Himanshu was behind the wheel, and Meghna sat beside him in the front passenger seat. Old Hindi songs played softly in the background, though they were unable to compete with the hum of the engine. This was broken only by the occasional chewing sound of Meghna munching on a packet of *bhujia sev*. Janvi, still lost in thought from her earlier interaction with Karan, turned to look at him. His eyes were closed, his head resting against the headrest with his arms folded across his chest.

Savouring the moment, she let her gaze study his profile, unhurried and unashamed. Even with his eyes closed, he exuded an imposing presence. His deep-set eyes, defined jaw, and sharp brows gave his face a striking, masculine edge. His straight black hair fell in a neat, controlled line, some strands brushing against his forehead. He wore a simple white, V-neck t-shirt that hugged his chest, subtly outlining the contours of his toned muscles. He embodied strength—not in the exaggerated way of a bodybuilder, but in a quiet, commanding way of someone who cared for himself without needing to flaunt it.

"So, Janvi, tell us something about yourself?" asked Meghna, breaking the silence. "Where are you originally from?"

Karan opened his eyes in that moment looking straight at her, unbridling her. *Busted*. She hoped he didn't notice it but the narrowing of his eyes and the slight, one-sided curve of his lip told her he knew exactly what she had been doing.

Damn you, Mr. Rathore.

"Um... I've been to many places across India," Janvi replied quickly, her eyes still locked on Karan, her voice a little shaky as she tried to recover. "But I'm originally from Mussoorie."

She watched Karan's brows furrow in confusion, his gaze sharpening slightly. She lifted an eyebrow at him, questioningly. He gave a subtle side-eyed look towards the front seat before gently shaking his head. She let it go, making a mental note to ask him again later when they were alone again.

"Oh, how beautiful. I've always wanted to go to a hill station. Tell me, is it as picturesque as they show it in photos?" Meghna interjected, her voice light and cheerful.

Janvi smiled, a soft, nostalgic curve to her lips. "It's even more beautiful than what you see in the pictures," she replied, her voice taking on a warmer tone as she spoke. "The air is so fresh, and the view of the mountains just... takes your breath away every time. The kind of peace that settles over you there is hard to find anywhere else." Her smile deepened as memories of the hill station came flooding back. "There's a small market where the air smells of pine, and you can hear the sound of the temple bells from the top of the hill. It's like time moves slower there."

She turned to look at Karan, who had an odd expression on his face that she couldn't quite place, as if he were caught between curiosity and something else—something almost reverent. She held his gaze for a moment longer than usual, but before she could ponder what she saw, Meghna's voice broke through.

"How romantic!" Meghna exclaimed.

"Well then, it's settled," Himanshu chimed in, grinning. "Our next trip should be Mussoorie. What say, Karan?"

"I'm right there with you buddy," Karan acknowledged, his voice steady, though something in his eyes lingered, still focused on Janvi.

19

SHIFTING SANDS

It was late afternoon by the time they arrived at the campsite, the temperature significantly cooler than when they left Jaisalmer. A gravel driveway guided their path to a large sandstone gateway with two-way openings, where a security guard checked their bookings. After confirming, he swung the manual boom gate open, revealing a spacious parking lot with ample room for their Bolero.

Another sandstone structure greeted them, a larger building adorned with intricate carvings and *jali* windows. A short flight of steps led to a large iron doorway which opened into a rustic reception area.

Meghna, brimming with excitement, rushed ahead, pulling Himanshu along for their obligatory Instagram post. Janvi smiled at the couple as she lingered behind to help Karan with the luggage.

"It's so quiet here, isn't it?" she remarked, watching him with a meaningful expression.

"It would be, wouldn't it, after driving in this bloody motor mower for the past five hours." Karan retorted, pulling out Meghna's heavy suitcase, not noticing Janvi's softer tone. *Did she pack her whole house?* he wondered.

"It wasn't that bad," Janvi chuckled sympathetically. "Besides, it more than makes up for the peacefulness here, don't you think?"

Karan looked up at her finally catching on. He lifted an eyebrow, unable to resist teasing.

"Oh, now you're all for it? After agonizing over every possible escape clause in the past few days?"

"Could you blame me?" she gasped mortified. "I was nervous. I know I was being unreasonable, but I'm trying to be nice now. Though, it rather seems like the motor mower has rattled your manners along with your eardrums."

They both stared at each other for a moment before bursting into laughter.

"Should we go in?" she asked.

Karan nodded.

As Janvi turned to go in, but Karan wrapped a hand around her wrist, turning her back to face him.

"Wait," his voice was softer now. "Janvi. In all seriousness, I understand why you were nervous. You probably still are. But I want you to know I haven't come here with the pretence of compelling you into something you don't want to do. Do you trust me at least in this?"

Janvi nodded speaking softly. "I do"

More than I do myself, she wanted to add. She wondered at her silent admission. Did she really?

At the reception area, a turbaned man relieved them of their luggage, while a woman in traditional Rajasthani garb greeted them warmly, putting on a welcoming *tikka* on their foreheads.

After they checked in, they were guided to another opening at the back, revealing a vast expanse of sandy dunes. White tents dotted the rust-coloured landscape at equal intervals in the distance, their canvas tops fluttering gently in the breeze. An open jeep awaited them, ready to take them toward the camping area. Himanshu and Karan helped their partners into the back of the jeep, their luggage having already been sent ahead in an electric buggy.

The jeep drove past the main camp, venturing further into the western dunes, where the haunting melody of the *sarangi* grew louder with every turn. The sun hung low over the Thar Desert, its golden light spilling across the sinuous mounds of sand and illuminating the vast blue heavens above.

They stopped near a table set up for afternoon tea, the delicate arrangement contrasting with the wild beauty of the desert. The photo enthusiasts eagerly walked away, cameras in hand, to capture the sinking sun painting the horizon in fiery hues.

Janvi, however, was drawn to the music. She walked toward folk singers seated a short distance away, their vibrant attire standing out against the muted tones of the sand. Instead of joining the tourists at the tables, she chose to sit on the warm dunes, the soft strains of the instruments weaving into the quiet rhythm of her thoughts.

"Chai?"

Karan's voice broke the stillness. She turned to see him standing behind her, holding out a clay cup of steaming hot tea.

"Thank-you," she smiled at him gratefully as he joined her beside him.

They sat together for a while in silence, the only sounds around them the gentle strains of the folk music and the soft whisper of the wind. Before them, the landscape burned redder with every passing second, the sinking sun casting its fiery glow over the endless dunes—a perfect reflection of the unspoken emotions simmering beneath the surface. Each was keenly aware of the other. His presence a subtle mix of strength and restraint. Her scent lingered in the air, a sweet blend of jasmine and sandalwood. And yet, for reasons neither could fathom, it felt right. Comfortable even.

Janvi broke the silence first, a lingering thought from the car ride earlier prompting her words.

"I wanted to ask you something," she began.

"Go on."

"Earlier in the car, when I shared that I was from Mussoorie. I could be mistaken, but were you trying to say something?"

"You... weren't mistaken," he began, a small smile tugging at his lips. "I had a passing thought. I just didn't want to say it in front of Himanshu and Meghna without opening up the floor for more awkward questions."

Janvi nodded emphatically, "I gathered as much."

"Well, what was it?" she prompted him a few seconds later giving into curiosity when he hadn't continued.

Karan sighed before continuing. "My boarding school was in Dehradun. You'd have been a mere hour away from me. How many times I would have gone into Mussoorie town from school during my time there. And how many times you may have ventured into Dehradun with your family. I wondered if we ever crossed paths."

Janvi's gaze softened the more he spoke. She'd seen his framed photos at the Rathore Haveli countless times. She'd also seen the ones with him in his boarding school uniform. She'd recognised it of course the first time she'd seen the photos, that uniform. She remembered having similar thoughts at the time. How many times she'd have seen that uniform on the young boys who'd visit Mussoorie on a school excursion? Would he have been one of them?

Karan continued, "I wondered, there's so much that I don't know about you. Like... what you would have been like growing up?"

Janvi smiled, hoping to lighten the somewhat reflective mood.

"Well, to put it rather succinctly," she said, "I definitely wasn't catching snakes."

Karan's laughter broke out unexpectedly, loud and hearty, catching Janvi off guard. She blinked at him, her brows lifting in surprise. She wasn't quite sure why, but hearing him laugh so openly made her feel... a little lighter.

"Alright, I'll admit. I might have been something of a wild child, Miss Goody-Two-Shoes," he said, his voice playful. "But haven't you done anything remotely adventurous?"

"Don't chastise me," she retorted, a hint of defiance in her voice. "You forget, I'm the daughter of an army man. I grew up in camps surrounded by handguns and rifles."

"I wouldn't know anything about that," he said with a hint of a smile, "but I have first-hand experience of your skills with a cricket bat."

Janvi laughed, "You're never going to let me live that down, will you?"

"Never," he said softly, his words hanging in the air, suddenly carrying a weight that neither of them had expected.

As the last rays of the sun dipped below the horizon, their guide called out, signalling it was time to head to the camp. Janvi rose reluctantly from the warm sand, brushing her palms against her dress. Karan followed, holding out a hand to steady her. She hesitated for a fraction of a second before placing her hand in his.

The jeep ride to the tents was short, and soon, they arrived at their accommodation for the next two nights.

They got off in front of tent 103, where Himanshu and Meghna quickly disappeared inside. The guide walked Karan and Janvi to a tent a little further away, to 107. They stopped at the entrance, the soft sound of canvas flapping in the breeze greeting them.

The tent was framed by sturdy poles wrapped in fabric, their dark wood polished to a soft sheen. The entrance flap was tied back, revealing a stone threshold beneath their feet. It felt cool against their shoes, a surprising contrast to the dry heat outside. Above them, lanterns cast a warm, flickering light.

"So, Mr. and Mrs. Rathore, here we are," the guide said. "We will start serving dinner from 7pm onwards at the restaurant. You may join at your leisure, and in the meantime if you need anything at all, you can call our 24-hour room service number and we'll bring it to you. Enjoy your stay."

Karan stepped inside first, holding the inner flap open for her. "After you," he said, his tone calm but carrying an undercurrent of awareness.

She hesitated for a moment, her hand brushing against the thick fabric of the entrance before stepping through. The air inside was cooler, scented faintly of earthy tones.

Her gaze was immediately drawn to the centrepiece of the room—a plush mattress placed on a bed carved from smooth stone, its edges softened by layers of crisp, white linens and cushions in muted desert hues. The sturdiness of it, juxtaposed with the inviting softness of the bedding, made her pause.

Behind her, Karan brought in their bags from the outer veranda, placing them next to a wooden wardrobe on the side.

"This is not what I imagined," she admitted softly, more to herself than to Karan.

"What did you expect?" Karan asked.

"Well... an actual tent?" she said with a small laugh.

She wasn't sure how to feel. Part of her wanted to be relieved that the room was much larger and more spacious than she had imagined, its grandeur almost reassuring. But another part of her couldn't help but feel a bit uneasy about the distinctly romantic ambiance that seemed to envelop the space. The soft lighting, the serene stillness, and the stone bed—it all suggested an intimacy that made her anxious.

On the far side of the room, an arched opening led to an adjoining space, where a small desk sat beneath another *jali* window, a small dressing mirror placed on it. A brass pitcher and matching glasses gleamed on its surface, catching the fading light. Beyond that, a doorway led to the bathroom, though she could only glimpse the stone basin and a hint of mosaic tiling.

Janvi drifted toward the veranda at the back of the tent. The view was breathtaking—a quiet expanse of dunes stretching endlessly into the horizon, their ripples painted pink in the dusk. A low parapet of carved stone framed the outdoor space, where a pair of wooden chairs and a table waited invitingly. She turned back to the room, her eyes darted from one corner to the next, as if searching for something to anchor her.

"Everything okay?" His voice was soft, almost concerned, as if he could see through her hurried thoughts.

Janvi gave a small nod, forcing a smile before looking back at the view. "Yes, just... taking it all in."

"Janvi, look at me," he whispered.

She turned to face him, finding him closer than she expected, the golden light from the tent casting a soft glow on his features.

"I meant what I said earlier," he murmured, his voice low and steady. "I won't push you into anything. But being here... with you... it feels right. I just want you to know that."

Her heart fluttered at his words, and for a moment, she forgot how to respond. The unspoken tension between them hummed in the air, fragile yet undeniable.

"Karan, I..." she began, but the words faltered on her tongue.

He smiled faintly, stepping back to give her space.

"Why don't you take a shower, freshen up before dinner? I'll go take a walk."

With that, he left the room. Strangely, she found his absence tormenting her more than the prospect of any kind of intimacy.

* * *

Karan leaned on the bar nursing the glass like a lifeline. The area was lit up with warm lights and shadows of soft water waves in the pool nearby were casted on the wall behind him.

Today had been... different. Even with that darned car and Himanshu and Meghna for company, he curiously found it enjoyable. Himanshu had grown up considerably. No longer the annoying, nosy brat from school. He should be thankful to him for this trip. Thankful to have gotten Janvi to open up and be more comfortable.

He couldn't forget the way she had tilted her head slightly, her eyes narrowing with curiosity as she asked, *"That night, in the study. Did you mean what you said? About wanting to stay in this marriage?"* The question had caught him off guard, not because he didn't know the answer, but because she'd dared to ask. She was opening up to him, step by hesitant step, and Karan wasn't sure whether to be relieved or terrified by how much he wanted to hold onto that openness.

And then there was the moment when their shared histories had unfolded like an unexpected gift. Mussoorie and Dehradun—so close, and yet, they might as well have been worlds apart back then.

Now, standing here with the evening breeze brushing against his face, he couldn't stop thinking about her—her voice, her laughter, the way her fingers absentmindedly traced the threads of her dupatta when she spoke.

In the privacy of their tent, he had told her again that he

wouldn't compel her into anything. It had been the right thing to say, the honourable thing. But even now, the memory of her so close, the warmth of her presence filling the space between them, made his pulse quicken.

He took a slow sip of his drink, letting the smoky flavour linger on his tongue. His restraint had been near-impossible. He was no saint. He wanted her—more than he had the words to express. To take her in his arms, to kiss her, to lose himself in her entirely. The ache of it was maddening. But he couldn't risk it—not yet. Not until she wanted it too, freely and without hesitation.

Karan exhaled deeply, setting his glass down on the polished bar. As he straightened and walked toward the path leading back to their tent, the lanterns lining the resort's walkways cast a soft glow on the sand. The sky above had darkened into indigo, stars beginning to pierce through the fading light.

When he returned to their tent, Janvi was seated at the desk, her pen moving across the pages of her faithful companion.

"Ah," he remarked, his voice breaking the silence, "I was wondering where that notebook of yours was."

She glanced up, catching his gaze in the mirror. A soft smile played on her lips.

"It was in my bag," she replied, her voice calm yet warm.

Karan nodded, stepping toward the outdoor bathroom. It was a charmingly rustic space—walled for privacy but open to the sky, where the evening air carried the scent of rain-soaked earth and distant jasmine. He let the cool water rinse away the weariness of the day, a brief reprieve from his thoughts.

When he returned to the room, droplets clung to his skin, and a towel sat low on his hips. He ran another towel over his damp hair, the muscles of his arms flexing with the motion. From the corner of his eye, he caught Janvi's gaze—fixed on his reflection in the mirror. She wasn't pretending not to look, and her attention lingered, unguarded.

"Do you like what you see?" he asked, a hint of mischief in his voice.

She quickly lowered her gaze, a faint pink blush rising on her cheeks. Janvi bit her lower lip, clearly flustered.

He chuckled softly, the sound rich and amused.

"You know," he said, stepping closer with deliberate slowness, "they say it's rude to stare."

When she didn't respond, he leaned down behind her, his hands braced on the edge of the desk. The movement made her tense visibly, but she didn't pull away. Their reflections met in the mirror, her wide, uncertain eyes staring back at him.

"But for you, Mrs. Rathore," he murmured, his voice dropping lower, "I think we can make an exception. For you see," he paused, a playful glint in his eyes, "I am all yours."

Her breath hitched, the smallest sound betraying her composure. He saw her grip the pen a little tighter. But then she recovered quickly, her chin tilting just slightly, a spark of defiance in her eyes.

"For now," she began, her voice measured but soft, "I'd prefer for what's mine to put on a shirt."

His chuckle rumbled softly as he straightened, giving her space again.

"Fair enough," he said lightly, walking to the dressing area. His movements were unhurried, and he couldn't resist the urge to glance back at her. Her gaze lingered on him for a split second before she snapped it back to her notebook.

He smirked to himself as he pulled on a shirt, the tension between them still humming like a quiet song.

* * *

They strolled toward the restaurant, the evening air cool against their skin, a stark contrast to the blazing heat of the morning. Karan took in a deep breath, his shoulders relaxing as a rare sense of ease settled over him.

"Do you suppose, Himanshu and Meghna would be joining us for dinner?" Karan asked, his voice casual, breaking the silence.

"Why wouldn't they?" Janvi replied, her brows knitting together in mild confusion as she shot him a questioning glance.

Karan's lips curved into a teasing smile as he slowed his pace, his voice dropping into a more playful tone. "Are you really this naïve, or do you reserve that special treatment just for me?"

Janvi's steps faltered for a moment, then she stopped, blinking in confusion. "What do you mean?"

Karan sighed, shaking his head. "Come on, Janvi. It's their honeymoon. And judging by how quickly they dove into their tent earlier, I don't think they're in any hurry to join us for dinner... or anything else."

"Ah, that," Janvi said, glancing down at her watch. Her lips curved into a cheeky smile as she replied, "In that case, assuming they've spent, say, fifteen minutes per session, they're probably in dire need of some much-deserved food by now. Don't you think?"

She looked up at him, her eyes sparkling with mischief, but Karan had stopped walking and was now regarding her with an unreadable expression.

"What?" she asked, her smile faltering slightly under his steady gaze.

"You know," he said quietly, his voice low and measured, "you're really lucky I'm a gentleman."

"*Matlab?*" she asked, her brows knitting together as she tilted her head in confusion.

Karan smirked, stepping past her as he muttered under his breath, "Figure it out, smart-ass."

Janvi stared after him, her mouth slightly agape before a slow smile spread across her face. Shaking her head, she hurried to catch up, her cheeks faintly flushed.

At the restaurant entrance, a turbaned *dwar-pal* greeted them with folded hands and a slight bow. His regal demeanour was softened by the bright smile visible through his impeccably groomed handlebar moustache.

"*Khama ghani, hukum, baisa,*" he said warmly. "*Aaiye, viraajiye.*"

"*Ghani khama,*" Karan replied, inclining his head as he motioned for Janvi to follow.

Janvi mirrored his gesture with a polite nod and a soft smile, stepping through the carved wooden door frame into a warm, rustic dining area.

Inside, the soft glow of warm lighting danced across the rich wood of the beams above. The air was filled with the comforting aroma of freshly made bajra rotis and spices. Colourful plush cushions surrounded low tables, inviting guests to sink in and relax. The walls were adorned with intricate tapestries telling stories of Rajasthan's history and culture.

They were guided to a table in an open area, from where they could see the wide landscape of a sandy dune bathed in moonlight. From their vantage point, they could also see the outdoor stage being set up with a bonfire for the evening folk dances and music.

Karan pulled out a chair for Janvi before settling into his own across from her. The table felt intimate, yet casual, a contrast to the vast, open desert around them. His phone lit up with a message, drawing his attention for a moment.

"It's Himanshu," he said. "They'll be joining us in ten minutes. Are you hungry? Should we order something now or wait for them?"

Janvi adjusted her dupatta, her fingers absently tracing the embroidery. "Let's wait for them," she said with a small smile.

Karan nodded, his gaze steady on her. Silence settled between them, unbroken for a moment. Then, as if the thought had suddenly struck him, he blurted out, "How about, for the next ten minutes, we pretend this is a date?"

He watched her closely, waiting for any sign of hesitation or retreat.

"Date?" Janvi repeated, blinking as her eyes widened in surprise at the directness of the question.

"Yes, a date," Karan said casually, leaning back in his chair. "You know—someone takes you out, makes you feel special, all that.

Haven't you been on one before?" His eyes glinted with mischief, clearly enjoying her reaction.

Janvi let out a nervous chuckle, her cheeks warming to a soft pink. "Well, no... I haven't really had time for that kind of thing," she admitted, glancing away as though the idea itself felt foreign to her. "I mean, I was in school... and then..." Her voice faltered before she finished softly, "We were... married."

For a brief moment, a flash of sympathy filled Karan's heart at her soft admission. But intent on changing exactly that he pressed on, his lips curving into a smirk. He leaned closer with a playful glint in his eye. "So, no boyfriends in school then? Not even one?"

Janvi hesitated, her gaze shifting away from his before she slowly shook her head.

Karan raised an eyebrow, his voice taking on a softer, coaxing tone. "Come on. Not even a little crush? A guy who made your heart race at least once?"

She turned to look at him, her eyes wide with curiosity, her lips parted slightly. Then, for a fleeting moment, her gaze dropped to his lips before quickly returning to meet his eyes, her breath coming a little faster.

Karan's eyes widened and his heart skipped a beat as understanding dawned. She looked away, her cheeks flushed with embarrassment, and he let out a quiet breath, his lips curling into a knowing smile. *Him.* The air around them seemed to thicken as his body reacted before his mind could catch up. He stilled, restraining the urge to pull her closer. The impulse was there, raw and immediate, but he held it back, focusing on maintaining control.

He poured her a glass of water, the sound of it filling the air as he handed it to her. She took it gratefully, downing it in one swift gulp.

"Well, this date is off to a wonderful start," he teased, keeping his tone light, even though his pulse was still racing.

Might as well keep it going.

A devilish smile curled at his lips as a thought crossed his mind.

"And seeing as this is your first... why don't we mix things up with a game?"

"A game?" Janvi echoed, her confusion evident, unsure of where he was going with this.

"Come on, humour me," he coaxed, his smile widening.

"Fine," she relented, her brow furrowing slightly. "What kind of game?"

"Twenty questions," Karan suggested, his voice light, eyes glinting with amusement. "Now normally, it involves someone choosing something and people use twenty attempts to guess what that is. But we'll do a variation. We take turns asking a question each, and we have to answer truthfully. Until we reach twenty. Essentially, we're just trying to getting to know each other."

Janvi paused, her gaze thoughtful as she considered his words. "Any question?"

Karan shrugged nonchalantly, a playful smile tugging at the corners of his lips. "Anything at all. No rules."

She looked at him for a moment, as if deciding whether to play along, before nodding. "Okay, sounds fair. But can I go first?"

"Be my guest," he replied, a quiet confidence in his voice.

Janvi tilted her head slightly, her eyes narrowing in playful contemplation before settling on her question. "What's your favourite colour?"

Karan raised an eyebrow, a teasing edge to his voice. "Really? That's all you could think of?"

"Why, what's wrong with that?" Janvi countered, her chin raised in innocent defiance. "Everyone has a favourite colour."

"Alright, fine," Karan relented, leaning back slightly. "Um... I suppose it depends on what it is—black for cars or electronics, grey for furniture, whites or neutrals for everything else."

Janvi laughed softly, shaking her head. "Mr. CEO," she teased.

Karan chuckled, his eyes twinkling with something more. "Exactly, efficient." He leaned forward slightly. "Alright, my turn. You've lived in many cities with your dad. Which one was your favourite?"

As Janvi was about to respond, Himanshu and Meghna walked into the restaurant, promptly joining them at the table.

"Sorry we're late!" Meghna said, offering an apologetic smile as she settled into the seat beside Janvi.

Karan quickly glanced at Janvi, his expression still playful, before his gaze shifted to the newly arrived friends. Without missing a beat, he leaned forward slightly, locking eyes with Janvi for a moment. "This isn't over," he said quietly, his voice low but certain, just for her to hear, her cheeks heating up at the words that sounded oddly like a challenge.

"So, what were you two lovebirds up to? Enjoying the resort so far huh?" Himanshu asked with a wink as he took the remaining seat next to Karan.

"Apparently not as well as you two honeymooners," retorted Karan looking at his watch, causing a riot of laughter.

* * *

"That was delicious!" Meghna squealed in satisfaction as she took a swig of her wine. "Oh, I think I have a food coma now, hashtag FoodGoals. By the way, did I take a picture of the kebabs?"

"Um, no, I think you devoured them before they even had a chance to cool down," Himanshu teased, casually twisting the neck of his beer bottle between his fingers.

"Oh, how sad." She leaned back, swirling her wine dramatically. "Still, totally worth it. Janvi, wasn't that paneer tikka just incredible?"

Janvi smiled politely, her fingers absently tracing the rim of her glass of water. "It was very good."

"Good? It was incredible, perfectly tangy and spicy!" Meghna countered, her eyes gleaming with mischief. She leaned closer, her voice dropping to a playful lilt. "And speaking of spicy things, darling, tell me, what's this tall, hunky thing in bed like?"

Janvi's eyes widened in shock, heat creeping up her neck. A quick glance at Karan showed he wasn't just amused—there was an intensity in the way he watched her, his gaze steady and unflinching as he took a slow sip of his beer. The faintest hint of a smirk tugged at the corner of his mouth, making her shift in her seat, suddenly acutely aware of him.

Janvi froze, caught off guard. "I… um—"

Meghna cut her off with a tipsy laugh. "Come on, you're married. You don't have to be shy! I mean, with all that energy of a young bride, I'm sure Mr. CEO can't keep up—"

"Meghna," Karan interjected smoothly, setting his bottle down with a quiet clink. His tone was calm but firm, drawing her attention like a magnet. "I think it's time you and Himanshu called it a night."

Meghna pouted, swaying slightly in her chair. "Fine, fine. Spoilsport."

Himanshu rose with a chuckle, gently pulling Meghna to her feet. "Thanks for dinner, Karan. And Janvi Bhabhi, don't let her scare you off—she's harmless, I promise."

Janvi smiled. "It's fine. Goodnight, Himanshu. Meghna."

Karan stood up, straightening his linen shirt. "You guys go on ahead, I'll get the bill," he said smoothly, offering a reassuring smile.

Himanshu nodded, appreciate. "Thanks Karan. You're a lifesaver."

Karan just gave a simple nod. "No problem."

As the couple wandered off, Janvi let out a soft laugh, shaking her head. "She's… lively."

Karan gave a faint smirk as he signalled for the bill. "Lively is one way to put it."

Janvi glanced at him, her embarrassment fading slightly.

Once the bill was settled, they stepped out into the cool desert night. The moonlit sand stretched in quiet ripples around them, the resort lights casting a faint glow in the distance.

They walked side by side toward their tent, the only sounds the soft crunch of sand beneath their feet. Karan slipped his hands into his pockets, his strides relaxed but steady.

Back in their tent, the figurative elephant in the room stared at them—the large concrete bed with its plush sheets and pillows. For a moment, they stood silently, staring at it. Eventually, Karan broke the silence.

"You take the bed. I'll sleep on the lounge chairs in the veranda."

"Outside? No, that's... not necessary, it's a big bed," she replied quickly. "I mean, there's enough space for both of us."

Karan's gaze softened at her words, "Janvi, I want you to be comfortable. And I think that—"

"I know," she interjected softly. "And I see it."

The idea of sharing a bed with him felt like a huge leap, but he had been nothing but respectful. "We can make it work."

"Janvi," he said raising his palm, "It's okay. It's just for two nights. I'm taking the lounge chair."

Karan picked up an extra pillow and moved toward the lounge chairs outside, but a soft hand on his elbow pulled him back.

"Wait, you don't need to sleep outside. Please," she said, her voice soft but firm. "It's a big bed. We can make it work."

Karan paused, his expression gentle. "Are you sure?"

She nodded, feeling a surprising sense of calm. "Yes. I trust you. And like you said. It's just two nights. We can make it work."

Karan hesitated, then nodded and moved towards the bed.

"I'll... go change," she said quickly, needing a bit of space.

She walked toward the bathroom, grateful for the brief solitude. Changing into a simple white kurta, the cool fabric was a relief after the desert's heat. She brushed her teeth, grounding herself in the familiar routine, the quiet offering a fleeting sense of normalcy.

When she returned to the room, they awkwardly brushed past each other. Karan was at the sink, brushing his teeth, and she tried not to notice the small, careful distance between them.

After a moment, Karan finished and waited, giving her time to settle into bed first before he joined her. Gently pulling the covers, he kept a respectful distance, lying down beside her without crossing the space between them.

For a while, they both lay in silence, staring at the canvas of their tent. Karan glanced around looking for the lamp switches, only to realize they were all on Janvi's side. Without thinking, he reached over her to turn them off. Janvi's breath caught in her throat, a slight panic rising as she shifted away. He quickly apologized, his voice soft. "It's okay. I'm just... turning off the lights."

They settled back into the dark quiet, the only sounds the occasional breeze brushing against the tent and the soft drip of water from the bathroom. Neither could sleep. Janvi tossed restlessly, the sound of her paayal breaking the stillness.

"Can't sleep?" he asked.

"No," she replied.

A thought occurred to him.

"You never answered your question," he said.

"What question?" Janvi asked.

"The game we were playing just before dinner—Twenty questions," he reminded her.

"Ah," he could almost feel her smile, "my favourite city with Papa. I think it has to be Jaipur."

"Jaipur, interesting. Why's that?"

"It was my first time in Rajasthan. I had grown up looking at tourism magazines from Rajasthan, reading about Rajput kings and their palaces. It was fascinating to finally see it all in person."

Karan considered her response for moment.

"So, do you actually like it in Jaisalmer? I know it's smaller than most Rajasthani cities, but do you actually prefer it over somewhere like... Mussoorie?"

"Mussoorie has its own charm, I suppose," she said, "and I grew up there so it's special, but yes, I do like it in Jaisalmer. I like learning about Royal history."

"So how many other Rajasthani cities have you seen?" he asked.

"Unfortunately, just two. Jaipur and Jaisalmer," she said.

A thought occurred to Karan.

"Janvi, we're only about an hour and a half away from Jodhpur. Do you want to go visit Mehrangarh Fort tomorrow? We can leave early, have breakfast in Jodhpur? What do you think?"

"Really?" she got up excited. "I mean... are you sure? If it's not too much trouble."

"Oh, trust me, I can get you there and back with my eyes closed."

"I'd like that very much, thank-you!" she asked.

"Well in that case, let's try and catch some sleep. We have an early day tomorrow. I'll check with Himanshu if we can borrow his car in the morning."

Karan settled back against the pillow, a quiet sense of satisfaction building in his chest. He hadn't expected things to go this smoothly tonight—just the fact that they were talking, that they'd made it to this point, felt like a small victory. It had been a long time coming.

Janvi was right there, just a touch away. He felt the urge to close that distance, but for now, he resisted. He would take what he could, and tonight, this was enough. Tomorrow was another step forward. And that was enough to keep him content for now.

Janvi closed her eyes, feeling the weight of the day start to ease. The promise of tomorrow, the adventure of it, was enough to lull her toward sleep. Eventually, the rhythm of her breathing evened out, and Karan let his own eyelids flutter shut.

20

JOURNEY TO LOVE

The first thing Janvi noticed was the early morning light pouring in from the veranda of their tent. She sat up in momentary panic, remembering where she was and who she was with last night. *Karan.* Turning to her left, she found him still asleep, rolled onto his stomach, his face turned towards her. His strong arms lay relaxed, one stretched above his head, the other resting close to his side, the faint outline of veins running down to his wrists. He was impossible to ignore. With a small pang of sympathy, she noted that, despite the vast expanse of the king-sized mattress, he was lying precariously close to the edge, as though even in sleep, all his subconscious could think of was her comfort.

In the safety of his slumber, she leaned against the bed frame and allowed herself this rare chance to watch him closely, letting her gaze trace the sharp lines of his face in the soft morning light. A light stubble dusted the edge of his jaw. She swallowed, suddenly hyper-aware of him. The faint scent of his cologne clung to the sheets, a mixture of cedar and something spicy, something inherently him.

Her eyes drifted lower, taking in the way his kurta had ridden up his back, exposing the toned muscles beneath his tanned skin. His hair, thick and straight, had fallen over his forehead, a few strands brushing against his closed eyes. It looked soft, too soft. Her fingers, almost of their own accord, reached out almost needing to feel the softness of his hair and to trace the edge of his jaw and feel the roughness beneath her touch, to trace the curve of his exposed back, but she stopped herself, biting the inside of her cheek.

Beneath her gaze, he stirred, as if attuned to the unbridled thoughts racing through her mind. Her so-far steady pulse quickened the moment his eyes fluttered open, locking onto hers with a quiet intensity—learning her, recognizing her in ways that left her feeling bare. She watched in silent defeat as the corners of his lips curved into the faintest smirk, catching her red-handed in her stolen moment of observation. Once again, she found herself ensnared by his perceptiveness, the warmth creeping up her cheeks betraying her further.

Is this how it would always be? she wondered. Would he always be able to read her so effortlessly, like an open book, growing more attuned with time?

"Good morning," he said, his voice low and husky with sleep, filling the quiet space between them.

"Morning," Janvi replied, her voice quieter than usual. She didn't move. She didn't want to. Instead, she remained where she was, her gaze fixed on him—the tousled strands of his hair falling over his forehead, the slow, steady rise and fall of his back as he stretched lazily, the way his strong arm lay so close, yet not quite touching her.

The weight of her lingering stare made him shift slightly, his dark eyes flicking toward her with quiet concern. "You okay?" he asked, his voice careful, gentle, as though afraid he'd done something to make her uncomfortable.

Janvi swallowed, hugging her knees closer to her chest. The polite concern in his voice only added to the restless frustration simmering beneath her skin. She didn't want to feel this way—hot and bothered by the very sight of him. She hadn't signed up for this. She'd agreed to come on this trip to let things happen naturally, to figure things out at her own pace. But right now? Right now, everything about him—the way he occupied space so effortlessly, the kindness in his gaze, the way his voice settled into her skin like warmth—felt too much.

She gave a small nod, hoping it would end the conversation, but Karan lingered, studying her with that quiet perceptiveness of his that usually made her feel safe. Today, though, it irritated her. Why did he have to be so... nice? So patient? It made things harder.

As if sensing her need for space, Karan finally stretched and, without warning, tugged his kurta over his head, tossing it onto the bed.

Janvi stiffened, her eyes betraying her as they dragged over the broad expanse of his back, the defined muscles shifting under tanned skin. He was all lean strength, effortless and composed, and the sight of him only fuelled the heat curling low in her stomach. She clenched her jaw, annoyed at herself, at him, at the whole situation.

She wasn't supposed to feel this way—not for him. Not for the man who had once walked away so easily, leaving her behind like an afterthought.

Karan, oblivious to the war raging inside her, stepped onto the veranda and started his workout. Each stretch, each pull of the resistance band, made her grip the sheets tighter. He wasn't doing anything to provoke her, not intentionally at least, but the sight of him—shirtless, focused, existing so effortlessly in her space—was making it impossible to breathe normally.

He glanced back at her mid-stretch, brows pulling together. "Are you sure you're okay?"

Janvi's lips parted, words tangled up in the frustration tightening in her chest. "I'm fine," she muttered, though it didn't sound convincing even to her.

Karan didn't seem to buy it, but instead of pressing, he wiped the sweat from his brow and offered an easy out. "You know, it's still your turn."

She blinked, her mind sluggish to catch up. "Huh?"

"Our game," he reminded her, throwing her a casual glance. "Twenty questions. You never asked your next one."

Her grip on her knees tightened as her gaze flickered back to him—standing there, bare-chested, acting like he wasn't completely undoing her. Frustration bubbled to the surface before she could stop it, and before she knew it, the words tumbled out—sharp, laced with something she couldn't quite name.

"Question two," she said, her voice carefully cool. "On our wedding night, you said you were never left wanting for anything. That you were used to the good life. Have you really always gotten whatever you've wanted in life?"

Karan froze mid-motion, the resistance band slackening in his grip. His gaze flicked to her, a mix of confusion and something else flickering beneath the surface. "What?" he asked, blinking as if he hadn't heard her right.

Janvi shrugged, standing abruptly before he could analyse her any further. "Take your time," she said lightly, though the words carried an edge, before turning toward the bathroom.

Karan stood still for a moment, clearly thrown off by the sudden shift in her tone. He ran a hand through his hair, staring at the space she'd just occupied, brows furrowing in thought, completely stumped.

Inside the bathroom, Janvi gripped the edge of the sink, staring at her reflection with wide, conflicted eyes. She let out a shaky breath, pressing her palms to her flushed cheeks.

What was happening to her?

She hated how this felt—how one moment of politeness, of him being him, could undo her so easily. And worst of all, she hated that deep down, she wasn't even sure if she wanted him to stop.

* * *

Karan adjusted his watch, glancing at Janvi through the mirror as she tied her hair into a loose ponytail. She had been quieter since coming out of the bathroom, calmer, but there was something different in the air between them—something he couldn't quite put his finger on. He tried to ignore it, focusing instead on packing up their things.

The silence stretched between them, comfortable yet charged, until he finally spoke. "You asked me earlier if I've always gotten everything I wanted."

Janvi paused mid-motion, her fingers stilling over her earring.

He glanced at her, offering a small smile. "The truth is... no. I haven't. I like to think I have, but life doesn't exactly work that way, does it?"

Her gaze lifted to meet his in the mirror, something shifting in her eyes—something softer, more thoughtful. "No, it doesn't," she murmured.

Karan turned, facing her fully now. "But I'm beginning to believe that whatever I did get, it has been worth more than anything I could have imagined for myself."

For a long moment, she just looked at him, and he saw it—the quiet vulnerability in her eyes, the way her lips parted slightly as if holding back words she wasn't sure she wanted to say. And then, before he could react, she stepped closer, her hand reaching up tentatively.

Karan barely had time to process what was happening before her fingers grazed his jaw, and she leaned in—hesitant, yet certain. His breath hitched. For a split second, he almost let it happen, almost let himself give in to the warmth of her touch, the pull of her presence.

But then, instinct kicked in. He turned his face at the last moment, her lips brushing lightly against his cheek instead.

Janvi froze. He could feel the way her entire body went rigid, the way her hand fell away from his skin as if she'd been burned. "I—" she stammered, stepping back quickly, her cheeks flooding with colour. "I'm sorry..."

Before she could turn away completely, Karan reached out and pulled her back with a force that startled her. He bent her hand behind her locking her, using his grip on her wrist to pull her waist into him. His grip was firm, almost desperate, his dark eyes burning into hers with something raw, something menacing in its intensity.

"What are you apologizing for?" His voice was low, rough, sending a shiver down her spine. With his free hand, he snaked his fingers in her hair, forcing her to look at him.

Janvi swallowed, caught in the weight of his gaze, her pulse hammering in her ears.

"What is going on in that mysterious head of yours? Do you

think I'm not attracted to you?" he demanded, his voice dark with unspoken restraint. "Janvi, do you have *any* idea what you do to me? Even now, it's taking every ounce of my strength not to throw you onto this bed and rip every inch of your clothes off. Believe me, if I allow myself, there is nothing more I want in this very moment than to have my way with you. And where we are, no one would hear your screams."

Her lips parted, her breath catching in her throat, but he didn't stop. He pulled her closer, his grip tightening ever so slightly. "Each time you're near me, I'm dying to pull you into my arms, to kiss you." His voice dropped lower, more dangerous. "That day... the Visarjan, when you came to the terrace wearing that yellow *saree*. Do you have any idea what it did to me? All I wanted was to drag you to my room and unwrap you out of it."

His thumb grazed over her wrist, his voice thick with restraint. "Every time you're near me, I want to bury myself in you, make love to you until you scream my name in ecstasy."

Janvi trembled, overwhelmed by the sheer force of his words, of him.

"But each day, it's a damn near struggle holding myself back." He exhaled sharply, his forehead nearly touching hers. "I know you plan on leaving after our contract ends, Janvi. I saw the school admission forms for Aman. The book-keeping night classes. I don't blame you. I've never given you a reason to stay." His voice softened, but the intensity never wavered. "And suddenly, here I am, asking you to."

Karan's gaze dropped briefly to the mangalsutra resting against her collarbone. His jaw clenched before he spoke again. "I'm not one to follow rituals. I don't believe in any of it. This," he touched the pendant lightly, "this doesn't mean much to me." He looked back into her eyes, his voice low but unwavering. "But I will promise you one thing. So, think very carefully before you make your decision."

He leaned in to her side, his voice a whisper in her ear, his breath warm against her cheek. "If we do this—if we cross that line—the moment we consummate this marriage... I swear on everything that's holy, there won't be any turning back from me. You will belong to me, heart, mind, body and soul." His fingers tightened around hers, his voice raw and unshaken. "And I will never, *ever* let you go."

A heavy silence fell between them, thick with unspoken emotions. Janvi's heart pounded in her chest, her fingers trembling slightly against his hold. Her lips parted, but no words came out.

Karan released her gently.

"I'll go get the car keys from Himanshu," he said stepping back before finally leaving her with her thoughts.

* * *

For the first few minutes, they drove in relative silence, the only sound between them being the steady hum of the engine. It was just past seven in the morning; the roads were empty, and the air carried a lingering coolness from the fading night.

The earlier tension hung heavy between them, thick and unspoken. Janvi stared out the window, watching the landscape blur past in soft hues of gold and ochre, her mind a tangled mess of thoughts and emotions. Absentmindedly, her fingers toyed with the locket of her *mangalsutra,* tracing its familiar contours as she replayed everything that had happened in the tent earlier.

Karan had been patient—so patient. Respectful, considerate, and composed in a way that only made her confusion worse. He had been the one to hold back, the one to give her time and space to decide what she wanted. So why did she feel this restless urgency gnawing at her now? Where was this sudden pressure to make a decision coming from?

A subtle clearing of his throat snapped her out of the abyss of her thoughts, bringing her attention to the man responsible for all of it. She turned to look at him. His eyes, hidden behind the tint of his sunglasses, remained fixed on the road, his right hand steady on the wheel, the other resting casually by his side. He wore a forest green linen shirt, the first two buttons undone, revealing just a hint of the dark hair on his chest. Her gaze lingered there longer than it should have, her pulse betraying her attempts to stay composed.

For a man who had just laid bare his feelings, Karan looked remarkably at ease—so calm, so self-assured. And here she was, a melting pool of emotions, struggling to keep herself together.

"My turn. Question two," he said, his voice steady yet laced with interest. "Why Pune?"

Janvi turned to watch the road ahead but her mind was miles away. She attempted to gather her thoughts, enough to be able to string them into intelligent sentences.

"My mother's family lives there," she began, her voice pensive.

Karan turned sharply to look at her, his curiosity piqued, hoping to be able to read her reflective tone, waiting patiently for her to continue.

"When she married Papa, they weren't happy," Janvi began, her voice soft yet steady. "They never wanted any of their daughters to marry army men. So, eventually, they cut all ties with her. But she missed them."

She paused, her fingers tightening slightly around the locket of her *mangalsutra,* as if drawing strength from it. "She used to try—calling them, writing letters. She even sent them baby photos of me, hoping they'd melt enough to let bygones be bygones. But nothing changed."

Janvi exhaled a weary sigh. "Still, she never let it make her bitter. She always remembered them fondly and wouldn't let me speak ill of them."

Silence stretched between them for a moment before Janvi continued, her voice quieter now. "I thought... if I moved to Pune, I could reach out. Get to know them. Let Aman be around them." She paused, as if weighing the words in her heart before letting them go. "I thought it might bring some peace to my mother, even if it's too late for her." A wistful smile flickered at her lips. "They're the only family I have left."

Karan's grip on the steering wheel tightened, his jaw flexing as he processed the ache beneath her words. He glanced at her briefly, his gaze unreadable behind the dark lenses of his sunglasses, but Janvi could sense the weight of his attention. After a moment, he spoke, his voice low yet steady.

"Janvi, whatever happens between us, whatever you decide, I'll make you this one promise—whenever you reach out to your family, I'll be right there with you." His words hung in the air, filled with a quiet conviction that made her chest tighten. Then, after a beat, he added softly, "And you're wrong. They're not the only family you have left."

Her breath hitched, feeling moved by his sincerity. She turned to look at him, but he remained focused on the road, his expression unreadable. Despite whatever confusion she had about him, one thing was undeniably certain—he was a man of his words.

A small smile tugged at her lips as she shifted in her seat, the weight on her chest feeling a little lighter. "My turn. Question three. What's your favourite hobby?"

"You mean other than trying to woo my wife?" he asked, a playful smirk tugging at the corners of his lips.

Janvi felt the warmth creep up her neck before she could stop it. She knew he was trying to make her laugh, to lighten the mood, but instead, he managed to make her blush. She turned her gaze back to the road, hoping he wouldn't notice the faint smile threatening to give her away.

"Let's see..." Karan mused, a thoughtful crease forming on his forehead. "I'm a little stumped, actually. The last couple of years, it's been nothing but work—office, meetings, research... and trying to stay on top of my health." He exhaled, a hint of self-awareness in his tone. "I guess I'm fortunate that my work is my passion. It's undoubtedly hectic, but honestly, I can't think of anything else."

"I can't decide if I should be happy for you or feel sorry," Janvi said thoughtfully, her voice laced with genuine curiosity.

Karan let out a soft laugh, shaking his head slightly. "Okay, my turn," he said, his voice lighter now. "Have you ever travelled overseas? And if not, where would you want to go first?"

Janvi tilted her head thoughtfully. "Oh... no, I haven't. But honestly, I've never really thought about it. There are so many places in India I still want to visit."

"That's fair," Karan nodded, his tone understanding. "But take your time. Surely there's someplace that's caught your eye?"

She pursed her lips, considering. "Maybe... Paris? I'd like to visit the Louvre," she said after a moment.

Karan smiled, leaning back slightly. "Paris is beautiful, I've been with Any—" He stopped abruptly, the name slipping out before he could catch it. A flicker of something unreadable crossed his face, and he turned sharply toward Janvi, gauging her reaction.

For a split second, the easy conversation shifted, tension settling between them like an invisible thread stretched too tight. Janvi didn't look at him right away; instead, her fingers fidgeted with the hem of her dupatta. But Karan noticed—the subtle tightening of her jaw, her lips pursed together, regret tearing at him.

"You know what? I think Paris is overrated," she said after a while, forcing a small shrug. "I'd like to go to Uzbekistan instead."

Uzbekistan? Karan thought, momentarily amused. But then it hit him—she was *envious.*

It wasn't like her to be so unguarded with her emotions. Karan leaned back slightly, watching her with newfound interest. Earlier that morning, she had tried to kiss him—crossing a line she'd never dared to before—and now this? Even if she wouldn't admit it, some part of her was staking her claim on him. *And he liked it.*

Smiling, he leaned back. "You know what? You're right. Paris *is* overrated," he said lightly. Then, after a beat, "Uzbekistan sounds perfect. I haven't been. If you'd let me, I'd like to come with you."

Janvi looked at him, surprise flickering in her eyes. Karan held her gaze, his expression sincere, unwavering. Then, just as suddenly, her expression shifted—her eyes narrowing ever so slightly, a new edge creeping into her voice.

"Four. How many girlfriends have you had?" she asked, her tone deceptively casual but laced with something he couldn't quite place.

Karan shifted in his seat, aware of how loaded the seemingly simple question was. Given the fragility of their relationship, the peril of answering it was not lost on him. He considered his options. Tell her the truth or give a diplomatic answer. The latter would be an insult to her intellect so he decided to risk everything and completely unburden himself. Give her the complete truth.

He exhaled, his grip on the wheel tightening briefly. "I've had a few girlfriends," he admitted, his voice steady but quieter than before. "My first serious relationship was in high school—Shahana. She studied at a girl's college while I was in boarding school at Doon. I lost my virginity to her." He glanced at Janvi, but her expression remained unreadable. "We parted ways after graduation."

Taking a breath, he continued, "Then, during university in London, I briefly dated an exchange student from Belgium—Sophia. It wasn't serious, more of a fleeting thing."

He hesitated slightly before moving on. "After that, I had a steady girlfriend in my last two years of university—her name was Isha. She was from Mumbai, the daughter of an industrialist. Our families met, and hers were quite keen on us getting married. But when I got into Harvard for my postgrad, they didn't want to wait. That's where it ended."

Karan's gaze flickered toward Janvi, trying to read her reaction, but she remained silent, listening.

"During postgrad, I didn't officially date much," he added, his tone shifting slightly. "Partly because of the heartbreak, partly because I was focused on my studies. I... did, however, have occasional flings and one-night stands." He cleared his throat, his voice laced with honesty but also a hint of regret.

"And then, after graduation, when Nathan and I began our start-up, Anya joined as an intern. Eventually, we started dating. To date, she's been my longest steady relationship."

He finished, letting the weight of his words settle between them.

The air in the car felt heavier now, and for the first time in a while, Karan found himself feeling exposed in a way he hadn't expected. Karan let out a slow breath, watching her carefully. He had expected curiosity, maybe even judgment, but instead, Janvi simply said, "Your turn."

Her tone was steady, almost too composed, and it unsettled him more than if she had reacted emotionally. She sat still, her gaze fixed ahead, her expression giving nothing away.

Karan studied her for a moment longer before speaking, his voice quieter now. "What did you hope to get out of that last question?"

"Clarity," she said without skipping a beat, her voice steady and unwavering.

His fingers tightened briefly on the steering wheel, but before he could respond, she continued, her gaze fixed straight ahead. "Five. Why did you break up with Anya?"

The question hit him harder than he expected. Karan felt the weight of the question settle between them like a heavy stone. This was no longer a game but a grilling. He realized with a sinking certainty that Janvi wasn't just making conversation anymore. She was sifting through the past, looking for answers, and since he was the one who had started this, he would have to see it through.

Besides, wasn't this the whole point? To finally be honest, to strip away the walls and get to know each other—the whole truth, no pretences.

He let out a slow breath, his fingers tightening briefly on the steering wheel. "I grew distant and she fell in love with Nathan." *The whole truth, Karan. The whole truth.*

His jaw clenched briefly before he added, "I caught them together in bed after I came home from a work trip."

The confession hung in the air, heavy and raw. Karan kept his eyes on the road, unwilling to see the expression on Janvi's face just yet. For a long moment, there was nothing but the steady hum of the engine and the faint rustle of the wind outside.

Finally, he risked a glance at her, but she remained impassive, her gaze fixed ahead, absorbing his words without reaction.

And somehow, that made it worse.

Say something, Janvi, please.

After what felt like an eternity, she finally spoke.

"Your turn," she said, her voice steady, giving nothing away.

The sinking feeling in his chest grew deeper with each passing second of silence, gnawing at him. He swallowed, forcing a lighter tone into his voice. "What's your favourite colour?"

"Blue," she responded almost too fast.

He opened his mouth to say something more, but before he could, Janvi's next question landed like a punch to his gut.

"Six. If you hadn't caught Nathan and Anya together, would you have come back to India?"

Karan's hands tensed around the wheel. For a moment, he considered brushing it over—smoothing it with something vague and meaningless. But that wouldn't be fair. Not anymore.

He exhaled slowly, staring straight ahead. "No," he admitted. "I wouldn't have."

Janvi nodded, her face unreadable, and once again, the silence stretched between them—heavy, filled with truths neither of them were sure they were ready to face.

"Your turn," she said.

"What's your favourite food?" he asked.

"Anything home cooked," she answered.

"Seven," she began, her voice suddenly quieter, carrying the faintest tremble. "What makes you think we could last?"

The words, spoken so softly, cut through him—sharper than any blade ever could.

Karan swallowed hard, shifting in his seat as a heavy weight settled in his chest. He wasn't sure what hurt more—her scepticism or the fact that he had brought her to this point.

Glancing at her, he found her looking so distant and wound up, as if bracing herself for an answer she wasn't sure she wanted to hear. A pang of regret twisted inside him, but he knew this question demanded more than simple assurances and elaborate words.

Without a word, Karan eased the car off the highway, pulling onto a quiet side road. He cut the engine, the sudden silence amplifying the tension between them.

Janvi looked at him, confused, as he removed his sunglasses, got out of the car, and walked around to her side. Opening the door gently, he reached for her hand and helped her out, closing the door behind them with deliberate calm.

Then, without hesitation, he leaned in, bracing his hands on either side of her against the car, his eyes locking onto hers with unwavering intensity.

"Before I answer yours," he said, his voice low and steady, "I'd like to take the liberty of asking my seventh question first."

Janvi swallowed, her gaze fixed on him, the proximity making her heart pound.

"In all this time that you've known me," he continued, his eyes searching hers, "from what I told you on our wedding night, from learning about me from a distance over the past two and a half years, and up close in these past few weeks… from everything I've said to you today—do I strike you as a man who makes empty promises?"

She stared at him, her lips parting slightly, caught in the weight of his words. The truth shimmered between them, undeniable and raw. After a long pause, she shook her head.

"No," she whispered, her voice soft but certain. *No. A resounding no.*

Karan exhaled, something in his chest loosening just a little, but his gaze never wavered. "Then here's the honest answer to yours."

He stepped back slightly, his voice firm yet laced with an unfamiliar vulnerability. "What makes me think we'd last? I don't know, Janvi." He paused, his expression unguarded. "All relationships are a gamble. We go into them putting our hearts on the line."

His voice dropped lower, rough around the edges. "And here I am, putting mine in your hands."

Janvi blinked, emotions flickering across her face too quickly to grasp.

"If you've learned anything about me at all," Karan continued, "it should be that I will not be the one to back out. So, essentially... I'm giving you the power to ruin me."

He took a breath, his eyes dark and unwavering. "So do with it what you will. I am at your mercy."

21

INTO THE MIRROR

They continued in silence for most of the way until they neared Jodhpur, where the roads grew more constricted and busier.

"You don't want to interrogate me any further, Janvi?" Karan spoke first, a rueful smile tugging at his lips.

Janvi folded her arms and looked out of the window. "Not now. I'm hungry."

Karan glanced at her, amusement flickering in his eyes. A soft laugh escaped him before he could stop it. He wasn't sure what was funnier—the fact that she had indirectly admitted to interrogating him earlier, or that she was merely postponing it because hunger took precedence.

After a quick stop for breakfast—Janvi indulging in crisp, golden samosas while Karan sipped on chai—they made their way to Mehrangar Fort.

Arriving at the base, Mehrangarh greeted them, tall and resolute against the morning sky. Karan walked over to pay the 200-rupee entry fee and the ten-rupee parking fee to the attendant. As he waited, his gaze inevitably found Janvi, watching as she stood in quiet awe of the imposing fort.

She opened the back door and reached for her white cotton bag, which held her trusted notebook and a bottle of water. The soft rustle of fabric drew his attention, and for a moment, he allowed himself to simply take her in. The sky-blue Georgette Anarkali swayed with every graceful movement, the flowing layers cascading effortlessly around her as if the wind itself were conspiring to make her look otherworldly. The intricate mirror embroidery along the square neckline shimmered under the sun, drawing his eyes with a magnetic pull. The delicate detailing framed her features in a way that left just enough to the imagination, and yet, it was too much for him to ignore.

His gaze trailed down to her long, sheer sleeves that revealed tantalizing glimpses of her slender wrists—elegant and poised, like the woman herself. The way she carried herself, with a quiet confidence that demanded no attention yet effortlessly commanded it, only added to the allure that had been driving him to the brink of distraction all morning.

He watched with a half-smile as she reached up to undo her straight hair, letting it fall over her shoulders, before adjusting her bindi in the car's side mirror. The small, everyday action somehow felt intimate, drawing him deeper into a dangerous spiral of longing. For a fleeting moment, his imagination ran wild—his fingers itching to pull her back into the car, to slide that diaphanous dupatta off her shoulders, to press his lips against the warm curve of her neck and trace a path down to where the fabric met her skin.

The thought hit him hard, raw and undeniable, making his breath hitch. He clenched his jaw, shutting his eyes tightly as if willing the temptation away. *God, give me patience.*

Brushing the thought away, he grabbed the tickets and walked towards the car, locking it.

* * *

Deciding against hiring a tour guide despite the many offers from persistent locals, Karan and Janvi walked into Mehrangarh Fort, the towering walls whispering tales of its rich history with every step. Since the fort had just opened, there weren't too many visitors yet, allowing them to ease their way through the winding corridors and expansive courtyards. Karan had expected Janvi to be curious, but he hadn't anticipated just how much she already knew.

With every turn of a corridor, every intricate carving they passed, she would mention a detail—a story about the Marwar

Kings, the fort's strategic placement, or the significance of a particular architectural feature. She carried herself with a stoic reverence, her love for history shining through in ways that intrigued him.

Every now and then, she would pause to jot something down in her notebook. Karan, familiar with the sight, was still amused when she held it up proudly. "I'm using a brand new one especially for today," she declared with a smile. "The one you gave me."

He raised an eyebrow, smirking. "I see it's already well broken into."

Janvi shrugged playfully and continued her exploration, stopping at various points to run her fingers along the walls, examining their textures with deep fascination. Then, to Karan's surprise, she did something he hadn't seen before—pressing a page of her notebook against the rough surface of an intricately carved pillar and gently shading over it with a pencil. He watched silently, intrigued by the focused expression on her face. Though curiosity burned in him, he chose not to ask. Instead, he stored away this newfound quirk of hers, another layer to the enigma that was Janvi.

The palaces fascinated her the most—Moti Mahal, Phool Mahal, and especially Sheesh Mahal. Karan had caught her twirling in the centre of the mirrored hall when she thought he wasn't watching. The delicate embroidery on her Anarkali dress reflected off the mirrors, scattering shimmering patterns around the room. He had been transfixed by the sight—by her. In that moment, surrounded by the fort's timeless beauty, she seemed almost ethereal.

As they wandered deeper into the fort, Karan found himself lingering in a grand hall, admiring the fading murals and ornate arches. When he glanced back, he saw Janvi had drifted towards a balcony.

There she stood, gazing down at the sprawling blue city below. A gentle smile played on her lips as the wind toyed with her hair, lifting loose strands across her face. She closed her eyes for a moment, letting the breeze wash over her, a picture of serenity and pure joy.

Karan felt something stir inside him—an ache, a longing,

an appreciation so deep it almost hurt. She looked breathtaking, effortlessly so, and he wondered how she could appear so lost in the moment while he struggled with every one of his.

Then he noticed them.

A group of teenage boys huddled in a corner, their phones angled subtly in Janvi's direction. A slow, simmering irritation built within him. Without thinking twice, he walked over and stood beside her, his broad frame blocking their view.

Janvi, oblivious to the situation, looked up at him with a bright smile, the wind playing in her hair. "Ready for question eight?" she asked, mischief dancing in her eyes.

Karan, no longer watching the boys, found himself drawn solely to her. "Go on," he said, his voice softer now, grounding himself in her presence.

"If you could live in any era of royalty, which one would you choose and why?"

It was then that he noticed it. Her hand resting lightly on his chest. Whether she realized it or not, the touch sent a quiet thrill through him, a sign of growing comfort he hadn't expected but welcomed.

He smirked, his gaze holding hers. "The Mughal era. Grand palaces, rich traditions... and kings who always got what they wanted."

Janvi rolled her eyes but didn't move her hand. "Of course. You'd pick the era of indulgence."

Karan chuckled. "What can I say? I like the finer things." His voice dipped slightly. "And the Mughals were known for their grand romances, weren't they?"

Janvi laughed, shaking her head. "You just want an excuse to build me a palace."

His smirk widened. "Would you let me?"

Her fingers curled slightly against his chest before she quickly withdrew her hand, as if realizing what she'd done. "You still have twelve more questions before I answer that," she said, turning away to continue walking.

Karan watched her for a moment before speaking again. "What about you? Which era would you choose?"

Janvi glanced at him over her shoulder, arching a brow. "Is that your next question?"

He shrugged, grinning. "Sure."

She tilted her head thoughtfully, then with a mischievous glint in her eyes, replied, "Rajput, of course. I'd defend my kingdom with valour against the conniving Mughals."

Karan chuckled, his eyes twinkling with amusement. "In that case, your highness," he said with a bow, "I'll be the Akbar to your Jodha."

Janvi's laughter echoed through the fort, light and genuine taking Karan's breath away.

As they explored further into the fort, they came across a section where an older man stood at the centre of a group of students, gesturing animatedly as he spoke about the intricate restoration work. His voice carried a quiet authority, and Karan could see the students listening intently, scribbling notes.

Janvi suddenly stopped beside Karan, her gaze fixed on the man with a flicker of recognition in her eyes. Without a word, she stepped away, leaving Karan standing there, watching in mild confusion.

He observed as she approached the man tentatively, speaking softly. The man paused mid-sentence, his expression shifting before a wide smile of recognition spread across his face.

They exchanged a few words, and Karan noted the warmth in their interaction, the ease with which they spoke. A moment later, Janvi turned back, her eyes searching for him. When she found him watching, she gestured for him to come over, her lips curving into a small smile.

Karan sighed, shoving his hands into his pockets as he made his way to them, curiosity burning within him.

"Professor, this is..." Janvi turned to look at him, a flicker of hesitation in her eyes before a small smile softened her expression. "My husband."

Karan felt an odd warmth at the way she said it—gentle, almost careful, yet not without a sense of quiet pride. The professor's eyes shifted to him, assessing, before he extended a hand with a warm smile.

"This is Professor Arvind Tyagi," she introduced him. "He works in the Conservation and Restoration department of the Mehrangarh Museum Trust."

"Mr. Karan Singh Rathore, your reputation precedes you. It's a pleasure to finally meet you in person," the older man said, offering Karan a firm handshake. "I've read all about your company, inSense."

"Thank-you," Karan replied gratefully, glancing at Janvi with a silent plea for help.

Janvi stepped in quickly to explain. "It was Professor Tyagi who helped me with restoring the old artifacts in the storeroom at Rathore Haveli for the museum," she said. "I reached out to him via email. He used to work closely with the former director of the Mehrangarh Museum Trust, who was very passionate about museums. Naturally, when I explained what I was trying to do, he was more than willing to help."

Karan blinked, absorbing the new information. "Wow," he said, genuinely impressed. "That's... incredible. I didn't realize how much effort went into all of this. I mean, I had a rough idea, but I had no idea how intricate it all was."

"Yes," Professor Tyagi nodded with a chuckle. "It's meticulous process. Needless to say, I was pleasantly surprised at such genuine interest and dedication to preservation. It's refreshing, to say the least."

Professor Tyagi suddenly grew quiet, as if a thought had occurred to him. "Say, Janvi, the Trust has some internship programs for scholars across India and overseas in conservation. Of course, they are typically open only to students with formal training, but seeing your portfolio of work, I'd be more than willing to put in a good word on your behalf. If you're interested, of course."

Karan glanced at Janvi, catching the slight widening of her eyes at the unexpected offer. His gaze softened, a newfound respect stirring within him. He had known by now she was passionate about history, but seeing her in her element—confident, knowledgeable, and held in such high regard—made him realize just how much more there was to her.

Janvi smiled, her fingers tightening around the strap of her bag as she looked between Karan and the professor. "That's... an incredible opportunity," she said, her voice measured but tinged with excitement. "But I'd like to think about it."

Karan looked at her, puzzled, but decided to remain silent.

"Oh, of course, take all the time you need. And I'm always here to help," Professor Tyagi added reassuringly.

"Thank-you so much, Professor. It was such a pleasure meeting you in person," Janvi said gratefully.

Janvi turned to Karan, who was watching her with a strange expression, his gaze lingering on her longer than usual.

"What?" she asked softly, a hint of shyness creeping into her voice.

Karan shook his head, a small smile playing on his lips. "Nothing," he said, his tone lighter. Looking at his watch, he asked "Shall we have lunch now and then slowly make our way back to the camp?"

Janvi nodded.

* * *

"There's a kachori shop right there. It doesn't look too busy," Janvi suggested, eyeing the bustling street vendors as they passed by.

Karan, however, didn't even slow down.

"Mirchi vadas?" she tried again, hopeful.

Karan's lips curled into a smirk, his gaze steady on the road. "Janvi, while I admire your simplicity, just for today, I had something... different in mind."

Janvi's brows furrowed. "Different how?"

"Something less... pedestrian," he added, throwing her a quick glance, the smirk still lingering.

Janvi narrowed her eyes. "Is it far?"

Karan chuckled. "Do you have a train to catch?" he teased. "Relax. It's just ten minutes down this road."

When they arrived, Janvi found herself stepping through a grand arched entrance into a quiet oasis hidden within the heart of the bustling old city. The noise of the streets faded into a soft hum of cascading water and the cool, fragrant air of the lush garden inside.

Her eyes widened slightly as she took in the scene—high walls wrapped in creeping vines, a shaded courtyard with sunlight filtering through palm trees, and a series of delicate fountains adding a tranquil rhythm to the atmosphere. It was beautiful. Serene.

A waiter greeted them with a polite smile. "Mr. and Mrs. Rathore, welcome to Raas."

Karan thanked him, his voice smooth yet appreciative. "Thanks for accommodating us on such short notice."

"Of course, sir. It was not a problem. Please follow me," the waiter replied, leading them through the garden toward a secluded dining area set up for two.

Karan's hand rested gently at Janvi's waist, a barely-there touch that sent a ripple of awareness through her. He pulled out the chair for her, waiting for her to settle before taking the seat opposite.

"Any drinks, sir?" the waiter inquired.

Karan glanced at the menu briefly, then looked up. "I'll have a glass of your house Merlot, please." He turned to Janvi. "Janvi?"

Her eyes widened slightly before she shook her head. *"Paani,"* she said softly.

The waiter offered a polite nod before stepping away, leaving them alone in the quiet intimacy of the shaded alcove.

Janvi's gaze drifted around the serene space, the sound of trickling water filling the air. She turned to Karan, her voice low. "What's all this?"

"A date," Karan said, as if it were the most obvious thing in the world. "A proper one. We deserve one, don't you think?" His eyes held hers for a beat. "At least, I know you do."

Janvi swallowed, feeling a lump form in her throat. He was making her swoon, and she was falling for it.

Shortly after, a server appeared with their drinks, the deep crimson of Karan's wine glistening under the dappled sunlight. Janvi watched as he took the glass with an effortless ease, swirling it gently before taking a sip. There was something unnerving about how composed he looked, and for a moment, she wondered if she was out of place.

Karan noticed her gaze lingering on the wine glass and smirked. "You sure you don't want to try it?" he asked, his tone teasing yet gentle.

Janvi shook her head again, reaching for her water instead.

Glancing down at the elegantly set table, her fingers traced the edge of the napkin. "I wouldn't know what to order in a place like this," she admitted quietly, her voice carrying a rare hint of uncertainty.

Karan leaned back, watching her with an easy smile. "Don't worry about it. I've arranged for their set menu."

She looked up at him, a small crease forming between her brows. "Set menu?"

He nodded, placing his glass on the table. "So that the disturbances would be... minimal," he added, his voice laced with something she couldn't quite place—part amusement, part intent.

Janvi's lips parted slightly, the meaning behind his words sinking in.

"You ready to continue our game? It's your turn," Karan said, his voice smooth but laced with something deeper.

Taking a deep breath, Janvi considered her next question before finally asking, "Okay, question nine. When did you change your mind about our marriage?"

There was an intensity in Karan's eyes as he looked into hers, unflinching. If he was surprised at the question, he didn't show it. His gaze held hers, steady and unwavering. "It was a gradual realization," he said, his voice low, deliberate. "At first, it was purely physical attraction—though that shouldn't come as a surprise to you now."

His lips quirked slightly, but it didn't quite reach his eyes. "But soon, it became more than that. A deep-seated respect and admiration for you. The way you took care of everything... with a maturity far beyond your years. And without resentment for what I did."

He paused for a beat, his gaze never leaving hers. "You broke through all my pre-conceived notions—about you, and about what marriage should be."

Giving her a moment to absorb his words, he eventually leaned in slightly, his voice almost a whisper. "Does that answer your question?"

Janvi nodded, her fingers tightening around her glass, the weight of his gaze making it hard to breathe.

"Good," he said, a slow smile tugging at his lips, the kind that sent a shiver down her spine. He leaned back slightly, his eyes never leaving hers. "My turn."

He let the moment stretch just enough before asking, "Why did you agree to marry me?"

Janvi was momentarily startled. Then with a sad smile she asked, "Is this payback for my behaviour in the morning?"

"One good turn deserves another," Karan said raising an eyebrow, his tone teasing. Then after a while he added softly, "No, its not, but I'm genuinely curious. I do have a deep-seated regret that I never bothered talking to you at the time. Never sought to understand you."

Janvi nodded then inhaled sharply, her fingers tightening around her glass. "I—A lot of it is a blur. When Viren uncle got sick, Bakshi Uncle let Aman and me stay at his place," she began, her voice growing quieter. "Aman was… scared. So was I. We'd only lost Papa two years before, and in many ways, Viren uncle had taken on that role. Papa's posting was in Assam at the time. That day... I... Aman—"

Her voice faltered, and she closed her eyes tightly, unable to continue.

Karan was out of his chair in an instant, kneeling before her. His hands found hers, his touch firm yet gentle. Regret flickered in his eyes, realizing too late that perhaps the answer wasn't as simple as he had thought.

"Hey," he whispered.

Out of the corner of his eye, he saw the waiter approaching. With a subtle gesture, he signalled for privacy, and they retreated discreetly.

Janvi's shoulders trembled. "I—" she cried.

"Shh... Janvi, you don't have to answer," he whispered, his voice low and soothing.

In a swift but gentle motion, he stood, lifting her effortlessly from her chair. She gasped softly, but didn't resist as he sat down in her seat, settling her into his lap, cradling her against his chest, his arms encircling her protectively. She collapsed into him, her fingers gripping his shirt tightly as sobs wracked her body. He stroked her hair gently, his heart aching at her pain.

"Aman was the one who found Papa," she whispered brokenly. "I was still in school. The neighbours took him to the hospital, but it was too late. I never got to say goodbye."

Karan's grip tightened protectively around her, feeling the dampness of her tears seeping through his shirt. But he didn't stop her. He knew she needed this—needed to let go of the burden she had been carrying for too long.

"I held on to Aman at the hospital. I didn't know what to do. They kept asking me questions, and I couldn't answer. Somehow, I remembered Bakshi Chacha and Viren uncle's phone numbers in my notebook. I called Bakshi Chacha first—he didn't answer. Then I called Viren uncle. He answered immediately."

She exhaled shakily, drawing strength from Karan's steady heartbeat beneath her ear. "The next day, they were both in Assam. After Papa's cremation, they used their army and government contacts and Bakshi Uncle's legal aid to draw up custody documents for Aman and me. They brought us with them to Jaisalmer."

Karan remained silent, holding her close, letting her continue.

"Viren uncle and Bakshi Chacha took care of us like fathers. Everyone was so loving. Laxmi Tai, Daadi... even Badri Kaka." Her voice cracked with emotion. "When Viren uncle got sick, Aman and I were distraught. It was like losing Papa all over again. But I had to stay strong for Aman. When Viren uncle asked me to marry you, I didn't know what to say. Daadi sa, Bakshi Chacha... they all encouraged me. Assured me you were a decent person."

She paused, taking a shaky breath. "I wanted to repay Viren uncle for everything he had done for us. And I had to think about Aman. I thought it would bring him stability. So, I said yes."

Finally, she looked up at him, her eyes swollen with grief. "If I had known you loved someone else, I'd never have agreed."

Karan pressed her back into his chest, his voice thick with emotion. "Shh... don't. None of this is on you. None of it."

He held her like that, his arms wrapped around her, absorbing every tremor of her pain until the sobs finally subsided.

Janvi stirred slightly, pushing back nervously but not attempting to get off his lap.

Karan watched her for a moment before picking up her glass of water and pressing it to her lips. "Here," he murmured.

She took a sip, her eyes drifting to his glass of wine. Karan caught it instantly. "You sure you don't want to trade this for something stronger?" he asked, smirking.

Janvi nearly choked on the water, coughing as a laugh escaped her. She punched his chest lightly in annoyance.

He chuckled, his grip firm but comforting. "Just saying."

Janvi shook her head, wiping her mouth, and Karan leaned in slightly. "Should we finish our lunch and leave?"

She nodded.

* * *

Despite their earlier tender moment at the restaurant, the ride back to the camp was comfortable. The bright afternoon sun cast dappled shadows through the trees lining the road, and the hum of the car engine blended with the occasional chirping of birds outside. Karan kept his focus on the road, but his occasional glance at Janvi betrayed his thoughts.

He no longer wanted to continue their game of twenty questions, but Janvi was having none of it.

"Question 10," she said, her tone both teasing and curious. "Do you drink a lot?"

Karan's lips pressed together for a moment before he answered. "I drink socially," he said finally. "And… sometimes, I need it to deal with difficult things—emotions."

His answer hung in the air, and Janvi nodded thoughtfully, sensing there was more beneath the surface but choosing not to press further. She wanted to keep things light, to bring back some of the ease between them.

Karan glanced at her briefly, a small sigh escaping him. "I don't have any questions for you, Janvi. You can ask me whatever you want. It's fine."

"No," she replied, raising an eyebrow at him. "Where's the fun in that? Besides, aren't you a man of your word? You started this game—you should play till the end."

He groaned softly, a reluctant smile tugging at his lips despite himself. "Fine," he relented. "Let me think."

The quiet stretched for a moment before he finally spoke, his voice quieter than before. "Do you… regret marrying me?"

Janvi blinked, the unexpected question giving her pause. A soft smile played on her lips as she thought about her answer. "No, I don't," she said, her tone steady. "Regardless of whatever's happened between us, the last two and a half years have been a blessing for me. I had a family again, Aman was well looked after, and I learned so many things. The work I do around the estate—I enjoy it. Restoring artifacts, digging into your family's history—it's fulfilling. And didn't I say I love living in Rajasthan?"

Karan considered her words in silence, his expression unreadable.

"Okay," Janvi said, shifting slightly in her seat to face him. "Question 11, do *you* regret marrying me?"

Karan shook his head, his voice barely above a whisper when he answered, "No."

He paused for a moment, his gaze flicking toward her before returning to the road. "But I regret leaving you."

Janvi's breath caught as he briefly turned his attention to her, the intensity in his eyes making her heart skip a beat.

"Your turn," she said quickly, trying to steady herself.

Karan furrowed his brows, thinking back to her earlier response. "Why book-keeping?"

"What?" Janvi asked, startled by the sudden shift.

"You clearly have a passion for restoration and conservation," he said, glancing at her briefly. "Why not pursue that? Why book-keeping?"

Janvi sighed softly, her hands fidgeting with the edge of her dupatta. "It's… practical," she admitted. "I'd be able to get a job quickly to support Aman and m—"

"Stop," Karan interrupted firmly, his tone gentle but resolute.

She looked at him, surprised, as he continued. "Janvi, haven't I told you that I'll be there for you no matter what? Take whatever financial help you need, but please—follow your passions. Do what makes you happy. Go to university, get the right degree, and chase the opportunities you deserve. After everything you've done for me and my family, I think I owe you that much at least."

Janvi swallowed, unsure how to respond.

Karan's voice softened, his sincerity unmistakable. "If not for yourself, then do it for Aman. Wouldn't you rather Aman see his sister thrive and be encouraged to follow his own dreams?"

His words lingered in the air, and Janvi found herself looking out the window, trying to process the sudden lump in her throat. She didn't speak right away, but despite her quietness, he knew his words had struck a chord.

Karan shifted in his seat, glancing at Janvi briefly before focusing back on the road. With a smile he asked, "No more questions?"

Janvi looked back with a smile.

"Question 12, if you weren't running inSense, what would you be doing?"

Karan chuckled softly, his fingers tapping against the steering wheel as he thought. "If I weren't running inSense... maybe product designing or consulting for other companies. Something still rooted in tech—creating, solving problems. That's my thing."

Janvi nodded, her curiosity growing. "What about something completely different?"

He glanced at her, his lips twitching with amusement. "Why don't you tell me what you think I should be doing?"

She tilted her head, her eyes narrowing thoughtfully before a mischievous grin spread across her face. "Acting," she said with mock seriousness.

Karan raised a brow, the corners of his mouth tugging into a smirk. "Acting?"

"Yeah," she replied, a playful lilt in her voice. "You're handsome enough for it, and you've got this broody, mysterious thing going on. People would eat that up."

He burst into laughter, the sound warm and genuine. "Handsome, huh? Is that why you've been staring at me all week?"

Janvi's cheeks flushed, but she quickly recovered, giving him a mock glare. "Don't get ahead of yourself. I just think you'd be good at it—convincing people to believe in something you're not."

Karan shook his head, still grinning. "Well, thank-you for the career advice, I'll keep that in mind."

"You're welcome," she said breezily, folding her arms with a self-satisfied smile.

Karan's laughter faded into a soft chuckle as he glanced at her again, his expression unreadable. "My turn. Is there something that you want to do that you haven't been able to?"

After a quick thought she said, "I want to learn how to drive."

Karan looked at her softly, "I think that's something we can easily fix. I'll be more than happy to teach you."

"Can I start now?" she asked.

"No, not in this car. I don't even know if the airbags on this thing work." Karan added with disdain. Glancing at her with a smile he added, "We'll make sure you learn properly—and safely."

"Fair enough," Janvi nodded. "Question 13, why don't you like Himanshu?"

Karan looked at her curiously, "What makes you think I don't like him?"

"Oh I—," Janvi hesitated, "I thought… I just felt some tension in you each time I brought him up… that's all."

Karan nodded, "You're not entirely off the mark. He was very different growing up, more nosy, flirty, arrogant and I suppose… had this way of inserting himself into things that didn't concern him. He loved stirring the pot, and I've never been the most patient person when it comes to that. I didn't consider that people do change for the better too sometimes. And now I feel he has grown quite a lot since we last met."

"My turn," Karan said, glancing at her. "From what I've seen so far, you're pretty tolerant of people. But is there something you absolutely can't stand in a person?"

Janvi's expression softened, her gaze turning distant for a moment. "I can't stand unnecessary cruelty," she said quietly, her voice tinged with sadness. "Like when parents yell at their children over something trivial, or when people hurt animals just because they can. It doesn't take much to be kind, does it? People forget how short life is. Everyone deserves the chance to live a little… love a little."

Karan glanced at her, momentarily caught off guard by her sweetness. "You make it sound so simple," he said softly.

"Isn't it?" she asked, tilting her head.

He looked back at the road, a faint smile on his lips. "Maybe it is. Not everyone sees it that way, though."

As the silence settled, Karan found himself glancing at her again, the thought unbidden but persistent—he wished this sweet, kind girl could be his forever.

"Okay, question 14," Janvi said, her voice steady but soft. She paused, taking a deep breath before continuing. "If I choose to stay... in this marriage, would we move to New York?"

Karan's hands tightened on the steering wheel as her words hung in the air. Hope stirred within him, sharp and unexpected. He allowed himself to picture it—coming home after a long day at the office to find her waiting in their apartment. In his mind's eye, he saw her moving around the space, her presence lighting up the sterile, impersonal world he had built for himself in the city.

He imagined wrapping his arms around her, burying his face in her hair, the noise of the concrete jungle fading into nothing. The thought of her being his oasis in a place that had always felt cold and unyielding made his chest ache with longing.

But as quickly as the vision formed, Karan pushed it aside. He couldn't let himself get carried away. This wasn't about what he wanted—it was about what she needed.

He glanced at her, his voice steady but warm. "Not unless you wanted to," he said firmly. "Janvi, I'd love to be with you wherever you are. If New York is where you want to be, we'd make it work. But if you're happy here, in Rajasthan, then that's where I'll stay too."

He hesitated for a moment, then added softly, "It's not about where we live. It's about being with you."

Janvi blinked, caught off guard by the depth of his answer. She turned her gaze to the window, her thoughts swirling as her heart thudded heavily in her chest.

Karan kept his eyes on the road, but his mind lingered on the fleeting vision of what could be, knowing that wherever she chose, he would follow.

"Your turn," Janvi quietly reminder him.

"Where in India have you lived with your dad?" Karan asks.

"Ugh... so many places. Mussoorie obviously, then the first teaching posting he had after the accident was in Jabalpur," she continued. "Then MHOW, Ambala, Jaipur, Udhampur, Secunderabad, Shillong... and finally, Tezpur in Assam."

Karan glanced at her, a small crease forming between his brows. "What's MHOW?"

Janvi smiled faintly, as if she had expected the question. "Military Headquarters of War. It's an Army training centre in Madhya Pradesh." She cast him a sidelong look, amusement flickering in her eyes. "For someone whose father was a Brigadier General, you're surprisingly unversed in Army life."

Karan huffed a quiet laugh, shaking his head. "I know enough. I just didn't commit every base name to memory."

"Mm-hmm," Janvi murmured, unconvinced. "I bet you don't even know where the Armoured Corps is based."

Karan smirked, sensing a challenge. "Ahmednagar."

Janvi raised a brow, impressed but refusing to show it. "Lucky guess."

He shot her a look. "I'm not completely ignorant, Janvi. I just… chose a different battlefield."

Janvi considered that response before asking her next question.

"Fifteen. Did you really not see eye to eye with Viren uncle?" she asked cautiously.

Karan's jaw tightened at the question. He thought hard about it.

"I suppose it doesn't matter anymore," he said finally, his voice quieter than before. "I don't really want to talk ill of the dead. He did his best."

Janvi nodded, her expression soft, understanding that this was all he was willing to say.

But just as she was about to move on, Karan swallowed and spoke again.

"…I do, however, want to add something." His voice was lower this time, almost contemplative. "In his passing, he did right by me." He paused, choosing his words carefully. "I was too blind to see it at the time, but I see it clearly now."

He glanced at her briefly before returning his eyes to the road.

"He couldn't have given me a better gift in life than you."

Janvi stilled.

The air inside the car shifted, something unspoken settling between them. She blinked, unsure of how to respond, warmth creeping up her throat.

"I'm going to ask you a follow up question as my fifteenth. Did you really stay in Udhampur with your dad? When was this?"

She turned to him, noting the curiosity laced in his voice. "I did," she said. "It was 2015. I was eleven."

Karan frowned slightly. "That was when the Udhampur attack happened, wasn't it? The one on the BSF convoy?"

She nodded. "A few months after we moved. Security tightened overnight. Papa wasn't home that night—he was at the base, caught up in military briefings. The lockdown happened so fast, and I was alone with Aman."

Karan's hands flexed over the wheel. "Alone? With a baby?"

"He was three," Janvi murmured. "I had to turn off all the lights, lock the doors, and keep him from crying. He didn't understand why we had to be quiet, why I wouldn't let him look out the window. He kept asking for Papa. I told him it was a game, that we had to stay hidden to win."

Karan exhaled sharply, his jaw tight. "And you weren't scared?"

"I was," she admitted. "But Aman was more scared. I couldn't let him see it."

A beat of silence. Then, softly, "That explains a lot."

Janvi turned to him. "What do you mean?"

His gaze remained steady on the road. "You don't break, no matter how hard things get. You stand your ground. That kind of strength... it can't be taught. It comes from experience."

"It doesn't mean I don't get scared. I do get scared. I also need help sometimes," she added.

"And yet you refuse to take it," Karan commented.

"Is this about the stalker?" Janvi asked.

"It just slipped out. Sorry, I didn't mean anything by it. Forget about it." Karan quickly added.

Janvi shook her head. "No, no, you're right." Her voice was

quieter now, thoughtful. "I should have done the responsible thing by allowing at least Daadi Sa or Bakshi Uncle to tell you. They really wanted to but I was just too proud, I made them promise to keep you out of it. Not out of resentment, I just thought, I was already so much trouble in your life. But the night of Janmashtami, when I realised it was you. I was so relieved."

Karan glanced at her, something unreadable flickering in his gaze before he looked back at the road. A long pause stretched between them, the quiet hum of the car the only sound filling the space.

Finally, he spoke, his voice lower, thoughtful. "I'm glad I came back that night."

Janvi inhaled softly, her fingers playing with the edge of her dupatta. "Me too."

Another silence settled between them, but this one felt different—less weighted, less burdened. There was no need for more words, not right now. Some things had already been understood.

The desert stretched ahead, golden and endless, as they drove forward, the road unravelling before them.

22

PICTURE PERFECT

Arriving back at the camp in the late afternoon, the familiar golden glow of the lanterns lining the pathways flickered against the deepening evening sky. When they walked back to the common area of the camp near the bar and pool, a familiar voice rang out.

"There you two are!"

Meghna practically bounced toward them, her eyes shining with excitement. She was already dressed for the evening in a breezy, embroidered kurta, her enthusiasm as infectious as ever. "How was your day? And—oh my god—was Mehrangarh as amazing as I remember?"

Janvi smiled, stepping into the shadow of the poolside bar. "It was incredible," she admitted. "I could spend an entire week there and still not get enough."

"I can imagine," Meghna said, then turned to Karan. "And you? Did you actually enjoy something for once, or did you just tolerate it?"

"It was fine," Karan said impatiently, "now can I please get a drink?"

"Okay, okay, but first—before we all settle in—I have a surprise!"

Janvi and Karan exchanged a look.

"You're scaring me," Karan muttered.

Meghna ignored him and turned to Janvi instead. "I hired a freelance photographer for some couple portraits! I thought it would be the perfect way to remember this trip."

Janvi's brows lifted in surprise, but before she could respond, Meghna kept going. "And guess what? I found these gorgeous traditional Rajasthani lehengas from the locals! I got one for myself, of course, but I found one for you too, Janvi!" She beamed. "It's stunning—you're going to love it."

Janvi blinked, caught off guard, but then smiled. "Oh?"

"Yes! Come, I'll show you," Meghna said, already grabbing her hand. "You have to change into it for the shoot—it'll be perfect."

Without much choice, Janvi let herself be dragged away toward the tents, a quiet decision already resting in her mind.

Karan watched them go, shaking his head before turning toward the bar.

Himanshu was already there, leaning against the counter with a glass in his hand. "Well," he drawled, smirking as Karan approached, "looks like you're about to have a very interesting evening."

Karan exhaled, "Why do I feel like I should be concerned?"

Himanshu chuckled, taking a slow sip of his drink. "You should be."

⁂

Janvi smoothed her hands over the lehenga, feeling the rich fabric settle around her. The deep reds and intricate embroidery were beautiful. She glanced at her reflection, adjusting the dupatta draped over her shoulder.

As she turned toward the entrance, ready to step out, she paused remembering something.

Her gaze drifted toward her bag beside the bed.

The gift.

Her fingers hovered before she reached for it, it was simple, but the meaning behind it anything but. She had almost forgotten about it, but now, with everything that had happened today, it suddenly felt… important.

She tucked it into her emptied out cotton bag

⁂

Karan swirled the amber liquid in his glass, the ice clinking softly as he leaned back against the bar. The late afternoon breeze barely registered, nor did the distant hum of folk music playing near the bonfire. Across from him, Himanshu was watching the musicians set up, while Meghna arrived with a triumphant look on her face.

"The lehenga looks even better on her than I imagined," she said smugly, taking a sip of her drink.

Karan barely processed the words. He had been about to ask about Himanshu—casually, just to move the conversation along—when something made him stop.

Or rather, someone.

Janvi stepped into his eyeline, and everything else ceased to exist.

The firelight from the camp cast a warm glow across her skin, highlighting the deep reds and intricate embroidery of her lehenga. The fabric shimmered subtly with every movement, wrapping around her just right, cinching at the waist, flowing down in soft waves.

Karan's grip on his glass tightened.

Her hair was different—not pinned up, not the casual waves he was used to. Tonight, it was styled in a way that did something to him, sleek and pulled back just enough to let her earrings catch the light. The bold silver jewellery, the delicate bangles on her wrists—everything about her was effortless, regal, breathtaking.

And then there was the way she carried herself.

She didn't hesitate. She didn't fidget, didn't adjust her dupatta like she felt out of place. She walked like she owned it. Like she had always belonged in it.

And damn if that didn't do something to him.

Heat curled low in his stomach, creeping up his chest, slow and insidious. His gaze flickered lower before he could stop it—to the dip of her neckline, the bare curve of her waist.

Fuck.

He dragged in a slow breath, lifting his drink to his lips, but the whiskey did nothing to cool the heat pressing against his skin.

Seconds passed. Maybe minutes. He barely noticed Meghna smirking at him over the rim of her drink.

Beside him, Himanshu nudged him lightly. "You okay, man?"

Karan blinked once, forced himself to take another sip of whiskey.

Cool liquid. Hot skin. Useless.

He set the glass down, flexing his fingers around the rim. "Yeah. Why wouldn't I be?"

Meghna snorted. "Oh, no reason at all."

Karan wasn't listening.

Because Janvi had just looked up.

And her eyes had locked onto his.

And then... she smiled.

Not a playful smirk, not a teasing glance—just a soft, knowing curve of her lips, like she had caught him staring and wasn't the least bit bothered by it.

Karan exhaled slowly, his grip tightening around the glass. This was dangerous.

She wasn't doing anything out of the ordinary. She wasn't trying to get a reaction out of him. And yet, she had him on edge.

His pulse drummed low in his throat, the space between them suddenly feeling too vast, too charged. The sinking sun bathed everything in warm gold, casting long shadows over the sand, the breeze lifting the edge of her dupatta just slightly.

For a split second, Karan wondered if she knew what she was doing to him.

Probably not.

That only made it worse.

Because he hadn't been expecting this. He hadn't thought tonight would be any different than the others.

But suddenly, it was.

And now, as they prepared to leave for the dunes, he wasn't sure he trusted himself anymore.

The sand stretched out ahead of them, golden in the fading sunlight, rippling in soft waves beneath their feet as they made their way toward the dunes. The air was cooler now, touched by the crisp evening breeze, carrying the distant sound of music from the camp.

Karan walked a few paces behind Janvi, his hands in his pockets, his jaw tight. He needed to focus on something else. Anything else.

But his gaze kept betraying him.

The way her lehenga skimmed the sand with every step, the way the last rays of sunlight made the silver embroidery glimmer, the way she moved—effortless, completely unaware of the fire she had ignited in his chest.

Ahead, Meghna chatted excitedly with the photographer, pointing toward the highest dune where the sunset would be the most dramatic. Himanshu, ever the supportive husband, nodded along as he carried their things.

Karan exhaled slowly, forcing his gaze to the horizon. This was just a photoshoot. Nothing more.

Then Janvi glanced over her shoulder—directly at him.

For a moment, nothing else existed.

The sun behind her cast a golden halo around her silhouette, the wind catching the edge of her dupatta, sending it fluttering slightly. Her eyes met his, warm and unreadable, as if she knew something he didn't.

Karan's fingers twitched. This was going to be a long evening.

The sun dipped lower, turning the sky into a breathtaking blend of burnt orange and dusky pink. Meghna and Himanshu stood a few feet away, posing as the photographer gave directions, their laughter light and effortless against the evening air.

Karan and Janvi sat a short distance away, the cool sand shifting beneath them. It should have felt comfortable, easy. But it wasn't.

Not when the space between them felt too small and too vast at the same time.

Karan rested his arms on his knees, watching as Meghna nudged

Himanshu's shoulder playfully before leaning into him for the shot. He exhaled slowly, pretending to focus on the photographer's instructions, but his mind was elsewhere.

"So," she began, breaking the silence.

Oh, thank fucking God.

"Question 16, how do I look?"

Karan blinked, turning his head to look at her properly. She was watching him, one brow arched, the barest hint of amusement flickering in her eyes.

His throat felt suddenly dry.

How did she look?

Like a vision he wasn't prepared for. Like a temptation he had no business entertaining. Like she had stepped straight out of a dream designed solely to test his patience.

He cleared his throat, forcing his voice into something resembling neutrality. "You look… fine."

"Fine?" she echoed, unimpressed.

Karan dragged a hand over his face. "You know how you look, Janvi."

She tilted her head confused.

He glanced away, back toward the photographer, willing himself to focus on something else. Anything else.

But then she shifted closer, just slightly, the movement unassuming.

And suddenly, fine wasn't even remotely the word he'd use.

"You're usually so creative with your responses," she said with a pout.

Karan huffed out a quiet laugh, shaking his head as he dragged his fingers through his hair. Of course, she wasn't going to let this go.

He looked at her then, really looked at her. The teasing curve of her lips, the way she sat there with absolute ease, her lehenga draped elegantly around her.

Creative?

Oh, he could get creative.

His jaw flexed. "You want a real answer?"

Janvi shrugged, but there was something expectant in her expression. "Isn't that the point of this game?"

Karan exhaled slowly, rolling his shoulders as he leaned back on his palms.

"You look," he started, choosing his words carefully, "like a rising sun in a land parched for light."

Her smile faltered slightly, something flickering behind her eyes.

Karan wasn't sure if he had said too much.

But for once, he wasn't going to take it back.

"Okay, my turn. What's in the bag?"

Janvi parted her lips to answer, but before she could speak, Meghna's voice rang out.

"Alright, lovebirds, you're up!"

Janvi blinked, glancing toward Meghna and the photographer, who were already adjusting the lighting for the next set of shots.

She turned back to him, a small, unreadable smile playing at her lips. "I'll tell you in a bit."

And just like that, she was up, brushing the sand from her lehenga before making her way toward the dunes.

Karan exhaled, running a hand through his hair before following her.

The photographer positioned them on the dune, adjusting his camera. "Karan, stand behind her. Janvi, look ahead—natural, relaxed."

Karan stepped closer, his breath steady, but his mind anything but. The scent of her, the bare skin at her back, the effortless way she held herself—it was too much and not enough.

Meanwhile, Janvi remained perfectly composed, unfazed, while he fought to keep his hands from shaking.

"Good," the photographer nodded. "Karan, a little closer."

He complied, jaw tight, fingers hovering near her waist.

"Janvi, soften your expression—look at him."

She turned, meeting his gaze.

Karan's breath hitched.

The sunset bathed her in gold, the wind teasing strands of her hair across her cheek. She didn't fidget, didn't break eye contact. If she felt anything, she didn't show it.

Meanwhile, he was unravelling.

"Question 17," she murmured, her voice almost lost in the wind. "If you could live another day of your life again, which one would it be?"

The photographer's camera flashed, but Karan barely registered it. All he saw was her.

Her question echoed in his mind—clear, direct, cutting through everything else.

If he could relive one day…

His answer should have been easy. He could have said something safe, something expected.

But the truth settled deep in his chest, heavier than he was ready for.

Karan swallowed, his voice low, almost lost between them.

"The day I married you."

Janvi's lips parted slightly, her breath catching.

He hadn't once looked at her that day. Hadn't taken in the way she had looked, hadn't held her gaze, hadn't given their wedding the attention it deserved. He had been too caught up in his own choices, too focused on what he thought he wanted.

But if he could do it again…

He would do it properly.

Before either of them could react, the photographer's voice cut through the haze.

"Alright, let's switch it up," he called out, adjusting his camera. "Janvi, turn toward Karan this time. Karan, place your hand on her waist."

Karan exhaled slowly, his pulse steady in theory, chaotic in reality.

Janvi moved first, shifting gracefully as if his words hadn't just shaken something fundamental between them. She turned to face him, her expression unreadable—too composed.

Meanwhile, he was still trying to process what the hell he had just admitted.

Karan's fingers hovered near her waist, breath slow and measured, but beneath the surface, he was anything but composed.

Janvi had moved into position effortlessly, her expression smooth, her movements fluid. But he felt it.

Felt it in the way his fingers flexed before they found the small of her back. In the way his chest tightened as he finally, finally touched her.

"Good," the photographer nodded. "Now, Karan, bend her back—gently."

Karan swallowed, gripping her waist just a little tighter as he slowly tilted her backward.

Her breath hitched this time.

As their eyes locked, something unspoken passing between them, Janvi's voice came softer, more uncertain than before.

"Your turn."

Karan steadied himself, inhaling slowly. She was waiting, expecting his next question as if she hadn't just knocked the breath out of him moments ago.

He could ask something safe. Something easy.

Instead, his voice came low, deliberate.

"If you could change something, what would it be?"

For a moment, she looked like she was thinking deeply, her expression unreadable. Then, just when he thought she might say something real, she smiled—soft, knowing.

"For now, I'd like to change the photographer."

Karan's chuckle ran deep and warm, shaking loose some of the tension curling inside him.

"Perfect!" called out the photographer.

The photographer gestured toward the soft, rippled sand. "Alright, let's go for something natural—comfortable but close."

Karan stilled, glancing at Janvi, but she didn't meet his eyes.

"Sit back, Karan—lean on one arm for support," the photographer instructed. "Janvi, sit between his legs, rest into him."

Janvi hesitated.

It was barely noticeable, but he felt it.

Still, she lowered herself into position, adjusting her lehenga carefully as she settled between his legs. Karan followed, bracing himself on one arm, the warmth of the sand pressing against his palm.

Then she leaned into him.

The shift was subtle, but it changed everything.

Her back met his chest, her weight light against him, but Karan felt every single point of contact. The scent of jasmine curled through the cool desert air, mixing with the faint traces of the bonfire smoke in the distance.

Too much. Not enough.

The photographer adjusted his angle. "Perfect. Karan, wrap your arm around her—just lightly. Janvi, relax into it."

Karan exhaled, forcing himself to stay steady as his free arm slid around her waist. His palm barely rested against the soft fabric of her lehenga, but the warmth beneath it burned through.

Janvi tensed—just for a second.

Then, just as quickly, she let out a small breath and eased into him.

He felt that too.

The photographer moved around them, adjusting his focus. "Good, good. Janvi, tilt your head slightly toward him—just like that."

Karan barely breathed.

Janvi was too close.

Her hair brushed against his chin, her heartbeat steady against him. And she still wasn't looking at him.

Because if she did—if she looked up right now—

It would be over.

The camera clicked one last time, the sound cutting through the thick silence between them.

"Okay, lovebirds, that's enough tension for one night!" Meghna's voice rang out, full of amusement. "Group photo time!"

Janvi moved first, easing away from Karan like she hadn't just spent the last few minutes pressed against him.

Karan let her go, though his fingers curled slightly before his hand dropped to his side.

The photographer laughed, switching lenses. "Alright, everyone in! Say cheese!"

23

SANDSTORM

The warmth of the bonfire flickered, casting long shadows across the sand. The distant sound of traditional instruments blended with the rhythmic clap of dancers, their movements fluid and mesmerizing against the night sky.

Janvi sat beside Karan, her arms wrapped around her bent knees, firelight painting soft gold across her skin.

Across from them, Meghna and Himanshu sat wrapped together, tucked comfortably into each other, their laughter easy, unguarded. Around them, other guests watched the performance, their voices hushed in quiet appreciation.

Karan exhaled, shifting slightly. His legs were crossed at the ankle, his arms resting loosely over his knees.

Too much space. Not enough.

Then, from the corner of his eye, he saw Janvi pull her cotton bag closer, fingers brushing over the fabric before reaching inside.

"You asked me what's in the bag earlier," she murmured.

She pulled out a hardcover journal and set it between them.

Karan frowned slightly, his gaze shifting between the book and her face. A journal?

His confusion must have been obvious because Janvi let out a small, knowing smile.

"This," she said, tapping the cover lightly, "is for you."

Karan hesitated, fingers twitching slightly before resting on his knee.

"At first, I packed it as a return gift," she admitted. "For the notebooks you gave me. But today—when I saw you hesitate to talk about Viren Uncle—I thought maybe you needed this more than ever."

Karan's frown deepened.

"When he brought Aman and me to Jaisalmer... maybe it was losing my father, your mother's passing, or just being so far from you, but... he wasn't the strict man you seem to remember." Janvi paused, searching his face. "He spoke about you often. He was so proud of you."

Karan's throat went tight.

"One day, I was helping him clean the study. He pulled out an old shoebox. He told me Gayatri *Chachi* used to fill it with souvenirs—photos of you, school articles, report cards. Everything you achieved. After she passed and you left for the States, he kept adding to it."

Janvi opened the book, flipping through the pages carefully.

"The box got tattered over time, so one day, Viren Uncle asked me to put everything together in a journal." She glanced at him before continuing. "I started organizing it all—chronologically."

Karan turned the pages, unable to believe his eyes.

Inside were pieces of him—things he had forgotten, things he didn't even know had been saved. His old school reports, newspaper clippings, a faded photograph of him holding his first trophy. Then, later, a lone article about the launch of his startup.

And after that... everything.

Janvi's voice was softer now. "After he passed, I continued our little tradition. I started collecting everything of yours I could find—online, in magazines, newspapers. I'd read them out to Daadi Sa and Laxmi Tai sometimes. Your video interviews? I made QR codes and attached them here instead."

She gave him a small, almost shy smile. "I even taught Daadi how to scan them so she could watch you."

Karan swallowed hard, the weight of her words pressing against something in his chest.

"I just want you to know," Janvi continued, "that your father was proud of you. Maybe he could have handled things better when you were growing up, but that doesn't mean he loved you any less."

She hesitated for a second before adding,"And as a consequence... I grew to be proud of you too. Whether you knew me or not."

Karan looked at her, the flickering firelight tracing the delicate curve of her face, highlighting the quiet steadiness in her posture. She was close, yet there was still something just out of reach—something he couldn't quite touch, couldn't quite name. He wanted to bridge the gap, to say something, to acknowledge the shift between them, but he didn't know how. So instead, his mind pulled him back.

To the night of Janmashtami—the moment she had run into his arms, gripping him with the kind of desperation that came from relief, not necessity. Had he ever truly questioned why? Or had he been too blind, too caught up in his own emotions to see what it meant? He had assumed she had had no reason to trust him, yet she had. Instantly. Entirely.

His thoughts flickered to all the other moments—the way she always seemed to be waiting on him, even when he had given her no reason to. The quiet, unspoken way she had hinted—without ever saying it aloud—that he made her heart race. And now, to tonight.

"I grew to be proud of you too."

The words curled around something deep inside him, refusing to loosen their grip. He had been wrong about many things before, but what if he had misread something staring him right in the face? The cogs in his mind turned.

Did she...?

The realization hit fast and hard, knocking the breath from his lungs. But he couldn't ask. Not yet. Not until he was sure.

Instead, he exhaled slowly, his voice even, careful. "Your turn to ask Question 18."

His heart pounded, but for the first time, he was the one waiting on her.

"Eighteen. Is there something about me that you'd want to change?"

Karan was momentarily stunned. That was a loaded question. He turned to look at the bonfire, watching, thinking.

"You know, I pride myself to be a very perceptive man. It's how I charm my way into getting my suppliers to give me the deal I want or my clients to choose me over competitors. But you," he turned to looked at her, the firelight flickering in his eyes, "you are that one puzzle in my life that refuses to unravel. Each time I feel like I've finally figured you out, you peel off another one of your layers. It's infuriating. And yet… I still wouldn't change a thing."

Amusement flickered in her eyes.

"Your answer," Janvi shook her head. "I can't decide if you're complimenting or insulting me and somehow… I'm the onion?"

Karan chuckled, shaking his head. "Not an onion. Onions make people cry." His smirk softened. "You? You just keep me guessing."

Janvi huffed. "So, I frustrate you?"

He exhaled, gaze flickering toward the fire. "You intrigue me."

She frowned slightly. "So, would you change it?"

Karan turned to her, his voice quieter now. "Let's put it this way. To an observer you might come across as a challenge. But I wouldn't change a thing. Because, I guess I'm a sucker for a good challenge."

Janvi blinked.

"Okay, my turn," he said. "Yesterday, when I asked if there was anyone who had ever made your heart race, you didn't answer—but it was definitely me. Don't even try denying it. I saw it in your eyes as clear as daylight."

He leaned in slightly, his gaze unwavering. "So, my question to you is—when was the first time I made your heart race? Was it after we married, after I returned from New York… or long before?"

It was Janvi's turn to look into the fire. If he had asked this question earlier, she wasn't sure she would have been able to answer it. But now, she understood it needed to be said. That had been the point of all of this, hadn't it?

"Long before…" she whispered.

Karan didn't move, but she felt the shift in the air between them, the weight of those two words settling over the space they shared.

He said he was intrigued by her. Maybe it was time he saw the final layer.

Janvi exhaled slowly, her voice quieter now. "I didn't expect it to happen," she admitted with a light shrug. "At first, it was just a project—I think he thought it would keep me occupied. That, after losing my father, after being uprooted from everything I knew, maybe if I had a task—something to focus on—it would help. And at first, that's all it was. A project. I didn't think much of it."

She paused, her throat tightening slightly. "But at some point... it stopped feeling like a project."

She turned to him then, her eyes steady, her words laced with quiet certainty. "That's how I first got to know you—not through anything you ever said or did, but through the eyes of your parents. By laying it all out, one piece at a time."

Karan's face was unreadable, his gaze locked onto hers, but she knew he was listening.

She let out a small, wistful breath, a hint of a smile tugging at her lips. "And I suppose, after a while... my young, foolish heart couldn't help but be drawn to you, too."

Karan didn't respond immediately. He just looked at her, absorbing this newfound part of her with interest. Feeling equally elated and overwhelmed.

"So, you liked me? I was never really a stranger to you. Is that why you...?" his voice quiet without even trying.

"Married you?" Janvi finished for him. She let out a soft, almost tired breath, shaking her head slightly. "No, I was naïve, but I wasn't stupid. I understood how relationships worked. I wasn't sitting around dreaming of marrying you. Or anyone else, for that matter. You were so much older than me anyway."

Her voice was steady, but there was a reflective brokenness in the way she spoke, like she was laying out parts of herself she had hidden away for so long and had lost all hope of ever letting it out.

"But I do know a thing or two. I probably changed more homes and schools than you ever have in your almost thirty-two years. So needless to say, I've seen a lot of things. I've seen my peers, time and again, hang onto boyfriends and girlfriends like their lives depended on it. So, it would have been *extremely* far-fetched for me to imagine you in New York still waiting for your one true love." She smiled faintly, but it didn't quite reach her eyes.

"So, no. I wasn't harbouring a deep-seated need to be a part of your life. But it is true that, in my heart of hearts, I did come to have something akin to a deep admiration for you. If that is what you want to define as a crush then that is your prerogative. But for me it was an innate respect that comes from understanding someone's true values."

Something in Karan shifted.

"But to marry you? We never planned for any of this to happen," Janvi continued, a soft smile painted on her lips as her mind recalling memories that Karan had no privy to until this moment. "Viren Uncle and I spent hours talking about what I wanted to do in life. He wanted me to go to university. Just like you. He became my mentor in a lot of ways. But I never believed in conventional learning. I already enjoyed helping him manage the estate, running errands for him. I wasn't going to spend another three years in a classroom, memorizing lectures, when I could already start getting things done. And isn't that what the internet is for?"

Her lips curled slightly, as if amused by her own stubbornness, but there was an intensity to her words—a raw, quiet conviction.

"There was always so much to do. So much to fix. So much to preserve. Not just at home, but in town, in Jaisalmer, in Rajasthan, in India." Her voice softened. "I saw how my father spent his life in service to this country, as did Viren Uncle. And I wanted to do exactly that. Maybe not in the patriotic sense of joining the army, but in ways that felt right to me. I wanted to make a difference at the root level. In things I cared about. And we agreed—he'd hire me after I finished high school, and we'd eventually work out a way to do just that."

She paused, her breath steady but her eyes shining with something more fragile.

"But man proposes one way… and God disposes another."

Karan didn't realize he was holding his breath until he saw the flicker of pain that crossed her face.

"His sickness came as a shock to all of us." Janvi swallowed, her voice trembling slightly. "And then he asked of me something I couldn't deny. I knew what he was trying to do. Holding onto what he promised me. He made me swear on his deathbed. But I had been so emotional at the time. I wanted to help out at the hospital but Bakshi Chacha and Daadi Sa were absolutely adamant that I focus on my studies. I had to remain calm for Aman but it was so hard. His sickness, the scary possibility of me getting married to you, exams at school, Aman's comfort. I was juggling so many emotions."

Karan continued to listen, unable to respond.

"I thought, perhaps, you wouldn't want to marry me. Maybe you'd refuse. I was living under uncertainty. I decided I wanted to speak to you in person to clear all this uncertainty. I waited for Bakshi Chacha to come home that night and tell him to introduce me to you. But that same night Bakshi Chacha came home to tell me you had agreed to marry me. Of course, I had no idea at the time about what you were going through."

Janvi blinked rapidly, trying to hold back the tears that threatened to spill. "And then, on our wedding night, it all became quite clear. Your hand was forced in the matter and you had no choice. Although, you left with guilt in your heart, I wish we'd have had a chance to talk. Perhaps I would have agreed to marry you anyway to help you out, and you wouldn't have had to go through all the guilt that you did."

"At the time, I didn't understand why Viren uncle wanted me to marry you when he could have just asked you to hire me. Until I actually *started* making the changes I said I would."

She let out a shaky breath, a tear slipping down her cheek.

"I realized—to my regret—that the Rathore surname opened doors for me in a way that wouldn't have as a mere employee of the

Rathore family. There were things I made happen as the *Rathore daughter-in-law* that I could never have achieved otherwise. And *he knew that.*"

She wiped at her cheek, frustration mingling with emotion. "He wasn't just trying to give me stability. He was gifting me his hard-earned reputation so I could go out and *do* what we promised we would do. He wasn't trying to trap *you*. He wanted to free *me*."

Karan felt his pulse hammering in his ears, his stomach twisting at the sheer weight of her words.

Janvi let out a breathy laugh, one that was more of a sigh. More of an exhale of years of buried truth. And then, finally, she looked at him.

"And you..." Her voice wavered now, her gaze locking onto his. "You were never a stranger to me. I could trust you with my eyes closed." She swallowed hard, another tear slipping down. "Because *he* trusted you. And I... liked you because *he* did."

Silence stretched between them, thick and fragile all at once.

Karan stared at her, feeling something deep inside him crack open, something he wasn't sure he would ever be able to piece back together.

He had spent all this while trying to figure her out. Trying to *earn* her trust.

And all this while... *he already had it.*

Not because of anything he had done.

But because she had *always* believed in him. Even before he had ever given her a reason to.

His voice, when he finally spoke, was hoarse, barely above a whisper.

"Janvi..."

But she shook her head, as if she already knew what he wanted to say.

"No." She smiled, small and weary. "You don't have to say anything. But you can answer question 19."

"Go ahead," he asked.

"Now that I have freed you from your guilt, knowing everything you know now, would you still want me to stay in this marriage?"

Karan exhaled slowly, his gaze steady as it met hers. His voice, when he spoke, was low, certain.

"If you think I asked you to stay in this marriage because of my guilt, then you haven't really been listening."

Janvi's lips curved into the faintest hint of a smile.

Karan watched her carefully, the firelight catching the shimmer of unshed tears in her eyes. She had given him so much tonight—more than he ever expected. And for a moment, he just sat there, taking it all in.

Then, just as the silence stretched, he exhaled dramatically, leaned forward, and smirked.

"Okay, my turn. Question 19."

Janvi raised an eyebrow, waiting.

Karan tilted his head. "If I was the last man on Earth... and your other option was Himanshu... would you still make me work this hard?"

Janvi blinked—then let out a startled laugh. "Oh, please. Himanshu is so sweet, I couldn't do that to him."

Karan stared at her, shaking his head. "Unbelievable."

Janvi laughed her heart out.

Before she could fire back, the beat of *dhols* and the sound of clapping filled the air. Their conversation was cut short as a group of dancers whirled onto the sand, the energy of the performance sweeping through the night. The dancers spun across the sand, vibrant skirts swirling, anklets jingling in rhythm. The firelight cast flickering shadows, the air alive with claps and cheers.

Janvi hugged her knees, watching in silence, the tension from their conversation slowly ebbing away.

She inhaled deeply, exhaling just as slow. Then, without turning to look at him, she spoke.

"Last question."

Karan glanced at her, sensing the shift. "Go on."

Janvi hesitated, her fingers tracing idle patterns over the fabric of her skirt. Then, finally, she spoke, her eyes still fixed on the dance in front of her.

"If I say, that I want to remain in this marriage... will you kiss me?"

Karan stilled.

His fingers, loosely resting on his knee, curled slightly. His gaze snapped to her, eyes sharp, searching.

The firelight flickered across his face, highlighting the way his jaw tightened, the way his breathing seemed to slow just slightly.

But Janvi didn't look at him.

She kept watching the dancers, her expression giving nothing away.

Karan looked back at the performance. The music swelled, the *dhols* echoing in the air. The crowd clapped along, caught in the hypnotic rhythm.

His voice, when it came, was even. "Before I answer that, I want to ask my last question."

He caught her frown but she didn't speak. Just a nod.

"Will you stay?"

Janvi turned to look at him. And then, softly—almost like a secret—she whispered, "Yes."

Karan saw the emotion in her eyes, the sincerity in her voice. But he didn't say anything.

He turned his attention back to the dancers.

And the silence between them stretched on.

The songs changed. The dancers changed. The audience watched, mesmerized. But the silence remained.

Seconds turned to minutes. They sat there in silence until an hour had passed.

Karan still hadn't said anything.

Not once looked at her.

She watched the rest of the audience, mesmerised by the dance. Smiles on their faces, couples in each other's arms, Meghna and

Himanshu. Whispering sweet nothings in each other's ears. But the awkward silence between Karan and her stretched on.

Had she misunderstood something? Said something wrong?

Eventually, unable to bear the awkwardness any longer, she got up and walked back to their tent.

* * *

A soft breeze drifted through the floor to ceiling netted opening in the veranda of the tent. The stars in the night sky shone like jewels embroidered on a dark velvet cloth. The full moon had reached its zenith illuminating beneath it a vast landscape of winding mounds of sand painting a picture of pure tranquillity.

Yet standing in front of it, beneath the canvassed roof of the luxury tent, plagued by her interminably mortifying and self-deprecating thoughts, Janvi felt anything but. If the past hour was an awkward reticence, then the last ten minutes in the solitude of the dark tent was a torturous perpetuity that grated at her dignity and pride.

Did she misread everything again?

The distant hum of the folk songs continued to assail her ears as though they were taking a front-row delight to her woeful stage.

Was he still sitting there?

A shuffle at the canvassed entrance answered her silent question. She felt him walk in, approaching her closer until he stood right behind her. He was so close that she could feel the warmth radiating from him and smell the spiced musk of his cologne. But she couldn't bring herself to turn and face him.

Before she could stop herself, the words escaped her lips of their own accord like the last fight of a diffusing ember, achingly soft like a whisper and hoarse like an untuned *ektara*.

"You never answered my question."

Seconds passed. She expected them to continue into a minute and then an hour but then what happened next turned all her concept of time into dust.

It started with the touch, a lone palm over her navel beneath the drape of her dupatta, strong and noticeable. Then a single backward pull, crashing her against a sturdy, imposing frame of pure muscle.

Before she could even recognise the sound of her gasp, she felt his breath against her ear, hot and unsteady. Then with a raspy voice that carried the depth of his desperation, he spoke the words that shattered every distorted illusion.

"Why don't I show you?"

The implied intensity ricocheted through her body like a lightning strike, rendering her limp and at the mercy of his hold that was getting tighter with his need, unbridled and unchecked. Heat pooled in the depth of her core as he brought his other hand to sweep her hair to one side, each movement slow and deliberate, his fingers burning her skin across her nape.

With the tip of his nose, he traced her frame, from an exposed shoulder to the hook in her neck, breathing in her sweet fragrance as if his life depended on it. She arched into him, when with a barely-there touch of his teeth, he grazed her skin.

He steadied her at the pelvis with his free hand, as the one on her stomach roamed higher, slow and torturous over her embroidered blouse. He didn't speak. Didn't need to. Didn't want to. He had exhausted all his words and now it was time to show her what he *really* felt.

Writhing under his agonizing hold, Janvi gripped the skirt of her lehenga on both sides, hoping to ground herself. She had lost all power of thought aware of nothing but his touch and an unfamiliar, unexplained yearning.

Suddenly he pulled his hand away, but just as quickly he returned it back to the same place, this time over her dupatta, scrunching it as if it had offended him. Using his hand on her hip and his lips on her neck, he held her in place as he slowly peeled the three yards of cotton *bandhani* that had been attempting to cover her modesty.

No longer from him.

Slowly, he let her go and turned her around. And then she saw it. Illumined by the moonlight, each line on his face telling the story of his desire for her. She watched him wear her dupatta like a medal around his neck and placed his hands in his pocket. Then he simply stood there, watching her. His gaze took in every curve of her body, as if her were silently undressing her.

He took a step forward.

She stepped backward.

Partly in hesitation and partly afraid of her own feelings. Her chest rose and fell with each difficult breath.

Eventually, he began walking closer causing her to retreat further. His movements were calm and controlled while hers were scattered and timid. Her legs hit the edge of the wooden coffee table on the veranda. She stumbled and sat on the table. When he reached her, he bent over her just enough to have access to the strings tying her blouse at the back. Janvi's heart raced faster with each slow tug of string, his unwavering gaze on her disarming her defences completely. At last, when his fingers touched her bare back, overwhelmed by her accelerated heartbeat and the onslaught of unfamiliar sensations, she closed her eyes shut.

But then he stopped completely.

She opened her eyes to find him kneeling in front of her, looking at her with a strange expression. *Compassion? Pain?* He brought his palm to her face, his thumb lightly grazed her cheek in quiet affection, a sad smile on his face. As though he were caught between a dilemma to choose between his needs and her comfort. Even before he moved, she saw the retreat in his eyes. Just as he dropped his hand and was about to get up, she reached out on impulse, curling her fingers into his shirt, urging him to stay. She was nervous, yes. But the thought of him leaving was even more agonizing.

He stilled, her unspoken yearning tugging at his heartstrings, but he remained where he was—kneeling in front of her yet just slightly out of reach. What happened next, however, was something he was entirely unprepared for.

At first glance, it looked like she was shielding herself. Her arms crossed, her gaze—lowered, thinking, processing. Then, as though shedding the last vestiges of her vulnerability, she began to slide her undone blouse off of her shoulders, her trembling fingers betraying her uncertainty.

And that shook him to his core.

She was offering herself up to him along with her pride and dignity, putting her trust in him wholly and unequivocally.

But she was priceless. And he was humbled.

The fabric had just slipped past her shoulders when his hands came down, firm and unyielding, stopping her before it could slide any further.

Before she could react, he pulled her into his arms with a force that startled her, his grip both desperate and careful.

Janvi's confusion melted away, giving way to tenderness as he bent his head, gently lowering his forehead onto hers. She could feel his breathlessness—ragged, uneven—mingling with her own, their closeness amplifying every unspoken emotion between them.

Calming down, he moved closer, his lips brushing against her forehead, planting in its wake a kiss. Sweet. Chaste. Reverent.

But then—he wavered.

His restraint unravelled, little by little, as his lips traced a path along her temple, trailing downward with aching deliberation. A kiss against her cheek. Another beneath her jaw. Each one deepening the ache inside her, igniting something she had no control over.

She melted into him, pliant and breathless, surrendering to the warmth of his hold as he gently eased her down.

A shiver coursed through her when the hot skin of her bare back met the cool surface of the coffee table.

She gripped the edges of the table, letting him take charge.

His kisses were still slow, but deeper and more insistent, as though he were seeking to merge into her, to claim her. As he moved lower, she turned her head to the side, baring her throat to him in silent invitation. A tremor ran through her the moment his lips found the sensitive skin there, lingering, tasting, branding her with every unhurried press of his mouth.

He continued for a while in this way, tracing a path along one side of her throat, then the other, his lips mapping her skin with a slow, deliberate hunger.

Each kiss was deeper than the last, each lingering touch leaving her breathless, heightening the warmth pooling low in her belly. His hands remained steady, anchoring her as he claimed every inch of her exposed skin, his mouth worshiping, savouring—until she felt like she was unravelling beneath him, piece by piece.

And then, he let one hand stray lower, his touch light yet purposeful, while his lips remained on her chest. Even with his desire burning at his peak, he kept his movements slow, no matter how excruciating it was. He refused to rush, refused to let urgency override the moment. Every touch, every lingering press of his mouth was deliberate, worshipful. Through the haze of longing, he remained acutely aware of her—watching, waiting—for the smallest flicker of hesitation, any sign of tension.

His hand drifted past her belly, skimming over the delicate curve with an aching slowness. Lower still, past her hip, his fingers traced a path as though memorizing her, before finally coming to rest softly over her thigh, where they lingered for a few seconds.

One achingly slow inch at a time, he began to gather the fabric of her lehenga. The movement was deliberate, unhurried, heightening the anticipation with every slow shift of cloth against flesh. With his head so close to her chest, he could swear he heard her pulse quicken. She was tensing, her breath coming in uneven waves, but she was trying so hard not to. That made him smile.

So, he did something that would hopefully distract her from what his hand was doing. With a roll of his tongue, he ran a slow, teasing line just above the crease of her breast.

And that seemed to work. Her head rolled back, lost in the new sensation, unable to register the breeze on her exposed legs.

Raising his head slightly, he paused to admire his handywork, a slow smile playing on lips. Her head fallen backward, arched at the throat and her exposed thigh lay beneath his hand. Her body taut and surrendered to his command like a musical instrument, waiting to be played—she was breathtaking.

Under her lehenga, his hand found its way to the band of her tights and underwear. As his fingers curled around the band, and his skin met hers, she suddenly tensed in instinct pushing herself up slightly. He paused here, his eyes on her silently willing her to trust him. He watched her swallow before laying back down and closing her eyes to give into the sensations he was promising.

And then, without any further hesitation, he peeled both pieces of garments down in one fluid motion, past the curve of her hips, along the length of her legs, until they slipped off entirely. He dropped them on the floor behind him, his gaze never once leaving her.

Then... he did nothing.

He simply remained there, watching her, letting the moment stretch, heavy with anticipation. His hands rested at her sides, his breath warm against her skin.

She opened her eyes, confusion flickering in them as she pushed herself up slightly. But he looked completely relaxed, his face giving away none of his thoughts.

And then, without warning, he stood.

Caught off guard, she scrambled to sit up, but before she could move, he placed a gentle, coaxing hand on her cheek, his thumb brushing against her skin in a soothing caress to calm her down.

"Shhh," he murmured, his voice low, steady. "Wait here."

Propped up on her elbows on the table, she watched him disappear into the darkness of the tent, her brows furrowing further. She straightened up, waiting a moment in silence, the only sound being her ragged breath and the distant singing of the folk songs still playing live at the bonfire. In the darkness, she thought she heard the sound of a zipper.

Was she mistaken?

As the moment stretched unbearably, she tapped the wooden edges of the table, nerves coiling tight in her stomach.

Should she go to him?

He told her to wait.

When he returned, there was a smugness on his face and the barest hint of a smile, as if he knew something she didn't.

Her heart skipped a beat.

This didn't bode too well for her.

Stepping into the moonlight, his features sharpened, the flickering glow illuminating every sculpted line of his face.

Definitely smug.

Then, she saw what he held in his left hand.

Was that a… toothbrush?

She opened her mouth, questioningly, but no words would form. Her gaze flickered between Karan's face and the toothbrush in his hand. Her mind reeled, her thoughts scrambling to make sense of it. A faint furrow formed between her brows, her expression torn between bewilderment and exasperation.

He simply stood there, watching her, his face unreadable save for the faintest hint of amusement ghosting over his lips. With slow deliberate moves, he rolled the sleeves of his shirt higher up, exposing the taut muscle beneath. The moment stretched.

Before she could react further, before she could fully process what was happening, he moved.

Swift. Decisive.

One moment she was grappling with her stunned thoughts, and the next, his hands were on her again—this time firmer, bolder, claiming her as if there had been no interruption at all.

The breath she had been holding left her in a sharp exhale, her body responding before her mind could catch up. His fingers curled around her waist, pulling her flush against him, his warmth branding her through every layer of fabric she still wore. His mouth found her throat again, picking up exactly where he had left off, his lips tracing fire along her skin.

Her hands, which had been frozen in midair, instinctively clutched at his shoulders for support. A shiver ran down her spine, her skin prickling with heightened sensitivity, her bewilderment fading into the onslaught of his passion. Her mind screamed for an explanation. But her body… her body no longer cared.

She closed her eyes and let herself fall back, trying to relax but the heat in the pit of her stomach was becoming unbearable. She wanted to ask for something but wasn't sure what.

When she felt his hand move lower, her heartbeat began to pick up. All her instincts screamed at her to push him away, her mind telling her these feelings are foreign but her body was having none of it. It wanted to remain, wanted to respond to him and his unspoken commands like he was her master.

Lower. She arched.

Lower. She steeled herself. Fists tightening, bracing herself.

She wasn't sure for what but her reactions were no longer in her control.

And then she felt the buzz.

Her eyes shot open in panic.

Gasping in shock, she tried to get up but he was holding her with the weight of his body, his lips still warm and moist on her chest.

The feeling first started at her thigh, and slowly began to travel up. She tried to make sense of it all but the vibrations were unlike anything she had ever experienced and it was unravelling her. She was incapable of thinking, much less deducing.

But through the haze of the tremors, she finally made out what it was.

The toothbrush. An electric toothbrush!

It travelled further up, igniting a wildfire in her, racing through her veins, scorching every ounce of rational thought. Her hands flew to his shoulders, gripping hard, trying to hold on.

Further up.

Her chest heaved, her stomach tightened, and her back arched as if seeking escape, yet her body betrayed her—leaning into him, into the sensation. Her nails dug into his bare arms, pleading but she didn't know for what.

And still, he didn't stop.

The incessant, tormenting object was dangerously close to the very epicentre of her being.

Her head fell back, her throat exposed, lips parting soundlessly as a shudder wracked through her. Her thighs trembled, caught between tension and surrender.

She tried to say something, anything. But all she could manage was a whimper.

And then the damn thing found it.

The very source of all her sensations.

The scream that escaped her lips was completely involuntary. She was at the whim and mercy of him and his bloody toothbrush.

It was as though her body didn't exist. It was just him and this unending onslaught of pleasure that just kept building and building with each passing second. Pushing her to the cusp of something, she knew not what.

Her body began to wind tighter and tighter.

She felt like she was about to break.

Just when she felt like she couldn't take it anymore, the tightness snapped.

The cry that escaped her lips was guttural, raw, primal. The world had suddenly ceased to exist. She felt as though she were floating in a cloud of bliss. She was weightless.

Her body still trembled, shuddering in the aftermath of it all. She barely registered the feel of the wooden table beneath her, or the cooling air against her flushed skin. Slowly, her breath began to even out, the rapid hammering in her chest dulling into a soft, languid rhythm.

And then—awareness returned.

The warmth of his body. The heat of his gaze.

Her lashes fluttered open.

Karan was still.

He had stopped.

He had not moved. Had not touched her. Had not continued.

Instead, he had watched.

He had watched all of it—every uncontrollable tremor, every desperate arch, every fractured breathless cry as she came apart before him.

The realization hit her like a physical force, heat scalding her cheeks as she took in the expression on his face.

Dark.

Possessive.

Hungry.

A raw, primal need burned in his gaze, so intense, so unrelenting that it left her breathless all over again.

Her stomach twisted, the moment stretching between them, her vulnerability exposed, her body still flushed from the aftershocks of what had just happened.

And just when she thought she could find solid ground again—

She heard it.

The buzz.

Her breath hitched violently.

No.

Karan's gaze did not waver, but something flickered within it—amusement.

Her stomach flipped.

No, no, no—

Her body was still too sensitive, too raw, too wound tight—she couldn't take another—

The vibrations touched her.

A higher setting.

Her entire body jerked, a sharp cry tearing from her lips as the sensation rushed back, relentless and all-consuming.

She trembled violently, fingers clutching at the table, trying desperately to fight it, to resist. But her body had already learned to yield to him, to every unspoken command, to the sheer power he had over her.

And that was exactly what he was doing now.

He was playing with her.

Toying with her.

Teasing.

Her eyes snapped to his, dazed, wild, helpless—and there it was.

The unmistakable mirth hidden behind his dark gaze, the wicked glint of amusement.

He was enjoying this.

The realization made her breath catch, made her insides twist with something humiliating and thrilling all at once.

She wanted to fight it, to push him away, but she was too weak.

Too overwhelmed.

And so, she broke again.

Her body betrayed her.

A sob-like gasp left her lips, her back arching as pleasure consumed her, her muscles clenching around nothing, her breath shattering in erratic, helpless cries.

It was too much.

Too intense.

The moment she came undone for the second time, he finally turned it off.

Silence.

Her body collapsed against the table, her breath ragged, her fingers trembling.

She lay there, gasping, unable to move.

Her mind barely registered anything beyond the sensation still lingering in her nerves, her body too weak, too exhausted to react.

Then she weakly opened her eyes and saw him continue to watch her enthralled.

She watched the corners of his lips twitch as he raised the toothbrush again. She tried to shake her head, her body twitching. Her entire being hyper-aware, knowing exactly what was coming.

Karan's hand was already moving lower, but this time, a desperate cry tore from her throat. She managed to push herself up, her hand pushing away the damn thing out of his hands. Janvi exhaled sharply, as her body gave up, falling into him, completely spent.

He caught her instantly.

She sagged against him, unable to fight it anymore. His heartbeat, steady and unwavering, pounded against her ear.

A deep, comforting exhale left his lips as he cradled her against him, his arms enveloping her completely.

His fingers threaded through her hair, smoothing it back, soothing her as her breathing slowly returned to normal.

And there they remained for a while, not moving. In the silence of it all, she registered the music again, still playing. They hadn't stopped, they were playing into the dark moonlit night.

When Karan finally moved, Janvi barely registered it.

One moment, she was melting into him, her body still trembling, her mind too hazy to think. The next, she was weightless. He lifted her effortlessly, still cradling her against his chest, her paayal clinking as they moved.

Her breath hitched, fingers curling weakly into his shoulders, but she didn't protest.

Didn't even try.

She simply let him take her.

The world blurred around her as he carried her further inside the tent, past the sheer drapes that billowed from the ceiling.

The bed met her back with exquisite gentleness, the sheets cool against her overheated skin.

He hovered over her for a moment, eyes dark, unreadable, before he straightened.

And then—

He began undressing.

The slow, practiced movements sent a fresh wave of anticipation curling low in her stomach.

First, his shirt.

It slipped off broad, sculpted shoulders, revealing the hard planes of muscle, the deep ridges that rippled down his abdomen.

The golden glow of the lanterns cast shadows across his skin, making him look untamed.

Then, the jeans.

The soft rustle of fabric. The slow, deliberate slide.

Janvi swallowed hard.

And then, he was back.

Hovering over her. Caging her in.

But he didn't move—not yet.

Instead, with lifted brows, he searched her face, a silent request for her permission.

She simply nodded. She was ready.

His hand came up, fingers brushing over her cheek, his touch featherlight, reverent.

When he spoke, his voice was low, hoarse. Careful.

"This might hurt."

Her breath caught.

He watched her, waiting, giving her a choice.

"Tell me to stop, and I will. Immediately."

Janvi's fingers trembled against his skin.

For a split second, she thought she might hesitate.

But then—she didn't.

Instead, she reached up.

Grasped his face.

And pulled him down.

Her silent yes.

He adjusted his stance, poised and positioned. His body shuddered against her, his restraint fraying.

He exhaled sharply, as if that one action had destroyed whatever control he had left.

And then—

His voice, a whisper against her lips.

"Then here is your answer."

The words barely had time to register before his mouth claimed hers, swallowing her gasp, her hesitation, her last moment of innocence.

And then—he took her.

A sharp, searing pain shot through her, a gasp lodged in her throat, but he was already there, devouring the sound before it could escape, his kiss deep and unyielding.

His fingers tightened on her waist, an iron grip, steady, reassuring, holding her still as he pushed deeper, his body tense, every muscle coiled and trembling under the weight of restraint.

He did not move.

Did not dare.

He was swallowing it all—her pain, her gasps, the tight, almost unbearable resistance that he forced himself to weather. The kind of control that sent tremors through his frame.

His breath came shallow, his forehead pressed against hers, lips parting but saying nothing.

Not yet.

He was giving her time.

Taking her pain so she wouldn't have to bear it alone.

His hands, traced slow, grounding circles over her skin, urging her body to adjust, to accept, to yield.

Janvi's breath came in uneven gasps, her fingers flexing against his bare shoulders, her mind reeling, caught between the aching stretch and the unbearable intimacy of being completely filled—of having no part of herself untouched by him.

Her pulse pounded against his lips where he hovered, watching, waiting, fighting himself.

She swallowed, eyes flickering up, searching.

And in the dim glow of light, she saw it—the agony in his restraint.

The way his jaw clenched, his arms shaking from the effort of not moving, his control stretched so thin it might have shattered had she asked him to stop. In the silence of his restraint, the folk music continued to seep through her consciousness. She barely register the familiar words.

This man—her husband—was giving her the choice, to stop

him if she wanted.

But she didn't.

Instead, her hands slid up, fingers brushing the nape of his neck, curling into his hair.

And then—she pulled him down.

Kesariya...

The gesture was small, but it broke him.

Baalam...

A ragged breath left his lips before he sank fully into her, the last of the barrier between them giving way as he claimed her, body and soul.

Aao ni...

Janvi's back arched, her nails biting into his skin as he groaned, the sound low and primal, vibrating through her, shaking her to her core.

And then—he moved.

Padhaaro ni mhare desh...

Slow. Deep. Unforgiving.

A slow rhythm that sent fire licking through her veins, that pulled her further into a place where nothing else existed but him. No space, no resistance—only him.

O ji kesariya... baalam...

Each thrust sent a ripple of fire curling through her veins, his movements deep and deliberate, unravelling her with an unbearable slowness. Every inch of her body responded to him, tightening, seeking, aching for something she couldn't name, something that lingered just out of reach.

She gasped, her head tilting back as her breath tangled with his, her body arching toward him, desperate for more.

But Karan wouldn't let her move.

His hands found hers, fingers threading through hers before he pinned them above her head, trapping her beneath him. A silent command.

Stay.

Feel.

Her lips parted in a soundless plea, her body trembling beneath his. The contrast was unbearable—his grip strong and unyielding, but his mouth… his mouth was soft, reverent, trailing open-mouthed kisses down her throat, across her collarbone, lower.

Every brush of his lips, every lingering touch sent liquid heat pooling deep inside her, her body wound so tight she could barely breathe.

He was everywhere, possessing her, consuming her, dragging her closer to madness with every devastating stroke.

His breath was hot against her skin, his desire dissolving into something desperate, something close to reverence.

And yet, even now, he held back.

His control was fraying, his body trembling with restraint, as if he was teetering on the edge of something he wasn't ready to surrender to just yet. But Janvi felt it—the way his fingers tightened around hers, the way his rhythm stuttered ever so slightly, his composure threatening to crack.

She was right there, just as lost, just as desperate. The tension coiled inside her, building, stretching, wound too tight to bear. She tugged against his grip, needing to touch him, to pull him closer, but he didn't let her. Her body was helpless beneath him as he thrust deeper, slower, more agonizingly controlled.

She cried out, her fingers curling against his, her back arching as pleasure crashed through her.

She couldn't hold on anymore.

And then, she shattered.

A sharp, broken gasp escaped her lips, her body locking around him, her legs tightening, her fingers clawing at his grip as wave after wave of pleasure tore through her. It was too much, too intense, stealing the breath from her lungs, drowning her in him.

Karan wasn't far behind.

The moment she broke, he followed—his body tensing above her, a deep, guttural groan torn from his throat as his control snapped completely.

His movements stilled, his arms trembling as he shuddered against her, buried inside her, utterly wrecked.

For a long moment, there was nothing but silence.

The distant hum of music drifted through the tent, the soft notes of the song weaving through the air like a whisper, an echo of something ancient, something inevitable.

He didn't move. Didn't let go.

Didn't dare.

Still inside her, his forehead fell against hers, their breath tangled, uneven, still lost in the remnants of what they had just shared.

His hand still clasping hers above her head, loosened, slowly sliding down to frame her face, his thumbs brushing gently over her flushed cheeks.

She barely had the strength to open her eyes, but when she did, she found his gaze already on her, dark and unreadable. A few strands of his dark hair lay glued to the beaded moisture on his forehead, highlighting the heat of his physical exertion.

Because in this moment, in the quiet aftermath, the truth was undeniable.

She had given herself to him.

And he had taken her.

Completely.

Utterly.

His wife.

And he would never—ever—let her go.

24
AFTERMATH

The first thing Janvi became aware of was the warmth that surrounded her. Then came his scent, rich and masculine. It caused her eyes to flutter open, though her mind was still caught between sleep and wakefulness. The weight on her waist, heavy and possessive, tipped the scales of her cognizance.

A contented smile painted her lips as she registered the solid press of his chest against her back, his arm draped securely around her. A stark contrast to the deliberately placed empty space between them the morning before.

With a soft intake of breath, she twisted in his embrace, careful not to stir him. It was unbelievable how much difference a day made. Yesterday, she was struggling with her conflicting feelings of whether or not to touch him.

And today, he was all hers.

His dark tousled hair, the faint crease between his brows, the slight part of his lips and the light shadow dusting his jaw—she could trace lines through them all with her fingertips without the fear of propriety.

Oh, the possibilities.

Instead, she softly touched the tip of his nose with her lips, lingering just long enough to feel the barest hint of his fingers twitching at her waist.

After allowing herself a few more stolen moments, she carefully slipped from his embrace and lifted herself out of bed. She turned to look, half-afraid she had woken him. But aside from the furrow deepening between his brows and his fingers clutching at the sheet where she had been, he remained fast asleep.

She stretched slightly, the movement bringing awareness to the ache—a delicious, lingering soreness. A reminder of everything. As she moved toward the dresser, the flowing skirts of her lehenga tangled at her feet, making her stumble.

Blinking, she glanced down.

She was stilling wearing her lehenga, an aside from the open strings at the back, her blouse was—still on.

Her fingers lifted absently, brushing over the embroidery on her chest. She turned to look at him. But Karan lay still in slumber, blissfully unaware of her mental reflections.

Last night, she was there, willingly giving herself to him, and yet all he had thought about the entire time, was her. Her comfort, her pleasure, her experience. Even at his breaking point.

The moisture in her eyes threatened to spill over.

Despite the admission of his attraction and the heated promise in his words yesterday morning, he had ensured her first time was completely about her. She was at his whim. He could have very easily made the whole thing physical, yet he hadn't. Instead, he respected her, revered her. He had held himself back the entire time by a tightly wound thread until she allowed him to unravel.

An awareness of something she was still scared to name, settled deep in her heart.

The pages in the journal, Gayatri chachi's lovingly recorded anecdotes, Viren Uncle's measured praise… and her young heart. None of them had ever lied. He was the same man in person as he was in those pages. Beneath the baffling mix of charm and impudence, he was deeply giving and respectful.

And she was falling…

At the foot of the bed, her gaze fell on his black, linen shirt. The memory of him pulling it off came rushing back. A shiver rippled down her spine, though it had nothing to do with the cool morning air filtering through the tent's veranda.

Her lips twitched.

She reached for the hem of her sleeves, slipping it off before pulling his shirt over her head instead. Grabbing the notebook from the desk, she padded toward the veranda.

Outside, the world was quiet, the desert just beginning to wake. A soft morning breeze drifted in through the netted opening, rustling the curtains, cooling the heat lingering along her skin.

Janvi sank onto the lounge chair, tucking her legs under her as she pulled her notebook and pen into her lap.

⁂

Karan stirred, noticing the emptiness beside him. His eyes blinked open and he turned in bed adjusting to the soft morning light filtering through the net in the veranda, where he saw her.

She was curled up in the lounge, writing away.

Of course.

A slow breath escaped his lips as he let his head fall back against the pillow, a rare, unwary smile breaking across his face. His chest rose and fell steadily, the weight of the past night sinking into his bones.

For the first time in his life, he was wholly, irreversibly, and undeniably married. Not just in the eyes of the world, not just in name, not just on paper—but in the most absolute sense.

And what startled him was how right it all felt.

What had he done to deserve this?

It had begun with confusion, then disbelief, shifting to regret, acceptance, desire and finally—the pursuit that he never expected to lead anywhere. But somehow, everything he thought was wrong came together to show him what a fool he had been. Being back home, learning about her, falling for her—the entire process of winning her—it was like a complex domino art, each piece slowly but surely falling into place in the most satisfying way.

And now, she was his.

And he was hers. Irrevocably. Completely.

Oh, she had been sweet. *So sweet.*

And now, he wanted more.

Karan let out a short chuckle, shaking his head at himself before reaching for his jeans. He pulled them on, fastening the buttons in place before stepping onto the veranda.

The moment he did, Janvi glanced up—and then she smiled at him.

Not a shy smile. Not a nervous one. A real, bright, open smile.

"Good morning," he murmured, his voice lower than intended.

"Good morning," she returned softly, eyes holding his.

Without thinking, Karan leaned down and pressed a kiss to her cheek, lingering just enough to feel her inhale at the contact. Then, he pulled back slightly, watching, gauging.

She didn't pull away.

Didn't tense.

Instead, she reached up and touched his face, her palm warm against his cheek.

Karan's breath hitched for just a second.

Her touch was soft, certain, and without hesitation. A slow smirk curved his lips as his fingers found the pen and book in her hand, gently slipping it away and setting it aside.

And before she could react, he bent down, hands curling around her waist, and in one smooth motion—lifted her off the chair.

Janvi let out a startled gasp followed by a half-laugh, clearly flustered. Her fingers instinctively gripped his shoulders. But before she could protest, he sat back down, settling her right between his legs, her back pressed lightly to his chest.

"Much better," he murmured against her ear, the heat of his breath making her shiver.

"How are you feeling? Are you sore?" he asked, his whispered voice featherlike in her ear.

"No. Not so bad," she answered.

"Good," Karan said, breathing in her scent as his lips found the same delicate area at the base of her neck that he had caressed the night before.

With deft fingers, the hand resting loosely at her chest began undoing one insidious button at a time. With his other hand at her belly, he pulled her closer into him.

"What are you doing?" she asked softly, even as her eyes shut and she leaned back into him.

"Finally getting to know them," he whispered scandalously into her ear, and on cue, at the end of his sentence, his hand slipped beneath the shirt, covering the soft mound of flesh in gentle possession.

Janvi could scarcely stand the heat ignited by his words and touch, but when he flicked the brazen nub that responded of its own accord, she could no longer bear it.

Twisting in his arms, she hid into his chest, her forehead on his chest, her hands gripping his arms, her breath erratic as tried to control it.

Then she heard his chuckle, rumbling through his chest, warming her and she couldn't help but smile through it.

Karan could almost feel her blush as he ran his fingers in her hair, protectively. Then, with a deep exhale, he leaned back, letting her rest against his chest. A few moments passed before he spoke.

"I really don't want to leave. Not yet."

Janvi turned to look up at him. He continued, tucking her hair behind her ear. "But… Himanshu said we are checking out early, so I think we should start getting ready soon."

Janvi nodded before settling back into him, feeling safe and happy.

He continued running his fingers through her hair, the act soothing her, making her eyes flutter shut.

"Do you suppose, we could at least get a little breakfast time payback, for keeping us waiting for dinner the other night?" he asked, his voice dripping with mischief. "And you did say fifteen minutes is sufficient time."

Janvi giggled, swatting his arm lightly, but not getting up.

"No," she said, "Meghna has an event tonight and she needs to be back as early as possible so she can complete her last-minute checks. And besides, its rude if we do. Technically, they are still our hosts."

"Fair enough," Karan acquiesced.

Janvi was almost drifting to sleep under his gentle touch when he spoke again.

"Janvi."

The seriousness in his tone caused her to look up. He gazed at her, his expression unreadable. Then, finally, with an unmistakable sheepishness, he asked—

"Can I at least borrow your toothbrush?"

Her eyes widened, the flush creeping up her cheeks giving away her thoughts before she even realized them.

And once again—she hid herself in his chest, her shy smile syncing with his roguish laugh.

Karan sighed in satisfaction.

Oh, he could really get used to this.

* * *

"I can't find the other *jhumka* I was wearing last night," Janvi fretted, rummaging through her things. "I have to return it to Meghna. She lent it to me."

Karan, mid-way through tying his shoelaces, glanced up with an easy smirk.

"Check the sheets," he suggested, eyes glinting with mischief. "It might have slipped off last night."

Janvi, too preoccupied to catch his tone, immediately began fluffing the sheets—only to freeze. Her breath hitched, and a soft gasp escaped her lips.

Pausing in his act, he looked up and followed her gaze, his smirk deepening the moment he spotted the tell-tale crimson stain that had scandalized her so.

Janvi turned to him with wide, mortified eyes, clutching the bedsheet like a student caught red-handed. "Won't the hotel staff be upset about… about having to clean that?" she whispered, as if speaking it aloud would make it worse.

Karan bit back a laugh at her wide-eyed innocence. "Sweetheart, we're at a five-star resort. In a country that sees an average of 27,000 weddings every day. I'm certain they deal with their fair share of… newlyweds. Trust me, we're not exactly making history here."

Janvi's face grew impossibly red.

"If anything," Karan continued, his voice dipping into that maddening, teasing lilt, "they'll probably be wondering what took me so long."

"Karan!" she shrieked, mortified, grabbing a nearby pillow and hurling it straight at him.

He caught it effortlessly and laughed—deep, rich and completely unrepentant.

And then, before she could launch another attack, he closed the space between them in two strides and caught her by the waist.

Janvi barely had time to yelp before she was flush against his chest.

Karan tilted his head, his smirk downright sinful. "Careful, Mrs. Rathore," he murmured, voice low, teasing. "Don't start something you can't win."

And just as she opened her mouth—whether to protest or gasp, she wasn't sure—he leaned in, brushed his lips deliberately slow against her ear, and let her feel his smirk.

By the time she registered what had just happened, he was already stepping back, smoothing his sleeves like nothing had happened.

Completely smug. Completely unfair.

Janvi stood frozen, breathless, hands still hovering mid-air where he had held her—her face so hot, she was surprised the entire room hadn't caught fire.

Her scandalized glare followed him as he strode toward the door with the suitcases, but somewhere beneath the mortification, was the tiniest, giddiest smile.

* * *

The drive back to Jaisalmer was rather uneventful, filled with warm, friendly conversations between themselves and their hosts. Casual banter was peppered with the occasional teasing between each couple, and a classic game of *antaakshari* between the girls and Himanshu had kept them entertained for much of the way.

In the sporadic silences that lay in between, however, lay stolen glances and the brush of soft, lingering touches, an acknowledgment of Janvi and Karan's changed dynamics.

At one point, still exhausted by the previous night's excursions and lulled by the warmth of the passing desert, Janvi had slipped into a comfortable sleep. When she stirred sometime later, she had found herself tucked securely in Karan's arms, his grip firm yet absentminded, as if he had been holding her there the entire time without a second thought.

When they reached Rathore Haveli, Meghna and Himanshu bid their goodbyes, promising to meet again soon. As Karan turned to help Janvi with their bags, his gaze flickered toward the entrance.

SP Bhargav stood by his jeep, arms crossed, expression unreadable. A slow, uneasy feeling crept through Karan's chest.

"Janvi," Karan said, his voice lower than usual. "Wait here. I'll go have a chat."

Janvi watched as he strode toward the officer, tension tightening his shoulders. She couldn't hear their words, but their serious expressions made her uneasy. She barely noticed when Badri Kaka approached.

"*Aa gaye beta,*" the older man greeted warmly as he and another staff member picked up their bags. "*Kaisa raha safar?*"

Janvi forced a small smile, but her gaze remained locked on Karan and Bhargav.

"*Ji, Badri Kaka. Bahut achha tha,*" she replied distractedly. Then, almost as an afterthought, she added, "*Aap saaman andar le jaaiye. Hum baad mein aate hain.*"

"*Theek hai.*" With a nod, Badri Kaka walked off, leaving her alone at the threshold.

Janvi continued watching as Karan turned slightly, his face

partially obscured by his sunglasses. Even from a distance, she could tell he was holding something back.

A strange foreboding curled in her stomach.

Then, he said something to SP Bhargav, who nodded. Janvi straightened as Karan started walking back toward her.

"What's going on?" she asked the moment he reached her.

Karan pursed his lips in hesitation. Then he exhaled sharply, rubbing his jaw.

"They have found a lead," he finally said. "Based on my description of the tattoo on your stalker's hand. It matches someone in Bikaner. So, they're sending a team. I'm going with them."

Janvi's heart dropped. "But why do you have to go? Just let them do their job."

"Janvi," he said, softer now, his hand coming up to cradle her cheek. "I have to." His thumb brushed over her skin in a soothing motion. "It's okay. It's just a day or two. Then I'll be back, alright?"

She swallowed hard, nodding reluctantly.

Still, she stood there—rooted to the threshold—watching him disappear inside to grab his bag. She was still standing there when he returned, his presence grounding her for just a second before he leaned in and pressed a firm kiss to her forehead.

She remained there as he climbed into the jeep. She remained there as SP Bhargav started the engine. She remained there long after the dust settled and the vehicle disappeared from sight.

And amidst the ache of his absence, one thought rang loud and clear—that in such a short span of time, he had brought her to this state.

That she could no longer imagine a life without him.

25

SEPARATION

That night, back in the familiar confines of her room at the haveli, in the bed that now felt too empty, Janvi struggled to sleep.

Earlier, after explaining to Daadi, where Karan had gone, she had resumed her role of daughter-in-law of the Rathore family as if nothing had changed.

She couldn't be more thankful for the calm that the older woman brought in her life. Where she had been grappling with the moral dilemma of telling an elderly woman her grandson had gone in search of a criminal, the older woman had brushed aside her concerns like it was an everyday affair.

It was this single-minded strength of Renuka Devi that had kept Janvi brave and sane in all her trials post marriage.

The initial sting brought on by an absconded husband. The discomfort that grew from the hushed judgment of a society that enjoyed blaming women for the actions of men. The fears that crept in with every stalker's note.

Daadi's equanimity was the rock of Janvi's life in the last two and a half years.

And while she was thankful for her understanding, there was a small part of her that was still debating between wanting to share the joy of her newfound relationship with Karan and keeping it to herself until he returned.

For now, though, she lay in bed, wide awake.

Karan's absence was not new to her. She had lived with it all this while. *So why was it so difficult tonight?*

In the silence of her empty room, a long-learnt lesson taught by her father came to mind. The perils of tying one's happiness to the fulfillment of one's expectations.

The first time Karan had left, there was a clear line drawn. He did not belong to her. There was nothing that she hoped to achieve from this relationship other than to help him get his birthright and eventually leave.

This time though, the stakes were higher. Now that he had opened her eyes to a new world of possibilities, a shared one between him and her, her belief in him and the expectation to live that dream had grown a hundred-fold. And with it, the pain of separation was being keenly felt.

Night turned to dawn, dawn turned to morning.

But Janvi hadn't slept a wink.

There was no call from Karan. No message.

Was he okay?

Janvi threw herself into her routine, forcing her mind away from the gnawing worry. After Aman had left for school, she tried to engage with tourists but her thoughts kept drifting, inevitably returning to Karan. So, she decided to do a stock-take of restaurant supplies, a task she hoped would require a little bit more focus than teaching ill-advised influencers that of the 19 languages spoken in Rajasthan, 'Rajasthani' wasn't actually one of them.

But even this, she realized with chagrin, was proving difficult.

Her eyes moved over the shelves as she flipped through the register, ticking off items and making notes.

Then she paused.

Her brows knitted. She looked up trying to find someone. "*Ghee ka stock kisne check kiya tha? Itna kam kyun hai?*"

The kitchen bustled on without an answer.

Her grip on the notebook tightened.

"*Nakul?*" She addressed the kitchen hand, her voice sharper than usual.

The boy froze, eyes darting to the shelf before he looked at her, nervous.

"M—main... pata nahi, Bhabhisa... shyaad bhool gaya—"

Then he stopped. His shoulders stiffened, and realization dawned.

"Aapne hi toh kehdo hoto... pehla purano ghee khatam karvo, naya stock ni jarurat ni."

Janvi stilled.

Oh. She *had* said that.

Heat crept up her neck, embarrassment curling around her. Her fingers tightened around the notebook before she exhaled, pressing her forehead for a second.

"Haan... theek hai. Main bhool gayi thi." She paused to regain composure before speaking again in a gentler tone. "Sorry, *tum apna kaam karo."*

Nakul nodded quickly, relieved, turning back to his task.

Janvi closed the register and walked out, pressing a hand to her temple.

She leaned against the column outside, exhaling.

What was wrong with her?

She looked down at her watch. It was almost lunchtime.

Where was he? And why hadn't he called yet?

The dread was eating at her.

At lunch, she barely ate a morsel, her stomach too tight with unease. She proceeded to make another vain attempt at doing something productive. But the numbers in the account books blurred, shifting meaninglessly in front of her.

Exhausted, she slammed the ledger on the study table shut and buried her head in her hands. The lack of sleep and constant worry had turned into a dull, throbbing headache. Outside the door, she heard Aman, who was just back from school.

Maybe she could help him with his homework.

But before she could ask, Aman was already running outside with the neighbourhood boys for cricket. She sighed, about to protest, when Daadi's voice rang out from upstairs.

"Janvi! Beta, zara mere kamre me aana?"

When Janvi entered, Daadi was seated in her armchair by the window.

"Yes, Daadi?"

The older woman gestured toward her. "Come, beta, sit here."

Janvi obeyed, settling near her feet.

Then she felt the cool drizzle of liquid on her overheated skull. Daadi's deft fingers began kneading the oil in her hair gently, working the tension from her head. The relief was immediate. Her body, tense and coiled all day, melted under Daadi's magical touch.

"*Tum logo ko kya lagta hai?*" Daadi murmured with a knowing voice. "That you all can simply hide everything from me and I won't figure out a thing? Karan also likes to think so. But these old eyes see and understand everything."

Janvi turned around to look at her, unsure of where this was going.

"*Karan ke liye pareshan ho na?*"

Janvi stiffened.

"Daadi… main—?"

"You've been here with me for almost five years now, beta," Daadi continued, her voice soft and kind. "In all that time, I've learned to hear even the things you don't say."

Silence.

"*Tum ek doosre ko pasand kar ne lage ho, hai na?*"

And just like that, the dam broke. Janvi dipped her head, pressing it into Daadi's knee, letting the tears flow. Daadi sighed, her hand resting gently on Janvi's hair.

"There, there, now. It's okay to cry sometimes, beta, instead of keeping everything inside."

Janvi let out a shaky breath, allowing herself the vulnerability. And when the tears finally stopped, Daadi nudged her up gently.

"Now look here."

Daadi's eyes held that gentle calmness that Janvi had always admired.

"Firstly, I am very happy about you and Karan. And secondly, I've seen many a person being worried in this household. I've stood by Gayatri every time Viren went off for service."

She tilted Janvi's chin up.

"I also know the difference between real worry and when your mind is playing tricks on you. Karan has not gone off to war. He's with the inspectors. And if he hasn't called, I'm sure he has a good reason. Right?"

Janvi nodded silently.

Daadi smiled, patting her cheek.

"Good. Now, wipe your tears and come lie on my bed for a while. You look like you haven't slept in days. Badri and Laxmi will take care of all the housework."

Janvi didn't resist. As her head touched the soft mattress, she finally let go. In the aftershock of the emotional exhaustion of the past twenty-four hours and Daadi's shield-like presence, her worries faded into deep sleep.

* * *

When she awoke, the first thing she did was check her phone, but there was still no call or message. The sleep had helped with the exhaustion but she still couldn't shake off the nervousness.

At dinner, she felt Karan's absence even more keenly, but everyone else was chatting as if nothing was amiss. Laxmi Tai and Daadi's usual banter, though she knew tonight they were doing it on purpose, did manage to put a smile on her face.

But after everyone had retired to their rooms, the silence of the haveli became unbearable.

At first, she tried to sleep too. But after tossing and turning for a while, she understood it was futile.

Restless, she finally gave up and made her way to the kitchen.

If sleep refused to come, she might as well deep clean.

She emptied the cabinets, wiped them spotless, and put the jars back one by one. She continued this for every cabinet in the kitchen.

The mundane task was strangely comforting, and before long, her worries took a back seat for the time being.

Eventually, when she was done, she grabbed a wet cloth and moved to wipe the counters clean.

And that's when she noticed it.

The warmth.

A presence behind her.

Close. Watching.

Before she could react, an arm wrapped around her waist from behind, pulling her in.

A hand clamped over her mouth, silencing her startled cry.

* * *

"Shh… Janvi, relax its me."

Karan!

Janvi whirled around, breath hitching.

For a second, she just stared, disbelief flooding through her.

Then, before she could think, she lifted herself onto her toes, throwing her arms around his shoulders, a sharp gasp escaping her lips. And for the second time today—she broke.

Karan caught her, his arms wrapped around her tightly, his hand sliding into her hair, soothing.

She felt the exhale of his breath against her ear.

Then with a hint of a smirk in his voice, he murmured, "I missed you too."

For a while, she stayed there, Karan's arms steady around her, giving her time. Then when her emotions finally settled, she pulled back slowly.

Then, frustration took over. She shoved at his chest, barely managing to move his tall, solid frame even an inch.

"Where were you? Why didn't you call?"

Karan let out a quiet breath, his hands sliding down to her arms, grounding her.

"Janvi, sweetheart," he murmured, his voice low, steady and aimed to soothe. "I promise you, I have the simplest explanation."

He held her gaze, giving her a second to breathe.

"My phone cable was packed in the other bag. I only realized it when I reached Bikaner last night."

His lips quirked, trying to ease the tension. "And would you believe it—none of the officers use an iPhone?"

Janvi didn't react. Karan sighed.

"I couldn't find time to buy one in the morning. Then I did… but look…" his voiced dropped low.

"I'll explain everything later. But for now…"

He stepped closer, his lips almost touching hers.

Janvi's breath hitched.

"For now, come with me," his voice barely more than a whisper.

A pause.

"Please?"

* * *

Karan had held her wrist in a firm grip as she walked behind him. Her heart fluttered in anticipation. Janvi's curiosity piqued when instead of turning up the stairs, Karan headed towards the main entrance. From the outer courtyard, he turned a sharp right. Her *paayal* tinkled in the dark, the path was lit by the outer lights.

Where were they going?

Ahead he turned another right. And then she gave a gasp.

The mandap area was decorated with sheer curtains, there was a daybed on the mandap floor. Around the mandap and behind it around the pool, there were candles lit.

He stopped abruptly in front of the pool.

"Karan… when—"

She wanted to ask when he had time to arrange all this, but the look on his face made her breath catch in her mouth. Unable to speak, she simply looked into his eyes that were menacingly dark and purposeful. For a moment, it scared her.

Instinctively, she stepped back.

But he wasn't having any of it.

His hand curled behind her waist and with one confident pull, he closed all distance between them.

Before she could think or protest… his lips crashed into hers.

And she forgot everything.

Her question, her hesitation, the restlessness of the day. Forgot everything that wasn't *him*—the feel of his lips, decisive and demanding. His hand, one firmly holding her waist, the other tangled in her hair, pulling her deeper into his kiss. The warmth and firmness of his body, his smell. Building the heat in her that she was now beginning to recognise.

Before long, he pulled the georgette *dupatta* away from her neck, letting it fall to the side.

As soon as he did, his lips found her neck and chest, kissing, nibbling. His actions felt demanding, urgent. Gone was the gentle and restrained man from two nights ago. In his place was a man who was struggling to breathe and she was his lifeline.

And she let him breathe.

If *she* had been restless without him then his actions told the story of *his* agitation.

Suddenly, he stopped.

But he wasn't ready to go anywhere. He put his hands in his pocket and took out his phone to put on the steps of the mandap.

And then, with swift hands, he effortlessly swept her off of her feet. Janvi gasped in shock and hung tightly to his neck. But his hands were steady and his grip firm.

Before she could make sense of what was happening, he began walking assuredly but urgently towards the pool.

She couldn't read him and his impulsive actions tonight any more than she could understand why she still trusted him so much. He was completely unsettling her and yet she was letting him.

She braced herself for the cold shock of the water but instead was surprised that it did nothing to cool the heat that Karan had ignited.

When they were both submerged up till their necks, Karan stopped for a while to adjust to the water. He held her firmly. Placed his forehead on hers. He was catching a breath, and it was then that she noticed she had been trembling. Trembling at the sensations that his urgency was creating in her.

But he wasn't done.

He slowly waded them towards the edge of the pool and when her back hit the tiled edge, she gasped.

He peeled off his long-sleeved t-shirt, placing it on the ledge behind her.

Then he swiftly turned her around placing her hands on the edge, effectively locking her in place.

With quick fingers, he undid the strings of her churidar at her nape, and with a slow deliberate movement, unzipped her.

And then he began to slow down. He ran an achingly slow finger from her nape, down the centre of her back, passing over the strap of her bra and then further down to her lower back.

Janvi shivered at his touch.

Then holding the churidar from the edge of her sleeves, he began peeling it down.

Janvi shuddered when the cool night air touched her wet skin.

He then turned her around to face him.

At first, she instinctively tried to hide herself with her hands, but, he gently nudged her hands away.

Tonight, he was desperate. For her. All of her.

He reached behind her for a candle.

He brought it close to her face, using its light to memorise her face. Her brows furrowed in the sweet distress of anticipation. Her lips parted, trying to fill her lungs with air because he was making her breathless.

He slowly lowered the candle, past her shoulders, down to the delicate dip of her neck, that disappeared in the valley of her breasts.

For a while his gaze remained there, taking her all in. Every delicious curve, and mysterious dip of her body.

The pure desire in his eyes was making Janvi weak and she could barely hold on.

He brought his finger to the centre of this dip, and when he began to run it up the curve of the mound, she tried to stop him, shocked by the sensations.

But he simply took her hand and placed it on his shoulder, training her to stay put.

There was no teasing smirk on his face, no calculation in his eyes.

Just a raw, dark, urgent need.

He wasn't going to hold back.

Not tonight.

And it was turning Janvi asunder.

He brought back the finger to the soft flesh, continuing it's journey up her shoulder. Hooking it in the strap of her bra, he pulled it down slowly, down her arm.

Janvi was panting, hot and sharp.

And when she felt the cold air on that delicate, forbidden skin, she closed her eyes shut tight.

She heard his slow deep breaths mixed with the gentle swirl of the water in the pool. Then his voice came hot and heavy, demanding.

"Janvi, open your eyes."

The claim in his voice caused her to obey.

In his eyes, she saw his intent. He wasn't going to let her hide. Whatever he wanted to do, she was going to have to watch and feel.

She watched as he bent lower in the water, his eyes still on hers.

And then, when he was in position, she felt his warm breath.

And then he took her in his mouth, and she cried out at the sensation. His mouth was warm and wet on her breast.

At first, he was gentle, swallowing, tasting. Then as she adjusted to the feeling, he increased the intensity of the action. Drinking, gulping.

When he pulled with his teeth, she had to bring her hand to her mouth to supress her scream.

He was relentless and the ache and need in her core was increasing.

Suddenly, he stopped, placed the candle in his other hand, and pulled down the strap on the other side, repeating the same actions again on her left breast.

The sensations were wild, otherworldly.

She felt wanton and somehow, it stopped feeling embarrassing. She wasn't thinking anymore. Couldn't. She was losing herself.

Karan continued his relentless torture alternating between each side until the throb in her core became unbearable.

Then he let her go, pushing himself up, waiting for her to catch her breath.

But not for long.

He turned her once again, and taking both her hands, he placed them on the ledge.

He brought one hand around her chest, holding her breasts, while the other roamed lower down into the water.

She gasped, when it found its destination under the band of her underwear.

But instead of pushing him away, she welcomed him.

The ache was unbearable and she needed release.

When he found the sweet spot, she was not too far.

But he was too slow and she pushed her hips to meet the rhythm she needed, her body instinctively knowing what to do.

He understood. He responded.

The sensations built up, stronger, hotter, heavier.

And right on the edge of it, he dipped his head in her neck.

The tight grip of his strong arm on her delicate breasts, the torturous lips on her neck and the pulse of his finger near her core.

Then she finally broke.

And he held her, catching every tremor until she finally collapsed into him.

Then he gathered her in his arms, her wet churidar still hung from her hips. He climbed the steps exiting the pool and walked towards the cushioned area in the mandap.

Karan laid her down on the cushioned daybed in the mandap and worked quickly to pull her out of her wet clothes. His hands moving with a gentle urgency as he ran the towel around her trembling form, wiping away the wetness. He then used the towel to pull her wet hair back.

The flickering candlelight bathed her skin in gold, soft and damp, trembling from the aftermath of his touch.

For a moment, he simply looked at her. Drank her in.

The erratic rise and fall of her chest. The deepening flush along her skin. The way her lips, kiss-bruised and swollen, parted as though she could barely catch her breath. She was wrecked. Because of him.

Janvi's breath was still unsteady, but she couldn't tear her gaze away. The way he loomed over her, still dripping, still fully clothed except for his discarded shirt. The way his chest rose and fell, his limit worn thin, the hard lines of his body tense with need. The raw, aching hunger in his dark, unblinking eyes.

But Karan did not move.

Not yet.

His hands, his breath, his entire being stilled, poised over her.

Karan swallowed hard, his throat thick, his body impossibly tense.

His fingers flexed against the dip of her waist, his thumbs tracing the soft heat of her skin.

A part of him wanted to slow down—to savour her, to prolong the moment. But the other part?

The part that had been unravelling for days—for weeks now—that part was too far gone.

And so, he decided. There was no stopping. No asking. No waiting. He was already past the point of return.

A quiet, shuddering breath left him.

And then, he moved.

His lips brushed against her jaw, then lower, down the length of her neck.

Janvi shivered beneath him, her breath catching.

But he didn't stop.

Didn't give her time to think.

He kissed his way down, his mouth hot, open, insatiable, worshipping every inch of skin, every soft, aching curve.

Then, he was on her.

His body caged hers, his weight sinking her deeper into the cushions.

She welcomed it. Welcomed him.

His hands gripped her thighs, spreading her open beneath him. A groan rumbled in his chest as his hips ground against hers, slow and devastating, the hardness of him pressing into her core.

Janvi arched against him, but Karan held her still, his weight anchoring her.

And then—

He took her.

The pleasure was instant, violent in its intensity, and Karan groaned, low and guttural, as he sank into her.

Janvi gasped, her fingers clutching at his shoulders, her body tensing for a fraction of a second before melting against him completely.

He filled her, consumed her, erased whatever boundaries had ever existed between them.

His body moved against hers, slow at first, deep, unrelenting, savouring the moment of being inside her, of being where he belonged.

Then she moaned—soft, breathless, wrecked—and he broke completely.

His control snapped, his movements growing harder, more desperate, more punishingly slow.

Each thrust sent a shudder through her, through him, through the very air around them.

She was tight, unbearably hot, her body gripping him like she had been made for him, like she had been waiting for this moment as much as he had.

Karan buried his face against her neck, groaning as he thrust into her deeper, gripping her hips with bruising force.

She wasn't stopping him. Wasn't pulling away.

She was welcoming him. Meeting him. Holding on.

And that—that was his undoing.

The air thickened, their bodies slick, tangled, the rhythm between them unbearably perfect.

The scent of wet earth, candle wax, and her—filled his lungs, drowning him in a pleasure he had never known before.

Janvi gasped again, a broken, breathless sound, her nails digging into his back. Her body clenched around him, gripping, pulling, demanding.

And Karan?

Karan gave her everything.

His thrusts turned frantic, uncontrollable, devastating.

His fingers dug deeper, branding her, claiming her, wrecking her.

The pleasure built, hotter, harder, consuming.

And then—

He shattered.

A deep, guttural sound tore from his throat as he buried himself deep inside her one last time, his entire body locking as pleasure ripped through him.

It was too much.

Too intense.

Too perfect.

His hands tightened on her hips, his mouth at her throat, his breath ragged, shaking, wrecked.

He felt her breaking too—her body trembling beneath him, her breath stuttering, her fingers gripping him like she never wanted to let go.

And he held her.

Held her through every single wave.

He collapsed against her, his chest rising and falling, his forehead pressed against hers, his body tangled with hers as though he never planned to move again.

The candles flickered, the wind whispered, the water in the pool stilled.

26

MISUNDERSTANDING

The distant calls of peacocks stirred Janvi awake. The sky was still painted in the dusky hues of early dawn, but the first hints of daylight were creeping in.

As reality settled, her heart lurched. *Oh, God.* They were still at the mandap. Panic surged through her as she bolted upright.

"Karan," she hissed, shaking his shoulder. "Get up! Someone will see us."

Half-asleep, Karan barely cracked an eye open before reaching for her wrist and pulling her back against him as she tried to reach for her churidar.

"Relax," he murmured lazily, his voice thick with sleep. "No one will see us."

Janvi wriggled against his hold, her exasperation mounting. "How do you know?" she demanded. "It will be daylight soon and all the staff will start showing up. Come on, let me go. I need to get dressed."

Karan sat up at last, watching her with barely concealed amusement. There was something oddly entertaining about seeing the ever-composed, ever-collected Janvi scrambling.

"Alright, alright," he said, pulling her close once again. Leaning back against the cushion and the mandap's column, he let her settle against him. "But, if it helps ease your nerves, let's find out where everyone is, shall we."

Before she could question him, he reached for his phone from where it lay beside his discarded jeans. He powered it on and with deft fingers, swiped through the screens until he reached an unfamiliar app. Janvi watched, confused at first—until the screen filled with a series of live video feeds.

She gaped at him. "Cameras? When did you install cameras in the haveli?"

Even as she asked, the memory of the scattered haveli schematics on the coffee table flashed through her mind. That's what he had been doing!

Karan barely hid his smug expression. "After the stalker incident. For security." Then, with a lazy grin, "So, no need to worry. We can stay here a little longer."

Janvi stared at him, half-bewildered, half-impressed.

And then—his smirk turned downright wicked.

"Oh, and by the way..." He leaned in slightly, voice teasing. "I also know how someone was absolutely tortured yesterday. I wonder—were they missing me."

Janvi's gasp was immediate.

"How dare you?" she shrieked, smacking his chest, her face burning. "You knew what I was going through and you didn't bother calling?"

Karan laughed, effortlessly catching her wrists. "Easy, easy, sweethe—"

"Don't 'sweetheart' me!"

His grin widened. "You know what? I really like this fiery Janvi."

Janvi huffed, wrenching her hands free. "I'm leaving." She scrambled to her feet.

"Oka, wait—stop." Karan reached for her again, tugging her back. "Let me explain."

When Janvi relaxed, Karan continued.

He exhaled, pulling her closer. "I was only looking at the recorded footage after I finally got a charger. I was so bothered and all I wanted to do was see you. I was really missing you."

His voice softened, and something in his expression shifted.

"And then I did. You looked exhausted. You weren't the only one struggling, Janvi. I felt the exact same way."

He paused, his lips quirking ever so slightly.

"Then… I had an idea."

Her eyes narrowed.

"On my way back, I called Meghna and had her whip up some of her quick event planning magic to decorate the mandap and pool area. Laxmi Tai helped out too."

Janvi's eyes widened and her brows shot up. "Laxmi Tai knows I'm here?"

Karan smirked. "So what? You're my wife Janvi. I don't think it's anyone's business where I spend time with my wife…" Then, his voice dropped, eyes gleaming mischievously. "…or how."

Janvi's breath hitched and a blush crept up her neck.

She opened her mouth, closed it, sighed, then finally gave in—leaning back against him once more. She couldn't win against his charm. Silence stretched between them for a moment, comfortable and warm, before a thought crept into her mind.

"Why did you seem so bothered earlier?" she asked, tilting her head. "What happened with that lead?"

Karan's expression darkened.

He hesitated. "I don't know if I want to talk about it."

Janvi reached for his hand, giving it a gentle squeeze. "Just let it out," she urged.

For a long moment, Karan was quiet as if trying to find his words. Then, with a sigh, he spoke.

"The police found the man with the tattoo I described. But he wasn't our stalker—he was the stalker's younger brother. I assume the tattoo was a tribal symbol so that's how the police may have found him."

His fingers raked through his hair as he continued.

"We met with his family. They live in a shack, Janvi. Their eldest son—the man we're looking for—was the only provider. But apparently, he's been suffering from a mental illness for years.

Something happened... they didn't tell us what, but it was bad enough that they had to throw him out."

Janvi remained silent, listening intently.

"They haven't seen him since," Karan muttered. "But he's delusional. Clearly unstable."

He exhaled sharply. "I don't want to humanize him in anyway, Janvi. Not after what he did to you. But..." His jaw clenched. "I can't help but think that maybe he needs help. Real help."

His voice dropped lower. "His younger brother had to drop out of school to take on the responsibility of providing. He isn't much older than Aman."

Janvi's heart twisted.

Karan pinched the bridge of his nose. "I wanted to do more. In the end I just left them some money."

He shook his head. "There should be better ways to help people like him. To help families like his. But all we ever seem to do is cast them out onto the streets."

Janvi was momentarily stunned. He had been so furious at this man and now he was advocating for him. *This* was Karan. A man who had every reason to hate and yet, still sought to understand.

Her heart swelled with something deeper than mere admiration.

And somewhere, between their growing closeness and her deepening respect for him, Janvi realized an undeniable truth.

She was completely and utterly in love with him.

* * *

"Bhabhi sa, hukum su milan koi aayo hai."

Janvi was in the kitchen. For all intents and purposes, she was refilling the lentil canisters but her mind had been far away still caught up in the magic of the night before.

Each time her thoughts drifted back to the feel of Karan's touch, the husky timber of his voice against her ear, the way his breath had stolen hers under the stars—a delicious shiver would race down her spine. And no matter how hard she tried to suppress it, a smile would stubbornly tug at her lips.

More than once, she had caught Laxmi Tai giving her a knowing look, the amusement in her eyes barely concealed. And each time, Janvi had groaned inwardly.

Damn Karan.

It was entirely his fault.

Shaking off the scandalous thoughts threatening to pull her under again, she turned her attention back to the house help standing at the doorway.

"Hukum sa toh tayar ho rahe hain. Mehmaan ko baithak mein le jao, main bas abhi aati hoon."

"Ji, Bhabhi sa."

As she walked along the corridor, she wondered who had arrived so early in the morning. A merchant? One of Karan's acquaintances? Perhaps a relative passing through Jaisalmer?

But her curiosity was short-lived.

Stepping into the formal living area, her gaze naturally landed on the lone figure standing by the window.

Anya.

For a brief moment, Janvi felt time slow.

Even in the soft morning light, she was striking—more beautiful in person than any photograph could have captured. Those deep blue eyes stood in sharp contrast to her jet-black hair, a striking combination that made her impossible to overlook.

It was easy to see how anyone could fall in love with her.

At the sound of approaching footsteps, Anya turned, their gazes locking for a moment.

A brief flicker of surprise passed through her eyes before she composed herself, offering a polite smile.

"You must be Janvi. I'm Anya."

Janvi inclined her head slightly, the corners of her lips curving into a gentle smile of her own.

"I know who you are," she responded, her voice warm yet composed.

Anya's expression remained unreadable, but something softened in her posture.

Janvi stepped forward, her hands resting lightly at her sides. "Karan will be here shortly. Please, have a seat." She gestured toward the *divan*, the hospitality in her tone instinctive.

For a fleeting second, Anya hesitated before lowering herself onto the seat, crossing her hands in her lap.

Janvi offered a small nod. "I'll bring some tea."

"Oh, there's no need to trouble yourself," Anya said, tilting her head slightly.

Janvi met her gaze with quiet elegance. "It's no trouble," she assured her.

And with that, she turned, gliding toward the kitchen, her steps unhurried, her posture as poised as ever.

She did not rush.

She did not fumble.

She did not even allow herself to linger on the strange, unfamiliar pull in her chest.

* * *

Karan stepped into the *baithak*, his gaze landing on the figure seated on the divan.

Anya?

The moment their eyes met, she smiled—soft, familiar, almost wistful.

Once, that smile had meant something. Had held a pull.

But now?

Now, his first thought was Janvi.

And that told him everything he needed to know.

Schooling his expression, he offered a polite, measured nod.

"Anya," he said evenly.

* * *

Balancing the tray of chai, Janvi stepped over the threshold—only to come to an abrupt halt.

Karan stood near the *divan*, his arms loosely wrapped around Anya in a fleeting embrace. It was nothing more than two old friends meeting after a long time, yet something unfamiliar stirred within Janvi, a feeling she couldn't quite name.

Before she could dwell on it, they stepped apart. Karan's gaze shifted, landing on her, and his face lit up with an easy smile—completely unaware of the flicker of hesitation in her eyes. Without a second thought, he stepped forward, taking the tray from her hands.

"Come in Janvi. I want to introduce you to Anya."

Janvi met his gaze with the same warmth she always carried, her expression unruffled. "Oh, we have met just a little while ago. You two have a lot to catch up on, I'll leave you be," she said, her voice smooth as ever, before excusing herself to give them space.

As she walked away, Karan's eyes followed her retreating form, lingering until she disappeared from view. When he returned his gaze to Anya, he found in them barely concealed amusement.

"I know that look," she mused, tilting her head. "You're in love."

* * *

Janvi walked back to the study, her steps measured, her expression composed.

She wasn't quite sure what she was feeling. It wasn't hurt. Not exactly. It wasn't jealousy either—at least, she didn't think so. But something about that moment, about seeing Karan and Anya in that brief embrace, had unsettled her in a way she couldn't name.

She exhaled softly, pushing the thought aside. There was no reason to dwell on it.

The curtains near the window billowed with the breeze, their edges fluttering against the desk. Frowning, Janvi stepped forward, reaching to pull them shut. But as she did, her elbow brushed against the edge of Karan's briefcase, sending it tipping over.

A quiet gasp left her lips as papers scattered across the floor.

Annoyed at herself, she knelt, quickly gathering the sheets, stacking them into a neat pile. But then—her hands stilled.

Her gaze caught on a familiar heading.

Divorce Petition.

The breath left her lungs.

Her fingers trembled slightly as she picked up the papers, her eyes scanning the lines. Karan's name. Her name. The legal jargon spelling out the severance of their marriage.

She couldn't move.

She couldn't think.

The world around her faded into silence, save for the rustling of the curtains, the slow, rhythmic thudding of her own heartbeat.

She didn't know how long she sat there, staring at those papers, the weight of them suddenly unbearable in her hands.

Janvi's breath turned shallow, her chest tightening as she continued to stare at the divorce papers. The neatly typed words blurred before her eyes, her mind refusing to make sense of what she was seeing.

Her fingers curled around the pages, but she couldn't hold them. She let them slip from her grasp, scattering once more onto the floor, as though releasing them would lessen the weight crushing down on her.

She needed air.

Her gaze darted wildly around the study, her body moving before her mind could catch up. She reached for the notebook on the study table—the only thing her hands could find, the only anchor she could cling to. Her grip was almost desperate, fingers clutching onto it like it might steady her, might hold her together when she felt like she was unraveling.

She couldn't stay here.

The walls of the haveli, once a place of warmth, now felt suffocating. The room felt too small, the air too thick.

Her mind whispered reason—There must be an explanation.

It's just a coincidence. Anya being here, the papers, all of it—just a coincidence.

But her heart wasn't listening.

Her heart was reliving a night long past. The night Karan had left her, without a word, without a promise to return. The weight of that night crashed into her, the ache in her chest familiar, suffocating.

She needed to get away.

Anywhere.

Just away from here.

Before she could think, before she could question herself, her feet were already carrying her out of the room, down the hall, out the haveli's grand doors—away.

A few steps past the gates of the haveli, Janvi's pulse roared in her ears, drowning out everything else. Her mind was still spinning, her grip tightening on the notebook as if it could ground her, but nothing could settle the storm inside her.

The weight of her emotions bore down on her so heavily that she barely registered the presence behind her.

Not until it was too late.

A strong arm wrapped around her from behind, trapping her in place. Panic flared, but before she could even gasp, a handkerchief was pressed firmly over her mouth.

The sharp, acrid scent burned her nostrils—sickly sweet, chemical-laced.

A muffled cry barely left her lips before dizziness crashed into her, her limbs turning sluggish. She fought, twisting, her nails clawing at the hand restraining her, but her strength was slipping too fast.

The edges of her vision blurred, blackness creeping in like an unstoppable tide.

Her notebook slipped from her grasp, landing with a soft thud against the dust-covered ground.

And then—

Everything went dark.

* * *

Anya placed the small velvet box on the coffee table, her deep blue eyes steady yet gentle.

"I'm not here to stir the pot, Karan," she said with a quiet smile. "I just came to return this."

The engagement ring.

"And to end things on a positive note," she added.

Karan exhaled, nodding. He had expected this, but seeing it now—seeing the weightless finality of it—he felt something shift inside him. A closing, an easing.

But Anya wasn't finished.

"I also wanted to explain myself," she continued, tilting her head. "Not to justify anything. Not to make excuses. But because I think you should hear it. I think, given our history, we owe each other that much at least."

Karan met her gaze, waiting.

"When you came back to New York after your wedding… you weren't the same. Not really."

His brows pulled together slightly, but he said nothing.

Anya let out a small breath. "You were distant. Even when you were with me, you weren't really there. At first, I thought it was guilt—that maybe, deep down, you felt bad for what had happened. But it wasn't just that, was it?"

Her voice softened.

"I think a part of you had already left, and I just hadn't realized it yet."

Karan's jaw tensed—not in denial, but in recognition.

Anya gave a small, wry smile. "At the time, I was relieved when you chose me. I wanted to believe it. But now I see it for what it was—you were never really choosing me, Karan. Because the choice was never yours to make. It had already been made for you."

Karan swallowed, something heavy pressing against his ribs.

"When I betrayed you," she continued, her voice quieter now, "it wasn't just my mistake that ended us. We were already slipping away.

You felt it too. I know you had. You had already left—long before you even knew it."

She hesitated for a beat, then spoke the words that neither of them had said out loud before.

"You didn't come back to Jaisalmer looking for closure."

Karan stilled.

"You came back to escape," she said simply. "You ran halfway across the world to outrun the hurt. But in the end, it wasn't just heartbreak that brought you here, was it?"

She studied him, her expression open, unafraid.

"Maybe we can call it guilt. Maybe it was fate. Maybe it was something as intangible as destiny. But whatever it was, it brought you here. And it brought you to her."

His heart pounded.

"No matter how much you fought it," she murmured, "you were always going to find your way back to Janvi."

Something inside him went still.

He had spent years convincing himself that life was nothing but choices. That he was the master of his own fate. That when he left New York, it was because he had chosen to.

But the truth had been waiting all along, lingering in the quiet corners of his mind, waiting to be spoken aloud.

He hadn't chosen this path.

It had chosen him.

Anya smiled then, the kind of smile that carried no resentment, only understanding. "We both need to let go now. To forgive ourselves and move on."

And for the first time since this all began, Karan felt no weight in his chest. No anger. No regrets.

Just peace.

"Thank-you, Anya," he said, meaning it.

She nodded, standing. There was nothing left to say.

As he walked her to the door, bidding her farewell, he felt lighter than he had in years.

A chapter closed. Neatly. Effortlessly.

And as he turned toward the study again, a quiet sort of joy settled in his chest.

Janvi.

Anya was right about one thing. He really did love her.

With an easy smile, he made his way to find her.

* * *

Karan stepped into the study, his gaze immediately falling on the scattered papers strewn across the floor. His brows furrowed as he crouched to gather them, but the moment his eyes landed on the bold, legal lettering, his breath hitched.

Divorce papers.

A sudden, gut-wrenching realization clawed at him.

Did Janvi see this?

Panic surged through him like wildfire. He shot to his feet, scanning the room as if expecting to find her standing there. But the study was empty—eerily so. His pulse thundered as he bolted out, his voice echoing through the haveli.

"Janvi!"

He stormed through the corridors, checking every possible place she could be. Her room. The courtyard. The kitchen. The terrace. The museum and restaurant. His panic grew with every empty space, every unanswered call of her name.

And then, with a sinking dread in his stomach, he pulled his phone from his pocket to bring up the CCTV feeds. His hands were unsteady as he rewound the footage, scanning every frame for her.

There—she was in the study. He watched as she reached for the window, knocked over his briefcase, and bent to pick up the papers.

His breath caught when he saw the way she stilled.

Even through the grainy footage, he could see it—the way the life seemed to drain from her. The way her fingers clenched around the notebook on the desk, clutching it like it was the only thing keeping her together.

His heart broke.

Frame by frame, he watched her leave the study. Watched her walk through the haveli, her steps unsteady, her face pale. He could see it now—she wasn't just leaving the room. She was *escaping*.

His panic deepened when he followed her movement to the gates.

And then, his blood ran ice cold.

A shadow moved behind her.

His entire body locked as he saw the moment she was grabbed. The struggle lasted mere seconds. A handkerchief pressed to her mouth. Her limbs going limp.

Then nothing.

The footage ended. She was gone.

Karan didn't think. He ran.

He tore through the haveli, past the gates, to the exact spot where she had been taken. His breath came in harsh, ragged gasps as he scanned the ground.

Then, he saw it.

Her notebook.

His fingers trembled as he reached down, picking it up with a grip so tight his knuckles turned white.

The world tilted beneath him.

Everything, everything inside him, had just been ripped apart.

Janvi was gone.

And he had never been more terrified in his life.

27
FIND HER

Diary Entry – 22nd February 2022

Dear Papa,

Tonight, your darling daughter got married. I could only imagine your happiness if you had been there, standing beside me, giving me away. I thought about it so many times—how you would have looked at me, your eyes shining with unshed tears, your voice steady as you placed my hand in his. I can almost hear you whispering, "Jaan, he will keep you safe. He will love you." And do you know who I married? Viren Uncle's son. Even in his passing, he fulfilled his promise to you. He made sure I was looked after, that I had a home, a family, a husband. Does that make you proud, Papa? He was your best friend till the very end. I wonder if the two of you ever spoke of this—if you ever sat together, maybe over chai on cold winter mornings, laughing about how one day, your children might unite your families. Did you ever picture this moment, Papa? Did you imagine that when the time came, you would place my hand in his with complete faith, knowing I would be safe? Would it have comforted you? Because it comforts me. Or at least, I wish it did.

Everyone told me today was a blessing. That my new life had begun. That I should step into it with grace, with joy, with gratitude. But if this is my new life, then why does it feel like I have already lost everything? I sat through the wedding rituals, Papa. I let them place my hand in his, my fingers trembling beneath the weight of unfamiliarity. I listened to the priest's chants, let the flowers rain over me as strangers blessed a future that wasn't even mine to begin with. And I waited. I waited for something—anything—to tell me that this was real. A glance. A nod. A flicker of acknowledgment. Even the smallest shred of warmth. But there was nothing. Nothing but silence.

At first, I told myself I was imagining it. I'm nervous. He's probably nervous too. After all, he doesn't know me. But then he spoke those words that turned my doubts into reality. "I love someone else. This is just for three years. After that, we'll go our separate ways." I sat there, frozen, as he spoke of a woman he had left behind in another world—one he never meant to trade for this one. He told me about her with the kind of quiet grief that only comes from real, unwavering love. And in that moment, I knew. I was never meant to be here. I was never meant to be his.

I thought of you, Papa. I thought of how you would have looked at him today, at the boy who grew up under Viren Uncle's shadow, the boy who was meant to be safe, familiar, mine. Would your heart have broken for me? Would you have stopped this wedding if you had known? Or would you have told me what I already know—that I have to be strong. That I cannot crumble, that I cannot weep, that I cannot let my pain consume me. Because I am not just your daughter, Papa. I am Aman's sister. He has already lost too much. He has seen enough grief in his short life. And if I let myself break, if I let my sorrow seep into the walls of this haveli, he will feel it too. I will not let that happen. I will not let him feel abandoned again.

So tonight, I will wipe my tears before he sees them. I will sit with Daadi and Laxmi Tai and let them believe that everything is fine. I will hold my head high when I walk through these halls because I refuse to let them see what I lost before I even had a chance to hold it. I will be strong, Papa. For Aman. For you. For the version of me who still believes that one day, I will be loved the way you always wanted me to be.

But when I lay down tonight, I will allow myself these stolen moments of weakness. I will let myself wonder how different things could have been. What if I had met him first? Before her. Before this life that he so desperately wants to return to. Would it have made a difference? Would he have looked at me then the way he looks at her in his memories now? Or was I always destined to be a placeholder? A name in his family's register, a signature on a marriage certificate, a mere obligation to be fulfilled? And if I was, Papa—why did fate have to be so cruel? Why did it have to be him?

I have spent the past two years hearing his name in this house, in the voices of people who loved him before I even knew what he looked like. I have seen the pride in Daadi's eyes when she spoke of him, felt the warmth in Viren Uncle's voice when he called him his greatest joy. I read about him in Gayatri Chachi's old notebooks, saw his achievements carefully tucked away in Viren Uncle's study, listened to stories of his brilliance, his sharp mind, his ambition. And somewhere along the way, I let my foolish, young heart admire him. Not because he was handsome. Not because he was powerful. But because he was everything I thought I could trust.

And yet, I was never anything to him. Not even a stranger. Because to be a stranger, at least he would have had to see me. But tonight, he didn't even look at me, Papa. Not once. Not when he tied the mangalsutra around my neck. Not when he filled my maang with sindoor. Not when we took our pheras around the fire. I could have been anyone, and it wouldn't have mattered. The only time he truly spoke to me was when he told me that this was temporary. "Three years. That's all. And then we go our separate ways." I don't know if I nodded, if I agreed. Maybe I did. What else could I have done?

I don't even know if he saw the way my hands trembled when I clutched my dupatta. I don't know if he noticed how my breath hitched when he said her name. I don't know if he heard the sound of my heart breaking inside my chest, piece by piece, with every word that fell from his lips. All I know is that when he walked out of the room, I stood there for what felt like an eternity. And then—when I was sure no one was coming back—I sank to the floor.

Papa, I have never felt so alone in my life. But I will not cry where anyone can see. Tomorrow, when the sun rises over Jaisalmer, I will wake up. I will smile. I will do my duty as a daughter-in-law of this house. I will make sure Aman never sees me falter. Because I am your daughter, Papa. And I will not break.

Yours,
Janvi

* * *

It felt surreal, holding her notebook.

Karan's grip was iron-tight, his fingers pressing into the leather as if it was the only thing tethering him to reality. The pages were still warm from his touch, but their words had left a cold, splintering ache inside him.

Janvi's voice—her pain—was woven into every line. Every word etched into those pages had shattered something inside him, something he couldn't quite name.

"He didn't even look at me, Papa."

His stomach twisted violently, but he shoved the feeling down. He had no time to dwell. No time to process.

Because Janvi was gone.

The jeep jolted as it sped over a rough stretch of road, but Karan didn't flinch. His eyes burned as he stared ahead, his thoughts a chaotic storm.

"Three years. That's all. And then we go our separate ways."

His grip tightened. She had carried that pain alone. That night. That moment. He had left her there to hold it all.

"I am your daughter, Papa. And I will not break."

But now—now she was broken. Somewhere out there, in the hands of a man who had been stalking her for years, she was alone. And for the first time, Karan was terrified.

"Sir, we got a location," Bhargav barked into his phone. "The truck passed through a toll booth not long ago. It's been traced to the abandoned industrial site near the outskirts."

A truck?

Something in Karan snapped back into focus. His fingers curled around the notebook, his breath sharp and uneven. A labourer, a drifter, someone who lived between states, between shadows. A truck was his home, his means to escape, to disappear.

"He could take her anywhere."

His pulse was a hammer against his ribs.

"Faster," Bhargav ordered the driver, his voice clipped.

The tires screeched against the gravel as the jeep shot forward. The dry desert wind howled past them, stinging against Karan's skin, but he barely felt it.

He forced himself to breathe. Forced himself to think.

"She's alive. She has to be."

He had never been this helpless before. Not when he lost his mother nor his father. Not when he had walked away from this place all those years ago. Not even when he had seen his life collapse before his eyes in New York.

But now, right now—this was the worst kind of helplessness.

His hands were fists around the notebook. He couldn't blink the image away—Janvi, clutching onto it, looking so lost, so stunned, as she read those divorce papers.

She had thought he was leaving her.

And before he could even fix it, before he could tell her it was never meant to be signed, she was gone.

A muscle ticked in his jaw. His entire body was coiled tight, ready to snap.

I will get to you, Janvi. Just hold on.

The warehouse wasn't far now.

And when he found that bastard—God help him—because Karan wouldn't.

* * *

The convoy of police vehicles screeched to a halt outside the sprawling industrial wasteland, a vestige of a forgotten period, its rusted metal structures clawing at the sky like skeletal remains. The moment the tires ground to a stop, officers spilled out, weapons drawn, their boots crunching against gravel as they spread out.

Karan barely registered the commotion around him. His heartbeat was a war drum in his ears, his muscles coiled so tightly he thought he might snap.

"Stay put, Karan," SP Bhargav ordered, throwing him a sharp glance as he gestured for his men to fan out.

For once, Karan didn't argue. He sat frozen in his seat, fingers still curled around Janvi's notebook, his mind racing through everything they knew about the stalker. The man was a drifter, a truck driver. He didn't belong to any place, didn't own anything substantial. And yet, he had stayed close. Close enough to leave those letters. Close enough to know her every movement.

"He was the only provider in the family. But they had to throw him out."

His younger brother's words replayed in his mind.

"They haven't seen him since."

"We don't know where he sleeps."

A flicker of realization jolted through him.

The police were combing through the abandoned warehouses, the vast halls where most criminals would hide hostages. But this man—this man had nowhere to go.

Karan's jaw locked.

He wasn't using one of the warehouses. He wasn't thinking like a man with resources.

He was thinking like someone who lived on the move.

A truck. A damn truck.

Karan's gaze darted across the sprawling site, his pulse hammering in his throat. The police were moving methodically, sweeping building by building, but it was too slow. Too damn slow.

If the stalker realized they were here, if he panicked—he could drive away with her in seconds.

His gut twisted violently.

No.

He couldn't wait. Couldn't waste time calling them back.

He moved.

Sliding out of the jeep, he ducked low and slipped into the shadows, his steps soundless against the dirt and steel. His heart pounded, but his mind was clear. He followed his instincts, his gut pulling him toward a more secluded stretch of the yard—where the old loading docks sat abandoned.

Where a truck could be hidden in plain sight.

* * *

Janvi's mind was sluggish, her senses clawing their way back from the heavy fog of unconsciousness. Her head throbbed, her body stiff from being sprawled on the cold, hard floor of what smelled like oil, rust, and dirt.

She blinked against the dim light filtering through the broken panels of the truck's rusted body. Her breath came in shallow gasps, muffled against the rough tape plastered over her mouth.

She tried to move—only to realize her wrists and ankles were bound, the coarse ropes digging into her skin.

Panic surged through her chest.

A sound.

A low muttering.

Her eyes flickered upward.

The first thing she saw was the torn shoes—dusty, frayed, held together by desperation more than anything else. Then, a hunched figure. Ragged clothes. Fingers twitching at his sides, his unkempt hair falling over wide, restless eyes.

The stalker.

Her stomach twisted in fear.

He was talking—to her, to himself, to something unseen in the dimly lit space.

"Maaf karna... mujhe aisa nahi karna chahiye tha."

("Forgive me... I shouldn't have done that.")

Her body tensed, every nerve on high alert but she had to stay calm. She had to think.

"Par main kya karta?" he continued, his tone uneven, almost wounded. *"Tujhe us aadmi ke saath dekhkar mera khoon khol gaya... Woh toh tujhe chod kar chala gaya tha. Toh phir wapas kyun aaya?"*

("But what else could I do? Seeing you with that man... it made my blood boil. He had left you alone. So why was he back?")

Her pulse thundered as he crouched down beside her, his shadow blocking the dim light filtering through the cracks in the walls of the truck. She willed herself not to recoil, but every fibre of her being screamed to get away.

"Par tu toh meri hai, na?"

("But you're mine, aren't you?")

The possessiveness in his voice sent a shiver down her spine.

"Bas thodi naraaz ho gayi hai, hai na?" he murmured, his voice softening, as though trying to soothe a lover's anger. *"Main samajh sakta hoon. Itne dino se tu akeli thi, par ab main aa gaya hoon. Ab sab theek ho jayega."*

("You're just upset, aren't you? I understand. You were alone for so long, but I'm here now. Everything will be fine.")

Janvi squeezed her eyes shut for a brief second, trying to steady herself. He was delusional. He wasn't just obsessed—he truly believed there was something between them.

Then, his fingers reached out, brushing over her hair. She flinched violently.

"Darna mat," he said softly, as if she were a frightened child. "Main tujhe koi takleef nahi dunga. Tu itni acchi hai. Hamesha dhyaan rakhti hai mera... yaad hai, ek din jab mujhe bhook lagi thi toh tune khana diya tha?"

("Don't be scared. I won't hurt you. You're so kind. You have always cared for me... remember the day you gave me food when I was hungry?")

Janvi's mind reeled. She had no recollection of him—not like this. But it wasn't impossible. She often helped those in need at the restaurant, giving extra food to the labourers who passed through Jaisalmer, never questioning if they deserved it or not.

"Bas tabse main samajh gaya tha..." His voice was thick with emotion. "Tu alag hai. Tu mujhe samajhti hai. Tu meri hai."

("'That's when I knew... you're different. You understand me. You're mine.")

Janvi's breath came in ragged gasps, her pulse pounding against her ribs. This was all in his head. A single act of kindness had become something monstrous in his mind.

She forced herself to meet his gaze, her heart hammering. But she did not see reason in his eyes. Only madness.

* * *

Karan crouched low, his breath controlled as he waited in the shadows. His eyes were locked on the figure of the stalker, watching as the man stepped away from the truck, muttering something to himself. It was only a moment—just a brief lapse in vigilance—but it was all Karan needed.

Without hesitation, he moved.

He slipped into the truck as silently as he could, his heartbeat hammering against his ribs. The stench of oil, rust, and damp cloth filled the cramped space, but none of it mattered when his gaze finally landed on her.

Janvi.

His breath caught.

She was slumped against the interior wall, her wrists and ankles bound, her mouth taped. Her wide, terrified eyes lifted to meet his, and something inside Karan cracked.

"Janvi," he exhaled, already reaching for her.

She whimpered, blinking rapidly, as if unable to believe he was actually there.

"Shh... I'm here." His hands worked quickly, fingers shaking slightly as he untied the ropes digging into her skin. The moment her arms were free, she flung them around his neck, her body trembling violently against his.

Karan pulled her into him, gripping her tight, his own relief almost knocking the air out of his lungs. She was safe. She was safe.

"Are you hurt?" he whispered against her hair, his hands already running over her arms, her back, checking for injuries.

Janvi shook her head frantically, her breathing uneven. "K-Karan..." Her voice broke as she clutched onto him, her whole body wracked with exhaustion and fear.

"Let's get you out of here," he murmured, steadying her up. "Can you—"

A sudden, searing pain exploded at the back of his skull.

Karan barely registered the impact before his knees buckled.

His vision swam. A grunt tore from his throat as he crashed against the truck's wall. The world tilted. His mind screamed move, but before he could react, hands were on him—rough, furious, desperate hands.

The stalker had come back.

Karan's head was spinning, but instinct took over. He fought back, throwing a solid punch into the man's ribs, making him stumble back. But the stalker was frenzied, his grip clawing at Karan's throat.

Then came the squeeze.

Karan choked, his airway constricting as the man's hands locked around his neck. His vision blurred. He struggled, twisting, trying to pry the iron grip off—but the stalker was strong, fuelled by something more terrifying than strength: his own delusion.

Karan's limbs started to weaken. His lungs burned.

Then—

A sharp, sickening crack split the air.

The stalker's body jerked before going eerily still. His grip on Karan loosened instantly, and he crumpled to the ground face-first with a heavy thud.

Karan gasped, coughing as air rushed back into his lungs. He stumbled, his vision still spotty as he blinked rapidly, trying to process what just happened.

And then he saw her.

Janvi. Standing there, breathless, clutching a cricket bat in her trembling hands.

His gaze darted between her and the motionless stalker on the ground. His chest rose and fell in ragged, disbelieving breaths.

She had done that. She had saved him.

Janvi's lip wobbled, her eyes wide, as if only now realizing what she had just done. A choked sound left her throat.

And then, before he could say a word, she dropped the bat and threw herself into his arms.

Karan caught her immediately, wrapping her up in his embrace, pressing her close as she clung to him. She was half-crying, half-shaking, her fingers twisting into his shirt as if to anchor herself.

Karan exhaled sharply, burying his face in her hair, grounding himself in her warmth. Relief flooded through him so fast it almost knocked him over. She was here. In his arms. Safe.

"Remind me never to play cricket with you again," he rasped against her temple, his voice hoarse from both the fight and the raw emotions ripping through him.

A small, breathless sound escaped Janvi—a half-laugh, half-sob. She hit his chest, weakly, as if she didn't know whether to scold him or cling tighter.

"You idiot," she sniffled, pressing her forehead against his shoulder.

Karan smiled against her hair, tightening his hold.

"I am. I am a complete idiot."

For the first time in what felt like a lifetime, he could breathe.

* * *

The moment the police stormed in, their voices sharp and

commanding, Karan felt the weight in his chest finally begin to lift. Officers surrounded the unconscious stalker, securing him in handcuffs before hauling him away. The air was thick with tension, but the danger was over.

Karan exhaled deeply, his arm still wrapped protectively around Janvi's trembling frame. His fingers found their way into her hair, cradling the back of her head as she clung to him, her breath warm and uneven against his chest.

SP Bhargav approached, his expression both relieved and grim. "Good work, Karan. Though I did tell you to stay put," he muttered, though there was no real reprimand in his voice.

Karan let out a wry breath, shaking his head. "Did you really expect me to?"

Bhargav gave a half-smile before glancing at Janvi, his voice turning softer. "She's safe now. You did well."

Karan nodded, his grip unconsciously tightening around her. "Thank-you… for getting here so fast."

Bhargav merely inclined his head before signalling his men to wrap up. The officers moved swiftly, clearing the area, the flashing red and blue of their vehicles illuminating the darkened industrial grounds. The night was finally settling into quiet.

Karan turned back to Janvi, brushing a loose strand of hair from her face. "Janvi… it's over," he murmured, his voice low, meant only for her.

She didn't respond.

His brows furrowed. "Janvi?"

A second later, her body went completely limp in his arms.

Panic gripped him instantly.

"Janvi!"

Her knees buckled, and Karan caught her just in time, his heart slamming against his ribs. He crouched down, cradling her close as he gently patted her cheek.

"Hey—stay with me," his voice was urgent, rough with fear.

Her head lolled slightly against his shoulder, her lashes fluttering but not opening. The world around him blurred, narrowed, his breath locking in his throat.

And then—

For the second time today, her world became dark.

28

MY ONLY DESIRE

A steady, rhythmic beeping was the first thing Janvi registered, punctuated by the faint scent of antiseptic. Her eyelids felt heavy, her body weighed down by exhaustion, but as she stirred, she became aware of two things—her right hand tethered by an IV drip and her left hand, held firmly in a warm, unyielding grip.

Karan.

He was slumped in an armchair beside her, his fingers curled tightly around hers as if anchoring her to reality. Shadows of exhaustion clung to his face—his usual sharp features softened by fatigue, dark circles marring his skin. It looked as though he hadn't moved in hours.

The door creaked open, and a small head popped inside.

"Didi!"

Aman.

Before she could fully process everything, he had bolted across the room, throwing himself into her arms. Despite the tug of the IV in her wrist, Janvi instinctively gathered him close. He was trembling. The poor boy had been crying—his face was blotchy, his eyes red and swollen.

The movement stirred Karan.

His grip on her hand tightened instinctively, his breath catching in his throat. His lashes fluttered, his brows furrowing slightly before his gaze snapped to her face. For a second, he just stared, as if making sure she was real—that she was truly awake.

Then, a sharp exhale left his lips, relief flooding his features.

"You're awake," he rasped, his voice hoarse, as though he hadn't spoken in hours.

Janvi managed a small, reassuring nod. "I'm awake."

For a moment, he didn't say anything. He simply held onto her, his thumb brushing absently over the back of her hand, his expression unreadable. Then, slowly, he lifted her fingers to his lips, pressing a lingering kiss against them. The moment between them was broken when Laxmi Tai entered, her voice gentle yet firm.

"Aman, *beta*, give your *didi* some space."

She stepped closer, resting a comforting hand on the boy's shoulder. "The child has been crying non-stop," she murmured to Janvi, shaking her head fondly.

Janvi offered Aman a soft, tired smile, brushing his hair back with her free hand. "I'm fine, Aman. See? No more tears, alright?"

The door opened once more, and this time, Daadi entered the room with slow steps, her face a picture of relief and concern. The lines of worry that had settled on her forehead over the past hours softened slightly as her gaze fell upon Janvi, awake and alert.

"Beta," she breathed, making her way to the bedside. Her hand, warm and familiar, cupped Janvi's cheek with a tenderness that made Janvi's throat tighten. "You, gave us quite a scare."

Unbeknownst to all, Laxmi Tai gave a knowing look to Karan.

"I think, now that we know Janvi is awake and well, we should make our way back to the haveli. Janvi is in safe hands, here."

"I agree," said Daadi.

"Come, Aman. Say goodbye for now. Let's go prepare at home for your didi's return."

Aman reluctantly gave Janvi a final hug before leaving with the two older women.

In the silence that followed, Karan continued to watch Janvi as if still unable to quite believe she was there. Eventually, he spoke.

"I was so damn scared, Janvi." His voice dropped, rough with emotion.

"When you lost consciousness, I was running on adrenaline. I just needed to get you to the hospital. And somehow after that, it's just been hours of torture hoping you were okay. The doctors kept reassuring me, but I was livid. I don't think I've ever felt so helpless as I have in the last twenty-four hours."

His voice dropped lower.

"Janvi I—"

They were interrupted by the arrival of the nurse and the doctor. The nurse took Janvi's vitals like any other patient. The doctor, however, beamed over her as though she were the only patient in the hospital.

"Mrs. Rathore! So glad to see you are up and well. Nothing to worry about at all—just lack of sleep, shock, and a bit of dehydration. There's still a little weakness, but you should be up and about it no time."

"And Mr. Rathore—once again, it's an honour to meet you!"

The doctor all but hovered over Karan, fussing over minor details that barely needed attention. Janvi watched the scene unfold, her curiosity morphing into amusement.

When they finally left, she turned to Karan, raising a brow.

"Why did the doctor look like he wanted to marry you?"

Karan leaned back in his chair and shrugged unapologetically.

"What can I say? My charm precedes me."

"Uh huh." Janvi said thoughtfully, narrowing her eyes. "Or?"

"Or I may or may not have promised a sizeable donation to the hospital."

Janvi rolled her eyes and shook her head but couldn't fight the laughter that was bubbling in her chest.

Karan watched her for a moment, drinking in the sound, savouring every note of her soft laughter like it was music to his ears. His expression softened, and as he continued watching, his smile faded as he gave into something more solemn.

"I love you."

It was barely a whisper.

But it stopped Janvi in her tracks.

Something about the way he said it—the weight behind it, the absolute certainty—made her breath hitch. She searched his eyes and found nothing but truth. Nothing but herself.

He reached to the side of the armchair, pulling out a stack of papers.

The divorce papers.

He held them up between them. Then, without another word, Karan tore them in half.

Then again.

And again—until they were nothing but shredded pieces in his hands.

Reaching for the paper bin beside him, he tossed the remnants inside with finality.

"I'm sorry, Janvi. For everything. For every pain I've ever caused you. And I know—no amount of apologies can ever undo what's been done. But knowing that each wound I inflicted, every moment of hurt, pushed you closer and closer to danger..." He trailed off, his voice thick with regret. "I don't think I'll ever forgive myself for that."

His jaw clenched, his throat bobbing as he swallowed hard.

"Coming so close to losing you forever—that's punishment enough. A lesson I will carry with me for the rest of my life."

Janvi's expression softened, sympathy flickering in her gaze. She shook her head gently, wordlessly telling him to stop.

But Karan wasn't done.

"Let me speak," he murmured, his thumb brushing over her knuckles. "I need to say my part."

There was a desperation in his voice. A need not just to be heard, but to be understood. To be forgiven—not by her, but by himself.

"This is what we are going to do. First of all, Janvi... I'm staying."

Her breath shuddered.

"Here, in India with you."

Tears burned at the corner of her eyes.

"I'm leaving the US operations of inSense in Nathan and Anya's hands," he continued. "We're moving to Jodhpur—you, me and Aman.

I've spoken to Professor Tyagi. You'll be interning with Mehrangarh Trust *and* I want you to get a diploma. I've lined up a few universities and courses that would help with your career in restoration and we can choose the best one for you after you come back home."

Her throat tightened, emotion welling so fiercely that for a moment, she couldn't breathe. He had always been decisive, always a man who carved out his own path without hesitation. But this time, he wasn't just making a choice for himself. He was choosing for *them*. Her fingers gripped the sheets beneath her as if they were the only thing grounding her.

"Karan..." her voice wavered. "You don't have to do this for me."

"I'm not," he said, his gaze steady, his voice unwavering and firm. "I'm doing this for us."

Her heart clenched.

"I've achieved everything I set out to do in life," he continued, his tone softer now, yet carrying the weight of finality. "And now it's time I step back and guide *you* through your dreams." He exhaled, reaching for her hand, his fingers tracing slow, steady circles over her knuckles. "Once you've accomplished what you need to, together, we'll make new goals."

His voice dipped lower, rough with conviction.

"As you said... we'll give back."

He smiled.

"And, I've already started on this grand plan of giving back," he exclaimed. "I've reached out to a psychotherapy institute. I'm creating an outreach and research program with university students to incorporate inSense technology in finding new solutions to monitor and collect behavioural data."

"You're right, Janvi," Karan said, his voice firm. "A degree is just a piece of paper if I don't find ways to use it for something greater. If I don't take what I've learned and apply it where it actually matters—in a society that needs help more than ever."

Janvi's heart swelled with pride at his genius and the warmth that he had taken her passion on giving back to the community to heart.

He cupped her cheek.

"So, my darling," he murmured. "I need you to get better quickly. You and I have much to do."

* * *

The grand doors of the Rathore haveli stood open, spilling warm golden light into the evening air as Janvi stepped out of the car. A gentle breeze carried the soothing scent of fresh flowers and smouldering incense, wrapping the air in a quiet sense of warmth and familiarity.

She barely had a second to take it all in before Daadi stepped forward at the threshold, a silver aarti thali in her hands, its small flame flickering in the dim light.

"*Hamaari Lakshmi ghar aa gayi,*" Daadi murmured with a fond smile, her eyes glistening as she took in the sight of Janvi standing before her, safe and whole. "Welcome home, beta."

Janvi swallowed against the sudden tightness in her throat.

Daadi raised the thali, circling it before Janvi three times, the small bells tied to the edge of the plate jingling softly with each motion. The rhythmic swish of her bangles accompanied the quiet murmurs of a blessing as she pressed a tilak to Janvi's forehead and held a small *mishri* to her lips.

"For sweetness in your life from this moment on," Daadi said gently, her thumb brushing over Janvi's cheek in an affectionate caress.

Janvi took the offering obediently, though her lips trembled slightly around the sweetness of the sugar.

Behind her, Aman hovered eagerly, his wide eyes drinking in the scene, while Laxmi Tai and a few of the older servants looked on with quiet relief. The atmosphere was thick with unspoken emotions—gratitude, love, and the weight of everything that had nearly been lost.

Karan stood beside her, his presence a steady anchor. He said nothing, only watching, his expression unreadable, but when

Janvi's fingers brushed against his, he closed his hand around hers instinctively.

Daadi finished the aarti and stepped back, beaming as she turned to Karan.

"Beta, take her upstairs. Rest a while before dinner."

With Karan by her side, Janvi walked up the steps. At the landing on the first floor, Janvi turned toward her room, but before she could take a single step, Karan's grip on her hand tightened.

She glanced up at him in confusion.

He didn't speak. He only turned her around to the other side.

Janvi was confused but followed him until they reached his room.

Karan walked in but her feet faltered at the threshold, her breath catching. She had not stepped foot in this room since the night of their wedding. Since the night Karan had walked away.

Karan paused and looked back. She looked up at him, uncertain, but Karan didn't give her a chance to hesitate.

Instead, he did something that made her breath hitch.

He walked back outside and scooped her up into his arms.

Janvi gasped, her hands clutching at his shoulders. "Karan! What—"

Without another word, with her in his arms, he carried her over the threshold of his room. She clutched his shoulders instinctively, her heart pounding. His grip on her remained firm, his expression unreadable but intent. Only when he reached the centre of the room did he finally lower her gently onto her feet. His hands lingered at her waist for a beat longer than necessary before he stepped back.

Janvi's gaze flickered uncertainly around the room. It was largely the same—pristine, sophisticated, with dark wood furniture and rich textiles.

"You belong here," he said quietly.

Janvi looked up at him, her lips parting slightly.

"This is your home, too, Janvi," he continued, his voice steady, firm. "You are the lady of this house. And this is where you belong—with me."

Her breath shuddered at the conviction in his words.

Then, before she could say anything, he reached into the drawer of his bedside table and pulled out a folded sheet of paper.

He placed it in her hands.

For a moment, she simply stared at it confused.

"Open it," he whispered in a quiet command.

As she unfolded it, her eyes landed on the first words.

To Janvi's Papa

Janvi's breath caught. She looked at Karan, her eyes already tearing up.

I have read your daughter's words. Words she wrote on the night of our wedding, when I was too blind, too broken, too much of a fool to see what had been placed into my hands.

I don't know if I would have ever been the man you envisioned for her. I don't know if, had you been there, you would have placed her hand in mine with complete faith. And if you had known the truth of how I walked into that marriage—with a heart still tethered to another—you might have stopped it altogether. Perhaps, if I had been in your place, I would have done the same.

But if you were here today, I would look you in the eyes and tell you this: I love her.

Not in the fleeting, reckless way of a man who stumbles upon love and claims it as his own. Not in the way of someone who sees love as a luxury or a convenience. I love her in the way a drowning man gasps for air. In the way the earth aches for the rain. In the way that I now know—I have always belonged to her, whether I was wise enough to see it or not.

You see, sir, I spent so long believing that I was a man in control of his own fate. That I carved my own path, that I dictated my own choices. But I have learned that fate is not something you outrun. It is something that finds you, despite every effort to escape it. And my fate? My destiny? It was always her.

From the moment she walked into my life, unknowingly carrying all the quiet strength of a storm waiting to be unleashed, she changed everything. She softened the walls I had spent years fortifying. She met my arrogance with unwavering dignity. She met my cruelty with unshaken grace. And even when I gave her no reason to, she stood by me. She was always going to be my undoing—and now, she is my salvation.

She wrote that night that I never looked at her. Not once.

I have spent every moment since making up for it.

I look at her now, and I see the woman I will spend the rest of my life proving myself worthy of. I see the resilience she carries, the fire in her spirit, the compassion in her heart. I see the strength of the daughter you raised, the sister Aman adores, the woman who deserves nothing less than everything I have to give.

And I promise you—I will give her everything.

I will spend every breath I have left making her laugh, easing the burdens she refuses to let the world see. I will be the man who stands beside her, who lifts her up, who protects her—not because she is fragile, but because she is precious. Because I cannot, will not, ever again let her stand alone.

She will never again question where she belongs.

Because she belongs with me.

For the rest of my life, I will love her. Fiercely. Unwaveringly. As you would have wanted. As she has always deserved.

I may not have been the man you hoped for that night.

But I swear to you, sir, I will be the man she deserves now.

And I will spend forever proving it.

With all my heart,

Karan

Janvi clutched the letter to her chest, unable to hold back the tears that slipped silently down her cheeks. When she looked up, Karan was already there, gently wiping them away with the pads of his thumbs.

He didn't say anything. He didn't need to.

Instead, he leaned in, brushing his lips over hers in the softest, most reverent of kisses—one that carried everything he couldn't put into words.

And this time, when he pulled her into his arms, Janvi didn't hesitate.

She was finally home.

AUTHOR'S NOTE

When I first dreamt up Karan and Janvi, I didn't know how far their story would take me—or how deeply it would reshape me.

This book is a love letter to longing, to fate, to the threads we can't explain but feel in our bones. It's for the girls who yearn and the men who are daring enough to change their minds. It's for second chances. And for those brave enough to take them.

If you've come this far, thank you for walking this journey with me.

— J.D. Raghav

A NOTE TO THE READER

If Duty and Desire moved you, I'd be so grateful if you left a short review online. Even a sentence helps more than you know—especially for independent authors.

To stay connected, get behind-the-scenes glimpses, and hear about my next novel, you can follow me here:

- Instagram: @jdraghav_author
- Goodreads: J.D. Raghav

Thank you for reading.

ABOUT THE AUTHOR

J.D. Raghav writes stories that linger—tales of devotion, desire, and the karmic pull between souls who are meant to find each other. Based in Sydney, Australia, she balances her time between writing, spiritual journaling, and dreaming up fictional men who ruin your sleep schedule.

Duty and Desire is her debut novel.